AuthorHouse™
1663 Liberty Drive
Bloomington, IN 47403
www.authorhouse.com
Phone: 1-800-839-8640

This book is a work of fiction. People, places, events, and situations are the product of the author's imagination. Any resemblance to actual persons, living or dead, or historical events, is purely coincidental.

First published by AuthorHouse   7/27/2010

ISBN: 978-1-4520-0546-1 (e)
ISBN: 978-1-4520-0544-7 (sc)
ISBN: 978-1-4520-0545-4 (hc)

Library of Congress Control Number: 2010907494

Printed in the United States of America
Bloomington, Indiana

This book is printed on acid-free paper.

GLORIA

a novel of new beginnings

JOHN OSBORN

authorHOUSE®

Other Books by John Osborn

MICHAEL

SAMANTHA

DANIEL

GLORIA MANSON RETURNS HOME FROM London to find her mother has become a penitent recluse. While working in the village pub and flirting with old school mates Gloria tries to bring her mother back into reality. Some friends from London come down to the village and help Gloria with her mother and cause her to restart her London career in a new location. Most of the action takes place in Fotheringham Manor Estate where school friends Gary and Freddie work. This Estate is the home of the Lord family where son Daniel is the resident manager. Hikers trespass through the Estate causing damage and upsets to both Daniel and his forester girl friend Katya. These hikers and the new Education Centre on the Estate mean there are more people in the forest and this constrains some of Gloria's plans. Daniel's sister, Samantha is a partner in Heritage Adventures, a company who helps tourists find their pasts, and she in turn upsets some of Gloria's activities. Over time the various parties clash through misunderstandings, jealousy, confessions, and fights and ultimately murder.

Waiting for the Jury

My name is Gary Templeton, although some days I really wish it wasn't. Today is one of those days. Within one hour I will be dead, well as good as. They may have done away with the death penalty but spending the next one, three, five or maybe twenty five years in gaol is as good as a death penalty. Bloody worse I expect.

The holding cell under the court is damp and chilly, and I shiver. Is it really the cold or is it remorse? Templeton, a name I was once proud of. Just think about it. There was my great grandfather Albert. He was a fine man. Fought in the Great War alongside George Lord and returned home a decorated hero. He came home to Fotheringham Manor to continue as George Lord's head gamekeeper but what a change to come home to. That must have been quite a shock for poor old great granddad. He'd left with George Lord when his job was all about shooting and hunting: rearing pheasants and keeping the woodlands open enough for the game. It would have been a quiet, slow and gentlemanly pace of life, a typical country seat. While he and George Lord were away that Lady Virginia had turned the place upside down. The rearing of pheasants was gone, the wildlife habitat neglected and some of the old woodland had been cleared away. In that space were those lines of exotic conifers. My

1

old great grandfather Albert had probably never seen so many conifers, certainly not row after row of them. And they were those long soft-needled white pines all growing like little rockets. Jesus what a shock that must have been but great grandfather held his head high and learnt a new business. Stayed on as head gamekeeper and forest foreman until he retired: proud man doing a good job.

Of course the other shock for Albert when he returned from the war was Edward his son. He'd never seen my grandfather Edward as the baby boy was born in 1914 after Albert had gone to France. Yes I thought, grandfather Edward Templeton was another good man of the forest. He was also proud of his name. Learnt from his dad and from Lady Virginia about the new approach to commercial forestry and he loved it. He welcomed the change of pace with more to do and a greater variety of operations in the forest. The job expanded to include tree nurseries, young plantations and the start of a new sawmill. Edward took over all of that plus learnt to be a mechanic as cars and machines became more common. Like his own dad my grandfather served his country by being an aeroplane mechanic and fitter and that wasn't surprising as George Lord's son Desmond was crazy about flying too. Like Albert, Edward came out of the war having done his bit and my dad gets born and the whole bloody scenario changes.

What was it everyone said about the post-war years? Christ, just listen to all the old folks going on as if it was something memorable. Everyone was living on rations: everyone had to go without but then not my dad. He decided to take anything he could get. Not for him the hard-working life in the forest. That was too much like hard graft and no opportunities to use his silver tongue. Quite early in life dad must have decided that the way to get on was to sell things to people. Seeing as most of them hadn't got anything it should be easy to sell them things, especially if you've got a silver tongue like my dad, and nobody could resist the "never-never". That wouldn't have been so bad if all he did was sell but he didn't did he? No ordinary thief my dad. Smart man, thinking man but the trouble was he thought with his cock. Perhaps that's where his brain really was, or maybe he had two brains because it was his cock that has ruled most of his life. So he stole other people's women. Not brutally mind you, nice and sweet and just what you like love.

'And I'll come back next week and check that it's working okay shall I darling, about the same time next Tuesday then?' Daughters, mothers, grandmothers, dad wasn't fussy – sort of driven like a dog in heat with its tongue hanging out and his flies already undone. Brian Templeton, father of Christ-knows how many of my half brothers and sisters in the West Country. I sat in my cell and wondered how many siblings I had in the village, or elsewhere for that matter. There was one sibling I did have though in the village and at the time I never knew. That girl was primarily why I was here. Well, she and several others I could name. Gloria Manson, precious Gloria, pretty Gloria, greedy Gloria, but o so wonderful Gloria. I could sing her song sitting here in the damp. How does it go, that old Bee Gees song? G, L, O, R, I, A, Gloria, sure that hot bitch who really wanted to make money the easy way. Well, I don't blame her now do I? I was going along for the ride and thought we were on to a good thing until bloody Freddie has to get jealous and that Daniel Lord and his sister have to go poking their noses into things that shouldn't concern them.

Last October it was that Gloria came home. Seven years she'd been living in London after she ran away back in 1991. She came back just after her dad died. Seems he was killed in a bloody great accident on the Motorway in the fog and being a truck driver for a petrol company he kind of went up in smoke so to speak. They said there was nothing left to bury: cremated on site if you know what I mean. I sat down in the cell and leant back on the bench. Last October there was a lot going on in our village. It all came to a head in mid October, that wild Saturday night when Gloria had just started working in our local, the George and Dragon. Old George Doone, the landlord, had hired Gloria to work behind the bar, and built the way she was it pulled in a few new punters. That was the night that weird Australian bitch tried to come on to Gloria and when that didn't work she picked up John Ferris. Who was she now, Vanda Whelks, Florence Whelks's granddaughter? Weird bitch but she could play darts though; drink too. That was the night she thrashed fancy pants John Ferris, our local brother killer and drank him under the table. John Ferris was out on bail and working with us on the forest gang up at Fotheringham Manor Estate, home of the illustrious Lord family.

Looks like I've got lots of time to spare here and so I'll tell you a little more about the background of my situation and why I'm sitting in this cell with just hours to go. It'll pass the time and the guard isn't interested but you look like you'd enjoy a good story.

Several of us in the village here work for the Lord family who own Fotheringham Manor Estate. The Lord family has been here for yonks and many of our parents and grandparents back in time have worked on the Estate. Right now the owners are Anthony and Sylvia Lord, who are close to retirement I hear, and so it is their youngest son Daniel Lord who is the Estate Manager and resident Forester. The older Lords' eldest son Geoffrey was killed in 1990 in an accident when he was climbing with his brothers, Michael and Daniel. Geoffrey's widow Christina still lives in Home Farm on the Estate along with her son and the Lord family heir Peter Lord. Funny thing about the Lord family is that they follow the old-fashioned tradition of the entire inheritance passing to the eldest son and only the eldest son. There is some fancy word for it I think but I've forgotten it. Primo something but what the hell. Anyway, Geoffrey died and so his son Peter inherited, even though he was only one year

4

old. Now that really pissed off the second son Michael who thought the inheritance should be his. Actually Michael was with Geoffrey and Daniel when the climbing accident happened but I heard that Michael just buggered off to get the rescue started and then fled the scene. The youngest son Daniel was left there with his dead brother and that had an effect on Daniel. Well, he's still a bit strange and mixed up over such things. However, we'll get to Mr. precious Manager/Forester Daniel in a minute. Now I was just a teenager when all this happened and still at school along with Freddie Dunster, Gloria Manson and Sandra Porlock. All four of us had been going out as a group for a year or more now and so we hung around a lot together. We heard all the tittle tattle up on the Estate 'cos Freddie worked up there as a gardener part-time and he developed a keen ear for anything that might help him. Freddie needed help because the forester on the estate at that time was a certain Norton Ferris. Now there was a nasty piece of work. Old man Ferris was a lazy, scheming and dim-witted bully and he used to give Freddie a real hard time. Although Freddie could usually get out of the way of Norton Ferris he also had to avoid the unwelcome attention of arrogant Michael Lord and Norton's two useless sons Idwal and John. As a kid Freddie was always getting the short end of the stick and that was something our Freddie never forgot, especially his resentment against the Ferris family. A lot of what has happened this past year, and very much related to my present circumstances arose from events back in 1990 and early 1991, some eight or more years ago. Geoffrey died and Michael the second son thought the inheritance should pass to him. But before Michael really pissed off too many people there was another death later that summer. Since some time back in the forties, and Jesus that's bloody ages ago, Anthony Lord's grandfather had hired two Italian prisoners-of-war to work on the Estate. They were Antonio and Enrico Branciaghlia. Now they were two really good men. If only my dad had some of their character I might be proud of my name again. The two Italians worked on the forest but as they were craftsman with big hearts they made lots and lots of sculpted and carved toys for the Lord family children and for several other children in the village too. I've even got a wooden soldier carved by Enrico and Freddie did have another at one time. As I was saying, that summer in 1990 Antonio gets killed in the forest. He and Enrico were thinning out some old large white pines and the top of a wolf tree snapped off and smashed his head. When Enrico went for help the only person he could find anywhere was Michael Lord. Trouble was young Michael Lord was only interested in himself and his inheritance and so he just told Enrico to piss off or so I heard. Enrico never forgot and his poor brother died alone in the forest. Mark you, Enrico was on the receiving end of Norton Ferris's prejudice too seeing as he was Italian. The story goes that Norton Ferris had got his face slashed by some local lads in Italy somewhere in the last war and he was down on Italians ever since. Actually I heard that Norton Ferris was down on most people and always blaming someone else for his problems. Still, he got killed too didn't he? Must have been early January in 1991 when old man Ferris was trying to steal some fence posts. Queer deal that was too and no one was ever sure what really happened. Freddie told me most of the details as he was there in the forest at the scene of the accident. Seems Norton was loading up fence posts in Michael Lord's Landrover for a quick sale to our local small-time village villain, Larry Whelks. Somehow a pile of sawlogs on top of the cutover got loose and cascaded down onto the Landrover, just when Norton Ferris was inside. No one ever found out who let the logs loose 'cos it didn't happen by accident. Some people think it was Enrico getting revenge for the death of his brother but we'll get to that in a moment. The logs smashed down on the truck and Freddie said it must have knocked the Landrover arse over teakettle into the stream below. By chance the Landrover ended up upside down and old man

Ferris drowned. It was all a little bizarre Freddie said 'cos it was Idwal and John Ferris who found the Landrover when they were out looking for their dad. Idwal suspected what his dad was up to and knew where there was a pile of fence posts because the gang had laid them out just the day before. Idwal and John Ferris thought it was Michael Lord in the stream as it was his Landrover. Well when they found it they rushed up to the Manor House and banged on the door for Anthony Lord to tell him what had happened. So there was a bloody great rescue Freddie said with Taffy Williams and his tow truck up from the village along with some of the forest crew. Sylvia Lord, Michael's mother nearly slipped into the stream as the whole slope was frozen and she was so anxious to recover her son. What a surprise though when they winched the Landrover out of the stream and who should be inside but Norton Ferris. That sort of floored everyone. Trouble was Idwal Ferris was convinced that Enrico had something to do with those loose logs.

Now Michael Lord might have escaped that accident but not the next one. Anthony Lord was about to fire all of the Ferris family and right after Norton's death he did fire Idwal and John. Some people thought this was a bit bloody minded but they were a useless and dangerous couple of layabouts. Freddie was bloody glad he told me. Anyway, a couple of days after that accident with Michael Lord's Landrover there was the shooting. Seems Michael Lord had really pissed off several people that year and some even wonder whether he was the target in his Landrover. Didn't matter did it 'cos some one shot him outside this old cave on the Estate. What cave you say? Now as kids we had all known about this cave. It was a slit in the cliff really and not any great shakes as a cave. After we had found it and discovered it didn't go anywhere we forgot about it. However, sometime around Christmas of that 1990, just before both Ferris and Michael's deaths there was some excitement in the Lord family about this cave. Freddie had overheard Daniel talking with Enrico about some secret. Now if there was one thing that Michael Lord couldn't stand it was someone knowing something about the Estate that he didn't, especially if it could be to Michael's advantage. It seems that Michael thought that this cave might contain something valuable and so he went investigating. As kids we had never found anything there and so we were surprised to hear that Michael had been shot right outside the cave. That January the police were all over the Estate. The death of Norton Ferris looked like an accident and that was the way it ended up but the death of Michael Lord was something else. That was cold calculated murder and a lot of people got questioned over that event, especially given the number of people Michael had pissed off. After several weeks though when the police couldn't find the murder weapon or even what actually killed him the case closed down into one of those, what do they call them, cold case files.

Now all this history came to life just last year in what turned into a bloody carnage on the Estate. Gloria was still away in London and Freddie and I had forgotten all about her. Her mum Tilley never said anything and she had been a good friend of Freddie's mum Rosemary Dunster. Actually they were cousins. Gloria's younger brother Wendell was just a teenage pain in the neck and he never really knew his sister anyway. I was working on the forest crew at this time, along with Freddie and several other people from the village. Also working with us was John Ferris, the younger son of Norton Ferris. The older brother Idwal had disappeared soon after he was fired but Anthony Lord decided that John deserved a second chance, and that looked like a good decision but then Anthony Lord has always been a people person. Looks after his people does Anthony Lord and helps trying to bring us together, work as a team he says, support each other. So John Ferris came back to work on the Estate and he married Betty Travers from the village and lived in his old cottage in the forest along with his two small children, Katey and little Paul. I suppose everything was going along quite smoothly until one day, right out of the blue Idwal Ferris appears, complete with some half-stoned tart apparently. I never saw him the day he returned but Freddie told me Idwal and John were in the pub that night drinking up a storm. The first I knew about that was the day we were working on a fence line and John hadn't been at work that morning. Bob Edwards our foreman was a little pissed off as he was expecting John, especially as John was a dab hand at straining up fence corners. Had the knack he had. Daniel Lord was out there that afternoon when John Ferris came flying up to us in some dusty little van screaming his head off. We found out soon enough what John was screaming about because Daniel Lord told us all to pack our things and get back in the gang truck. Along with Bob Edwards we drove through the forest to Enrico's cottage and that's where we learnt why John was screaming. Christ it was a mess. Apparently, according to John Ferris, his brother had returned with this mad idea to avenge the death of his father. Idwal was convinced that Enrico had let loose those logs back seven or more years ago that rolled down onto his dad. Screaming revenge John said, acting like a madman. As it so happens Enrico was in hospital at the time, although none of us knew that then but when Idwal couldn't find Enrico at his cottage he decided to take the place apart. The kitchen was a mess of smashed furniture, opened cupboards and their contents spread, smeared, splashed all over everything. Food, juices, vegetables, jars, crockery you name it was strewn in an incredible jumble all over the place. In the rest of the rooms there wasn't much to spread about but Idwal hadn't left a piece of furniture untouched. We spent the rest of the afternoon trying to see whether there was anything left to salvage and bundling the broken pieces into the lorry to carry away. After we had cleared away most of the bits and pieces we set about mopping and sweeping up. Daniel Lord didn't want Enrico to come home to such a fearsome mess and so Bob Edwards had

9

us make it clean and tidy even if it was very empty. But, it didn't end there did it because Idwal was still out there in the forest on the rampage and we had more work to do. Daniel Lord had several friends staying at the Manor that night. His sister Samantha had recently come over from Canada and also in the house were a Mr. Donald MacLeod and a slender little black lady called Danielle Made I think. This Danielle was there with her son Tony. Daniel Lord even had his sister-in-law Christina and her son Peter stay up in the Big House because he thought Idwal might have this silly hatred his dad had about Italians and Christina was Italian. Anyway, with Idwal Ferris on the loose Daniel Lord and Mr. MacLeod worked out a search party routine for the work gang and so we were all involved looking over various parts of the Estate. Didn't make me feel any happier when I saw both Mr. Lord and his friend carrying shotguns. Now Daniel Lord and John Ferris had gone down to John's cottage earlier but there was no sign of Idwal there and so we were all on tenterhooks wondering where the silly bugger was and what he would do next. According to John Ferris Idwal had gone nuts. Sure enough, just as it got dark someone shouted that the stables were on fire. We all rushed back to the yard to see Samantha Lord and this Danielle Made frantically opening stable doors and the family horses galloping for safety. Mr. Lord got us organised into a bucket and pail line trying to throw water on the fire while he telephoned for the local fire brigade. Freddie and young Les were sent to look after the horses and make sure they were safe and away from the smoke. Soon after that the fire brigade arrived and they soon had the fire under control. Daniel Lord got Bob Edwards to thank us and send us home but to be back for police questioning next morning. Little did we know as we went home what was about to happen that night in the Ferris cottage. I only heard about it the next morning when we went to the yard and got questioned by the police. It appears that Idwal had set the fire in the stables and then rushed back to his brother's cottage.

According to the rumours Idwal assaulted John's wife, shot his girl-friend and ended up getting killed when John rushed in. Daniel had taken John and PC Meadows down to the Ferris cottage because John thought that was where Idwal might go next. Now I overheard Timmy Meadows, the local plod, say he told Mr. Lord and John Ferris not to go in as he had heard that Idwal had a gun. Still, when John heard his wife scream he just charged in and ended up nearly getting shot. In his rage, while fighting his brother, John slashed his brother's throat. I heard there was blood from wall to wall, like a slaughter house it was. So the next day, it was a Friday, when we were all up in the yard waiting for the police we heard all the rumours and Bob Edwards told us a little more about the murder and mayhem in John's cottage. I'll give Daniel Lord his due though because when the police had finished with all of us he sent us home with full pay and a sincere word of thanks for cleaning up the mess in Enrico's cottage and helping with the fire at the stables.

These events took place towards the end of September last year and my work continued in the forest. Anthony Lord put up the bail for John Ferris and obviously the authorities thought he was no further danger to anyone and so he came back to work. Well Freddie of course couldn't leave him alone. You have to remember that old man Norton Ferris had always bullied Freddie a while ago and the two brothers gave him a hard time too and Freddie is not one to forget. So, now John Ferris is back on the gang and has to keep his nose clean seeing as he's out on bail and Freddie has a chance to make his life miserable. Of course Freddie can be an annoying little shit when he wants to be and he thought it was payback time. John Ferris had some real limitations associated with his bail. He had to live in his cottage in the forest and wasn't allowed to see his wife and kids who were back living in the village with Betty's mum and dad. He could only come into the village on Saturday and that meant he was in the George and Dragon most Saturday nights. Right from the day he came back to work after his court appearance Mr. Daniel came out to talk to all of us. Bob Edwards must have told him there was some muttering in the gang and so just before we had lunch Daniel Lord had us all stand there and listen.

'Okay, just a quick word please. First I want to thank each and every one of you for the job you did last week over Enrico's cottage. I know it was a mess but you all did a really excellent job and I know Enrico will be pleased. At the moment he is out of hospital as most of you know and staying with my sister at Home Farm. Needless to say Enrico is not letting things sit still and he is carving wooden figures for my new nephew Tony. I understand it will be a soccer player as young Tony is a fan.'

He made some joke after this about young Tony playing on the village team and George Crawford the team coach said he could use some new talent as most of the team he had now were no-hopers but then he went on, 'I also want to thank you for work on the patrols and fighting the fire in the stables. Thanks to you, and my sister and Tony's mum we saved all the horses with no damage and we only lost part of the stables. It could have been a lot worse and it was your efforts that made sure it wasn't. Finally, you all know what happened after the fire and John here was the one who put an end to that. Now I realise that each and every one of you has some feelings about this. Understood, but it is likely that none of you know the whole story so I would ask you to accept two things. First, John has been charged and will go to court but in the meantime he is here, out on bail and our family has agreed to have him work for us. My dad stood bail for him so that gives some idea how we feel. I've just come from a meeting we arranged with special permission from the court between John and his wife Betty to decide a few things. That done John works here and continues to live in his cottage and so that leads me into the second thing. If any of you feel you don't like this arrangement then say so, not now and not here but sometime later speak to Bob or come and see me. I'm quite sure we can find ways of keeping you employed and comfortable in your own thoughts. We realise that life would have been a lot easier, a lot more peaceful if Idwal Ferris hadn't returned but he did and what happened has happened. So learn to live with it one way or another. We have.'

So now we all knew but Freddie couldn't leave it alone could he? He sniped away at John in the forest and in the end Bob Edwards got so pissed off he moved Freddie to some other job away from the gang. That only made Freddie worse and so on Saturday nights when we were all in the pub Freddie continued. That very next day, the Saturday Freddie was in the George along with Danny Masters who's a mechanic in the local garage. I was in the pub too that night but I was across the room drinking with my dad and one of his sales associates. The evening hadn't started too well for Freddie. Samantha Lord had come in to see one of the coppers who had been around over the Ferris case and she had startled this copper who was sitting at the bar talking to George. So the copper turns round quickly without noticing he still had his beer in his hand and of course most of it splashes out over Freddie who is already half cut and just looking for some aggro. Freddie starts mouthing off when he notices Miss Samantha there and she cut him off at the pass. Paid for a pint for Freddie and Danny and wheels lover boy away to a table. Now Freddie is ready to burst his boiler and who should come in at that moment but John Ferris. Poor bugger, he'd hardly got to the bar to order his pint before Freddie is all mouth and shouting the odds about knife-wielder or some such. George the landlord had a sharp word with Freddie and funny enough it wasn't long before Freddie and Danny were playing darts against John Ferris and Bert Frazer. Seemed a friendly game but every now and then I would catch the look on Freddie's face.

Next Saturday night we had the big darts match against the lads from the Red Lion and so most of us were watching the game. We all knew that John Ferris was a good darts player and had been on the team for a while but Harry Biggins the team captain had never really liked the Ferris family and so Harry dropped John after the murder. Didn't do our team any good but Harry nursed a long time grudge. John had come in quietly and was talking to George about something when Freddie had to go and wind him up again didn't he? I didn't catch all of the conversation but I heard Freddie accuse Idwal of killing Larry Whelks and John got right pissed off about that. I'd never heard any mention of this before and I didn't realise its significance until a week later when all hell broke loose for John Ferris and that was partly because of my Gloria.

But, before we get to that weekend you have to understand what had been going on that week out in the forest. Daniel Lord and Bob Edwards had gone through a young Douglas fir plantation and marked several of the trees with silver paint. Bob had given each of us five rows and we were to work our ways up the rows cutting down the marked trees. In forestry terms it is called a thinning and lets the remaining trees have more light and nutrients and so they are supposed to grow better. Well us bozos working in the forest aren't supposed to know all that, just cut down the marked ones. Freddie was being his usual pain and eventually Bob moved Freddie out to the end of the crew and had him stacking cut logs, well away from Ferris. John seemed to be working steadily enough and I thought all was well but next morning there was no John in the yard for seven thirty. Bob Edwards asked whether anyone had seen him and when no one had it seems that Daniel Lord went to find him himself. The next thing we know is that the police are back again crawling all over John's cottage. None of us knew why and the rumours went flying around like wildfire. It turned out in the end that John had stumbled on some bones buried in the floor of his cottage. On the Wednesday John was back at work but kept very much to himself and I could see that he was troubled and puzzled. Thursday was similar but then Daniel Lord was out for a long talk with John and after that John didn't say a word to anyone. Rumours started flying again about more bones and someone said the first lot were dog bones. Of course all of us who had been around some time kept asking ourselves whether we could ever remember any animals at the Ferris cottage. I don't know what happened on the Thursday night but Freddie seemed a little stressed out on the Friday morning. It was like he was high on something but when I asked him he just told me to bugger off. It wasn't long though when Bob Edwards was involved with one of the lad's chainsaws that Freddie decides to go a little nuts. I had been trimming one of my trees when the next thing I know Freddie is hammering John Ferris with an axe handle over the shoulders. I heard the thump and turned round. John was flat on his back and Freddie was sitting on his chest trying to pound with his fists.

'Bloody murderer, that's what you are. Killed my cousins. I know you did.'

Bob heard the commotion and was over in a flash hauling Freddie off. Seems Freddie had some story about the bones in John's cottage. Anyway, Daniel Lord arrived just at that moment and next thing we knew Daniel is hauling Freddie out onto the forest ride between the plantations and listening seriously to Freddie's ranting. Bob had us all back to work but I noticed Daniel Lord take Freddie away for over half an hour and when he came back Freddie wouldn't say a word. He wouldn't even say where he'd been. Lunch time came and who should return but Daniel Lord again and this time he spent a long time talking with Ferris but that obviously wasn't good enough because then he's grilling Bob Edwards and finally Freddie's back into the conversation. The rest of the gang sat around eating lunch but you could tell we all had our ears pinned back and we were trying to hear what was going on. Whatever it was we never learnt that day although within forty-eight hours I suppose we all knew. Freddie wasn't in the pub that Friday night and I reckon after I knew what was going on Freddie was stewing in his own guilt and misery. So we arrived at that rather climatic Saturday night, October the seventeenth. Several things happened that night and some of them resulted in my sitting in this cold and dreary cell waiting for the jury. The guard won't look at me as he reads his newspaper so I'm all alone. Mum was in court but my dad's nowhere to be seen of course. He's probably too bloody worried about the fall out from what everyone heard in the court and some of their guesses from things that weren't said. Anyway, enough of that: let's get back to my story. Saturday night and Gloria Manson came waltzing back into my life. That afternoon Freddie and I had been out to watch the local football team and pretty useless they were too and so we were looking forward to watching some real footie on the tele in the pub while drinking away the boredom of the past week. Come to think of it that past week hadn't been as boring as usual what with the rumours over bones and the busies swarming everywhere. Still, you've got to drink haven't you? We walked in to the George and lo and behold there was gorgeous Gloria behind the bar. Well, what a reunion but of course Freddie had to make the big play and he and I ended up arguing at the bar until George told us to behave. Three of Freddie's village mates were sitting at one of the tables and we joined up with them although I didn't usually associate with that crowd. There was Danny Masters the mechanic, Lester Rainer who pretended to be a house painter and Don Winters who was a large oaf working in some lawyer's office. Nobody ever really knew what Don did as making the tea was probably beyond him but he was a big bloke and I just kept my mouth shut. The pub was pretty crowded as usual on a Saturday night and we were chatting and watching the football match on the tele. Although it was two London clubs playing we still got excited as the quality of play was a bloody sight better than we had seen that afternoon. Arsenal had just scored and Freddie was up waving his arms about when he suddenly noticed who was playing darts.

'Watch him darling. Cuts people up does our John,' as Freddie's voice rang out across all the noise in the room. Of course this brings George over and he tells me to put an anchor on Freddie.

'Gary, keep a hand on his shoulder lad. Make sure he stays seated.'

Now the five of us listened to George but all our eyes were watching who was playing darts. She'd been in the day before apparently and George said he'd never seen anyone throw darts the way she did. According to George, who you can only believe half of the time she'd thrown three darts in every number in sequence from one to twenty and then repeated the same feat using the doubles ring, all without missing. John Ferris was a good darts player and I listened to Freddie telling me she was suckering him, leading him on the way she was playing 'cos she let John win the first two games. The scores were close but John won. Now you've got to realise that our local was a typical small village pub and most of the patrons were village folk who looked normal. The bird playing darts against John looked anything but normal. First of all she was fairly slender with long flowing black hair. She was wearing a long black dress and a kind of sleeveless half jacket. Her skin was pasty white so she almost looked like one of those mimes you see on TV or in a circus what with the black clothes and white body. But it was the face that was really weird with black lipstick, black eye shadow, a stud in her nose and three rings through each eyebrow. I learnt later she was a Goth but I wouldn't have known what a Goth was so what the hell. I drank my pint and decided to get another round in and spend some time with Gloria doing it. Gloria is built like a lady and instead of covering her body up like little miss weirdo playing darts Gloria had this blouse that virtually poured her tits all over the counter. Obviously George thought he might

17

be on to a good thing and I wasn't complaining as I leaned forward and could almost suck Gloria's nipples. Freddie wasn't having any of that of course and so he had to get up and give me a hard time about drinking at the milk fountain. Supposedly on the way to the gents Freddie wanders over to the dart board and needles John about this Vanda bird. Tells him that she is leading him by the nose, or perhaps by his cock and that he Freddie wouldn't want her pulling his cock. George came up from the cellar just at this moment and clips my ear for not keeping an eye on Freddie. Quick as a flash Freddie scampers down the corridor to the gents out of harms way. The rest of that night, leastways the parts that I can remember Arsenal won, Freddie got really legless, I copped a couple of promising kisses and fondles with Gloria and managed to get home before I fell down sadly alone. It was the next day, much later the next day that I learnt about the real excitement of that Saturday night. We were back in the pub on the Sunday evening and all anyone was talking about was the murder.

'What murder?' I asked.

'You haven't heard? Christ, you been asleep all day or something?'

'Got pissed last night didn't I? How come you know all about it? About what or who I suppose if it is murder?'

'John Ferris of course; knife-wielding, brother-slayer, bones-in-the-cottage Ferris that's who.'

'So who has he killed this time, although I'm surprised it's not you Freddie with all the aggro you've been giving John?'

'He didn't kill anyone you stupid bugger. He's the bloody corpse isn't he?'

'John's dead?'

'Wash your bloody ears out Gary. You fucking awake in that head of yours or are you still having wet dreams over Gloria's tits? Every time you went to buy another round last night you came back with a hard on.'

18

'Shut the fuck up Freddie. She's a nice girl.'

'In your dreams mate. What the fuck do you think she was doing up in London? I'll bet she was peddling her arse. Look, when she gets a free moment we'll ask her. She was always our mate back when we were kids. The four of us went everywhere together, well four of us until Sandra topped herself. Actually, I'd be interested in knowing why she's come back here to the middle of nowhere. Funny that seeing as her dad was killed just over a couple of weeks ago. She wasn't down for the funeral or anything.'

'Freddie you stupid prat there wasn't any funeral was there? Walter Manson got incinerated in his fucking tanker. Anyway, bugger all that, what's all this about John Ferris? You say he's dead?'

'I heard he went home with that weird bitch. Did you know she was old Flo' Whelks's granddaughter? Apparently Larry's younger brother Phil came back here from Australia or somewhere fucking wild and he brought this bitch thing with him.'

'But John was as close to legless as you were last night. He couldn't drive anywhere.'

'Didn't drive did he? His car's still out there in the parking lot, or it was earlier. Perhaps the cops have taken it away before you got here.'

'Bugger the car Freddie, what happened to John? He was playing darts and drinking with that Australian black and white minstrel. Perhaps she's part abo? Did Phil Whelks have a wild fling with an abo? Now there's a thought. No, screw that, tell me about John.'

'The way I heard it she walked him back to Flo's cottage and they ended up in one of the sheds out back. Old Ben heard John had been tied up and there was some kinky sex involved. I don't know all the details but they were both stoned as well as drunk and sometime in the orgy this bitch realises who John really is. You may remember Gary about eight years ago Larry Whelks got killed up in Bristol. Well I think it was

19

Idwal Ferris who killed Larry and that's why Idwal was away for so long. He was in gaol for manslaughter or murder or something. Sometime Friday Phil was in here asking George all about his brother Larry and who Larry was dealing with. Larry was always dealing and just after old Norton Ferris got killed I know Idwal and Larry had something going on. I was so fucking glad that Norton Ferris eventually got what was coming to him but I do remember John and Idwal being fired and something going on.'

'So what's that got to do with this Australian bird?'

'She went bonkers when she found out she was with a Ferris and it was a Ferris who killed her uncle. Ben heard that she knifed him.'

'So how did anyone know he was dead or where he was?'

'Your friend and my friend Daniel Lord came looking this morning didn't he. Pissing with rain it was and blowing a bloody gale but Daniel was out with his Yank girl friend and his sister looking for John. Don't ask me why but they'd reasoned that Saturday night John would be in the pub.'

'But you said Ferris was in old Flo's shed.'

'Actually he wasn't but that's where he got killed supposedly.'

'So where was he?'

'Under Flo's garden path.'

'You mean the one the police have been digging up, what Friday wasn't it?'

'People are saying that Flo's bloody stupid dog started barking last night and Phil found the pair of them in the shed. He panicked and old Flo' had to sort it.'

'But she didn't if they found John?'

'No, well I suppose Flo' thought that the police had finished digging up her bloody garden path looking for all those funny stones. Actually I heard they were gold pieces. That Inspector bloke was giving me a real going over on Friday about that. Showed me one he did and it looked just like the one my cousins had found.'

'Freddie, now what the fuck are you talking about?'

'It's a long story Gary and I'll tell you another time but it seems that Flo' thought the path was disturbed already and so more digging wouldn't be so obvious. It was her dog who done her in. I'd have shot the stupid bleeder. Who the fuck calls their dog Goebbels anyway? What sort of a name is that for a dog?'

'So when did all this happen?'

'This morning you hungover sod, while you were still dreaming or pulling your cock thinking of Gloria.'

'So Daniel Lord found John?'

'He was there, him and his girl, his sister and a couple of cops. They were all in the cottage with old Flo' and Phil.'

'Where was this Vanda whoever?'

'Tucked up asleep in bed I heard, probably still stoned out of her mind. Later someone heard there were two ambulances but who went where I couldn't tell you. All of them ended up leaving the cottage, either to hospital or to the police station.'

'You two talking about last night?'

'Hi Gloria. Yea, and this morning too I understand.'

'The pair of you just going to sit there yapping or are you going to drink? George was telling me that this ain't a social club but a pub, for drinking like. Two pints is it?'

'Yes, sure love. Gloria, you got a minute, for an update?'

'Might have, might depend on what you want updating.'

'Gary here wants to put another notch on his cock.'

'Wash your mouth out Freddie Dunster. I didn't come back here to be slagged off by the likes of you. You used to be a nice little boy.'

'But I grew up into a randy teenager if you remember right darling and you used to....'

'Shut it Freddie. Two pints Gary?'

When Gloria came back with the pints she told us that she was on a break and so she sat down with the pair of us. Freddie insisted she sit between us so she could put her hands on both of us Freddie added. Gloria nearly poured Freddie's pint all over him but I interrupted to get some more news on John Ferris.

'When I came in at lunch time George told me he had had Daniel Lord down here early in the morning banging on the door looking for John. Next thing George knew there were ambulance sirens and then police car sirens. Soon after we opened the police were in here questioning George and me. When did John Ferris come in? Who was he with? When did he leave? How did he leave? Jesus it was non-stop questions and that Inspector Field is a very quiet but ruthless bugger.'

'Now poor Freddie will have no one at work to pick on any more, will you Freddie?' I said.

'Then I'll just have to pick on you Gary you useless sod.'

'Solves one of Anthony Lord's problems though doesn't it?'

'How'd you mean?' asked Freddie.

'Yes Gary, what difference does to make to Anthony Lord? Thought I heard my mum tell me he and his wife Sylvia had retired. Didn't they sell that Company of theirs, and doesn't their son Daniel run the Estate? Talking of the Lord family why is Samantha back? My mum said she got married and took off to Canada. Heard there was some flaming row with her mother but then that crazy bitch was always competing with everybody.'

'Gloria how about you and I go and have a nice evening out somewhere and I bring you up to date on all the real gossip in the village?'

'Nice try Gary. Since when has Gloria been your property? Anyway, you don't know the half of it, especially about the Estate.'

'Look blokes, tomorrow's my night off so why don't we all meet down here for a slow social drink and the pair of you can fill me in.'

'Right on,' said Freddie. 'I'll fill you in all right.'

'Freddie, get your brain out of your pants for just a minute mate. Sounds good to us Gloria 'cos there's a lot happened since you went away. You staying by the way?'

'Day by day Gary but at the moment the answer is probably yes, for a while at least.'

The rest of that Sunday evening Freddie and I played darts, drank a few pints and listened to the rumours and stories flying around the pub. Just before closing I managed to catch Gloria in the back corridor and we played tongue dancing and pelvic dancing before George shouted for last orders and Gloria had to go back into the bar.

The cell I am sitting in hasn't got any warmer and I shiver. What made me do it? Thinking back I suppose there were so many bits to the story and part of it was to do with the coins and Freddie's cousins. It's probably easier if I give you the long version, especially as it looks as if I'm not going anywhere in a hurry and it will help pass the time: so, gold coins. As I said before the Lord family have been here for a long time and many many years ago they made some money illegally, probably in the slave trade as most of the local bigwigs were into that through Bristol and one of the Lord ancestors buried some treasure on the estate. All of that was long forgotten until little Peter Lord, when he was just a nipper upends an old box full of papers and discovers a "treasure map". Well at the time no one knew what it was but Daniel Lord, who has always been a snoopy bugger looking into hidden places decides to find out more. Remember, he was only a teenager himself at this time as he is a year or so younger than Gloria and me. With the help of his dad and then Enrico Daniel found out that the map portrayed part of the estate and showed some kind of cave. Well when we heard about this and that Daniel had gone up to see where on the estate we all thought it was a hoax. As kids we had gone all over the estate and Freddie and I and several others knew about the cave and we knew there was bugger all there. Still, the Lord family didn't know what we knew and it all came to a head just after New Year 1991. Daniel thought there was treasure but he was keeping this a secret until he found out more. Seems his elder brother discovered Daniel's secret somehow and so Michael had to have it. Then we heard that another person or persons used the place as bait for Michael and killed him outside the cave but still no treasure. End of story, well for the Lord family it was but unknown to all of us it was the beginning of the story for Freddie. It was just after New Year and there wasn't much going on but Freddie was supposed to be working in the estate yard just the same. As Freddie told me it was just the week before all this mayhem and murder happened and he was skiving off work at home. His mum was out shopping in the village or something and just when he thought all was peaceful and quiet he gets invaded by some long lost family. Two teenage boys, called Jack and Lennie Cotton suddenly appear at Freddie's mum's house and claim to be his cousins. They were the twin sons of Freddie's mum's younger sister. Well after Freddie gets over the shock he thinks this is neat and he gets real excited but the twins want to hide away for a couple of weeks to make sure no one is looking for them. They had run away from home up in Liverpool and didn't want to go back. Seems their stepfather was trying to hire them out as rent boys. Without too much thought Freddie hid them up in the estate yard in one of the barns but he realised that they could be found there so he has this brainwave, which is a very dangerous thing for Freddie. He'll hide them up in the old cave. It's dry, relatively warm, has a spring for water and it's away from any prying eyes. Just what the twins wanted: absolute fucking brainwave.

Trouble was the twins were from the streets of Liverpool and had never seen trees before and the forest freaked them out. They also got bored with the confines of the cave and Jack ended up climbing the big old oak tree right outside the cave just for something to do. Next thing Freddie knew was the pair of them going nuts about needing a rope and being rich. Now Freddie had been going up to the cave every lunchtime with some grub that he pinched from his house. After he listens to the twins unlikely story he legs it back to the yard and gets some rope. When Freddie got back to the twins he finds Jack up in the tree hopping up and down with excitement and Lennie at the bottom grasping his precious gold piece. Yes, that's right, a gold piece. Seems Jack had been digging around in the fork of the tree and unearthed this dirty old coin thing and when he cleaned it up it looked like gold so he dug around some more. Well, found the box didn't he? And of course he thought it would be full of coins 'cos it was so heavy. What box you ask? Seems Jack got gold fever after finding the first coin and so he dug around some more up in this tree. It was there he found this box. When they got the box down out of the tree and Jack had come down beside Lennie the three of them tried to open it. Sure the box was heavy and part of that was because it was really well bound with iron bars and clasps and so they couldn't open it. Now Freddie said he was already late and someone would miss him so he didn't have time to go and get a hammer to open the box like the twins wanted him to do. They didn't have enough sense to have one of the twins go down with Freddie and get a hammer and so said Freddie that was the last time he ever saw them. When he went back the next day with a hammer the box was gone, the twins were gone and so was all their clobber. The fact that it was so neat and tidy bothered Freddie a bit 'cos if the twins had just scarpered they would have left some mess behind, but then who could he ask? No one knew the twins were even there. There never was any inquiry. Freddie said his mum never heard anything from her long lost sister and from what the twins had said Freddie wasn't surprised. Seems their mum was drunk most of the time or out on the streets peddling her arse. So Freddie just kept quiet. You've got to remember he was only sixteen at the time but he didn't forget. Right after this though, the following week there was the drowning death of Norton Ferris and even more frightening the shooting death of Michael Lord right outside the cave. So Freddie just kept his mouth shut.

Now I never knew any of this and so it came as a real surprise that Friday back in mid October when suddenly in the forest Freddie is having a go at John Ferris. Slowly the various bits and pieces got put together by rumour and hearsay. The bones in John Ferris's cottage did turn out to be the twins and although the box was never found some of the coins unearthed up by the cave were the same as those along the garden path of Flo' Whelks's cottage. Seems Idwal Ferris must have seen Freddie going up to the cave and found the twins and their box. Perhaps he lured them down to the warmth and civilisation of the cottage and buried the poor little buggers. Then Idwal was supposed to have this deal with Larry Whelks that went tits up so he killed Larry and did time. When he came back supposedly looking for revenge on his dad's death he was also coming back for the gold coins. John kills Idwal in the cottage and then John himself gets killed by Miss scary pants from Goth city. What a bloody mess all over some long ago buried "treasure" and all of that really didn't affect me directly but it did affect Gloria.

Bob Edwards, Bob Edwards I muttered as I sat in this dreary cell. I told you earlier I was proud of my name originally and now I felt both embarrassed and really pissed off. Great grandfather had been the gamekeeper and then his son Edward had moved into being the forest foreman, but when my dad had copped out of the forest the Lord family moved Ernest Edwards in to the foreman position. Before that the Edwards family had just been labourers. Bob Edward's grandfather George had been the same age as my great grandfather but he had been killed in the trenches in France. His son Ernest was much the same age as grandfather Edward and he too worked as a labourer on the estate, well he did until my grandfather died in 1978. Dad wasn't labouring in no forest and so Ernest became foreman and our family lost out. Old Ernest had married Gwen Biddle and they had two kids, Tilley and Bob and it was Bob Edwards who became foreman when his dad died in 1988. So our family got dumped from being in charge to being back on the bottom of the pecking order and that pissed me off even more about my dad and my name.

'No good you mutterin' to yourself mate. They'll decide when they're good and ready and not before. Still, I've no doubt the judge will have something tasty up his sleeve for you you little tosser. Fancy getting riled up with your mates all over some tart. Why can't you blokes realise cunts are all the same.'

I flung myself off the bench against the wall and grabbed the bars of the cell.

'You don't know nothing mate. You don't know fuck all. You've absolutely no idea in that pin size head of yours. You're so fucking stupid you don't even realise that you've been pretending to read the newspaper upside down. Perhaps you're an Abo from Australia. Jump like a roo do you? You're dark enough to be an Abo although you ain't got no hair so it's hard to see whether it had been frizzy.'

The guard folded his newspaper and put it down by his feet. 'Maybe mate but I'm the one on the right side of the bars.'

GLORIA'S TALE

AFTER THAT EVENTFUL WEEKEND WHEN John Ferris played darts, played kinky sex and finally played dead and the police had interviewed anyone and everyone it was time for some quiet explanations. As Gloria had promised us that Sunday evening Freddie and I went back into the pub on the Monday to meet up with her for a quiet drink and an update. It was her night off and the three of us almost decided to go somewhere else to drink but what the hell, it was our local.

'You show us yours and we'll show you ours,' Freddie suggested with a smirk on his face, 'just like old times.'

'Freddie mate, get your mind out of the gutter for a moment. I'd like to know what this lovely lady has been up to. You know Gloria you just up and left without a word and none of us knew where you had gone. Your mum never said anything, not even to Freddie's mum and they had been good friends. Your dad wouldn't say a word about you, except to tell us to piss off and good riddance.'

'Well he would wouldn't he?'

'Why's that then?'

'Look, I can tell you part of it 'cos you might be able to help me but keep it to yourselves. People might come asking questions and I tried to get away from all that.'

'All what, and who's coming asking questions Gloria?'

'What've you done girl? You're running aren't you?'

'Freddie, don't push it. Let Gloria tell us what she wants us to hear. When you've heard it you may not want to know and some heavy will come down here and give you the third degree. Thought of that you stupid git?'

Freddie sat back in his seat and supped at his pint. I could hear the wheels going round in his pitiful brain. Gloria looked at the pair of us. 'Mouths shut?' she asked.

'Sure love. At the end we might have one or two things for you that you don't know about, seeing as you have been away a while and some of us have grown up.'

'That include Freddie?' Gloria giggled.

'Have a feel darling. That should answer your question.'

'Is he always like this Gary?'

'No Gloria, I think he's just a little embarrassed because a good looking girl hasn't talked to him for a long time and he doesn't know how to behave. I'll put a leash on him, or perhaps a gag would be better.'

I watched Gloria suddenly change her expression and her face hardened a little as she seemed to size Freddie up. It was almost as if she was seriously considering what I had suggested and imagining Freddie on a leash, gagged.

'Come on then Gloria. It was just over seven years ago and it all happened so suddenly.'

Gloria put her glass down on the table and leant back in her seat. She seemed to look inside her head and I can only assume she was thinking how much she would tell us and perhaps how best to spin the story.

'What's your mum ever told you Freddie about my mum? They're cousins as you know and they used to be good friends when they were kids.'

'Nothing,' said Freddie. 'What would she have said? Sure I know that my mum's dad was the elder brother of your mum's mother. Jack and Gwen Biddle they were but so what?'

I watched Gloria and she obviously realised that maybe that wasn't the best way to start what she wanted to tell us. She swirled her beer around in her glass.

'What do you two know about my dad?'

'Walter Manson was a big man, a lorry driver who came from somewhere down in Devon didn't he? Married your mum about the same time as Freddie's mum got married.'

'No Gary, my mum got married in 1972, about a year before Tilley Edwards,' said Freddie.

'And yet I'm older than you are Freddie and I got born soon after my mum got married.'

'You saying your mum had to get married?'

'Work it out you two. Freddie wasn't born until 1973, after me.'

'Yes but so what?'

Here Gloria went back into her thinking mode.

'Gloria girl, what's all this got to do with fucking off and then coming back here? Your dad's dead so what's it got to do with him?'

'That's part of it Gary. It's because he's dead that I've come back. Well, as I said that's part of it.'

'You saying you ran away because of him?'

'Like you said my dad was a big man and yes he was a lorry driver so he wasn't around all of the time but when he came home he wanted his dues didn't he?'

'What dues?' asked Freddie who obviously was at a loss. 'Gloria this is doing my head in. What are you talking about?'

'He wanted his weekly Saturday night under the covers fuck you stupid prat. Jesus Freddie, to think we are vaguely related makes me want to puke on occasions. You're so thick.'

'Watch who you're calling thick.'

I put up my hands. 'Back off you two. Let's take this one step at a time. We've got all evening and I'll get another round of drinks in. Same again you two?'

'What are you three planning over there?' asked George

'George we're having a quiet drink and talking over old times. Freddie and I are helping Gloria catch up on the gossip in the village so she can be really good behind the bar for you. Not make too many fuck-ups if you know what I mean.'

'So you think that you and Freddie really know what's going on in this village do you and it's me behind the bar here who knows nothing?'

'Maybe George but we know all of the stuff happening up on the estate and that's where most of the action has been taking place of late. Been in the thick of it George Freddie and I have what with the fire, the cottages and the knifings. It's all go up there George.'

'Gary son you're full of it but here's your drinks. Just don't fill poor Gloria's head with any stupid stories. I think she had a tough time up in London recently.'

When I took the drinks back to the table Gloria had obviously told Freddie to listen for a change. 'Fine darling, we all grew up here like good little kids and had a grand time as teenagers, even for a fuck-all village like ours. There was you and me Gloria, and Freddie with Sandra Porlock. Remember the fun and games we had in our house? Mum used to work in the supermarket and dad was out on the road wherever and we had the house to ourselves. Learnt a lot that year before Sandra topped herself.'

'Yes,' said Freddie, 'the year we all learnt to shag our brains out.'

'Freddie!!' Gloria turned to Freddie and drew her finger across her throat signifying he'd be dead meat if he opened his trap again. 'I told you to shut it.'

'Gloria, you were sort of hinting about your mum and dad. What are you telling us?'

'My mum must have been a bit of a handful when she was a kid. Think about it. She grew up when the Beatles, the Stones and those other wild bands were starting. You've seen the pictures with all those teenage girls screaming their heads off. Long time ago I even found some old scrapbooks with newspaper clippings and photos.'

'So she was a normal kid growing up in the fifties and sixties. They were all a bit wacky then I thought. Everything had changed from their parent's time and so the kids went wild.'

'Yes Gary but look at my mum now. Something happened. She's got religion and now she's a born-again Christian or something. When I found those pictures I couldn't believe it and so I went and talked to Freddie's mum Rosemary.'

'What did my mum know about anything? She's never told me anything about pop stars. I don't think she even likes music. Dad had these old country and western crap tapes from somewhere in Yankieville but mum just watches the tele.'

'Maybe Freddie but your mum says my mum really changed about the time I was born and that started the problem.'

'What problem?'

'The Saturday night under the covers problem Gary Templeton you stupid bugger. I don't know what my dad ever got up to when he was out on the road but when he came home he wanted his bit of the other.'

'So?' said Freddie, 'why not? Bloke comes home from a hard day's work he wants his tea on the table and his......'

'Freddie, we get the message.' I turned back to Gloria. 'But your mum had gone holy, or frigid, or cold or something Gloria? That's what you're telling us.'

'But where's the problem?' asked Freddie. 'He sits on the bog looking at a girlie magazine and jerks off. Easy, end of story.' Suddenly Freddie thumped the table and all three glasses jumped. Fortunately they all came down straight and we didn't suddenly get a bath in beer.

'Watch it you silly sod. What's your problem?'

'That's the point, there wasn't one was there Gary? Your old dad must have got his end away Gloria 'cos then there was that little wanker of a brother of yours, dearly beloved Wendell. Don't tell me the fairies brought him? I know he's gay, or at least he pretends to be but as far as I know he came into the world the same way as all of us. Head first sliding out of your mother and the end result of good old Walter romping away under the covers on a Saturday night, or whatever night.'

'Jesus Freddie you've got a crude mouth on you at times, you really have.'

Turning away from looking at Freddie I realised that Gloria had that hard look back on her face. I wasn't sure whether she was really angry or very upset: whether she was holding back tears or about to thump Freddie in the face. I reached over and put my hand on hers to gently catch her attention. 'Forget it Gloria. Freddie's missed you and so have I. It's great to have you back here. Don't worry about why you left 'cos you're back now and said you're going to stay.' I watched Gloria slowly let out a great breath of air and felt the tension ease off a little as she looked at me.

'Gary, I've got to tell someone and who could be better than my old mates.' She turned to Freddie and said, 'You're part right Freddie although you may not know it. Yes, I've no doubt my dad banged away on Saturday nights and yes Wendell got born into our loving household and what a loving household it turned out to be.'

Gloria got up from the table. 'I've gotta pee and I'll get another round in when I come back. Then I'll tell you a story that'll curl your toes up about happy families.' She walked across the room and down the corridor to the ladies. 'Freddie, think before you open your trap mate for Christ's sake. Can't you see the girl's hurting? She needs to tell us something and you're not helping. Let her talk for fuck's sake.'

'Okay okay Gary. I hear you mate but she sure sounds one fucked-up bird and we haven't heard anything about why she came back from London. I'll bet there's more to that as that's just recent and she has this look about her, like she's expecting something or someone to come walking back in through the door.'

'Here you go lads. That feels better. George could really do with some work being done in that ladies lav though. There's quite a long list of phone numbers on the wall and all sorts of suggestions about the length of cock on the end of the phone. Didn't see your number there Freddie. Playing hard to get?'

'Gloria, I've told Freddie here to button it while you get a chance to explain. As you said, if you need to tell someone then who better than your old mates?'

'After Wendell was born I think the Saturday night sessions stopped completely. When I think back on those years I'm not sure whether my brother wasn't born out of mum being raped. Dad was always tense, edgy and I tried to keep out of the way but the trouble was I was growing up. It must have been about a year after Wendell was born that dad first came to play happy families.'

I was about to say something when I remembered what I had told Freddie and so I just lifted my glass and swallowed. We all had a drink and Gloria just looked at the pair of us with a mask of a face.

'Happy families and I was eleven. I couldn't hide and he told me I couldn't tell mum. It would upset her and dry up her milk or something. At first he tried to turn it into a game as if he was teaching me something. Told me it was important I learnt about these things 'cos they wouldn't teach me this at school and a girl should know these things. Who was better to teach his daughter about bodies and sex than a father? Looking out for me he said he was and making sure that I knew how to be safe. Making sure I knew how not to get pregnant, how not to get diseases, how to make a man happy. All one big happy family we were my dad said. I didn't know any better and I will admit he was a good teacher but fuck it he was my dad.'

I didn't know where to look or what to say. Freddie was silent too, staring across the room.

'You never said Gloria. All the time we were going out together you never said.'

'No Gary, I never said. As I got older and started to understand what was happening dad threatened me never to tell anyone. He was a big man remember. He never hurt me, in fact he was quite gentle for a big man but he told me never to tell anyone or else. What could I do?'

'But we went out for a couple of years. We were......'

'Yes Gary and I can still remember the first night for you.'

'Do I really need to hear this?' Freddie asked.

'No Freddie, I'll skip that bit but there is something you need to know too.'

I watched Freddie blush but wasn't sure what he was thinking. Gloria turned back towards me. 'Gary, you know that it's no secret we all four of us fucked each other. We had a couple of those strip poker sessions when

35

we all got pissed out of our minds and ran around your house bollock naked. Well you and Freddie were. I suppose Sandra and I were pussy naked or something. It ended up with us all over each other and I know you and Sandra were together so Freddie and I fucked each others brains out too. Fine, so we all know all that.'

Freddie blushed again and Gloria put her hand on his. 'Freddie, it was good and we all enjoyed ourselves. We were kids growing up and it's what everyone does.'

'So why did Sandra top herself? She was having a good time with us. I thought she and I were really an item but something happened. Something happened after your birthday party Gary, your sixteenth I think. Your parents were out, well most of the evening and we didn't drink too much as we knew they would be back before the party ended. Gloria what happened that night? I don't remember saying or doing anything with Sandra to piss her off. Why did she top herself?'

This time it was Gloria who was quiet and sat staring out across the room. She looked at me and she looked at Freddie. 'Time for some more home truths guys only this time it wasn't my happy family. Freddie you were always careful with Sandra weren't you? We used to joke about rubbers and we even had that one evening when we came up with a funny routine about when and how to put them on.'

'Yes Gloria, we were all kids and Sandra sure didn't want to get pregnant. We were at High School and Sandra wanted to go on to College or something. I remember her telling me she really wanted to be a teacher and help kids learn to read and write. She thought ankle-biters were cute but she sure didn't want any of her own while she was still a teenager.'

'Then how did she get pregnant?'

'But she never did.'

'Yes Freddie, Sandra was six months pregnant when she slit her wrists in the bath.'

Freddie slumped back in his seat. 'Never, never, she never said. She never told me. I know she felt sick for a while and all that but she never said why. Then I come home from school and the police are talking to my mum, asking all about my relationships with Sandra. They asked all about sex and I explained that we always used a condom. She didn't want to get pregnant I told them and I explained why.'

'They didn't tell you anything? They never explained why they were asking about sex and condoms?'

'No. I was scared. Mum and dad were really angry about my having sex at my age. Dad really had a go at me and mum wouldn't let me go out anywhere for a while. Christ it was like being in bloody prison.'

I sat there quietly wondering whether Gloria was going to tell me it was her dad who got Sandra pregnant. The two girls did a lot together and Sandra was often over at Gloria's house.

'Who get her pregnant Gloria? Was it your dad? Did he decide to fuck your friends as well as you?'

As soon as I had said this I wished I had kept my mouth shut. What a stupid and cruel thing to say I thought but Gloria just sat there and looked at me with a kind of sad expression on her face. 'No Gary,' she said eventually. 'What happened the night of your birthday party? Do you remember or were you too pissed like Freddie here. I can remember how legless Freddie was but how drunk were you?'

I tried to remember but it was a long time ago. 'Jesus Gloria that's a lifetime ago.'

'Sixteenth birthday Gary, rather special.'

'Yes but none of us were virgins by that time. You've just brought up all that earlier stuff when we played strip poker and such. I don't remember anything special.'

'Where was Sandra living at that time?'

'She lived by the post office, down on the High Street.'

'No, think again.'

'She'd just moved,' said Freddie as he lurched forwards off the back of his seat. 'The family had just moved to one of those new houses out on the council estate. Just that week if I remember right, but so what Gloria? What has that to do with anything?'

'So how did she get home Freddie? None of us had cars. You didn't even have a pushbike let alone a motorbike.'

'Dad took her,' I blurted out. 'Mum and dad came home around midnight and dad took her home.'

'So?' said Freddie.

'Think Freddie. Mr. Brian cocksman Templeton takes a rather drunk and sexy Sandra home. It had been a great evening and we were all feeling wet and warm. Your dad Gary couldn't keep his hands off anything that wore a skirt and I doubt whether Sandra had put her wet knickers back on. Kind, sweet loving man your dad is Gary with his silver tongue and wandering cock. Poor Sandra wouldn't have stood a chance and your dad Gary wouldn't have thought she wasn't on the pill like every other woman he shagged. Everyone was on the pill. Even I was by that time but I know Sandra wasn't.'

'My dad?'

'Yes Gary, your precious dad couldn't resist. She was a good looker was Sandra and your dad must have thought he'd died and gone to heaven. Such a sweet young thing and nice and juicy after the party that night. Bet he came home later that night than was expected although I doubt whether you could remember. You were probably sound asleep by that time.'

'Brian fucking Templeton,' cried Freddie and then put his hand over his mouth when he realised where he was. 'Your dad arsehole, your dad fucks my bird and she ends up slitting her wrists. Someone should castrate your dad Gary. No, that's only taking his balls away. They need to cut off his cock too.'

'Seem to remember your mother getting really worked up after my party,' I said to Gloria. 'Everything sort of went pear-shaped after that party. Your dad started to give me a hard time too.'

'Well I was working wasn't I as well as trying to study to get to University. I put long hours in working in that poxy tea-shop and I was having troubles at home. Wendell was starting to be a sneaky little bastard in my things and mum was quoting from the Bible all times of the day.'

'Did Wendell ever know about you and your dad?' asked Freddie. 'I'll cut the balls off the little cock-sucker if you say yes. He's already a bully for many of the young kids in the village and I hear he's been in and out of Tom Daley's place too often.'

'Wendell's too smart for his own good,' said Gloria, 'and I've found out since I've come home that he's become another computer nerd.'

'Probably poring over porno sites with Tom Daley. Seeing who can come on the screen first.'

'Wash your mouth out Freddie.'

'Think about it Gary. He really is a little shit. Sorry Gloria but I don't count him in your happy family.'

'Well that last year it wasn't very happy now was it? Sandra tops herself. I was working all hours and my dad was getting rather demanding.'

'So you fucked off?'

'I'd had enough Gary. Remember Val Gordon at school?'

'The girl who was a lesbie? Well we all thought she was. She sure didn't have any time for blokes and always had a gaggle of little girls around her. Still, she could sure play football. We could have used her

39

on the boy's team in that last year at school. Anyway, what about Val Gordon?'

'Remember when she left school?'

'The whole family left,' said Freddie. 'Didn't her old man get some cushy job up in London? He was the driver for some Company President wasn't he and when his boss got promoted to London he took Ken Gordon with him and the whole family up and moved. That was at the end of our last year wasn't it?'

"That's when you went Gloria, or right afterwards.'

'Yes Freddie, you're right about the Gordons, and yes Gary I ran away to London and stayed with Val for a while. They had relatives up in the East End, somewhere in Whitechapel and I lived with all of them. They knew their way around and I had a friend in Val.'

'But you weren't no lesbie Gloria.'

'Gary by that time my fucking dad had taught me a lot and needs must. Val and her family were good to me and she really helped me get started in London.'

'Did her parents know? Jesus, I don't know Gloria. That kind of turns me off. What kind of thrill is it for two birds? Does my head in that does just thinking about it.'

'What about you Gary?' Gloria asked. 'How do you feel about lesbians?'

'Live and let live I say Gloria. Whatever turns you on. Given the right time and place I could see myself getting in the scene.'

'Jesus Gary you're one fucked-up bloke you are. Pardon me if I sit with my back to the wall here before you get any other weird ideas.'

Gloria laughed as she looked at the pair of us. 'It's good to be home,' she said. 'At least the world down here isn't quite so fucked-up as it is in London.'

'But what about last Saturday night?' I said. 'That Australian bird was coming on to you if I remember right. What was it she said, something about half an hour on the couch in the back room?'

'Yes Gary and she was a typical city product. George said she came from Sydney and that is one of the major homosexual cities in the world. They even have some Gay Pride parade down the streets – typical Australian in your face sexual freedom.'

'So you ran away to get away from your dad and you never told anyone?'

'Just think about it Gary. Who was I going to tell? When I got up to London I told Val and at least she understood. She thought I had done the right thing and she helped me find a job in the end. Well her folks did.'

'So what did you do?'

Once again Gloria went into a thinking mode and Freddie and I supped on our pints waiting. What we didn't know at the time were some of the other things that Gloria hadn't told us. I found out later when Gloria and I were alone but I don't think Freddie ever realised exactly what Gloria was like. As a little girl she hadn't been horrified and terrified by her father's "teaching" but she'd liked it. She told me later that her dad taught her all sorts of things I'd never dreamt about let alone considered doing. Going up to London to live with Val Gordon was nothing new to Gloria. By that time she'd spent time with men and women in all sorts of activities and I'd never known any of this. One real reason she ran away she told me was she thought it would drive her mother mad. She thought her mother already knew about her and her dad and chose to ignore it but sooner or later it would lead to madness or murder she said. When she had the chance she ran.

'Well I had worked as a waitress in the café here and so I got a job as a cocktail waitress up in the West End.'

41

'Working in one of those pubs were you?' asked Freddie, 'or one of those posh wine bars? Christ, some of those wankers get up my nose. There were a couple of ponces in here a few nights ago, before you came Gloria and they wanted some special wine. Had to be at the right temperature landlord or it spoils the taste on the palate. George was fit to be tied and he nearly broke open the bottle over their heads but in the end he pulls the cork and offers a sample to one of the blokes. You should have seen the bloody pantomime with this geezer sniffing, sipping and looking for somewhere to spit.'

'What happened in the end Freddie?'

'Silly bugger looks at the label doesn't he and asks his fruity mate whether it was the right year. George quickly adds that this was the bottle and year he had asked for and that would be twenty five quid please. Didn't give the silly bugger a chance to hand it back.'

'And they drank it?'

'Fucked if I know. Once George got his money I lost interest and we went back to watching the tele.'

'You never said Gloria. You never said where you were working.'

'It was a night club, the "Oasis", somewhere off Marshall Street, just round the corner from Carnaby Street. You must have heard of Carnaby Street you two?'

'Of course Gloria, street of the clothes or somesuch back in the sixties or whenever.'

'You work there all the time or was that just where you started?'

'I suppose I worked at two places Gary over the years and the Oasis was the first one. You gotta' realise that the East End, well Whitechapel anyway is just like a big village even though it's part of the city. Like this village the people who are somebody know each other and one hand greases the other. Val's Uncle, Ken's brother-in-law I suppose knew some of the local heavies and they had two or three clubs up in the West End.

After I'd been there a couple of weeks Val took me up to the West End and we met Vince Tobin who was the manager of the Oasis. The club itself was owned by the Westgates but I never got to meet them. Not that I'd want to if what Val told me was true.'

'Why, what did the Westgates do?'

'Freddie, the less you know the better off you'll be. Trust me.'

'So you worked at the Oasis and some other club just waiting on tables. That's a bit of a drag Gloria, especially after you wanted to go to College. You were all keen that last year at school. Why didn't you try up in London?'

'I had to work Gary didn't I? I had no money. In fact I had fuck all really. I'd run away with a few clothes, a few quid and wanted to get lost.'

'Sounds like my cousins,' said Freddie sadly. 'They just wanted to run away from being abused. Poor little buggers didn't have a chance did they? That fucker Idwal Ferris killed them and then buried them.'

'Freddie, don't get so mournful mate. That's all done with and Idwal Ferris is dead and so is his brother so forget them mate. Here, I'll get you another pint while Gloria tells us the rest of her story. We haven't heard why she came back here yet and I'm sure it wasn't just to see you Freddie, gorgeous as you might be.'

'Piss off Gary and get those pints in. Next thing I know you'll want to kiss me. Christ, the very thought makes me want to puke.'

'Gary, go and get the pints in before Freddie does himself an injury. I'll tell you a little more before we call it quits. It's getting late and George will be calling for last orders pretty soon. Shift it Gary.'

Over the next half an hour before George called for last orders Gloria told us a little bit about life in the Clubs. Never having been very far, well I've been up to Bristol a few times but never up to London so Gloria's story was like a different world. First of all nothing started until our normal bedtime. Shit, as a forest worker you clock on around seven and we finish around four. That leaves you time for tea, a bit of a wash up and down to the pub until closing. Bed by eleven 'cos you've got to be up soon after six. Gloria's said her world didn't come to life until eleven and typically finished around six in the morning. First there was the crowd who might drop in after the flicks or the theatre. Then there were some of the young rowdies on the Club scene and finally the hard core punters who were usually into something illegal one way or another. Weird tourists would come in at any hour and the cops would float in and out depending on what they had heard.

'So did you just wait on tables? Did the Club have any floor show or music? Was there a band? Hey Gary, that would have been neat with Gloria in the band. Didn't you do some singing when you were younger Gloria? I seem to remember you did some dozy musical for a couple of years at school. So, did you sing?'

I watched Gloria as she listened to Freddie prattling on. She seemed to laugh within herself as if some of Freddie's suggestions were hilarious.

'No Freddie I didn't sing but there was a floor show.'

'So if you didn't sing what did you do?'

'There was a stage for dancers, complete with a couple of poles and a few other props I suppose.'

'What did you do with these poles then? This sounds like some kind of high wire act.'

'Freddie haven't you seen any TV shows about nightclubs and dance routines? Haven't you seen girls wrapping themselves around poles?' Here Gloria stopped and giggled. 'Jesus I can just imagine you Freddie coming into the Club and sitting down with your eyes out on stalks mate. Mark you I would probably have to pick you up off the floor when you heard the prices we charged for drinks, even though most of them were well-watered.'

'Any lap dancing?' I asked. Gloria turned to look at me. 'No Gary, not really but some of the tables were up close to the little stage.'

'And a couple of little rooms behind the stage?' I asked.

'Not directly Gary.'

'But close by?'

'It was a Club Gary not a bleeding brothel.'

'But some of the girls had regulars?'

'Some of the girls had habits too.'

'What do you mean had habits?' asked Freddie. 'Nuns wear habits and my mum tells me I've got bad habits so what are we talking about?'

'Freddie I'll tell you some other time mate,' I said. 'Tomorrow at work. It's time to leave before George locks us in. Night Gloria. We'll be in tomorrow and you can finish up your story then. In the meantime I'll educate our dear little friend here about the facts of life in the big city.'

'Hey Gary, I don't want none of your unnatural sex talk mate. I'm strictly a bird man myself and I'm out of here. Night Gloria.' Freddie left and I managed a quick snog with Gloria before George threw me out too.

Gloria was working that Tuesday evening and so Freddie and I had a game of darts before Freddie's mates came in and he wanted to join them. So he went off to drink with Danny, Lester and that great oaf Don and I continued to throw darts at the board until Gloria came over on her break.

'Christ my feet are killing me,' she said as she slumped down on the bench seat. 'I thought I'd find it easier than working up in town but George keeps going on at me to find things he's forgot. Seems Freddie has left you for that useless lot over in the corner. Whatever does he find in those three layabouts? Danny Masters was always taking things apart at school but never got the hang of putting them back together again did he? What's he now, a so-called mechanic? His boss must be a trusting soul Gary.'

'He works for Taffy Williams and he's a bloody genius with motors.'

'Old Taffy still around? He must be in his seventies by now? He was old when we were still at school.'

'Freddie likes to feel he's the leader and with that lot I suppose he is. Lester Rainer paints houses and anything else near the house the way he slops paint around and none of us know what Don Winters really does. He goes in and out of the offices of Tilson and Betts, you know the solicitors but what he actually does none of us have ever thought to ask. Still, enough of them Gloria what about you?'

'What do you mean what about me?'

'You never told us last night why the runner back here.'

'Who said I did a runner?'

Before I had a chance to continue questioning Gloria a new voice cut across the pub floor.

'Freddie, excuse me a minute but isn't one of your friends here Danny Masters?'

'Sure Miss Samantha, this 'ere is Danny. What's he done now?'

'Nothing Freddie. Evening Danny. I've brought some folks here to meet you. Seems you and they are related from a long time back. This is Mr. and Mrs. Stark and they've come over from Vancouver in Canada to find some old relatives.'

'Hi folks, I'm Lloyd Stark and this is my wife Candice. As Samantha said we've sort of traced our family back a way and we think that our great grandparents are the same as those of Brian and Ethel Masters who are your parents aren't they Danny?'

'Yea, they're my parents but I don't know about no what did you say great grandparents or anyone. I know dad's father was from here 'cos I can remember my old granddad but before that God knows.'

'Well before that Danny your great grandfather on your dad's side came up from Buckfast in Devon and that's where the family seems to have started.'

'Anyway, what's it got to do with me?'

'No offence son, Danny is it? We're just interested in where we came from and thought we'd try and find out where all the relatives went. Seems you father and grandfather came up from Devon to here whereas we have been to see some of the other relatives who stayed in Devon and some who moved further east. That was the New Forest wasn't it Samantha? Seems funny to think that area should be called the New Forest but we've learnt so much on this trip.'

'Well I can't do anything for you,' said Danny. 'Me I'm just a mechanic and still live with mum and dad.'

'Sure Danny, we've just come from your parent's house,' said Samantha, 'and they told us you'd be here. We just came to say hi. Lloyd and Candice wanted to see where and how all their relatives lived. It's a sort of education for them, a special kind of holiday if you like.'

'Can we buy you lads a pint?' asked Lloyd.

'Sure,' said Freddie quickly, 'as great great whatevers of Danny we'll join you in a drink. Friends across the ocean or something.'

'What's all that about Gary? Isn't that Samantha Lord with those two foreigners?'

'I'm not really sure Gloria but I heard Miss Samantha had started some new flaky kind of job. Seems there are rich folk somewhere in this world who want to know where they came from.'

'Christ, most of the time I was just wishing I could forget where I came from. I used to take pills to help me forget. You saying that folks pay to find their relatives like Danny?'

'Apparently.'

'Gary it's got to be a con of some kind. Nobody's naff enough to want to find Danny, or his mum and dad for that matter. They're all a bunch of losers.'

'Well I'll bet our Miss Samantha ain't doing it for free Gloria love. She's offering a service. Just like you did up in London?' Here I looked at Gloria as I posed this remark. Her face went through an array of portrayals and she finally brought her gaze back to me. 'Suppose you're right there Gary. Offering a service. Don't we all?'

'It paid though Gloria.'

'Fucking right it paid Gary but I also paid. They were supposed to protect me you know. Keep all the weirdoes out of my face but you could get some right bastards who wanted their money's worth.'

'So it was more than waiting on tables?'

'Val knew what I liked and what I could do Gary. Vince Tobin wasn't too bad a boss and most of the other lads in the Club were okay too. Sure there were a couple of right wankers but Vince looked after me. Part of the problem actually came from some of the other girls. We had all sorts in the two Clubs including several girls from Europe and even a couple from Africa.'

'So what was the problem? They all speak English? Were some of them illegals? You know you read about that kind of thing in the Sunday newspapers but you were right there girl.'

'The Oasis wasn't too bad but the other Club was a little different. I'm not really sure who owned that place but Vince was supposed to manage both. Trouble is he could change faces between the two places. At the Exotica he could be a real bastard, real cruel. Most of the girls at the Exotica were from Europe and many of them were hooked on drugs. I never liked going there.'

'Night Gary. Night, Gloria isn't it? Gloria Manson? Seems we've both been away for some time.'

'Night Miss Samantha. You finished with Freddie and his mates?'

'Yes Gary, we've just introduced Danny there to some of his long lost relatives.'

'Danny's been long lost Miss Samantha, relatively speaking.'

'Clever Gary. Good night.'

'What did she want?' asked Freddie.

'Just being sociable Freddie. She didn't want anything mate. I don't think Miss Samantha wants for anything. That family seems to have most of the things it needs in life.'

'Get killed though don't they. Two eldest boys dead and I heard Miss Samantha's husband got burnt alive somewhere in Canada.'

'Jesus you're a morbid couple. I'm off back to work Gary. Your three mates leaving Freddie?'

'Yea, that Canadian couple spooked Danny. He's off back to check whether his dad had told him the whole story. He's worried he's got some starving relatives in Africa somewhere and they want his pay packet.'

Later that evening I managed to notice Gloria slip away up the back corridor and as Freddie was glued to the TV I quietly excused myself to take a leak I said to Freddie. He sort of grunted and concentrated back on the tube.

'Well darling, you got time for a kiss and a cuddle?'

'Gary give over. I'm just off to find some packets of crisps for George. He'll expect me back in a jiffy. Gary get your hands out of there.' Gloria suddenly went quiet as I slipped my tongue into her mouth and continued to slide my hands under her panties. 'Hold it right there.'

'Gladly,' I said.

'Later Gary. Later, after closing time. I'll see you later. Mum'll be asleep by the time I get home. Wait for me outside somewhere and we'll walk home.'

'Promise?'

'I never make promises Gary but I'll see you later. Now get your paws off the pussy and go and piss.'

Very quietly Gloria unlocked her front door and slowly tiptoed indoors. She held my hand and whispered 'Watch the step.' Still holding my hand she led me into the front parlour and once inside she slowly closed the door. 'Now quietly. Mum's bedroom is upstairs at the back and she sleeps pretty soundly but I never know when she's in one of her holy moods and gets up to pray at some weird hour in the night. Gave me a bloody fright the first time she did it when I came home. She mutters and when I went to look there is this white-gowned apparition on her knees chattering into space. Christ, I thought I'd seen a ghost or something. I'm not even sure whether she is sleep-walking or whether she is actually awake but spaced out somewhere in a trance. Anyway let's keep it quiet.'

All through this little monologue of Gloria's I had been slowly peeling her clothes off which just goes to show that blokes can do two things at the same time because I was also listening to her voice. Lastly I slid my hands inside the elastic of her panties and eased them down her legs. As I knelt to slip them off her feet I brushed my lips across her pelvis. Gloria wrapped her hands around my head and pulled me tightly against her body.

Half an hour later we lay on our sides looking at each other in the darkness. 'You enjoy that Gloria don't you?'

'What do you think?'

50

'Answering a question with a question but yes, you enjoy it. Was the job up in London like that most of the time?'

'No, not really. Sure for some special customers Vince asked me to put out but I enjoyed it and he knew it so it wasn't any great hardship. Val used to come up to the Club sometimes and we'd do threesomes or foursomes. She always got a kick out of that. There were several girls at the Oasis who could swing every which way. Sure Gary, the Oasis was primarily a night club with a floor show, backroom gambling, expensive liquor and a couple of small private cubicles but Vince also had some of us party with special guests but that was separate from the Oasis. I had one really good friend at the Oasis, Lola Martinez and I think she was from Spain. She had this costume as a matador but she was a dominatrix complete with red corselet, red cape, red high-heeled boots and a whip. Sometimes I would just watch her with a client. Primarily she worked with women and she could really turn some women on but sometimes she and I would team up with one or two johns. Depending on the blokes the scene could go any number of ways and Lola and I really enjoyed working together.'

'Who were the blokes?'

'Nobody you'd know Gary Templeton.'

'You never did drugs?'

'No way. I've seen too many girls hit rock bottom doing drugs. Mugs game Gary but we were lucky. We got well enough paid and looked after. I've never seen a need to get spaced out after leaving being a teenager. Sort of "been there done that" if you know what I mean. It was a great scene for a while. In this last year we had a new girl come in. Belle Katz she called herself. She was a real Londoner and a cheeky bitch full of practical jokes. I worked with her a little bit but she preferred going solo with punters. She looked really young and had a waif-like appearance with almost a little girl's figure. Some of the older johns really liked her when

51

she'd dress up as a little school girl with a gymslip that hardly covered her bum and a loose top. The naughty school-girl routine with gentle canings, kissing it better and sitting on teacher's lap was a great success. Some of the older blokes would come before the lessons got very far. The problem Belle told me was getting some of the white-haired clients to even get stiff. She had all sorts of toys to help some of them get it propped up.'

'So how come it ended Gloria? If it was that bloody good how come you're down here?'

'Not sure you really want to know Gary. What you don't know you can't tell now can you?'

'Jesus Gloria it couldn't have been that bad.'

Gloria rolled onto her back and stared up at the ceiling. Rays of pale moonlight shafted across the room and everything looked black and white. 'Come on Gloria. You might as well get it off your chest. Who else are you going to tell down here? What's the problem?'

'Murder Gary, that's the problem. Well, I suppose not the murder itself although that wasn't necessary poor kid but the problem was I saw it.'

'Where was this?'

'Look, you keep your trap shut now if I tell you or quite likely they'll come looking for you too.'

'Who will Gloria, who'll come looking?'

'Gary, like I told you, the Exotica Club was more hard core and the clientele was a lot more brutal. Most of the girls there were European and I guess many if not all of them were illegals so there was a lot of pressure.'

'What do you mean pressure?'

'Gary they had to pay off getting into England and the owners made sure they paid. Also a couple of the girls I know were couriers to and from the continent and most of them used drugs. It was a much rougher scene and many of the johns were East Europeans who had some disgusting tastes. Also there was some money laundering going on although I'm not sure exactly how that worked and I didn't want to know.'

'So who got murdered?'

'I was working at the Exotica that night and had gone off on a break and I was hiding away out of trouble in a back room. Suddenly I heard a lot of shouting and swearing and four guys burst into the next room dragging two girls. They also had Vince along with them and it seemed they were trying to persuade Vince that he should hire these two new girls. Vince was a little reluctant and there was a lot of loud talk in what sounded like Russian or Polish or somesuch. I just sat next door but the trouble was the door between the two rooms was open and I expected someone to come looking and check. Shit Gary I was scared.'

'So what happened?'

'Seems they persuaded Vince and he left and then the trouble started because after one of the men shouted something at the girls they started screaming. From the sound of it one of the guys slapped one of the girls and the screaming stopped for a moment but this was followed by a loud shout which must have been "no" of some kind. Next thing I know the guys are laughing and I hear the sound of clothing being torn and again the girls are back screaming. Now I made the stupid mistake of moving in my little room.'

'And they heard you and found you?'

'No but I just wanted to see what was going on.'

'Could you?'

'I watched the four guys rape this poor kid. She didn't look older than fourteen or fifteen. They just took turns. All the while one of them held the other kid so she could watch and see what her life was going to be like.'

'So what happened after that? You said someone got murdered.'

'The other kid was crying by this time. I suppose she expected it was going to be her turn next. One of the guys said something to the crying girl and I heard her start and catch her breath as if what was said really frightened her. Next thing I could just see was another of the men pick up the one they had just raped and standing behind her he pulled her hair so her head stretched backwards. The one who I thought was the leader said something to the other crying girl and it was all over in a flash. It happened so quickly I nearly screamed in fright when I saw what they had done. It was horrible Gary.'

'What?' I said. 'What happened?'

'They cut her throat and they all laughed. The man holding her just dropped her naked body like a sack of coals. Her eyes were staring and the blood gushed out of her neck. He just dropped her. Someone said something to the other girl but I couldn't understand. Then they all left leaving the dead girl lying on the floor.'

'What did you do?'

'I tried not to puke Gary. I was so shocked at what I had seen but then I realised where I was. I must have closed the door between the two rooms and sat on the floor trying not to throw up. Before I knew it I heard the door open next door and two of the guys who worked at the Club came in swearing and arguing about having to clear up another of Vince's messes. I just sat tight curled up in a little ball trying to be as small as I could be. Eventually the two guys finished whatever it was they did and left. As quietly as I could and as fast as I could I slipped out of the rooms and went to the toilet to wash my face. I was shaking like a leaf I was so bloody frightened.'

'But no one saw you?'

'No Gary but almost as soon as I came out of the lav I bumped into Vince who wanted to know where the fuck I had been 'cos I was supposed to be working at the tables. Well I told him a girl has to pee sometime and tried to brush past him. Trouble was he caught my arm and looked at me. I probably shivered with fright and quite likely I looked scared too. Anyway he asked again where I had been and why I looked so pale. Told him I had my monthly rags on and did he really want to check, right here in the corridor? That sort of shut him up but I could tell he wasn't convinced. He thought something was up.'

'So you did a runner?'

'No you daft berk, not right away. That would have been too bloody obvious wouldn't it? I worked for another couple of weeks although I tried hard to be at the Oasis as much as I could.'

'Did you ever go back to the Exotica?'

'Yes Gary I had to. I must have gone back there for a couple of nights but I was bloody terrified all the time I was there.'

'Did you see the girl they made watch? You know the one they just held?'

'Yea I saw her. She was too young to dance or anything and so they didn't want the general public and certainly not the police to see her. She was definitely underage.'

'But they kept her there, at the Club I mean?'

'Yes Gary and I expect she spent most of her nights performing in some back room but I never saw her in action. When I saw her she was really made up to look like twenty but she was as pale as a ghost.'

'So after those two weeks you scarpered? Did you ever see any of the four blokes again, Russians you said?'

'I saw two of them one night. I nearly shit my knickers. I was waiting on tables and I never noticed who they were until Vince told me to take them a vodka drink or something. It was always quite dark in there Gary you know and so it wasn't easy to see who was who. I managed to put the drinks down without spilling them all over the place as my hands were shaking that much. Trouble was one of them grabbed me when I had served them and sat me on his lap. He said something to his mate and they both laughed. I probably wriggled trying to get free and he just took that as an excuse to paw me all over. We didn't wear a lot you know when working at tables and so he thought he was well away with his fingers before I managed to swing my tray around and catch him over the ear. He cursed and let go and fortunately his mate laughed and probably told him that served him right for being a pillock. Anyway I managed to get free and walk back to the bar. Fortunately Vince had seen the whole charade and when I complained he told me to forget it but just keep clear of that table for the rest of the night. Actually I suppose I used that incident to partly explain why I was leaving. I told Vince I had some family problems, my dad getting killed like and mum needing help. I never told Val what really happened. I just gave her the same family spiel and although she knew I had never been strong on my family I think she bought the idea of seeing mum after dad was killed.'

'So why the worry, why a problem? Everyone could find out that your dad did get killed and that your mum could do with some help. Seems a good reason why you came down here.'

'Hold me Gary, hold me. It makes me go all cold just thinking about that poor bitch. Those four Russian whatevers were bloody animals.'

We rolled back together face to face and I held Gloria and could feel her trembling. I didn't know whether it was fury or fear but she shivered. Slowly this time we kissed and Gloria rolled on top of me. I held her tight and she built up a passion and aggression that took my breath away. It was as if she wanted to get the thought and emotion out of her entire body and she pounded away on my pelvis like a woman possessed until she collapsed in a slither of sweaty body and an orgasm that almost wrenched my cock off. It was like an exorcism.

Next day at work I felt absolutely knackered. The crew were working in another plantation and we were felling bigger trees than before. I could hardly lift the chain saw to pull the starter cord and once it was going I didn't have the strength to pull the trigger.

'You can't take your pints any more Gary you useless wanker. Christ we only had a few last night. Actually, where did you bugger off to? I was watching some nutter on the tube try and win a few quid and then you weren't there.'

'Freddie I told you I was going for a piss mate. Got in the next round didn't I? You were still arguing with the idiot on the box although I could tell he wasn't listening to you.'

'You two ever going to do any work or are you just going to spend the day jabbering like two old women? It's the middle of the week lads and that means work. Remember work do you? Freddie get your self away over here to help old Tom. He's getting past swinging an axe to any effect and his trimming is bloody useless. At least you've got strong arms to go along with your non-stop mouth.'

'Sure Bob I'll go and help Tom. Actually it's Gary who needs some help this morning.'

'Templeton. Gary Templeton, come down a little in the world haven't you lad? Used to be your family that was in charge here. Your granddad and his dad before that. Your grandfather Edward was the foreman when I started here as a lad but that's all changed now Gary so you get you arse back in gear and pick up the pace. I don't see a lot of production in your rows and you're falling behind the rest of the gang. Let's move it eh?'

'Fuck you Bob,' I muttered under my breath. 'I'll cut the bloody trees mate and drop one on your head if you don't let up.'

'What's that you said Gary? I didn't catch that.'

'Just fighting a bit of a cold Bob but I'll do my share, don't you worry about that. I'll cut my quota boss.'

'We'll see,' said Bob and he stomped away to harass some other poor bugger in the gang. Wasn't the beer Freddie my old son, it wasn't the beer. Christ this is a boring job after listening to some of Gloria's stories. Wonder if that's the whole story of why she came back? Sounds like she was on to a good thing; plenty of booze and not too hard a job. Christ, she even liked it.

That evening Gloria decided she didn't want to go to the pub. It was another night off for her and she said she had seen enough of George for a while. Apparently she had worked there at lunchtime and something got said between her and George and she was right pissed off. She wouldn't tell me what it was but she said she needed a place to unwind.

Just out of the top end of our village there is a fair size stream and a public footpath runs alongside.

'Remember when we were kids we used to come along here?' said Gloria. 'We used to swim in the pool just round the next bend. Let's go and look. Never told you I kept up my swimming in London did I Gary?'

'Gloria, you've never told me much about what you did in London. Sure, you lived somewhere in the East End and worked in the West End but you've never really told me what your life was like up there.'

'Let's go and look at the pool? It's too cold to swim this late in the year but come spring, if I'm still here you know I might come back here to swim. That's one thing I did do up in London Gary. Val and I both used to go to the local Baths. Actually they had a really good swimming complex. Well I suppose it was more than just swimming 'cos there were all sorts of other things there too but we used to go to the pool. Val could swim really well and she liked to dive too. Used to be funny to watch her at the pool. She had a really good figure and all the blokes would watch her dive and laugh and nudge each other. They all thought they should have a go to pull her but none of them could dive as well as she could so they had to find another angle. Well one day they obviously staged some sort of impromptu fight in the pool and bumped into Val and pretended they had to rescue her. Of course the hands got everywhere but Val can be pretty brutal when needs be and several of the lads emerged from the pool with very bruised cocks. Just to add insult to injury she walked over and wrapped her arms around me and gave me a deep long kiss. Christ it was funny to watch their expressions but she never got any hassle after that.'

We walked on down the footpath as the light faded away. It was a quiet and peaceful evening and the pool lay still. Gloria knelt down and put her hand in the water. 'It's still fairly warm after today's sun but the deep part will be bloody cold Gary. I'll wait until spring time.' She turned and I wrapped my arms around her. We kissed gently.

'My mum's giving me the gears about seeing you,' Gloria said. 'She reckons you're a bad lot or something. I'm sure she never heard us last night but she gave me a right earful this morning.'

'I've never given your mum any aggro Gloria. Still, come to think of it she was never very keen on us going out together when we were teenagers. Remember we had to pretend you were going out with Freddie and I was with Sandra.'

'That's why she was so disgusted with you when Sandra killed herself. My mum never realised that it was your dad who get her pregnant.'

'Sure, but didn't she eventually find out who the father was?'

'No Gary. I don't think anyone in the village knows who the father was, well except your mother perhaps.'

'And mum wouldn't have said. She knows dad strays a bit but she never says a word. She likes to keep the house as peaceful and happy as she can.'

'Well be warned. My mum's really got it in for you so we'd better be a little careful where we're seen. Now dad is dead mum's all over the map. She ranges from holier than holy to excessive cleanliness and now it's joining every gardening group imaginable. It's like she's in a frenzy most of the time but I feel some sort of responsibility Gary. I'm all she's got now.'

'What about Wendell?'

'Wendell only thinks about himself and he's a secretive little bugger. Anytime he's home he's wanking away on the computer in his room. I'm sure he's gay 'cos he's down at Tom Daley's place a lot of the time and he's still the village pervert.'

'He's also the village computer nerd expert so I've heard.'

'Well Wendell just thinks mum's there to give him anything he asks for. He couldn't care less about mum and any of her feelings. Since I've been home I've found Wendell has become a real pain in the arse. Several people have already told me in the pub that he's a bully and he's supposed to have abused several of the younger boys. Down at Tom Daley's I'm sure he gets some more ideas about sex and perversion. I told you I caught the little bugger going through my clothes the other day?'

'No, well I don't think so. What was he doing?'

'Cheeky bugger's looking through my undies. He's beginning to give me the creeps but mum never sees any of this. I'm not even sure that she sees him at all.'

'Yes sir, what'll it be?'

'A pint of bitter and whiskey chaser mate. No, make that a double whiskey.'

'Coming right up. Come far have you? You sound like a Londoner.'

'Could be.'

'So what's brought you to this neck of the woods?'

'Got rooms have you, just for the night?'

'Sure, single is it, just the one night?'

'Don't see no one else mate. I'll see the room though. Never feel comfortable this far from the city. Strikes me as wild and uncivilised. So, the room?'

'Yes sir, just come along here and up the stairs. Got a nice big single overlooking the front. Breakfast in the morning?'

George let the man settle in to the room and went back behind the bar. 'Freddie, seen Gary today have you son?'

'Course George, he was at work wasn't he? Not that he was good for anything today you know. Pretty bloody useless he was. He looked like he couldn't lift a feather let alone a chain saw.'

'Where is he now then?'

'How should I know George? I ain't his keeper.'

'Here a minute Freddie. A word in your ear.'

Freddie came over to the bar and George leant over and whispered in his ear. 'Jesus, you don't say. Sure, sure I'll try and find him. Bloody hell, after what Gloria said we don't want any trouble. We've got enough of our own what with the bloody Ferris slaughterhouse.'

'Keep it to yourself Freddie. We don't need the whole bloody world to know. Go and find Gary and ....yes sir, the room suitable is it? Another drink then?'

'Room'll do landlord and same again. This the only pub in town?'

'Yes sir. George and Dragon we are and the only pub in the village so we look after everyone. They all come in here you know. Centre of village life is this pub. Writing a book are we sir or just travelling around?'

'Gloria work here then?'

'Gloria, Gloria who is that?'

'Gloria Manson she called herself. Said her dad got killed a couple of weeks back and had to come home to see her old mum. Well, that's what she said.'

'Well part of that's right for sure. Tilley Manson's husband Walter did get killed some four weeks ago now. Crashed his tanker he did on the Motorway and ended up in a ball of fire they tell me. Seems the whole lorry just exploded. They never did find any parts of old Walter. There wasn't anything for Tilley to bury and it was a sad day at the church for the memorial service. Suppose most of the village was there as Walter was well known here.'

'And Gloria?'

'No, she wasn't here. Ran away she did. Must be six or seven years ago now that she ran off. We all thought she'd run away to Bristol. It's the logical place for kids here to go to. Although it's a big city they still speak much the same way as we do here. Most of the village kids who take off end up in Bristol although we don't have many leave. We've still plenty of work here and then there are several places in the nearby town. Easy to get to work there too what with the bus.'

'So no Gloria?'

'No squire, not seen her since she ran off. Her old mum was on her own when they all said goodbye to Walter. How about one on the house sir? I'm just about to call for last orders. Same again is it?'

Freddie stood outside the George and scratched his head. Where the fuck was Gary and perhaps more importantly where was Gloria? Christ if that bloke was down from one of those Clubs where she worked and he looks a right bruiser then I'd better find her. But where? Freddie looked up and down the street. Gary didn't say anything at work so did he just go home tonight? No, Gary wouldn't have gone home unless he was sick so he's got to be with Gloria. At her house then?

Turning away from the George Freddie walked down the village main street to find the laneway where Tilley Manson lived. Upstairs in the big room overlooking the front the man moved the curtains a little and watched Freddie walk away. Tomorrow he thought. Maybe a little more looking tomorrow. Small dump and everyone knows everyone else's business. Maybe that little yokel will tell me. He looks like he'll squeal if I squeeze him. Why do people live out here in the bloomin' wilds? It's ten o'clock and the whole bloody place is dark and shut up tight like the birds in a nunnery.

There was enough light to walk back up the footpath and around into the village main street. We passed the pub but all the lights were off and George had closed up for the night. It was so quiet and peaceful and we just had our arms around each other as we slowly wandered down to Gloria's home.

'Gary, Gary that you?' came a whisper.

'Christ Freddie, you almost made me piss my pants jumping out like that mate. What's your problem?'

Freddie explained.

I got more of the story, embellished with all sorts of fancy suppositions from Freddie during the next day at work. We decided to lay low that evening and not go to the pub. Freddie was sure that George would have told Gloria who was there and what George assumed. Still, it seems we need never have worried as George's paying guest disappeared around lunch time.

'Sitting over by the window he was,' said George when we were back in the pub on Thursday night, 'Eating one of my pork pies. He had completely smothered the flavour,' George said in a disillusioned voice. 'He had covered the whole pie with sauce, HP sauce that is. How could he have tasted anything when it was buried under that brown muck?'

'So why'd he leave?'

'Left in a real hurry he did too. Fortunately for me he had already paid his bill. Apparently he'd been prowling around the village much of the morning and asking questions. He seemed quite chuffed when he came back for lunch and I thought "Oh no, now there's trouble".'

'You never said why George. Why'd he leave?'

'Funny really when you think about it. Never can find one when you want one but then we had two and our city pal legged it pretty fast.'

'Two what George? For God's sake George who chased that London heavy out of here, pork pie and all?'

'Well it was Terence Field wasn't it, and some other copper. The pair of them came in and Inspector Field says good morning and they ordered a couple of pints. Next thing I knew the pork pie had gone along with the mouth with no taste.'

'So our friend from London was no admirer of the boys in blue?'

'Suppose not. As is usual with coppers Terence Field looked around when he came in and he did say something to his mate but I never really noticed what was said. He didn't introduce his companion but I could tell he was another copper. Dressed smart though he was but there's always the look. The eyes are going everywhere and he must have noticed and recognised our visitor. Inspector Field had no sooner got his pint back to a table in the corner and he and his mate settled before I realised the window seat was empty.'

'So Gloria's safe? She can come back to the bar? Right panic she was in I can tell you George. Still, thanks for the heads-up. She managed to tell a few people early Wednesday morning to keep their mouths shut and that she wasn't back here. Don't know what story she told them but most people here look after each other.'

'Well don't go getting her hopes up too fast Gary son because Detective Inspector Terence Field was asking questions too. Well, I suppose it was the other bloke who was asking most of the questions. Now I couldn't stall with him because Gloria was in here this past Tuesday when Miss Samantha was here with those Canadian folk. Remember, they were those long lost relatives of Danny Masters? Miss Samantha may be from the village but she's also a good friend of Terence Field so I hear. I didn't want to run any risks of upsetting Terence Field because he already knows Gloria's back in the village. He'd also know from the questions he was asking after the murder of John Ferris so I just listened to this copper from London. He was asking after Gloria too.'

'Christ Gary, you can run in this bloody country but you sure can't hide.'

'Freddie shut it. I'm thinking.'

'Well pardon me for being here then mate.'

'No, listen up for a minute. Gloria's got nothing to hide from the cops. She worked in a couple of Clubs that were legit and no doubt the cops in London would have known all about them. Like she said she heard that her dad got killed and came down to look after her mum. No sweat.'

I turned to George. 'George, what did this copper from London ask about? What did he want?'

'Wanted to speak to Gloria Manson didn't he?'

'Yes, sure, I know that but what did he want to speak to her about?'

'Didn't say. Well he wasn't going to tell me now was he? You know coppers. Ask questions and never tell you anything.'

'What we going to do Gary?'

'Nothing Freddie, everything's cool. Gloria's story is straightforward and she's got nothing to worry about. Did Inspector Field say when he'd be back George?'

'No Gary Templeton, Inspector Field didn't say when he'd be back,' and I felt a hand on my shoulder. Turning round I found myself face to face with Detective Inspector Field and another bloke who I assumed to be the copper from London.

'So George, keeping the locals up to date are we?'

'Yes Inspector Field. I like to make sure we all know where we stand. Close knit community this village. We may have our differences and occasional spats but for the most part we live in a friendly fashion.'

'Like rape, fraternal murder, sex-crazed slayings and other friendly fashions I could mention in this village with its occasional spats George?' Here Terence Field turned to his companion and said, 'You know Barry this little village has kept me in business nearly full time over the past couple of months and all because of the occasional spats as the landlord describes them.'

'And here was I thinking the countryside was a land full of peace and quiet Terence. It sounds like we have a relatively dull life back in the Met. Perhaps I should put in for a transfer?'

'No sir,' George said, 'it's been a bit unusual over the past couple of weeks. Normally the biggest disturbance is when some kid breaks a window or one of the farmers lets his livestock out on the road. Peace and quiet is normal here.'

'Sure George' and Terence Field spun round and looked straight at Freddie. 'So Freddie, what have you been up to lately? No more cousins you want to tell me about? No more coins hidden somewhere?'

'No, no,' stuttered Freddie, 'There's nothing new going on Inspector, honest.'

'And you Gary?'

'No Inspector Field,' I said. 'Since the Ferris family has all gone we've lost our bad apples. It's like George said, it's quiet and peaceful.'

'So why's Gloria suddenly gone missing again?'

'Girl's got to get a day off now and again Inspector,' trilled Gloria as she walked up behind us. 'Hi George, sorry I'm a little late this evening but my brother was giving my mum a hard time and I had to offer some TLC before I could come to work. So, who's ordering or are you all just propping the bar up like it's a men's social?'

'Gloria, if George can spare you for a few minutes we'd like a brief chat,' said Terence.

'Well George, you're the boss,' said Gloria cheerfully.

'George we'll have two pints please and Gloria can bring them over. We'll sit over there in the corner and Gloria and the two of us can have a quiet talk for fifteen minutes or so. Keep your noses clean lads.'

Later that evening Gloria got a chance to briefly tell us what had happened with Inspector Field and his mate Barry Gates. 'Didn't know the face,' Gloria said, 'but I think he's in some special unit to do with illegal immigration. He never told me more than he was Sergeant Gates and worked in London. Wanted to know about some of the girls at the Clubs where I worked. When had I last seen so and so? What did I know about whoever?'

'What did you say?'

'Played dumb didn't I? I was just a waitress come dancer. Go ask Vince Tobin I said. He was the manager. He'd know who he hired. I just worked at the Clubs and lived with Val Gordon's family in the East End. I never knew any of the girls this Barry was asking about.'

'So it's all over? You think that's the end of it?'

'One day at a time Gary but for the moment I'll keep my eyes and ears open and live the peaceful life.'

Daniel's Birthday weekend

Several things happened the next weekend, must have been October 24 and 25 I suppose. They affected Gloria and I but we weren't directly involved. It was only later that I heard about these events and they certainly helped put me in this cell. In addition there were two other major things that happened during the next week that also had a significant bearing on subsequent events. One concerned the fate of the Ferris cottage in the forest and the second revolved around Samantha Lord's new occupation. I'll tell you first about Samantha Lord, or maybe I should call her Mrs. MacRae now. It's funny though, I still think of her as Samantha Lord although she got married. I never knew or saw her husband and so I remember her as a young woman charging round the forest on horses, or motorbikes or anything else that caught her fancy. When I think about it she is only a year older than I am but she spent her schooling in Switzerland and her University years at Cambridge and Oxford before chasing off to Canada with her forester husband. We poor village folk never got to know much about her because she was rarely at Fotheringham but when she was home you sure knew she was around. Samantha Lord was Anthony and Sylvia's third child and my mum told me that Sylvia Lord was delighted when she had a little girl. However, the delight didn't last as Samantha turned out to be a boy in a girl's body. She had this competitive thing where she had to be first at whatever she did. As she was quite similar to her mum there were major battles in the household and that is why Miss Samantha ended up schooling in Switzerland and rushing off to University. But, despite all that she was good at whatever she tried. Schooled in the Lord family traditions Samantha had learnt to ride, to climb, to sail and to ski. You know, all the sorts of things we do in the village every day. About four years ago she suddenly appeared back at Fotheringham complete with a baby. We did understand there was a husband somewhere but he had gone job hunting in Canada. Apparently he was another forester although Daniel Lord once explained to Bob Edwards that Andrew MacRae was a research forester only interested in forest fires. Seeing as there are not many forest fires in our part of the world it made sense for this Andrew MacRae to look elsewhere for work. Anthony and Sylvia Lord looked after the baby James for a year before Samantha came rushing back from wherever and took off after her husband to the fire ravaged forests of Canada, or so the story went. Everyone in the village heard the stories about the antics of Miss Samantha, especially the fights with her mother and so it was something of a shock when she came back to Fotheringham in September last year with her son James. The rumour was that husband Andrew had gone looking at one fire too many and ended up in smoke. At first we all thought her parents had brought her home to recover from the loss of her husband. Anthony and Sylvia Lord had planned some sort of peace and quiet but that all got shot to hell within a week with the return of Idwal Ferris, the vandalism of Enrico's cottage, the fire in the stables, the death of Idwal and his bird, and then another knifing murder up in the Manor. So much for peace and quiet as Miss Samantha ended up in the middle of most of this frenzy of activity. I heard from Bob Edwards that there had been a temporary reconciliation between

Samantha and her mother which amazed all of us but then Bob told me Miss Samantha had jumped into another venture in some crazy company called Heritage Adventures. Bob wasn't sure of the details but it seems one of Miss Samantha's old school friends had come down to visit and she had this company helping tourists find their past. Now why anyone would want to find their past seemed a bit beyond me until I started wondering about my own family. After I heard this I got to thinking that night if I had gone away, say to Canada or Australia or wherever would I really have ever wanted to come back and find out about my ancestors, or would my kids? The more I thought about it the more I could see how some people might be interested. I had been proud of my name and I did have an interest in my ancestors and I'd never left the village. Seems there were people from abroad who did want to find where their folks came from and so this Heritage Adventures deal helped them. Well that week after all the knifings and murder Samantha Lord had gone up to London and returned with two Canadians who were looking for their ancestors. Now the only reason we knew about this in any detail was Samantha brought them into the pub on a couple of evenings. Seems they wanted to sample the local yokel's lifestyle. Still, as it turned out some of us were actually related to this pair of Canucks. This couple explained that back at the start of the century a relative of Freddie's friend Danny Masters had emigrated to Canada. Just being a dumb mechanic Danny didn't know anything about this but during that week Danny filled us in on some of the details. The actual history of Danny's relatives wasn't really relevant but Miss Samantha decided that this was a good new career for her and that came back to haunt me later. Just like her younger brother she had to go poking her nose into things.

The other important event of that week revolved around John Ferris's cottage. When John married Betty Travers the Lord family gave them one of the Estate cottages as a wedding present. However, after the slaughter and mayhem of ten days previously Betty Ferris moved her kids to her parent's house in the village and understandably didn't want to go back to the cottage. In fact she wanted to sell it and after John got killed that was obviously going to happen. Sometime during the week Betty and the kids went up to the cottage and collected some personal items but as there wasn't much room in the Traver's household and she didn't have anywhere else to live for the moment most of the cottage stayed furnished. At the same time two of Daniel Lord's nephews wanted to do a school project and in their enthusiasm they opened up a new mess of evidence to do with Idwal Ferris and the cottage. When Freddie eventually told me the story of his cousins it became clearer what the two boys had found. It seems that Peter and Tony Lord had to do some school research thing associated with nature. Young Peter Lord, who is now the ultimate inheritor of the Lord Estate decided he wanted to do a project that was scientific. There had been some rumours going around that the Lord family might try and develop the Estate to include an Education Centre and both boys had been excited at this idea of learning in the forest. So Peter wanted a project that could be an example for such a Centre and of course Daniel thought up something for the boys to do. It sounded like hard graft to me but then I wasn't a forester and certainly not interested in too much bloody digging just for fun. Sometime towards the end of the week Daniel Lord had taken the two boys up to the Ferris cottage to help clear away some things that Betty wanted but couldn't carry herself. At the same time Daniel had explained to the two boys how to dig and describe soil pits. Even I can understand that different trees grow better on some soils than others and that looking at the hidden parts of the tree can be useful. So he could keep an eye on them while he was working in the cottage Daniel had them dig a soil pit on the edge of the cottage backyard. The cottage itself was set in a fair size clearing in the forest and Betty had developed a little garden area in the six years she had lived there and Daniel laid out a plot shape just outside this garden. You can imagine that for two kids digging a large hole can be a bit of a lark but Daniel had them do it right and he showed them how to trim the end cleanly so they could see the different layers of the soil. I never knew bugger all about this until after it all happened but it did make sense when you saw it. The kids had to measure the different layers and explain what was important about each area.

On the Saturday it was Daniel Lord's twenty-fourth birthday and so there were a fair number of people around the forest and the Big House. Being the weekend Daniel also had his American girlfriend, Katya something in tow. Never heard a bird's name called Katya but what the fuck do Americans know about English? As usual Samantha's son James was tagging along with both Peter and Tony and they all ended up at the Ferris cottage. Being a little kid, who I think is four or five James has to copy what the older two boys were doing and of course playing in the dirt suits little boys fine. So there were Peter and Tony cleaning up their first soil pit and trying to keep James from messing up the cut face. When they finished this soil pit Daniel must have decided they could all help tidying up inside the cottage but first everyone had to be sluiced down. Now we have an even better situation for little boys – dirt and water, and so the three kids were quite wound up by the time they got back into the cottage. Somehow, in their rushing around inside the kids ended up making another mess but one that was really amazing. That cottage is full of surprises. It seems Idwal and John Ferris had a mother. Freddie told me that was fucking obvious but neither of us knew anything about any mother. Then Freddie remembered Enrico telling him a long time ago that Norton Ferris's wife had died before they moved here but Norton had kept his wife's ashes. Enrico never knew where but Norton would have these drunken remorse periods when the whole world was against him and he would sit and hug his wife's ashes. It really is bloody amazing the rumours that run around our village. Still, this rumour turned out to be true, well the bit about his wife's ashes being huggable. Peter, Tony and James were in the cottage helping Daniel collect some heavier items and generally tidying up after John's death. The police had been all over the cottage I don't know how many times and it really was a bit of a shambles so Daniel decided to make it clean again. I can only assume that the Lord family were thinking of hiring some replacement labour and maybe moving them into the cottage. Seems that Peter and Tony were larking about a little and a large urn on the mantelpiece fell to the floor and smashed. Packed in the ashes were a whole mass of gold coins and those all tied into Freddie's story about his cousins. Jack and Lennie Cotton had found a chest which we all assumed contained all of the original coins. After the police investigation at old Flo' Whelks's cottage we all knew about the coins lining the garden path. When they found the coins in the smashed urn it seems that Idwal had hidden some of the coins in his own cottage and only some of them he moved over to Flo's cottage. Freddie always said Idwal was a crafty bastard and liked hiding things in front of your face.

Now Freddie is generally an idle bugger and when Freddie and I first heard about this soil pit thing we thought it was fucking stupid but Freddie sure changed his tune when the kids dug a second pit. Sunday it was and Daniel and his bird had gone to play golf but young Peter and his cousin had come back into the forest. After they had dug the first pit on the Saturday Peter got real keen and scientific, well for a nine year old that is. Not satisfied with just one trench Peter wanted to see whether a second pit further into the forest would look any different so he and Tony went back into the forest a little and dug a second soil pit. Trouble was they found more than soil. None of us heard about this until later in the week but there were police all over the Ferris cottage again. Seems the two lads had dug up some old clothing and away we go again with the police questioning all of the Estate staff. In the process Freddie recognises something about the clothing, the jacket I think and so it seems that confirms the fact that the twins were somewhere in or around the Ferris cottage. Anyway, out of all that series of disasters the Lord family ended up buying the cottage back from Betty. I heard she planned to use part of the money to expand her pie-making enterprise and I'll tell you all about that later but on the estate we now had a semi-furnished cottage that used to belong to John Ferris and another empty but unfurnished cottage where Enrico used to live. I overheard Daniel Lord telling Bob Edwards that Enrico had decided to stay at Home Farm with Christina, Peter and Tony. These two cottages became part of my nightmare.

Before we leave Daniel Lord for a moment though I should tell you some more about his birthday and expectations. As I told you before the Lord family has been here for generations and it appears Daniel's birthday was a chance for the relatives to come together. Anthony Lord was the son of Desmond Lord, who had been a fighter pilot in the Second World War. Although Desmond himself was dead his younger sister and brother were still alive and in their eighties. This would have been Daniel's great Aunt Veronica and great Uncle Matthew. In the next generation Anthony Lord had a brother Charles and a sister Stephanie. Just like Michael Lord Charles had been the second son and begrudged the family tradition of inheritance. Seems Charles Lord went a little crazy climbing somewhere in France with his French wife and the pair of them ended up getting killed. However, they left behind three children who were all younger than ten when their parents got the chop. Rather surprisingly it was Anthony Lord's younger sister Stephanie who adopted all three kids and brought them up in England. In the village we see quite a lot of Dr. Stephanie Lord. She is a vet, although she doesn't practice a lot but she does a lot of breeding research with the animals at Home Farm, mostly with sheep. Charles Lord's three children, well they're adults now and older than me included Marcel, Henri and Giselle. Marcel became an International yacht racer, whatever that means and we never see him. Marcel's wife Marie lives somewhere down in Devon and she had two sons until Michael Lord drowned one of them. No, that's not quite true that Michael drowned Jean but the kid did drown while he was out sailing with careless Uncle Michael. Jesus he was a self-centred bugger. The second son Henri, another Lord second son with a chip on his shoulder got into finance and investing or something in Bristol, which was where he had grown up as a teenager. He was down at Fotheringham occasionally and was a surly bugger if you met him. Big man he was and I'd heard he had been a climber like his dad. A couple of years back he had married some journalist who was always stirring up trouble in the papers. Seems the pair of them was a pain. Now the third child was Giselle Lord. She was quite some lady and although she was about ten years older than me I would have liked to get to know her. Don't know what I would have said to her though 'cos she speaks three or four languages, over and above English that is. Still, she is quite a looker. The close family were all there too and that included Christina, Geoffrey's widow with Peter and Tony, plus Samantha and her son James. Somewhat surprisingly Samantha invited Terence Field. I told you a while back that Samantha had come back to Fotheringham following the death of her husband, supposedly for R&R. However, our Miss Samantha was never one for sitting and thinking and so before a couple of weeks were out she decided to stay in England, get a job and get a man. I heard she sold her house in Canada and put the money into this new Heritage Adventures Company with some old school friend. Getting the man part though was typical Samantha Lord. After Idwal Ferris had set fire to the stables up in Fotheringham Manor's yard he ran off back to his brother's cottage in the forest. We can only assume that

Idwal wanted the van he had or he was going to collect the urn with the ashes and the gold coins. Now Idwal had assaulted both Betty Ferris, John's wife and the weird bird he brought with him and tied and gagged them in some cellar in the cottage. He must have done a good job though because when Daniel Lord and John Ferris went to look earlier in the day they didn't see or hear the two women. That sort of confirmed that John Ferris really didn't know anything about the cellar where they later found all the bones, including Freddie's cousins. Anyway, Idwal rushed back to the cottage but Betty had got loose and she had untied this Lola bird. So in charges Idwal and he got confronted by the two women. Rumour has it that Betty knifed Idwal but somehow in all the struggles Idwal shot Lola and then held a knife to Betty's throat. Idwal was in the process of raping Betty when John came rushing in having heard Betty scream and, well you know the rest. Idwal tried to shoot John and John slashed Idwal clean across the throat – end of story, but then again not quite. Miss Samantha has to come charging in playing Florence Nightingale or somebody. Daniel must have phoned the Big House and described what had happened after he had called the police. So, here's Samantha Lord with hands so badly burnt from rescuing the horses she had to have Danielle Made drive her to the Ferris cottage. Poor PC Meadows is standing guard at the cottage door with strict instructions from his sergeant not to let anybody in to disturb the crime scene. Well our Miss Samantha hasn't got time for such niceties when poor Betty Ferris has just been raped and is feeling like shit. Somebody needs to hold and care for Betty and that somebody is Samantha Lord. She bowled right over PC Meadows threatening another assault if he got in her way and has John Ferris go and sit down in a corner while she slides down beside Betty and offers comfort. You know this all might make sense and be a good human act of kindness and compassion but Miss Samantha of course has disrupted the crime scene. Next act in this

76

madhouse is the entrance of calm, quiet but very by the book Detective Inspector Field. He starts by giving poor PC Meadows a right bollocking for letting anybody into the cottage. Next he walks carefully over to Miss Samantha, who he has never met before this moment although he had heard of her and gently and politely tells her she is fucking up his crime scene and would she please move. It seems Inspector Field was thoughtful enough to bring WPC Nicols with him and he assured Miss Samantha that WPC Nicols was very familiar with such situations and could help Betty Ferris very adequately. Well of course Miss Samantha can't believe anybody is "familiar with such situations" seeing as the kitchen looks like the scene of a chainsaw massacre with two dead bodies, a murderer and a rape victim all neatly arranged around the room. But it's amazing because it turned out; well you know it looked like it turned out to be "love at first sight". So, there in the middle of guts and gore rather than candlelight and soft music Miss Samantha gets a man. Human beings are funny animals don't you think?

At the birthday party that Saturday Daniel had his girl friend there too of course. This was an American girl who spoke with a distinctive accent. We all found out over time she was going to Oxford and studying forestry so Daniel and she could talk about the birds and the bees quite professionally like. Turns out it was some of this Miss Katya's thoughts and ideas that threatened to bugger up some of Gloria's plans but that didn't happen that past October but the following summer. All we heard about her at the time of Daniel's birthday was her involvement with Peter and Tony and digging up the soil pits. Seems there were two parts to Daniel's birthday party on the Saturday, well over and above the episode in John and Betty's cottage with the digging the dirt and playing for the ashes. There was some quite elaborate dinner but as was typical of Anthony Lord he took the opportunity of having all the family there to discuss futures. I'll say one thing for that family. They've almost always had someone in charge who manages today very well and keeps looking forward. I suppose anyone who deals with forestry has to have their mind in both places because so much of what gets done in the forest today relates to tomorrow or even the next day. It may not be true in other parts of the world but here in Somerset the trees grow slowly and so you have to think long term.

'I thought I'd take this opportunity with nearly all of us being here for Daniel's birthday to talk a little about the future. I suppose it's only Marcel who is not here with us?'

'He's in New Zealand Uncle,' said Marie. 'We got an email just yesterday. Actually Daniel he did remember and he does wish you a happy birthday. He also says he hopes to see you when he's back home at Christmas. He reckoned you were the most sensible one and he wishes you every happiness. He also said he was very pleased to hear you had found a girl.'

'Most sensible one indeed,' snorted Samantha. 'Just tell him Marie that he'd better have a marlin spike with him if he comes visiting here at Christmas. I'll give him sensible.'

'Now now Samantha,' said Anthony, 'Christmas is for peace and goodwill. Your cousin knows that you are the competitive one and that's the life he lives by and so he finds Daniel a refreshing change.'

James, Samantha's son had slowly been building up a head of steam and eventually he exploded. 'Uncle Daniel didn't find Katya grandpa I did. I found her, and I found King Delaney and Queen Deidre. Uncle Daniel was still outside the carriage when I found them.'

'James MacRae you are absolutely right,' said Sylvia, 'and your uncle Daniel is so pleased he'll kiss you.'

'Ugh, no thanks. Anyway, he'd sooner kiss Katya. He does every time they say goodbye at the railway station. Doesn't he Katya?'

'But a little bird told me that you do too Master James,' said Stephanie with a twinkle in her eye. James blushed and Anthony took the moment when James was quiet to continue.

'Quick recap then about the family and after that I'd like you Daniel to explain where things might go next. We've had a couple of close family get-togethers and Sylvia and I have talked with most of you by phone over the future of Brainware and the Estate. Sylvia and I thought it was about time we passed some of the day to day responsibilities over to the next generation and so we tried to find some successors. Neither Samantha nor Daniel was interested in the future management of Brainware. I think it's fair to say they both thought that the new world of software development was too far removed from their areas of expertise. It just wasn't their thing. But, the family wanted to keep the products, the expertise and the good reputation of the company in England if we could and so we have approached a London company with whom we have done a lot of business in the past. Some of you may remember Cohen and Townsend who specialise in security and have installed and maintained several of our products. Sylvia and I have been up to London and talked with Rosalind Cohen, her partner and her financial people. Anyway, to make a long story short Rosalind is going to buy Brainware completely, leaving the Lord family estate with a considerable sum of money. We are still discussing how best to invest this money but it does relieve Sylvia and I from some considerable stress which we were finding hard to take.'

'So how do we all benefit from this sale?' asked Henri.

'Think back Henri,' said Matthew. 'Think back to how your father was involved in Brainware.'

'But he wasn't. He never had any money and he and our mother died young.'

'And so you have answered your own question.'

'It's the truth Henri,' added Giselle, 'although Aunt Stephanie did give us a few shares for our birthdays when we were growing up. She gave each of us some of her shares, to Marcel, to you and to me.'

'But I traded mine a long time ago to Marcel.'

'Henri, I'm sure the family will sit down and think how best to manage the money for the benefit of the entire family when the sale has gone through,' said Sylvia. 'At present we are still discussing payment schedules with Rosalind Cohen and no money has changed hands as yet.'

'Just as long as you don't forget us,' exclaimed Henri. 'Leslie reminded me to make sure we got our share and not get fobbed off with this second son stupidity. It's time this family moved into the real world Anthony. Leslie thinks it is archaic and cruel.'

Anthony could sense some bristling animosities around the room and decided to move on as it was Daniel's birthday and not the right time for an extended family brawl. With a quick glance across the room to Sylvia Anthony continued. 'So we found a preliminary answer for Brainware and I will make a brief apology to Uncle Matthew and Auntie Veronica who were most supportive and constructive in the early years. We tried to keep it in the family but we think we've done the right thing with Rosalind.'

'Anthony, times change and I for one think you've made a good strategic decision. My old Rear Admiral husband was a great believer in knowing when to stay with your strengths and when to shed the bits you couldn't defend. Always looked at the big picture. What do you say little brother?'

Matthew looked around the room with his old-fashioned National Health spectacles and smiled at his sister's appellation. 'The little brother says right on Anthony and Sylvia. That software world has become exceedingly competitive and I'm delighted to hear that Samantha and

Daniel are honest enough to realise it isn't their world. But I would be interested in hearing from Samantha, and Daniel. I'm intrigued to hear what they think is their world.'

'Samantha, do you want to let everyone know what you are up to now?'

'Why don't I tell everyone what mummy is up to grandpa? I'm sure I know what mummy is doing 'cos she tells me every night before I go to sleep.'

'James my love I don't think everyone wants to know what I tell you every night.'

'But you never said it was a secret, about Terence I mean. And then Uncle Daniel said you were going to work with that other hot woman.'

'James, hush my love. Remember this is uncle Daniel's birthday and I'm sure great uncle Matthew really wants to hear what Daniel wants to do, especially as it involves the Estate.'

'Does that include Dainty?'

'Daniel can you take over brother and talk while I try and gag my little angel here?'

'I suppose there are a few things I should say. Actually the first is thank you mum and dad for such a memorable birthday party. It's not often we manage to get virtually all of the family together and I will look forward to seeing Marcel at Christmas time Marie. And, as James has told you earlier, he did find a girl for me and that is truly memorable too, that particular day. Okay, well as you all know I have been managing the forestry part of the estate since I left university a couple of years back. With the background support of mum and dad we've done most of the right things but we've also reached a question mark about where best to go from here. This question mark is somewhat related to the sale of Brainware, well it could be. Commercial forestry is competitive, just like the software development market I suppose and we've been talking about how to diversify: how to become more resilient to change, more adaptable. You can imagine that is not easy, well certainly not fast in forestry activities. Once you planted the trees you can't change them or where they are but you can change how they are used. Over the past two or three weeks, along with a few other exciting incidents we have been thinking about diversification. For example we have been talking about using the estate as an Education Centre and this idea has some appeal to young Peter and Tony here. Think of it this way. Instead of cutting the forest down and selling the products to people outside in the town lets bring the customer into the forest and have them "consume" the knowledge of the forest, the science of the forest, the training opportunities in a forest. Now this is not an either/or scenario but an additive idea. We might even change part of the forest into shrubs, grasslands, wetlands instead of just a "tree farm". Anyway, that's an idea but before we leave that there is one other thing I suppose I should say seeing as dad asked me to explain where I wanted to go.'

'Uncle Daniel I still think that's a smashing idea.'

'Yes Peter, it could turn into a very instructive long-term proposition. Over time the Fotheringham Estate could gradually change again as it has done over the past one hundred years.'

'That's all very fine and high-faluting Daniel but would it generate any money? Leslie told me that I really have a claim on the revenues coming out of this Estate you know. I want to make sure I get my fair share.'

'Perhaps you and Leslie could compete in the other idea I have to generate revenues from the Estate,' suggested Daniel.

'Which is?'

'Competitive Orienteering,' replied Daniel. 'You climb, you're fit. We could put a "Lord" team into any competitions we hold here and win the prize money. Leslie could earn his share.'

82

'There Henri,' said Stephanie, 'you and Leslie could join in a real Lord effort.'

'Does Leslie run too Henri? I thought he/she was a writer, a journalist? Perhaps he/she could do the advertising and the publicity for Uncle Daniel's two ideas?'

'I think that is very unlikely Peter. It's not an important enough story. Leslie's away at the moment chasing a society scandal up in London. Something to do with illegal immigrants at night clubs in the West End.'

'Daniel, explain about the more recent finds here. I don't think all the family knows about our more recent discoveries on the Estate.'

'Sure mum.'

'Some more Lord family treasure to divide up?' asked Henri.

'No Henri,' said Daniel. 'This is rather sad in a way and we will probably convert this treasure into a memorial to both Geoffrey and Michael. Actually, given the number of tragedies in this family it may become a memorial to more members. Still, let me explain very briefly.'

Daniel spent the next ten minutes recounting the story of the maps, the cave, Michael's explorations and ultimate death, the find by Katya, the bones in the Ferris cottage, the golden garden path of Flo' Whelks and finally the conclusion that the "treasure" had been found. Terence Field kept very quiet sitting next to Samantha but he carefully watched the reaction of the people around the table. Samantha noticed and smiled to herself. Always the policeman she thought, ever attentive.

'So we are thinking of two things really,' said Daniel. 'First, we are thinking of putting some kind of plaque up on the cliff face beside the cave and the old oak tree. I would like to remember my brother in a friendlier outdoor place than a graveyard. Much of his time Michael was an outdoors person and I think the forest and the cliff face a suitable place for a plaque. Personally I would sooner go and think about the good times with my brother in the wild of the forest.' Daniel paused and looked around the room. 'But,' he said, 'on a more positive note we would also like to commemorate both Geoffrey and Michael in the name of the new Education Centre. Geoffrey was always looking to the future and he was so happy when Peter arrived. Christina, I hope this idea meets with your approval?'

'Daniel, I think it is a lovely idea,' Christina said and she half-sobbed with emotion.

'Mum, it's wonderful,' and Peter gently held his mother's hand. 'Dad would be delighted.'

'You know Sylvia, perhaps we should take this idea of Daniel's a little further,' said Anthony. 'Just looking around the table maybe we should consider a room or presentation cabinet describing the memories of all the family people we know who would have endorsed the idea of an Education Centre. Just think, sad I know but let's remember Charles and Helene, Henri's parents, little Jean, Geoffrey, Michael, Andrew and Danielle.'

'Dad, if you think along those lines I would suggest, no I would insist that we include Antonio. Without trying to embarrass Enrico here beside me I have always felt Antonio and Enrico are part of this family. So, to end this on a positive note please raise your glasses to the happy future of the extended Lord family. The Lords.'

'The Lords.' Glasses clinked.

'Daniel, you still haven't said whether you are going to stay on here as the Forester or play golf for a living?'

'Great Uncle Matthew you always were one for listening to the details. Never miss a trick do you?' Matthew laughed and wagged his finger at Daniel.

'Just like you Daniel my elder sister keeps me on my toes and I have to try to keep one step in front.'

'Get away with you Matthew. The only place I could keep ahead of you was on the ski slopes. You were always stopping and trying to see how the bindings really worked. You would have taken them to pieces up on the slopes if your fingers weren't so cold.'

'Golf Daniel, explanations please before my elder sister here lectures me. I can see that Katya sitting next to you is also interested in your answer. They tell me the weather is very nice in winter in Florida.'

'It's a little premature to decide. I'm still sitting on the fence.'

'You didn't sit on it Uncle Daniel. You knocked it down. You flattened it. Then you lay down to listen for earthworms. Mummy why did.....'

'Hush James. Have another cake.'

'Scrumptious.'

'So you left us all sitting on the fence with you Daniel, please continue.'

Daniel looked at his sister and then he turned back to face his great uncle. 'Sisters seem to be the bane of our life uncle. Still, golf and sitting on fences. Well, mum and dad now have some more time on their hands and I know they will not just sit on them. It isn't in their character so running the Estate may be less demanding for me, although this Education Centre may change all that. In the meantime I am playing golf twice a week fairly seriously and I have talked with Katya about Florida, perhaps the winter after next when she has finished at Oxford. So that's on the other side of the fence.'

'But then again Daniel Katya may decide that she likes the weather here in Somerset just fine.' Samantha turned and grinned at Katya as she said this.

'Katya could watch me ride Dainty,' said James, 'when we play polo.'

Katya laughed and she held Daniel's hand. 'Daniel and I are just taking things one day at a time thank you very much. I am still eight months away from trying to graduate and that is important right now.'

'Katya and I very successfully combine both sides of the fence because Katya comes out on the golf course and caddies for me. We have become a very successful team on the golf course and can talk professional forestry other times – both sides of the fence.'

'Sylvia, why don't we all go and sit more comfortably in the drawing room? I see that James here has devoured everything left on the table.'

'Right Anthony. Perhaps that would be a good place for Samantha to explain a little bit more about Heritage Adventures.'

In the drawing room Sylvia persuaded Samantha to briefly explain her new business activities and let Alan and Shirley Doone describe why they were here in Somerset from Canada.

'So you see we have all sorts of people who are fascinated in their history, especially people like Alan and Shirley here who live in Revelstoke in western Canada. I know some of this you can research and explore on-line with internet but it is even more exciting and emotional when it is real-life.'

'It's true folks,' said Shirley Doone. 'It really has been an interesting trip both in finding who my great grandparents were and where they came from, but also combining that with visiting another country. Samantha here found out that my great grandfather came out to Canada to work on the Canadian Pacific railway line. He finally settled in Revelstoke which is a small town in British Columbia. So we have seen some of the usual tourist things plus Samantha here has introduced us to many of the other "locals" whom we wouldn't have met and enjoyed without our special quest and guide. As Samantha says it is much more real-life than on the internet. Our daughter Elizabeth back in Canada first showed us some of the things we could find about our name and family but we are old-fashioned I suppose and wanted to see things first hand. I know we will go home and describe to all our friends what an interesting experience this has been.'

'Daniel, are you going to hire your sister to investigate the earlier days of the Lord family?' asked Matthew with a twinkle in his eye. 'You may find some more non-forestry facets about the Estate. If I heard correctly that could help Katya here add to the array of attractions of Fotheringham. What was it you were looking for Katya, green revenues was it?'

'We're looking for some interesting things to include in our Education Centre great Uncle Matthew,' added Peter. 'Tony and I think uncle Daniel's suggestion for an Education Centre here at Fotheringham is a smashing idea and we would like to include a wide array of topics, not just trees and sheep.'

'Should I suggest we keep llamas and alpacas then Peter?' asked Stephanie. 'We could collect the different wools and have a spinning and weaving class in your Education Centre.'

Now I have included some of this in my story because it shows that there were likely to be a few changes coming about on the Estate and all of these events had some bearing on what happened in the next year. Gradually, what had been a relatively quiet straightforward farm and forest operation started to expand and include other activities. This in turn led to other people coming to visit and more people starting to poke their noses into the background and opportunities in the forest. One other funny thing though had stuck in Gloria's mind. I mentioned earlier that Miss Samantha had brought these long-lost relatives of Danny Masters into the pub. Now this had embarrassed Danny as being a mechanic he was somewhat lacking in social graces. Maybe he could talk to carburettors and other parts of a car but people were never Danny's strong point. Anyway Gloria must have remembered this meeting and when we saw Miss Samantha with another foreign couple it niggled away. It may have been that this new couple's surname was Doone, the same as George the landlord of our pub; although it turned out they were not related. Anyway this all started Gloria thinking.

'Mum, where did our dad come from?'

'What do mean Gloria, where'd he come from?'

'Well he wasn't from around here now was he?'

'What's that got to do with the price of sugar? What's that Wendell done with the TV flipper? You seen it Gloria? That boy hides things all round the house he does. Now where's he put it?'

'Mum it's here. It's right here by your gardening magazine. But what about dad? He was from Devon wasn't he?'

'Gloria give over love. I want to watch this programme. There's something special on about flowers that bring peace and harmony to people praying for their sick relatives. I think I should grow some in our garden. They will help me.'

'That's on tomorrow mum. Here, you've marked it on your magazine. Right now mum it's some quiz show or other. It's the same old people doing the same old things. They just guess the price of all that useless clobber. Mum I want to know.'

'What Gloria? What do you want to know? I suppose I'll get no peace with all your going on.'

'How about you then mum? Bob Edwards is your brother and your parents were old Gwen Biddle and Ernest Edwards? That right?'

'Yes love. You know all that. My old mum and dad were alive when you were a kiddie. You used to go over to their cottage. What's this all about Gloria? Why the sudden interest?'

'That Miss Samantha Lord, although now I suppose she is Mrs. MacRae you know. Well, she was in the pub earlier with a couple of foreigners. Actually she's been in with another couple too and they were related to people here in our village. I found it kind of spooky but she has this weird thing going helping people find their past. It was like a cloud of cold air wafting into the room. Like someone walking over your grave. I wondered who we might have who was going to come invading our lives.'

'Gloria you've got your head in the clouds love. Living up in London changed you. On my dad's grandfather's side, the Edwards, the family has lived here for generations. My mother Gwen was a Biddle. Her dad Christopher Biddle was the blacksmith here in the village. He had been a gunner in the Great War and went deaf. Now his wife though was a little different. I can still remember her 'cos she was still alive when I was little. Mary Jones she was and her family were part of a tribe of Welsh tinkers. They must have been around the village just after the war and done some business with my grandfather at the forge. She was weird though. Spoke Welsh and would lapse into spouting spells or something. Frightened me she did. I can remember that dreadful year when she went mad. Granddad was dead a few years by then but Gran' Mary still lived alone in her little cottage. She started crying out about foreseeing the future and that the family would have devil's children. She would cook up the most awful concoctions in her cottage and run around naked chanting in Welsh. In the end my uncle Jack Biddle locked her up in her cottage. He was the blacksmith here by then and he barred up the cottage. She must have died within the year but she cast all sorts of curses on everyone around her.'

'Christ mum, I never knew we had anybody that crazy in the family.'

'Only you Gloria.'

'Wendell, where have you been? You've missed your tea. It's all cleared away now.'

Gloria's brother Wendell was a sixteen year-old waste of space. Everyone in the village knew he was a bully but Wendell was also sneaky and had a spiteful streak. Somehow he had become the friend of Tom Daley who we all knew was the local dealer. According to hearsay Tom Daley was a computer geek and knew all the secrets of everyone in the village. Now Gloria had told me that Wendell also lived on his computer and it is possible that Wendell knew as much about people in the village as Tom did, and that was a frightening thought. Tom Daley was very laid back which wasn't surprising as he reeked of grass if you got near enough. Wendell Manson however was a vicious little tyke. Gloria told me some of these things about her family background a little later. When she mentioned the curse about having devil's children I thought about the Manson family. On the male side of the Biddle family it went down from Jack to his two daughters, Rosemary and Violet. Now Rosemary Dunster was still alive and she seemed normal. But then Freddie had told me about the younger sister Violet who had run away to Liverpool and had the twins. That's the same twins that Freddie had befriended and had ended up being killed by Idwal Ferris. That Violet could claim to be a devil's child from the stories that Freddie told me. But what about the female side with Gwen Biddle? Sure she had seemed sane enough but just look at her daughter Tilley, Gloria's mother. She might not be a devil's child but she sure was weird. Gloria said her mum had gone all holy. She wore those plain dull clothes buttoned up to her neck and was always praying Gloria said. Had all sorts of crosses and icons in her bedroom with candles and even incense if I'm to believe Gloria. So Tilley had gone a little cuckoo and then along came that little bugger Wendell. Gloria had hinted at one of our teenage foursome get-togethers that Wendell might have been the result of a night of rape. She could remember one night when there had been a fearful fight in her house with both her parents screaming. She had been very frightened that night and thinks that may have been when Wendell was conceived. She could remember her mother getting even more wrapped up in herself after that and her dad was away more often. So that Wendell could be a devil's child. I kept these thoughts to myself as it seemed that the whole revelation had spooked Gloria more than she wanted.

One other thing happened just after the end of October and that really freaked me out. I told you that Gloria had tried to find out about her parents and grandparents. Well I didn't have to find out about mine because it came and hit me in the face. Right back in the beginning of this story I told you how I was ashamed of my name. I used to be proud of Templeton but then events really screwed that thought up. In the last week of October the usual bunch of losers were drinking in the George and we were half-heartedly playing darts but none of us were really good enough to be on the team. Anyway, who should walk in but Miss Samantha Lord again with another couple of foreigners. Seems this job or whatever you might call it that Miss Samantha had landed produced all sorts of weirdoes.

'Twenty Gary. You need twenty mate. That's right up the top of the board in case you've forgotten. We need twenty to go out.'

'All right, all right. I can see it. Heh, hold on, don't we need a double to go out? Twenty is no good. We need double ten you useless prat.'

'S'right. Yea, double ten then. That's, that's.....'

'I can see it Freddie. I'm quite capable mate without the running commentary.'

I threw and the dart landed in the ten.

'Now you need double five you silly wanker. Don't miss that or we'll need double two and a half.'

I turned and glared at Freddie. 'Can it. Just can it. Let me throw.' By chance my dart landed in the double five ring and stayed there. 'Bloody marvellous, absolutely bloody marvellous. Now that's talent Freddie. I should be on the team.'

'Gary, you got a minute please?'

For a moment I thought Freddie had changed his voice and then I suddenly twigged that it was Miss Samantha. Christ and she had those two weirdoes in tow. The clothes they wore didn't help because they looked like they had come from some Church charity sale. They were certainly out of date and way out of any fashion that I knew. The bloke wore a jacket like I'd seen in the flicks, a Second World War picture. Named after some President or other I seemed to remember but the lady had on a dress that was floral, flouncy and might have been worn at a summer garden fete. It too looked like it came out of the ark. You know, around the fifties. I had time to look at the faces and both of them were in their forties I guessed.

'Gary can we have a word please?' Samantha repeated.

'Sure Samantha. You got two more foreigners chasing their long-lost relatives? How come you end up with all the weirdoes who think their folks came from this neck of the woods?'

'I'd like you to meet Lewis and Shirley Peters Gary. They live in Melbourne Australia. Just recently they came into some money. A month or so ago they also learnt something that really surprised them, shook them I suppose. Anyway they wanted to find out more about this something they learnt a while ago. Sit down Gary. This may come as a bit of a shock to you too.'

'Hey up Gary mate. This here is the missus, Shirley, and I'm Lewis sport. Come over here on a bit of a bender. Yours a pint then is it? You want another Shirl? 'ow about you Sam?'

'Naw luv, she's right. I'm fine with this one.'

Samantha waved her hand and looked at me with a funny smile on her face. 'Take a drink first Gary and we'll explain why we are here. Actually I'll let Lewis explain as it's his story.'

'It's like this mate. Seems we have a long long ago connection. Your granddad, no I suppose it would be great granddad was an Albert Templeton. Have I got that right?'

'Yea, he worked here on Miss Samantha's family Estate. Gamekeeper I think he was.'

I looked back at this bloke Lewis and wondered how he knew this.

'But he went out and served King and Country in Europe didn't he Gary? You know, the big one in '14.'

'So what?'

'Came back though didn't he? Came back with Sam here's great grandfather. Who was it Sam, George Lord? Is that right?'

'Right Lewis but carry on. This is long before Gary's time. Those folk all died sometime in the fifties.'

'Well Gary, we've just learnt that Albert had a younger brother, a much younger brother who was called Reginald. Now it seems that Reginald was fourteen at the start of the war in 1914 but he got called up in 1917 and ended up in France by mid 1918. If what this Reginald says is true he was terrified fighting in the trenches and he deserted. Trouble was the silly bugger chose the wrong time. If he had waited another couple of weeks he'd have been fine 'cos right after he'd gone AWOL they signed the Armistice thing. Well Reginald was stuck. He was a deserter and he felt everyone would label him a coward. After the courageous action his elder brother had seen Reginald felt he couldn't come back here to his village. He was too ashamed and so he smuggled himself away on a ship and ended up in Australia.'

'See why I told you to sit down and have a drink Gary,' said Samantha.

'Yea, but what's all this got to do with me?' I said. 'I don't know anyone in Australia and my dad and even my old granddad never said anything about old Albert having any brother.'

'Reckon they all thought he was killed and never found I suppose,' said Lewis. 'With all the mud and collapsed trenches, shell holes and whatever there must have been lots of blokes buried and never found. Anyway Reginald Templeton, 'cos that's who he was decided to change his name in Australia. He called himself Reginald Peters. By chance he headed up to a place called Halls Gap in the Grampian Mountains in Victoria. Lot of logging went on up there in the early days and young Reginald had worked on the estate here so he knew a bit about trees and such. Seems he made a go of it and proved he could handle hard work. Up in western Victoria he met an Austrian girl called Marie Freidl. Reginald never let on that he'd been in the war fighting against the Germans or the Austrians. Anyway, Reginald Peters carries on working in the bush and he and Marie end up with three kids. There was George, Sophia and a lad they called Lazlo. When World War II started the family moved to Melbourne and by this time little Lazlo is five. Now you have to realise Gary that Lazlo was tiny, really an undersize little pisser but he loved horses. This family story now revolves around Lazlo 'cos he became a jockey and all the blokes in Oz are punters Gary. Where else in the world does a whole country stop work for a day when there is a horse race mate? The Melbourne Cup stops everything. We all bet and Lazlo became a top jockey. Won a fortune he did and he was careful with the money. Well sometime in the middle of 1958 old Reginald ups and dies but he was a crafty old sod. The family had made a bit of money in Melbourne and what with Lazlo doing bonza we were fairly well off. Now Reginald left a fifty-year time capsule but he never told anyone except his solicitors and to shorten this story up a bit we learnt about it just earlier this year.'

I took a sup of my beer and looked at this Australian couple. It was a little difficult understanding what he said with the accent and all, but I was starting to get both a little intrigued and worried with the story.

'So what jumped out of this time-capsule thing then?'

'Bear with us Gary mate. Let me take a pull here on me beer. Thirsty work all this talk. Well Reginald had these three kids as I said and the eldest was George and he's my dad. I was born in Melbourne and that's where I met Shirl here. Pulling pints she was and right easy on the eyes weren't you luv?'

'Lew go on with the story and put poor Gary here out of his misery. You're cutting into good drinking time.'

'Reginald's time capsule told this story Gary, about who he really was and where he'd come from. When the family heard about this we were all gob-smacked.'

'But Peter thought we should check up didn't he luv?'

'Who's Peter?' I managed to interject.

'Yes Shirl, Peter went looking on this web thing. Internet or whatever.'

'Who is Peter?' I asked again.

'He's our son Gary, Peter's our son and just turned sixteen he is. Really smart with computers and all this net thing. He spends a lot of his time chasing crazy information all over the world. Anyway Peter started looking up about Reginald and where he came from. He looked up the name and we decided that it would be fun to come and see whether it was real.'

'Their Peter looked up our Heritage Adventures Gary. That's the name of the company I work for and Lewis and Shirley here arranged with us to help them look for their roots.'

'So Sam here picked us up in London yesterday and brought us down to Somerset. She thought it was quite amazing as both your great granddad and your grandfather worked here at the Lord estate I understand. Small world eh?'

I must have just sat there. They were really Templetons I thought. Albert's brother Reginald to George to Lewis here and a son Peter to follow. Christ it was too much to take in.

'You okay there Gary? You look a little pale son. Bit of a shocker ain't it? Made all of us sit up a little back in Melbourne too. Still, Sam here's going to take us around the estate tomorrow and show us where old Albert and Edward worked. Your dad never worked on the estate did he Gary? Sam said that your dad was a salesman or something.'

'No, no Lewis that's right. My grandfather Edward was the foreman but he died when I was still a nipper. Dad decided to do something different. Working with his mouth really as opposed to his hands. Not much for the outdoors my dad.'

'But you work for us Gary? You've come back to us.'

'Yes Miss Samantha, I've always wanted to be like my granddad. My grandmother would tell me all the tales of how good he was. How he taught himself to be a mechanic and helped with the machinery on the estate. Then how he was a fitter in the war. You know he used to service the plane your grandfather flew Miss Samantha, Mr. Desmond that was. My old gran had lots of stories about them days. Then he worked for you for nigh on thirty years Miss Samantha as the foreman. All through the activities after the war with the replanting, fencing, and the real changeover from horses to machines. He must have been a grand old man.'

'You're proud of him Gary. I can hear that in your voice.'

'Yes Lewis I suppose I am. Seems like he lived an honest life and did a lot of good for people and the estate here. I'd like to think I could do something like that.'

'We can understand that Gary. Although old Reginald may have started off with a shaky beginning in the trenches and such, he pulled his finger out later on. We all did well and my uncle Lazlo has become a real champion. Made us realise that despite being pint size we can all make our way in this world. Our Peter thinks he is someone special.'

'So Gary is that enough of a shock for tonight? Never know in this quiet little village who is going to walk out of the woodwork next do you? I was telling Lewis and Shirley here about the couple I had from Canada who were related to Danny Masters. Shook him up too that did.'

Gradually, as the months passed from an event-filled September and October into November everything quietened down. The police finally had seen enough of both the Ferris cottage and the Whelks cottage and finished interviewing all of us about the past events. Even the members of the Lord family settled into a quieter routine. Operations on the forest returned to something like normal and our life in the village slipped back into a slow pace. True enough we still had the Saturday nights in the George with a more regular series of darts matches as we all moved into the winter season. Looking back the only really relevant thing that happened was the visit from two of Gloria's friends from outside the village. The two girls had come down from Bristol but I learnt later that they had both been with Gloria up in London too. In the same Club scene I think. It was sometime around Christmas if I remember right and the two girls were in the pub one night when I went in to chat up Gloria.

'The usual Gloria love please?'

'Wait your turn Gary. Can't you see I'm looking after my two friends here? So Gina, things pretty slow in Bristol? How long you been down from the city now?'

'Sheena and I left pretty soon after you did Gloria. Christ, it got pretty heavy right after you left. The cops were all over and there were some other blokes, Immigration or something I think. Who was it Sheena?'

'Dunno Gina. I was trying to keep out of sight. Immigration don't take too kindly to the Irish, nor the cops for that matter. Soon as you speak everyone thinks you're part of the IRA.'

'Anyone come down here Gloria? Anyone looking for you?'

'Gloria, my tongue's hanging out love. Let me 'ave my pint and I'll leave you chitty chatting. Where's George?'

'Gary shut it.'

'Hi girls, I'm Gary, Gloria's friend although you wouldn't think so the way she talks to me now would you? If I heard proper you're Gina and anyone with hair that colour love has got to be Irish and so you're Sheena. Pleased to meet you.'

I put my hand out friendly like and the two girls smiled.

'Hi Gary. Sorry we've held up your order. Here, let me buy you your pint. We're just catching up on old times with Gloria. Haven't seen each other for a while have we love? Come on Gloria, let the bloke cop his pint. What do you say Gina, shouldn't Gary get his drink? Claims he's a friend of our friend Gloria here.'

'So how's Bristol ladies?'

'None of your business Gary. Gina and Sheena are my friends. Here's your pint. Now bugger off.'

I took my pint, thanked Gloria, smiled at Gina and Sheena and carried my glass over to Sandy Leyton.

'Who are the two birds Sandy? Did they come into the village on the bus?'

Now Sandy Leyton drove the local village bus connecting us to the town on the main road. He usually knew who had come into the village.

'Heard 'em chatting on the bus this afternoon,' said Sandy. 'Come down from Bristol but just listening to the accents that ain't where they're from. The tall busty bird, Gina I think is certainly European. I think you worked out that the other one is Irish.'

'They have any luggage?'

'Yea, both of them had overnight bags. Think they're both staying here.'

The pub door swung open and five lads from the Crown walked in.

'Looks like the opposition has arrived. Who's playing on our team tonight?'

'The usual lot Gary.' Sandy looked around the room. 'There's George Crawford, old Harry, Ray, Tommy and young Ken Carter. All the usual crew.'

'Know who any of the opposition are?'

'See the tall fella, the one with a short crew cut? That's Bert Rawlings. Now he's good Gary. I'm not sure about any of the others though.'

'Can I have five pints please love? I need to get my team settled and relaxed before the match. Anything special I should know about your team? Got any ringers tonight?'

'No, just the usual blokes,' Gloria said as she pulled the pints.

'Who takes the bets?' asked Seaun. 'I've got a good feeling about our team tonight.'

Bert laughed as he turned to look at Seaun. 'You've always got good feelings Seaun you have. You're the ever optimistic Irishman. Anyway, thanks for the drinks love.'

'What did he want Gloria?' I asked. 'He seemed pretty inquisitive.'

'Gary all he wanted was drinks for his team. Jesus Gary, I'm the barmaid here and being friendly is part of the game.'

'So who are your girlie friends then? I heard they came in on the bus today. Staying are they?'

'We might be, and then again we might not be. Just depends who buys the drinks.' Gina leant on the bar and looked me up and down. Hell, it was as if she stripped me then and there.

'Gina don't let your paws stray too far over that one. You don't know where he's been. He usually sweats all day out in the forest and then comes in here to pester me.'

'Gloria that's fine. A naked sweaty male body can be quite a turn on you know. We should let Sheena dance for him and then he'd be a naked sweaty horny male body and that can be an even bigger turn on.'

Gloria laughed. 'Sure, we'll tie him up and tease him. Gary would probably like that.'

I felt the situation was getting out of hand and that the three of them were taking the piss. 'I'll see you later girls,' I said but I didn't realise at the time exactly what that would mean. It was only later that I saw them, much later.

Gloria's experiences in London slowly faded away and there were no more visits from either the heavy mob or the boys in blue. Seems she escaped. However, within a couple of months of being down in the quiet of Somerset Gloria herself started to get restless. Freddie and I were in the pub pretty often and I was still trying to get back in Gloria's good books, well into her knickers really. For some reason she wasn't having any of this, which I thought was a bit weird given what she had been doing up in London. I suppose the whole village shut down like the forest did over the winter. We all hibernated. Perhaps it was just the calm before the storm given what happened the next spring.

RAMBLING ON

THE EIGHT HIKERS PLUMPED THEMSELVES down on the soft grass tussocks on top of Damehole Point. Bright sunshine shone this early May Saturday morning and most of the members gazed northwest towards the Isle of Lundy in the clear air. Earlier that morning the group had driven down from Bristol and started their hike in the picturesque village of Clovelly on the North Devon coast. Rupert Oldshaw was the oldest and the de facto leader of this loose band of ramblers. It was a curious array of young people but they all were or had recently been students at Bristol Uni. Rupert himself was now a graduate student at Oxford. Ted Dexter was a recently graduated historian with Doris Lyon his girlfriend. There were two other men: Arnold Church, a fanatic, passionate about wildlife and wildlife areas and Rory Flanagan who was much more laid-back as an Irish poet, musician and supposedly wildlife biologist. The other three members of the merry band were also passionate in their own ways. Mavis Taylor was a close personal friend of Rupert, but mostly because Rupert's father was someone senior in films, and then there were Philippa Robson and Margaret Letterman. These last two young ladies were strong hikers but even stronger in their beliefs of God and the Biblical creation of the world.

Every Saturday the group assembled and travelled to a new hiking locale. This was the first time this year that they had traversed any part of the South West Way, the coastal path around the cliffs of south western England. The route from Clovelly to Hartland Quay was just over sixteen kilometres and embraced some great views out over the Bristol Channel. They had passed Blackchurch Rock, Chapman Rock and on to the lighthouse at Hartland Point. Rupert had led at a leisurely pace along the north coast and earlier in the morning they had paused at the memorial plaque at Becklands. Just below here a Wellington bomber had crashed into the cliffs in the nineteen forties: an event and a period far removed from the memories of the eight ramblers. After Hartland Point the coast turns sharply south and the eight young people walked onwards with the sunshine in their faces.

'Ever think what happened to the donkeys?' asked Rory with a grin on his face.

'I don't see any donkeys,' said Margaret.

'He means the ones that used to be in Clovelly Margaret,' said Philippa.

'Perhaps they turned them loose with the ponies on Exmoor,' added Rory. 'They could mate together and evolve into a wild animal capable of walking up and down staircases.'

'You're a beast Rory Flanagan. You're a fallen Catholic. You have no respect for God and all his bounty.'

'That would pollute the environmental state of Exmoor,' complained Arnold. 'Those ponies are unique to that locale.'

'I reckon they are in the glue holding my paper lunch bag together,' said Ted. 'Seriously though Rory, the donkeys at Clovelly were rather unique historically. There aren't too many English villages where the main street is a staircase. Actually, talking of old oddities I came across a map the other day showing ancient drovers' roads. You know the routes where they used to drive cattle in the old days.'

Rory started humming an old Irish song about droving but Rupert's voice cut across the melody. 'Any of the paths interesting Ted? I think the group could do with a new kind of challenge rather than just walking on established paths. Were these maps of this area?'

'I found them in the archives of the University and there were a couple covering this part of England. One of them included an area around the Mendip Hills in Somerset.'

'I wonder whether any of them are still legal Rights of Way?' pondered Doris. 'Do you still have the maps Ted? It would be an interesting legal challenge to see whether we could re-establish some of them. Most landowners are strongly in favour of closing those old paths. They don't want the public traipsing through their property but I think it is good to challenge them. It's our English right. Don't you think so?'

'Too true Doris,' said Ted.

'Well Ted, did you keep these maps as Doris asked?' questioned Rupert. 'We could fire up our merry band with a good challenge, opening up the country for the freemen.'

'No, I couldn't take the originals out of the archives but I could photocopy them. I remember the one covering the Mendips showed a drovers' road through Fotheringham Manor.'

'That's the place with that new Education Centre isn't it?' asked Arnold. 'The owner is trying to diversify his estate and turn his commercial forests back into more natural woodlands or something. It would be an interesting area to hike Rupert.'

'I heard there was some controversy over that Education Centre,' said Philippa. 'Wasn't there an article in the paper about some of the teaching there? I read there was some local Minister lecturing against evolution and the Lord family was a little upset, as were some of the kids' parents.'

'Sounds just like the sort of the place we should hike,' said Doris forcibly. 'Sounds like a legal battle about to break out over and above any mundane Rights of Way.'

'Doris you're just a radical love,' said Rory. 'Live and let live that's my motto.'

'And look where that got your country mate,' said Ted.

'Hold up there Ted. Keep your energy for the hike. We've still got to finish down to Hartland Quay and then walk back into Hartland village. Still, this area of Fotheringham sounds interesting for a whole lot of reasons. If Ted can make a copy of the map we should go there next Saturday.'

Tony Lord dived neatly into the pool.

'Jesus, blimey Uncle Daniel, you didn't tell me it would be this cool. It's bloody freezing if I put my feet down.'

'Just swim in the top inch then Tony,' laughed Daniel. 'The sun has warmed that part.'

Football was coming to an end and Tony had been bottling up his need to swim. Back in London where he had grown up he had spent most of his summer swimming at the local Municipal Baths. However, he remembered he had heard his uncle Daniel talk about swimming in the pool of the river just above the village. He also remembered the antics his wild auntie Samantha had got up too playing in the river. God I miss my mum thought Tony wistfully but the family down here is sure different. Ten years ago Tony's mother, Danielle Made had escaped from the horrors of the civil war in Mozambique and fled to England with her own mother. Danielle had met Michael Lord, Anthony and Sylvia Lord's second son, and become his mistress. Danielle had planned to have a child with Michael and persuade him to marry her. Unfortunately for Danielle only half of this plan worked. Sure Danielle had Tony, brazenly named after Michael's father, but Michael wasn't going to marry someone without money or power. Even after Danielle moved with Tony down to the village beside Fotheringham Manor Michael still kept Danielle as just his mistress. In January 1991 Michael Lord was shot outside a cave on the Lord family estate. To this day no one knows who or why. Right after the funeral Sylvia Lord wanted Danielle and Tony to stay at Fotheringham as Tony was a Lord grandchild but Danielle wouldn't have any of that and she fled back to London taking Tony with her. During the summer of that year it was Anthony Lord who slowly re-established contact with Danielle and she came to visit a few times. Last year, 1998, a part of Danielle's past came back to haunt her. In fact it came back to terrorise her. In Mozambique one of the rebel leaders believed Danielle's mother had stolen something of great personal value and he wanted it back. He sent two men to find it. Danielle knew that the story was false but she also knew the identity and reputation of the two men sent to find her. She and Tony fled to Fotheringham and the Lord family to find sanctuary in late September. Tony trod water in the pool and shivered. He wasn't sure whether it was the cool water or the memory of that fateful night. The two men, Senor Mendosa, a Portuguese mulatto, and Moboto, a three hundred pound black giant had followed Danielle and Tony down from London. They invaded Fotheringham Manor, knifed Danielle and tried to kidnap Tony. Fortunately Daniel Lord and two friends managed to disarm the attackers, rescue Tony and solve the problem with the two men from Mozambique. Tony remembered the wild ride with his auntie Samantha into the hospital in town. His mother was bleeding seriously in the back of the car and both he and little James were still in shock. And his auntie! Tony laughed to himself. There was auntie Samantha with her badly burnt and bandaged hands like two large white paws wrestling with the steering wheel on that crazy rush to the hospital. Everything was full speed ahead with auntie Samantha. But, he thought, it didn't end happily despite the rush. Danielle, his mother died in hospital from loss of blood and torn apart insides. I do miss you mum muttered Tony.

'Keep moving Tony or you'll catch cold son. Should we set up some kind of laps for you?'

'No I'm fine Uncle Daniel. I was just having a flashback about last September and shivered. But I was also remembering my auntie Samantha.'

'Now there's someone who will make anyone shiver,' said Daniel laughing.

'But she came with me to say goodbye to my mum Uncle Daniel. It was she who came to the hospital with me. And it was she who cried.'

'Tony son, my sister really loved your mother. She always told me your mother was someone special. But, you're right, my sister is a very confusing and eccentric lady. You made a good choice when you decided to stay with Christina and Peter. Where is Peter by the way? I thought he was coming to swim.'

'I'm here Uncle Daniel, I'm here I'm here,' and a loud splash followed as Peter jumped into the pool. 'Wow, ow, holy smoke it's cold. Tony why didn't you tell me you swim in ice cubes.' Peter splashed fiercely about in the pool trying to get a little warmer.

Daniel had brought down eight old plastic milk jugs and some string. Using a few rocks from the bank of the stream he set up a few buoys in the pool to resemble some kind of swimming lane.

'Do you have a routine Tony? Did you have a training system of any kind?'

'Not really Uncle Daniel. I did laps of various strokes and I practised life saving dives picking up objects from the floor of the pool. The water here is a little murky and it is hard to see things underwater, especially after Peter jumped in and stirred up the bottom. Still, thanks for the idea of the buoys. They will help with any lap routine.'

Soon after Peter's arrival Christina arrived beside the river with Samantha and James.

'Can I go in Mummy? I want to go in. Will you take me? Uncle Daniel will hold me.' The barrage of questions was muffled as James struggled to get out of his clothes.

'James, hold up a minute darling. We didn't bring any swimming trunks for you. We'll come down tomorrow if it stays fine and you can go in.'

'Peter be careful near the end of the pool. There must be a current with the river coming out of the pool.'

'Sure Mum. Actually I might come out pretty soon as it is bloody.... oops, sorry, jolly cold in here. I don't know how Tony stands it.'

Tony was swimming steadily and rhythmically up and down between the buoys, changing strokes at each end. He showed a powerful and controlled movement through the water.

'How cold is it Daniel?' asked Samantha.

'Colder than I'm used to,' answered Daniel, 'but I'll stay here and look after Tony. Peter, are you out of here?'

'Yes Uncle Daniel,' said Peter as his teeth chattered. 'I'll just get dressed and look after James. I won't let him fall in the river auntie,' Peter said to Samantha.

'Safer if we all walk I think Peter,' said Samantha. 'James is full of energy this afternoon.'

The ramblers on the top of Damehole Point weren't exactly full of energy as Rupert stood up and packed away the lunch materials in his rucksack. He folded the small groundsheet he and Mavis had been sharing and slid it into a pocket of his sack.

'Once more to the breech dear friends, or something like that.'

'You going to fill up the walls with your English dead?' asked Rory.

'Only if you fall off the walls of the stone bridge over the Abbey River just below us,' said Rupert. 'Still, it is a bit of a walk through Stoke and Hartland to get back to the cars. Ted, tell me more about this map over the Mendips. Was the path very well marked or will we be thrashing about in the weeds?'

'Hell Rupert, I don't know. I sure couldn't tell that from this old map. Get the Ordnance Survey map for the area. Here, looking at my map it looks like number 182 in the Landranger series, or maybe 172. That should be good enough to start with. If the area is really interesting and we go back we can look and see whether there are any maps at larger scales for that area.'

As the sun slowly moved around towards the west the eight young people left the coastal path and navigated their way back to Hartland village. They had left one car there and while the group waited, Rupert, Ted and Philippa drove over to Clovelly to fetch the two other cars. Margaret was the passenger in Philippa's car on the drive back to Bristol.

'Did you read all of the article about the teaching going on at that Education Centre at Fotheringham Philippa?'

'Yes, why?'

'The Minister's name was the Revered Godschild wasn't it?'

'If I remember right yes, I think so. So what?'

'The name is familiar. I'm trying to remember where I have heard his name before. Did the article say anything else about him?'

'Only that he had come into the village recently, some time just after last Christmas I think. Anyway, he was new and it appears that he has been stirring up some passions over and above his teaching at the Education Centre. Seems there are several people in the village who believe quite strongly in the biblical origin of the world. Rory's comments were quite uncalled for today don't you think? Donkeys are donkeys and ponies are ponies. It has always been that way.'

'Gabriel Godschild, that's it. His name was Gabriel Godschild.'

'Who was?'

'The Minister's name Philippa. He left a parish somewhere up in Yorkshire. I can't remember the details of where and why but there was some scandal. The parishioners drummed him out of the village I think.'

'Now wouldn't Doris love to find out about that? She really is quite catty at times, viciously spiteful. I think it goes with her job. Solicitors always seem to be looking for the bad things about people.'

'Arnold will be happy though. He loves anyone trying to look after wild areas, or trying to make wild areas.'

'Yes,' said Margaret rather softly, 'back the way God meant it.'

'Daniel, are you going to stay playing porpoises all afternoon?'

'Katya, I didn't know you had left the Manor. I thought you were going to spend the afternoon with mum looking at the bookings for the Centre.'

'I came down with Samantha and James Daniel. James insisted I was his special friend and I had to come down to the pool and see him play water polo.'

'James can't even swim Katya.'

'Daniel I know that but he heard his mother talking about water polo and James being James he just assumed it was a wet kind of polo. Tony, how's the routine coming on?'

Tony rolled over onto his back and looked back to the bank. 'Oh hi Katya. It's fine. Uncle Daniel has fixed up these markers for me. It's smashing.'

'Like smashing birds Tony, when we first met?'

Tony blushed when he remembered his exclamation when he first met Katya Howard with his uncle Daniel. To hide his embarrassment Tony swam over to Daniel.

'That's enough for today Uncle Daniel. Thanks for the buoys. They'll really help if I am going to swim seriously here. Thanks for being here too. Auntie Christina wouldn't let me come on my own, even though I told her how well I can swim.'

'She loves you Tony and like everyone she loves Christina is very protective. It's who she is. You're happy at Home Farm aren't you? You get on really well with Peter.'

Right after the death of his mother Samantha had taken Tony into the hospital to say goodbye. On the drive back to Fotheringham Samantha had asked Tony who he would like to stay with. Danielle didn't have any family in England and so the Lord family welcomed Tony to Fotheringham. Samantha herself was recovering from a series of traumatic events including the death of her husband in a forest fire in Canada. She was somewhat relieved when Tony told her quite clearly that he would like to live with Christina and Peter at Home Farm. Last September Tony had gone to school with Peter and now the two of them were virtually inseparable.

'Yes Uncle Daniel. Although I do miss my mum auntie Christina is wonderful and I'm really happy at Home Farm. Of course Enrico keeps us all in order as he's a grand old man. It's a cool home Uncle Daniel.'

'Maybe I should get Enrico to carve some smashing birds for me,' said Katya with a twinkle in her eye.

'Katya don't tease,' said Daniel. 'Look, we'll dry off and go and find the others.'

'That's a neat idea,' came a new voice.

The three of them by the pool looked up to see who had spoken.

'Hello Gloria. Yes, Tony here wanted to swim seriously in the pool and so I thought they would help. He tells me he used to swim laps back in London in a real swimming pool.'

'I do life-saving too,' added Tony as he looked at Gloria Manson.

'You could save me any time,' said Gloria as she stepped forward and offered her hand to Tony.

'Hold up there Gloria. Tony's only ten.'

'That's as maybe Mr. Daniel but he's from London and boys grow up fast there. Don't they Tony?'

Unable to stop himself Tony blushed. 'But you're not from London,' he said, trying to cover up his embarrassment. 'You don't talk like a Londoner. You're from down 'ere.'

'But I lived up there for a while Tony. Worked up there for some time.'

'Gloria, have you met Katya Howard? Katya, this is Gloria Manson who does come from this village as Tony suggests. Gloria works in the George.'

'Hi Gloria. Pleased to meet you,' and Katya stepped forwards and held out her hand.

'Me too,' said Gloria, and she shook Katya's hand. 'She sounds different too young Tony?'

'Yes, Katya's from Florida I think. That's right isn't it Katya? It is Florida?'

'You're right Tony, as is Gloria. I suppose I do sound a little different. It's funny how you can't hear the differences in your own voice and accent. I'm living in Oxford at the moment but I'm also trying to get Daniel here to make some changes at Fotheringham.'

'Yes, Gary and Freddie have been telling me that there are some changes going on.'

'Is that the Freddie of Freddie and the cousins Daniel?'

'The very same. Actually, aren't you and Freddie cousins Gloria, or is it second cousins? Don't you both have Biddles as grandparents?'

'Hell Mr. Daniel I wouldn't know.'

'Just call me Daniel Gloria. You don't work for our family and we're much the same age. Just Daniel please.'

'Okay then Daniel, but I wouldn't know about such things. My mum tends to play silent and holy about her past and my dad came from somewhere in Devon. Perhaps you should get that crazy sister of yours to investigate us, for free of course just as an example of a quaint English village. Should interest your American friend here. Perhaps Katya will find out she is related to all of us if you go back far enough. Young Danny Masters got a real shock the day your sister brought that Canadian couple in last autumn. None of us really know what skeletons we have hidden in our cupboards now do we?'

Gloria turned to look at Tony who was standing there towelling dry and listening to the conversation.

'You swimming tomorrow young Tony? I like to swim and it's good to have someone else here to look after each other. Did I hear you know about life-saving? I'd like to learn a little more about that. Think you could teach me?'

'Sure,' said Tony, 'it'll be a gas. I used to help with all sorts of people up in London, not just kids you know. I'll give it a go. Where'd you live up in London then? We lived on the edge of Kensington, just down the road from the museums.'

'Don't know about no museums Tony. I lived in Whitechapel but I worked in the West End. That's not far from Kensington is it?'

'Tony you finished drying off son? We should find Peter and James before they get up to mischief. See you later Gloria. Maybe Katya and I will come down the George some night. Don't you have darts tournaments over the weekends?'

'Saturday nights usually Daniel. Yes, come on down and see life in the village. I'll keep your forest crew in line so they don't give you a hard time. Freddie can get a little mouthy after a few pints but I can gag him. See you tomorrow then Tony, if the weather's fine.'

Katya, Daniel and Tony picked up their swimming gear and set off down the stream to find Peter, James and their respective mothers. Gloria walked back into the village thinking over what she might learn from Tony. Life-saving sure, but maybe we can learn a little more about that Education Centre and who is doing what in the cottages. Betty sold hers, that I do know and she put the money into expanding part of Marples the baker. Got the place enlarged with new ovens or somesuch so she could expand her pie-making. She also hired the elder of those two younger sisters of Lester Rainer to help with the preparations. Even George has bought several of the pies and offered them with his lunch menu. Quite a going concern that Betty Ferris, but an empty cottage she's left behind and that gives me some ideas.

That Saturday evening Daniel did bring Katya down to the George to watch the darts match. Samantha had persuaded her parents to keep an ear out for James but she thought he was pretty tired after an energetic day with horse riding in the morning and walking alongside the river watching the swimming in the afternoon.

'No special clients tonight Miss Samantha? No one with you to terrify the locals about there long-lost deported criminal great grandparents? Danny hasn't really recovered you know. Every time he comes in here he peers carefully round the door to see whether you're here. Then you went and brought those two Australians in here. Now Gary's all mixed up about being proud of his name and embarrassed because of this long lost Reginald.'

'Go on Gloria. Stop trying to pull my leg. Katya, what will you have?'

'A white wine Samantha please.'

'A white wine and two pints of bitter please Gloria.'

'Can we go and watch the darts match Daniel? That is something else I have never seen live.'

'Don't they play darts at any of the pubs in Oxford? Come on then but you'll have to keep quiet.'

Gloria watched them go. It's funny being back here in the village she thought. Things move a lot slower than up in the West End and people are more friendly, more considerate. Now, I need to know more about what is happening where at Fotheringham.

'Samantha, things all settled down now up at Fotheringham? Did Enrico ever go back to his cottage? You know, the one that that madman Idwal Ferris smashed up?'

'No Gloria, he's still living at Home Farm with my sister-in-law. I don't think he'll ever go back to that cottage now. Actually my mum was talking just the other day about hiring some new staff and maybe moving them into there. When she asked Enrico he thought that made sense.'

'Did Betty sell her cottage? I see she has expanded her business as part of the bakery. You offered to help with all that didn't you?'

'Yes Gloria I did. After John got killed and Betty decided to live here in the village again we bought the cottage from her. How come you're so interested in the estate?'

'Well it's Gary. With him and Freddie both working up there I suppose I get a lot of chit-chat about the estate but it's mostly what the blokes are up to. They never know what's really going on. Gary keeps giving me a hard time about not knowing what's happening right under my nose. He thinks I'm still wanting to go back to London and leave him behind.'

'Are you going to go back to London?'

'Not sure. But what ever happened to that idea of Daniel's here, well Daniel and that American girlfriend of his I expect? Didn't they want to put up some school in the forest somewhere? I heard Katya was all gung ho for teaching all about the birds and the bees up in the woods. She some back to nature freak? Americans always have funny ideas. Up in London they were the weirdoes. Must be something to do with their weather. Anyway, Gary was telling me there was some building put up but he hadn't seen it. He heard Bob Edwards talking about it with Daniel one day.'

'It's finished now Gloria. Has been for a while now. The local school does use it a little but it's mostly schools from the further away that have booked it. You must have seen that there are more kids around in the village. Haven't you had some of the people staying here?'

'So there'll be more people running around your estate then?'

'More useful for you there will be more people running around the village and coming in here. Some of the groups will end up staying here in the village and others will come in by bus but I expect there will be more people around.'

'So who is Tony, the kid I met this afternoon down at the river? He was there with your brother and Katya. Said he came from London.'

'He's my older brother's son, Michael's son.'

Samantha was about to briefly tell Gloria the story of Michael and Danielle and their son Tony when the darts match ended and the teams invaded the bar wanting drinks to celebrate their success or drown their sorrows. Gloria pulled pints and thought about Tony.

'So you did come then. I'd jump in if I was you. The water's still too cold to just wade in. It's fine once you're in though and do a few laps.'

Gloria stood on the edge of the pool and shivered. The May Sunday morning sunshine was bright and actually quite warm but the water did look cool. She laughed as Tony did handstands and all she could see was his feet. Taking a big breath she jumped and came up screaming.

'Jesus Murphy Tony but it's cold.'

'Swim then, swim hard, up along the line of markers. After a couple of laps you'll feel much better.' Tony rolled over and swam powerfully up the string of buoys. Gloria followed suit.

'Can you do the crawl as well as breast stroke?' asked Tony watching Gloria.

'A little bit Tony but I get my breathing messed up after a while.'

'Try and breath in when your head's on one side and you have created a wave and a hollow. Like breast stroke breath out when your face is underwater. Here watch.'

Tony stroked away and Gloria could see the hollow Tony's head made in the water and how he breathed in. She tried but came up spluttering after half a dozen strokes.

'You all right? You okay?' asked Tony as Gloria trod water and coughed.

'Yea, fine thanks Tony. You're right about the water though. It's not bad after a few minutes. What can you teach me about life saving?'

Tony went through a series of routines of how to approach a troubled swimmer or drowning person. He explained how to help them depending on whether they were tired and sensible or terrified and struggling. First Tony had Gloria as the victim and taught her to swim on her back while resting her hands on Tony's shoulders as he pushed her placidly to safety.

'That's the easiest way and if someone's calm or just tired with cramp that works fine. Trouble is most people you try and rescue are thrashing about and bloody frightened. Then you have to subdue them, almost strangle them before you can help them. Come here and I'll show you.'

Again Tony towed Gloria across the pool but this time he was on his back with his arm across Gloria's chest and holding her hand up across her body. After ten minutes or so Tony switched roles.

'Okay, that's the easy part now let me be the victim and you rescue me.' They went through the routines again and in the last exercise Tony put up a real struggle before he let Gloria suppress him.

'You have to really take charge Gloria. You have to really hold me tight.'

For a moment Gloria's mind flittered through other thoughts about holding a struggling man tight but then she shivered with memories of other struggles.

'Tony I'm getting chilly. That's enough for today. Thanks for the lessons. I'd like to do this again. Get some more practice in and swim some more but right now I've got goose bumps. I'm going to dry off.'

'I'll help you. You did good.'

They both climbed out of the pool and picked up their towels. Tony turned and looked at Gloria.

'You look real cool in that bikini.'

'Come here you cheeky young sod. I'm old enough to be your mother. Let me dry your back.' Gloria rubbed her towel vigorously over Tony's back.

'My turn,' Tony said. 'It's easier if someone else dries your back. Turn round and I'll rub.'

I was driving into the village that quiet Sunday morning when I had to stop my car so quickly that I stalled the engine. In a flash I was halfway out of the driver's side before the engine had coughed itself into silence.

'Oy, oy!! What you think you're doing? Leave off.' I rushed across the road and down towards the river.

'Hi Gary. What's all the commotion?'

'What you two think you're doing? In broad daylight too. Christ Gloria he's only a kid. And you, who the hell are you and what are doing feeling up Gloria here?'

Gloria moved around until she was between Tony and me. She thrust out her finger and pointedly jabbed it into my chest.

'Now listen up Gary Templeton and listen up good mate. This here is Tony Lord and you should know that he lives up on the Estate, at Home Farm if you must know. He is one of the Lord family and don't you forget that Gary. Over and above all of that Tony here was good enough and helpful enough to give me life-saving lessons. You're just lucky you didn't see him giving me mouth-to-mouth resuscitation. That would really have wound you up.' Gloria stood there and giggled. She turned and moved beside Tony.

'Tony this here is Gary Templeton. You may have seen him working up in your forest as he is part of your uncle Daniel's work crew.'

'Hello Gary. I was giving Gloria here swimming lessons, really I was. She wanted to learn about life-saving and I'm qualified. Up in London I got a certificate as part of the junior programme. She did real good, didn't you Gloria?'

'Yes, sure kid,' I said and I shook Tony's offered hand. 'Didn't know what you were up to now did I?'

'Gary I've got to go and get changed. I'm getting chilly standing here. Tony was keeping me warm with his towel rubbing until you came along. Tony you okay love? You've got your bike haven't you? If the weather stays warm can we do this again next Sunday? I really need to learn and get better. You're a good teacher.'

'Yes Tony, you bugger off now and I'll look after Gloria here. Won't I Gloria?'

'See you then,' cried Tony and he jumped on his bike and rode off.

'Christ Gary, can't a girl get a little action in without you having a hissy fit?'

'Come here gorgeous and let me keep you warm,' I said and I wrapped my arms around her.

'Gary give over. Let me go and get some clothes on for Christ sake.'

'I'd sooner you took them off and I'd really keep you warm,' I muttered in her ear. 'Ouch, that's my balls girl. I'll walk funny all week now.'

Gloria laughed. 'Come on Gary,' she said. 'Run me home and we'll have a nice hot cup of tea with my mum. She'll make you kneel and pray though before you can drink it. She's slowly going bonkers Gary what with all her praying. It's starting to give me the creeps. And Wendell, I'll brain that useless brother of mine what with his messing around with my clothes. Jesus Gary I live in a household of nutters. I think I might even move back to London. Everything seems to have gone quiet and no-one has been down here looking for me. Maybe I'll just leave again and find a new life.'

'Gloria, no you can't do that, not after you've come back again. Look, let's look around here and find something else to help you stay in the village. Can't we find some action for you down here? What about those friends of yours from Bristol who were down last year? Who were they now? There was a thin skinny Irish lass and some Italian-sounding bird. Greta, Claudia, no Gina that was it. It was Gina wasn't it?'

I watched Gloria going inside her head. 'Run me home Gary and I'll think about it. There was something that Samantha Lord said last night in the pub that's given me an idea. Maybe I will talk with Gina and Sheena. I may stay.'

She turned and jabbed me again in the chest. 'I may stay but you'll have to help.'

'You know me Gloria. I just want you to stay here. Get back together like before.'

'What about Freddie? You going to find a new girl to make up a foursome? You know my mum gets real mad if she sees us together. You'll have to find a new girl for Freddie.'

'Let him find his own girl.'

'No you stupid prat. We need a fourth to keep my mother off my back. How about one of Lester Rainer's sisters? You know, the girls that are working for Betty Ferris? Young Dora's okay. She's a bit young I know. Eighteen isn't she?'

'Lester will give Freddie shit if he tries anything on with his kid sister.'

'Yes Gary but it's you who is supposed to be going out with Dora and Freddie is with me. I know Freddie and I are second cousins or something but me mum never worried about that. It was you she didn't like. Worth the effort though don't you think?' and Gloria looked at me and smiled. She folded herself back into my arms. 'Didn't you want to keep me warm and help me stay here in the village?' she asked. Jesus, women I thought, women and that scheming Gloria. I drove her home and tried to be polite to Mrs. Manson. Fortunately Wendell was out somewhere. Holding my mug of tea and trying to make conversation I wondered what Gloria was thinking of doing. Said I'd have to help her. Now what's she got in mind?

A BLAST FROM THE PAST

LOOKING BACK I MUST HAVE got complacent that month of May. After our little chat that first weekend I got used to the routine of Gloria going swimming on Sundays. I mean to say, Tony was only a kid now wasn't he so there was no need for me to be jealous there? Every now and then Gloria would tease me by telling me how she was learning mouth to mouth resuscitation but I would show Gloria how it was really done in the village. Gloria would giggle and tell me all the bizarre experiences she had had up in London. There was one incident though that probably set more in motion than I understood at the time. It was on the middle Saturday of the month and as usual Freddie was partly to blame. Freddie had had a bad week with his mother for some reason. I had always thought Mrs. Dunster put up with a lot from Freddie but then she wasn't my mum. Because there was an important football match being shown on the TV that afternoon Freddie decided to watch it in the George. Back in our house my dad had taken over the TV for some reason so that wasn't an option.

'What's the big excitement Freddie?' I asked. 'You're not usually this keen on any northern team. What's so special about the "reds"?'

'Two reasons mate,' said Freddie, and he laughed as if he had said something funny.

'What's so bloody funny about two reasons?'

'Well I was thinking of the twins, my long-lost cousins if you must know and as there were two of them and I have two reasons I thought it was funny you know.'

'Freddie you've lost me mate. Another beer?'

'Thought you'd never ask. Aye.'

I came back with the pints after asking George to turn up the volume a little so we could hear the silly prat on the commentary box state the obvious.

'Games about to start. Talking of games Freddie I was chatting to Gloria about getting a foursome back together.'

'Hush up and let me hear who's playing.'

'Man it's Liverpool and they're playing Spurs. Anyone can see that. The reds versus the black and whites. So which team is special?'

'Liverpool, where Jack and Lennie came from.'

Freddie that was years ago. I was saying about a foursome. You know, you, me.....'

'Shut it. I want to hear who's playing for Liverpool.'

I sat back and supped on my pint and Freddie had his eyes glued to the box. He was silently mouthing the names of the team and then the substitutes.

'Shit, stupid gits. Don't they know Peterson can run rings around them? He should be playing. Coach is a moron.'

'So you're not interested in the game any more? Actually I should be. That's Spurs they are playing and they're the team that young Tony Lord supports. He was telling Gloria how well they have done this year. All I seem to hear from her is Tony did this and Tony said that. I went down to the river to watch last Sunday you know. Gloria could have been feeding me a line about swimming lessons. Still, they both swam and that young kid can really swim. Then he played the dummy and had Gloria rescue him. Told her she was learning really fast. Freddie are you listening to a word I've said mate? Muttering to the TV won't do any good you know. The bloke on the other end ain't listening.'

'What Gary, what were you saying? Bollocks to the lot of them then. They deserve to lose. What foursome? We ain't got no foursome. Sandra topped herself remember.'

'So how about we find another charming young lady to make up a foursome? Who do you fancy?'

'In this village? As a foursome with Gloria? Like before?'

'Yes, could be. You had a leg over recently that I don't know about?'

'Who have you been chatting up then? Who'd want to go out with us three, like old times? There ain't anybody left we was at school with.'

I drew a deep breath and looked at Freddie. He had stopped giving the TV a hard time and was guzzling at his pint.

'I was in Marples a couple of times this week and chatting up young Dora Rainer. She's a cheeky bitch and likes to throw herself about a bit. I offered her a chance to see more of life and she rolled her eyes and wriggled and giggled. Told her it was in a foursome and so it was good clean fun. She told me she was disappointed and hoped it would good and fun and maybe something else. I told her to keep my pie warm. Freddie you gone to sleep again or are you back arguing with the referee now?'

'Silly git missed a clear cut foul there. Should have been a free kick for Liverpool. No Gary. I'm being real clever. I'm doing two things at the same time. My mum keeps telling me that that's impossible. Men can't do that she says. Well I'm proving her wrong mate. Come to think of it I'm probably doing more than two things at the same time' and Freddie lifted his glass and managed to pour most of his pint down his throat. 'There,' he said, 'how about that? Watching, thinking, listening and drinking all at the same time. I'm a bloody wonder Gary.'

'Dora Rainer Freddie. Girl with the bright eyes, cheeky mouth, cuddly body and looking for good something fun.'

'What does Lester say?'

'Splish splash usually Freddie as he slops paint from one side of the wall to another. He really is a messy painter mate. Wouldn't be so bad if he changed clothes before coming in here but I'm always careful where I sit after he's been in.'

'Gary Templeton, you're one to talk. Seem to remember you coming in here and smelling of chain saws covered in sawdust and pine resin. Like a sticky bun you are sometimes Gary.'

'Don, how come you're in so early?'

'Half day in the office Freddie for some reason. Just told to go home by old Mr. Lacey. Seems there was a death somewhere in the family and they shut up shop.'

'Don what do you actually do in that office?'

'Mine to know and you to find out nosey pants,' said Don.

Freddie got in three more pints and we shot the shit and screamed at the referee but none of it made the slightest difference to what happened that evening.

That Saturday was a wet day and this upset the plans of the Ramblers from Bristol. Ted Dexter had gone back into the archives and managed to photocopy the old drovers' map. He'd also purchased the two Ordnance Survey maps covering the area. His girlfriend Doris was really pissed off because Ted didn't do this quickly enough and so they had walked in the Forest of Dean the previous Saturday when Doris was looking forward to some form of confrontation at Fotheringham. Philippa had telephoned Doris and told her about the controversial preacher speaking at the

Education Centre and so Doris was extra keen on such a visit. Although the rain may have upset the Rambler's plans it was Katya Howard who upset Daniels.

'Daniel I'm so close to completing things I can almost taste it love,' she told him down the telephone. 'I have finished my thesis with all the necessary references and now all I'm doing is getting my oral thoughts in shape. You know I have to defend my thesis and that is done through a *viva voce*. I need to get my thoughts in order to ensure I've got my arguments lined up correctly. This is the last and hardest part Daniel. Can you understand that? Of course you can as you have been through this yourself and so you understand. I knew you would understand.'

Sure I understand thought Daniel as he told Katya he missed her and hung up the phone. Still, that doesn't make it any easier not to be with you. Okay, if you can't come to me thought Daniel I will go out into the forest and think of you. I'll go and see what there is out there where we can put some of our ideas into practice. I can check to see what is happening at the Education Centre and perhaps look at our two cottages. We could always think of converting them into small-scale residences for people at the Centre. Alternatively we could tear them both down and let the forest revert a little back to woodlands ecosystems and show people the effects of disturbance. Then mum was talking of maybe hiring some new staff and they might want a home. Daniel convinced himself that he could put up with missing Katya if he was doing something that would normally involve her. He took himself off to the forest.

Late that afternoon a small black sedan slowly drove into the village from the London road. It wove a rather erratic route as it entered the village and coasted to a stop by the George and Dragon. The driver didn't get out immediately but appeared to be half asleep at the wheel. Several of the locals took a passing glance but there was no emergency and so they walked on. Two kids came flying along the street on their bicycles and just as they passed the car the driver's side door opened and almost pushed them into an oncoming tractor. Fortunately the tractor was going very slowly hauling a loaded wagon and so no harm was done but the driver did realise his error.

'Sorry, I'm sorry kids,' he uttered but the two kids had already dismissed the incident and were halfway out of the village. The tractor driver put his machine into gear and trundled on muttering about town folk. The car driver straightened up and looked up at the pub sign. This showed a very courageous and splendid George on a dashing white horse with his long lance neatly skewering a hideous red dragon.

'Gloria,' muttered the driver. Standing up tall the driver was all of five feet six and he wore a smart if somewhat rumpled three piece suit which fitted well on his compact frame. Shiny black shoes, clean white shirt and plain red tie completed the ensemble and the driver scanned up and down the street before stepping across and into the door of the public bar.

'What'll it be sir?' asked George.

'This is Gloria's local isn't it?'

'Who's Gloria?' asked George.

'A friend,' said the driver, 'a very old and loving friend. Gloria Manson with a cremated petrol tanker dad and a mother who's gone holy. That Gloria. Ring any bells landlord? And believe me she really is a friend.'

'Seems you know a bit about this Gloria then? How come you think she's here?'

'The George and Dragon,' said the driver. 'She used to tell me all about this place and how the village revolved around the George and Dragon and the Fotheringham Manor Estate. Well this is the George and Dragon. Is Fotheringham further on then? Where can I find ….?'

and the driver hesitated for a moment, 'Oh yes, Gary and Freddie, that's who?'

'Who's looking mate? You looking for Samantha MacRae, or maybe Samantha Lord? You looking for Heritage Adventures, although you sound like a Londoner rather than a real foreigner?'

The neat little driver looked at George across the bar. 'You've lost me there squire,' he said. 'I don't know any Samantha and I do think I'm in the right pub. Just to allay any concerns you might have I'm not Gloria's old boss, I'm not from the Bill, and I'm not a collector for Her Majesty's Income Tax Department. How does that grab you? I'm just an old friend of Gloria's popping in because she told me to look her up if I was ever down this way. I've been visiting friends in Barnstaple and thought I'd come and find her lovely village. There were times in London landlord when Gloria was quite lonely, despite the job she had. Times when we would sit together and she would tell me stories of what her life was like before she came up to the city. She missed her home and her friends but she was determined to make a go of things for herself. She's got guts that girl.'

'Sounds like our Gloria George,' said Freddie coming up to the bar for refills.

'What sounds like our Gloria?' said the lady herself as Gloria swept into the bar from the backroom. 'Sorry I'm a little late George but mum wasn't herself this afternoon and I've been tendering TLC, holy water and listening to confessions. Toby Dobbs, by all that's holy. God you're a sight for sore eyes. Mate how are you?'

Gloria had sudden noticed the dapper little man standing by the bar opposite George. She charged around the open end of the bar and embraced him in a boisterous hug.

'You found me, you found me,' she exclaimed. 'But how are you my love? Christ you look good, but then you always looked smart. My, just let me look at you. No, another hug is in order. You are a little darling.'

I suppose I must have just stood there by the bar beside Freddie with my mouth open. Gloria's reactions had startled George and Freddie too because when Gloria finished wrapping her arms all over Toby whoever she turned and looked at the three of us. She laughed. In fact she put her hands on her hips and positively roared.

'You should see the three of you. You're standing there open-mouthed and star-eyed like you've seen the Holy Ghost or something. Christ you all look funny. Aren't they a right sight Toby? Have you ever seen such a startled lot of fellas?'

'Only when Sheena danced Gloria. She used to open some eyes too you know.'

Gloria turned from looking at the three of us and she smiled at Toby and cupped his chin in her hand. 'Sweet memories Toby, and you're so right my friend. Sheena turned a few heads.'

'Gloria you staying over that side of the bar love or you here to serve?' asked George, shutting his mouth and thinking about business. 'This cove says he knows you.'

Gloria giggled and slowly walked around the bar while still trying to hold Toby's hand.

'George this is Toby Dobbs who really is an old friend. He was my friend up in London and I told him where to find me if he ever left the city. Now he has and I'm glad.'

She turned back to look at Toby. 'Toby, the landlord as you so rightly call him is George Doone, my boss, or so he thinks,' and she giggled again. 'And this here is Freddie Dunster and Gary Templeton. Boys, this is my old friend from the big city. Meet Toby Dobbs.'

Well we all shook hands 'cos it was polite to do so. I had been looking this Toby up and down and he was a snappy dresser. Nothing flash like but neat and tidy and in keeping with his shape and age. Freddie seemed to alternate between intrigue with this old geezer as a friend of Gloria's and some sort of jealousy as his little mind wondered how good an old friend this Toby was: up in the big city so to speak and all that. The pub door opened and in came Lester Rainer and Danny Masters. Freddie left the three of us by the bar and went over to the table where Lester and Danny had sat down with Don. I stayed at the bar looking at this Toby fella and ogling Gloria who was bustling up and down behind the bar getting things the way she liked them.

'You got rooms here Gloria? Seemed to remember you told me your pub had rooms?'

'Sure Toby. We're not full are we George?'

'No Gloria, we've still got a couple of rooms. Just the one night is it mate? Just the Saturday night?'

'Yes please landlord. It's too far to drive back to London tonight and a quiet evening here will do me fine. If Gloria gets a moment we can talk over old times but otherwise I will just relax and look at the people. Gloria used to describe this place and it will be good to actually see it in person. If Gloria ever told you I'm a people person. I work as a negotiator in several different ways and so watching and listening to people is my bread and butter. Make a nice evening just watching the world go round landlord. I'll buy my share, don't you worry. In fact Gloria, once I've dropped my bag off I'll have a pint. I'll just go and move the motor into the parking lot and be right back.'

Toby Dobbs walked smoothly and very quietly I noticed over to the door and went to move his car. As I turned back to look at Gloria I noticed the wistful expression on her face. 'Old friend?' I said.

'Yes Gary, he is both a friend and he is old but he is a good old friend. Toby helped me more than you could imagine. He was usually there when I needed someone.'

'And you were there for him?'

'Gary, I told you he was, no is a good friend. We shared some worrying and some wonderful times together. Yes Freddie love, what can I get you?'

Freddie leant over the bar and cupped Gloria's chin in his hands. 'A French kiss, four pints and thirty minutes in the back room.'

Gloria startled Freddie by leaning forward, kissing him full on the mouth but I'm not sure about the tongue bit and then leaning back again quickly to put a pint glass under the tap and pull the first of the four pints. 'Freddie you wouldn't last thirty minutes love with me in the back room so how about you settle for five minutes darling? Will that satisfy your friends back there? Will that show them how we're going steady? Just you and me love?'

Freddie carried the tray of four pints back to his mates and they all looked back at Gloria.

'You're in there mate. You said you had a good thing going with Gloria but we never believed you. Did we Don?'

'No Lester, right on. Thought you were pulling our chain Freddie but that Gloria's a bit of a goer eh? You got the legs for it Freddie? Can you go the distance mate?'

'Of course,' bragged Freddie.

'Well how come your bird is draped all over that old fart who's just walked back in again?' asked Danny. 'If she was my girl I wouldn't let her do that. Just look, he must be old enough to be her dad. Still, that can't be true as old Walter got incinerated.'

'Christ you're a foul-mouthed grease monkey at times Danny Masters,' said Freddie. 'Incinerated! Poor bugger swerved to avoid some clowns racing in souped-up old bangers and ended up redesigning the overpass. Had no chance I heard. Trying to save others he was. Just for that I'll team up with Don here to beat you at darts. Come on Don, lets beat this pair of wankers. Gloria knows who she's really going out with Danny and she's only saying hi to an old friend from London. Always the friendly bar-maid is my Gloria. Helps make the punters feel comfortable and wanting another pint. Talking of pints it's your shout Lester. Go and get them in while Don and I set up the darts.'

Toby had walked back in again with a small overnight bag in his hand.

'I'll look after your friend Gloria,' said George. 'You keep the locals happy in here. I wouldn't want you showing Mr. Dobbs here how comfortable our rooms are.'

'Get off with you George. Go and be officious and I'll pull pints. I'll sit and talk quietly with Toby when he's settled.'

'Danny, is it four more pints love. How's my Freddie tonight? He's special you know. Lester you going carry those two? Which hand do you paint with Lester? You use a brush and not your hand eh? Christ you're quick with it tonight. Actually, sometime tonight Lester you and I need to have a little chat. No, it's not to make Freddie jealous you stupid git. Freddie and I are fine. We know each other real good. Yes Lester, real good as in real good mate. No, it's about your sister Dora. I want to talk with her about a party.'

Freddie called across the room. 'Leave off the chitty chat with my bird Lester and get those pints over here mate. It's your throw and Danny has already disgraced your team.'

Gloria turned back to me. 'I need to convince simple soul Lester that I'm with Freddie and so Dora will be with you. I'm not sure Lester would accept Freddie going out with his younger sister. Can you live with that Gary?'

'Makes sense to me Gloria. Actually, maybe I should pop out and see whether Dora is in. I could carry on with my story about good clean fun and see what else she might have in mind. I won't bring her back here though. I think her brother might try and cramp her style. Maybe a quiet little drive in the country or walk down beside the pool. That's an idea and I can tell her all about your swimming with young Tony. That'll lead into life-saving, resuscitation and mouth-to-mouth with no problem. How's that for good clean fun Gloria?'

'What's that Gary? What did you say love? Toby, there you are. All settled in? George found you a comfortable room? So it's a pint right? This one's on me Toby and let's drink to old times. You off then Gary?'

I left and Gloria and Toby toasted each other and shared old memories. I had new memories to create and I walked out to my car and planned my memory-making moves with young Dora. Freddie and Don had won the first game and although it was Lester's turn to pay it was Freddie who came over to the bar.

'Move over old-timer,' said Freddie. 'Toby wasn't it? Well, it's time for you to sit back and watch people or whatever while I get some loving here from my Gloria. Lester's on his way over with some money Gloria but I'm on the way over for my thirty minutes and the other half of my French kiss.'

'Jesus Freddie, you're like a dog in heat darling. Four pints Lester? You want change for that note? Keep it, well ta love. Freddie keep your paws that side of the bar. Lester calm him down a bit. This is a public bar. Toby here will get the wrong ideas about country life. Man's from the city Lester, from London. Toby here and I go back a few years, don't we Toby. Toby this 'ere is Lester Rainer, one of Freddie's mates. Lester this is Toby Dobbs. Negotiator he is Lester. Know what that is painting maestro?'

Lester stood there with his head turning from Gloria to Toby and back again like he was watching a lengthy tennis rally. He was still switching his head from side to side when Gloria's last question went straight past his head like a well-placed backhand.

'Lester, you in there mate? Knock knock, anyone home?'

Freddie laughed. 'Geez Gloria, you're some talker you are. Knock knock. You just knocked him out darling. It's all right Lester, you can come down to earth now mate. Just pay the lady and carry those two glasses back to the darts and your ultimate loss. Your head was flopping to and fro like your bloody paintbrush man. No wonder you can't throw straight with all that side to side action. You'd be good playing on a boat though. Should go on a cruise Lester. Do you a world of good. Start painting at the front and just as you reach the arse end you could start back over again. Job with no end and play darts between shifts. You'd be rolling in money.' Freddie doubled over with laughter.

'Freddie, you okay down there? What's so bloody funny?'

'Rolling in money,' said Freddie and he doubled over with laughter again.

'Lester take him away before he does himself an injury,' said Gloria.

'Rolling, don't you get it?' asked Freddie. 'On a boat, in a rough sea, rolling,' and he nearly fell over this time.

'Should I talk to him quietly?' asked Toby with a wry grin on his face.

'No Toby, he's just over-whelmed with my presence. I'll roll all over him in a minute though if he doesn't smarten up.'

'Rolling,' laughed Freddie and this time he did fall on the floor. Gloria watched Lester struggle to lift Freddie up and walk him slowly back to the darts corner.

'How's life in the big city Toby?' Gloria asked as she wiped the bar clean.

'Not the same without you Gloria,' answered Toby quietly. 'I miss your other girls too,' he added. 'You were always such a lively and friendly lot. It's not the same without you and Gina.'

'A couple of the girls were down here last year Toby. Gina was down and so was Sheena. They're both in Bristol now. I don't know where Lola is, or Belle for that matter. You seen either of them Toby?'

'Lola was still working at the Oasis Gloria,' said Toby, 'but I haven't seen or heard about Belle. I'll ask when I'm back there next week. I'll tell Lola that I've seen you.'

'Well don't go telling the world now Toby,' said Gloria with a frown of concern on her face. Toby gently placed his small manicured hand on Gloria's. He looked Gloria in the face and very sincerely said, 'Of course not my love. I think we know each other better than that. We had some good times together you and I.'

Gloria leant over the bar and let her hand slide gently down the side of Toby's cheek. She rolled her finger softly over Toby's lips and tapped lightly. 'Yes Toby,' she said, 'we did.'

'You did what?' demanded Freddie.

'My other life Freddie, my other life,' said Gloria turning to face Freddie. 'I see you've managed to stop rolling. You need another round already? Is this to celebrate a win or just drown your sorrows?'

'Darling I always win,' bragged Freddie, 'and I've come over here to receive my prize.'

'Packet of scratchings then is it Freddie?'

'No Gloria, scratching isn't a turn on but kissing and cuddling is love. Shove over Toby and let me glory in my winning with Gloria here.'

'Since when Freddie Dunster did I become the floor prize? Here, kiss George instead. I've got customers to see to. Yes Mr. Standstead, what will it be for you and your good lady? A white wine and a glass of stout. Coming right up sir.'

The Saturday night wound down and the village went to sleep. Daniel Lord stirred and thought of Katya, her thesis and her caddie advice. Samantha Lord stirred and dreamt Terence Field had taken off his police uniform. Gloria went home to her mum's house to find her praying and Wendell's bedroom door locked but with the light on. Knocking yielded a muttered 'piss off'. Freddie and his mates separated and all ended up snoring beer fumes in their respective solitary bedrooms. Dora and I enjoyed some good clean fun in an array of Kama Sutras positions although neither of us had ever heard of such a classic. Just goes to show that education isn't everything and one can get much too intellectual about these things. The only one not asleep was Toby Dobbs. He lay in his comfortable room in the George and looked up and through the low white-painted ceiling. It was not one of Lester's painting masterpieces and so the surface was smooth and featureless but Toby could see far into the night sky as he recalled memories of days past with Gloria. He had been her father-figure, her mentor, her shoulder to cry on, her mouth-piece with people in power, her lover and best of all her friend. I'll see her tomorrow Toby thought and arrange to come back down next weekend. We'll get some time together my love. We were so good for each other. Eventually the memories morphed into peaceful moments and sleep came to Toby too in the quiet village.

The rain on Saturday had cleared the air and freshened up everyone's spirits. Daniel Lord played his best round of golf this season and hoped that his good form would last into July and the Club's Open Championship. Back in Oxford Katya Howard went back over her forestry thesis for the umpteenth time to make sure she had her story straight. Samantha Lord had cancelled her planned rock climbing for Sunday and wondered how best to spend the time and as usual took the bull by the horns and phoned Terence Field for a quiet drink later that evening in the George.

'Mum let's go for walk this morning?' suggested Gloria. 'Come and see where I swim with Tony Lord. You've not seen where I get my lessons from that young soccer star. He's a laugh mum with his London expressions and positive thoughts about life. He's lived through his dad being shot and his mum knifed to death and still he's full of go-go-go.'

'Gloria I've got to go to church.'

'That's later mum. It's bright and cheerful right now. Drink up your tea and put your shoes on. A walk up by the river will be pretty right now.'

'What about Wendell? He hasn't had his breakfast yet. Where is that boy?'

'Mum he was up late last night and he is probably still sleeping. He's quite capable of getting himself some breakfast. Come on mum so we can have a chat. Look, here are your shoes. You look just fine.'

Gloria eventually managed to wheedle her mother out into the bright already warm sunshine and the mother and daughter walked slowly up though the village and over to the river.

'Friend of mine was in the George last night mum - friend from London.'

'One of those wicked women you used to be with Gloria? That must have been a sinful place you worked. You told me the hours you started and any god-fearing person would be in bed at those times. I should never have let you be friends with that Val Gordon and her family. Working for a monster Mr. Gordon was. Driver for the devil and good riddance when they all went up to London. But you tagged along and sinned daughter.'

'Mum, hold up there a minute. The friend wasn't Val Gordon or any of the Gordon family, and neither was it any of my girl friends from work. It was a man.'

'There you go again Gloria. A man from London and probably a foreigner. You were always talking about foreigners. Was he down to kidnap you back to London again? City of sin that place. Home of the devil.'

Gloria laughed gently and tucked her arm through her mother's. 'Mum, mum give over do. He's middle-aged, very much a cockney gent but well-dressed, very well-mannered and works as a negotiator. He helps people with problems. He listens to one side and then the other and tries to bring the two parties together. He tries to have each person see the other person's point of view. You'd like him mum. He may not go to church every day but in his own way he helps people, just like church people do.'

Toby Dobbs woke and rolling onto his back he could see the ceiling in the bright light of the morning. Right on cue George knocked on his bedroom door followed by a cheerful 'Good morning, how about a cup of tea? Have a good sleep Mr. Dobbs?'

'Right on landlord. Slept like a top. Must be the fresh air down here. Breakfast's at nine is it on a Sunday?'

'Aye, we run a little later and slower on a Sunday down here. It's a grand morning though and that rain of yesterday has perked everything up no end. We were getting a little dry down here so a drop of rain is welcome. Still, this morning looks bright like a new pin with the sunshine. I'll leave you to your tea then and go and find breakfast.'

Toby slowly stirred his tea and mused over his thoughts of last night. Gloria my dear, what a different place this is from the West End.

After his leisurely and tasty breakfast Toby Dobbs decided to take an investigative walk around the village. One way led past Tom Daley's door and when Tom opened it just as Toby walked by the scent of grass rolled over the street and caught Toby's nose. He smiled at Tom propping up the doorpost and offered a bright 'Good morning.'

'Aye mister, right on' and Toby kept right on before reaching the bend and the new gate standing guard over an exceptionally ramshackle overgrown garden that fronted a low old cottage. The two windows overshadowing the mass of vegetation suggested frowning eyes with their thatched dormers as eyebrows. Place with character thought Toby not realising the recent history of Florence Whelks's cottage. As the houses stopped at this point so did Toby and he turned in the sunshine to retrace his steps. Walking back into the village a clatter of hooves sounded behind him which was soon drowned out by a young and very excited voice.

'Look Mummy, I can make Dainty high-step. Just like a prancing pony. Turn now Dainty. Stop and turn. Now let me swing my mallet. Stop Dainty stop. Hold!'

As the volume of the voice increased Toby turned to see a young lad on a small horse attempting to make the horse turn in small circles. Alongside a fit looking young woman was smiling as she watched her son try and work with his horse.

'Gently James, work as a team love. Dainty will listen. Be patient but firm. Guide with your knees and thighs, not just pull on the reins. Talk to her James. Let her hear your voice. Oh, good morning. You were standing there so still and quiet I almost didn't see you. Lovely morning.'

Toby smiled as he looked at the pair. 'Nice to see your youngster learning. Fine looking horses. And yes, it is a lovely morning. Talk gently young 'un. The 'orse will listen.'

James MacRae looked at Toby Dobbs standing by the side of the road and looking quite different in a three-piece suit, a clean fresh white shirt, bright red tie and now dusty but polished black shoes. Putting on his thinking serious face James asserted 'I'm nearly five and this is my horse Dainty. She's learning to be a polo pony. Mr. Rogers from California says I can play polo with his children. And Peter's tree fort is awesome, isn't it Mummy?'

The young woman laughed and a beautiful smile spread across her face and she turned to Toby and said 'I apologise for the flood of words. My son is apt to be a motor mouth. We hope we haven't disturbed your peaceful morning stroll. Come on James, we'll turn back into the woods and we'll gallop home.'

'Whoopee,' cried James and Dainty spun round as if she was as eager as her rider to speed up the pace.

Walking past the pub Toby saw a few more people about and the local village shop was open. He walked inside accompanied by the jangle of the bell at the door.

'Morning love. What can I get for you?' asked Mrs. Larkin.

'Do you have the Sunday Telegraph please?' asked Toby as his eyes scanned around the shop.

'No sir, all the papers are just up the street where the Post Office is. Dora Telford will have the Sunday papers. It's only a few doors along. From your voice you're a Londoner. Can always tell a voice I can. Just along the street sir, can't miss it. Lovely morning for a visit. Come far?'

Toby politely thanked Mrs. Larkin and returned to the sunlit street accompanied by the jangling bell. He found Dora Telford's, which he couldn't miss and bought a Sunday Telegraph. The headlines read doom and gloom which seemed very inappropriate thought Toby as he looked at his peaceful warm and bright surroundings. The Sports section told him that West Ham were lucky to win at home and that Arsenal thrashed Newcastle. Not being a fan of Spurs like Tony Lord just up the road he didn't really worry about the moaning and groaning at White Hart Lane. Folding the paper under his arm Toby continued his stroll and as it was a little village ten minutes saw him reaching the bend where the riverbank is close and there was someone he knew.

'Toby, what a lovely surprise this bright morning. Mum, this here is Toby Dobbs from London. I told you I met him last night in the pub. Well here he is in the flesh. Remember I told you he is a negotiator, helping people? You remember? Toby, I'd like you to meet my mum. Mum meet Toby Dobbs.'

'Good morning to you Mrs. Manson. And yes I am pleased to meet you this lovely morning. Gloria used to tell me all about you and life here in the village. I can see now why Gloria was often sad and homesick when she came from such a lovely place. How are you this glorious morning?'

Tilley Manson was quite taken aback. She almost gasped and Gloria looked at her mother. 'Mum, you alright? You've gone as pale as a ghost.' Gloria put her arm around her mum because she looked like she was going to faint. Suddenly, as if a wave of emotional memories flooded through her veins Tilley straightened up, smiled and offered her hand. 'You're Toby the Fixer. You used to promote music. You used to bring bands to Bristol. You were part of my growing up.' As she shook hands Tilley was looking intently at the face. Toby held the hand and stood there calmly smiling and gently nodding.

'That's a few years ago now my dear. We've both journeyed a little since those days.'

Gloria stood there on the riverbank looking first at Toby and then at her mother.

'Mum you know Toby?'

'No Gloria, not really but I do know of him, or rather what he did. He used to be the light of my life. No, that's not quite true as it was really the music that was the light but this man, the Fixer made it happen. He brought the music from all over down here. Big names, wild music, screaming fans. You've never seen the likes Gloria. There was never anything like those times. All gone now. All changed. Everyone's gone to the devil,' and Tilley seemed to shrink back inside herself.

'Mrs. Manson, the music is still there. People still play. People still sing. The kids still come although that's not my scene anymore. I work with more troubled people now but the job is much the same. I bring people together to take away the problem and let them live again. You said the music was your life. Obviously you enjoyed it and the happiness it brought you. I still do the same thing although it may not be music, or bands, or even singers that do the helping. There are other ways to help people. We should talk you and I. Maybe I should come and see you. Gloria, do you think I could come and see your mother?'

Gloria's head was swirling around and around. What had started as a simple walk in the sunshine to try and liven up her mother had turned into an unexpected therapy session. Toby Dobbs, her Toby Dobbs was Toby the Fixer, not that she knew anything about Toby the Fixer but obviously her mum did. What you don't know about people thought Gloria.

'Gloria, what do you say? Think I should come down next weekend? I'd like that and maybe I can sit with your mother and we can recall old times. They were good days back then Gloria. As your mother infers they were easier days, exciting but less stressful; days of fun and happiness. I like this place. It is peaceful. I think I'll come back next weekend. I'm pleased to meet you Mrs. Manson. Your daughter was a good friend to me and I will come back and repay her. Have a fine morning. Bye.'

Toby turned and with more of a spring in his step he retraced his path to the George. Could turn next weekend into a very pleasant and memorable time he thought.

'Landlord, George isn't it? Can I book a room for next Friday and Saturday night please? I've just met a very charming but needy lady who

I think I can help. I want to return here next weekend and see whether my old moniker still works.'

George stood behind the bar and puzzled over the words not realising that Toby the Fixer wanted to return next weekend rather than Toby Dobbs.

'The two nights you say? Sure, I'll book you in. You off back to London now?'

'Yes George. Needs must and I've work to do this week but I'll be happy to be back here on Friday evening. I'll just get my things and settle up for last night.'

The pub was crowded that Sunday evening. Somewhat surprisingly my dad had suggested we go down for a drink. This made me suspicious straight away and I was waiting for him to tap me for some favour, away from my mum I thought. Looking around I saw Freddie lording it over his three mates and caught fragments of the conversation. Despite the nicey nicey with that old bloke from London yesterday Freddie was going on about him and Gloria. The three other lads were giving him the gears but Freddie reckoned he was on to a good thing. Sitting quietly in one of the window bay bench seats were Daniel Lord along with his sister and that quiet copper. Wonder what he was sniffing about for I wondered? I looked quickly over at dad but he didn't seem too concerned. Gloria was cheerfully chatting with George and she looked happy. Dad emptied his glass and before he had a chance to ask me whatever it was he was going to I walked over to the bar for a refill.

'You look bright and cheerful this evening Gloria,' I said. 'Win the lottery or something?'

'Chances are Gary,' she replied. 'No, I had a surprising and enlightening walk with my mum this morning Gary if you must know.

Seems she's a long lost acquaintance of that mate of mine who was in here last night. You know, Toby Dobbs?'

'How's your mum know that old berk?'

'Me to know and you to guess Gary but he brightened up my mum no end he did. Brought back part of her past and she came alive for a moment. Almost like old times it was. Smiling as bright as this morning's sunshine.'

'Two pints love.'

'Gary mate, how did you make out with Dora last night?' asked Freddie as he came over to the bar. 'Those mates of mine are giving me a hard time after Gloria here was swanning all over that old city bloke last night. We need to show them Gloria and I are an item. You convince young Dora she's love's sweet dream. Old Lester will have a fit and paint himself all over if he knows what his sister is up to. He'll probably try and tar and feather you when she tells him and she's bound to tease and tell him. Flirty piece she is to be sure.'

'Freddie we're all set for Wednesday evening. That work for you Gloria? Wednesday's your night off isn't it? Freddie and I arranged to take you and Dora out for an evening of good clean fun, although Dora wanted to change the words. Think we can recall some of the old routines?'

I watched Gloria look at me and then look inside her head. What I didn't know was Gloria thinking back over some of her old routines. Some of the routines with the four of us kids, the routines with Walter, and then the routines up in London with Lola, Belle and the other girls. Recall some of the old routines Gary Templeton?

'Sure Gary. Wednesday night you say. Should be a blast.'

'Can I join in the fun?' asked my dad as he walked over to throw an arm around my shoulders. 'You seemed to be an age getting those drinks in son so I thought I'd come and join your party. Hi Gloria darling. You're looking your sexy self as usual I see. I wouldn't mind having a blast with you love. Think you can fit me in after looking after these two youngsters? They won't have the stamina but I think I could show you a blast or two. How about it then love? You should try a mature experienced male now and again Gloria and stop tiring out these children here.'

'That's two pints wasn't it Gary? One for you and one for the old gaffer here?'

Gloria pulled the pints and placed them softly on the counter while looking my dad straight in the eye. Christ she's hard I thought, but you know where you stand. Takes no bullshit and flannel does my Gloria. Back off dad I muttered under my breath.

'What's that son? What did you say?'

'Here's your drink dad. Let's take them back to the table. Or I could give you a game of darts. Haven't seen you play for a while and so maybe I'd give you a run for your money.'

'In your dreams son, in your dreams. I can run rings around you drink for drink, dart for dart, and woman for woman. I'll probably beat you playing left-handed.'

'Try again dad,' I said. 'You are left-handed.'

Gloria walked around the room collecting up empty glasses.

'Evening Gloria. No darts match tonight?'

'No Daniel, that's usually on Saturday nights but there wasn't one last night. Just our local team practising you know. Evening Miss Samantha and Mr. or perhaps Detective Inspector Field isn't it?'

'Hi Gloria,' said Samantha. 'I see Danny Masters didn't try and hide when I came in this evening.'

'No', laughed Gloria, 'and even Gary has got used to having some long-lost relatives from Australia. Still, we're always curious when you come in though 'cos we never know who you might have in tow. Funny old job you've got.'

144

'How's the swimming and life-saving coming on with Tony then?' asked Daniel. 'Actually I'm rather glad you're there as my sister-in-law would really worry if he went swimming alone.'

'I think we're both enjoying ourselves Daniel,' Gloria answered. 'Tony was telling me about your Education Centre. Apart from telling me it is smashing and awesome – yes I think those are the words he uses most often. Well, apart from that he tells me there is some controversy going on about some preacher or other. Actually some of the talk is around the village. People in here are chatting about it. Some bloke thinks we all come from Adam and Eve or something. Wham, bam and suddenly there are instant human beings searching to find God. I thought we all came from apes and monkeys but this holy man tells everyone that's not God's word. Even my mum has been listening but she's dead set that he's a phoney.'

'Well some of what you say is true Gloria but it's interesting to hear variations on the rumours. What do you say Samantha, should we put rival schools in our two empty cottages and then have a final all-out debate in the Ed. Centre. Evolution versus Revolution reads the banner,' chuckled Daniel.

'So do we put the god-fearing instant human crowd in the bare and empty cottage and the less holy crowd in the Ferris cottage which still looks a little more lived in. Sort of let the Darwin school enjoy the comforts of home while the God-given school endure the piety of bare walls and scrubbed floors,' said Samantha as she joined her brother in jest.

Terence Field sat quietly in the corner and just listened and watched with his eyes. Ever attentive Terence didn't say a word. He detected the situation and the reactions. Gloria just hoped that Tony would continue his lessons as she was "coming along smashing" according to her instructor and she took her collection of glasses back behind the bar.

Wednesday was a hot day at work and I felt knackered when I came home. Still, after a bite to eat and a wash and brush up I felt excited about the evening to come. We hadn't been out in a foursome for a while and past memories surfaced as I started to really look forward to the possibilities. It had been a day off for Gloria and she had washed her hair, put on a pretty summer dress and looked a treat as she opened the door.

'Freddie there you are,' she said. 'You look bright and cheerful for a warm summer's evening. Give us a hug then.'

Of course Freddie had forgotten he was supposed to be partnering Gloria and stood there like a stuffed rooster until I gently moved him forward with a not so subtle press from my hand in his back. After Gloria had finished wrapping her arms around Freddie and winking at me over Freddie's shoulder she stepped back and said, 'Hello there Gary. Is Dora in the car or are we picking her up?'

She turned and called back down the hall 'We're off then mum.'

'Bye Mrs. Manson', called Freddie.

Wendell appeared behind Gloria and looked at the three of us. 'When you back?' he asked.

'None of your business,' Gloria retorted.

'Just keep your hands on your keyboard,' added Freddie, 'rather than your joystick,' and he smirked. Wendell just gave Freddie a defiant glare and turned back into the house.

'Off then,' said Freddie and he grabbed Gloria round her waist and hustled her back to my car at the kerb. Freddie jumped into the back seat and half hauled Gloria after him.

'Let's go Gary mate. We'll pick up Dora and have some fun. I'm feeling good tonight. How about you Gloria? You feeling good tonight, or you feeling naughty? What was it Dora said Gary? She didn't want good clean fun. Cheeky bitch. We'll teach her won't we Gloria? We'll teach her what the three of us can get up to. Just like old times Gary this is. Put the motor into gear Gary and let's find the good and something fun Dora.'

We drove over to Dora's and she walked down her garden path followed by a shout from her dad about being home by eleven mind. The voice also reminded her she had work tomorrow and Betty Ferris didn't take kindly to late helpers. Dora giggled as she slid into the front seat when I opened the door for her. I went round to the driver's side and looked around inside the car as I got in.

'Come here gorgeous and give us a kiss then,' said Dora and she wrapped her arms around my neck. A waft of scent and young clean body with just a hint of baking enveloped me and Dora enthusiastically clamped her mouth on mine. Within seconds her tongue was pushing between my teeth and she giggled and kissed at the same time.

'Neat,' she said and she turned and looked at both Gloria and Freddie. 'Heard you three used to turn the world upside down with Sandra Porlock. All of us kids heard all the stories. I just hope some of them are true,' she said. 'They are true aren't they Gary?'

Turning back to look at me Dora wriggled in her seat and put her hand on my thigh.

'Be good if we move from my front door Gary or my dad will be out checking us over. Wouldn't want him to see me having some good clean fun now would I? And tonight Gary especially for you I'm clean all over. Every little bit of me and you can check it out if you don't believe me.' Her fingers pressed affirmatively into my thigh.

I put the car into first and eased away down the street. We got Dora home by eleven. She was starry-eyed and we had convinced her that the stories she had heard were true. Gloria had brought a bottle of vodka and some orange juice. After a hot hard day at work and no head for

147

liquor Freddie was soon somewhat wiped out but not before an hour of active involvement which had Dora giggling her head off. Of course Freddie wanted to know whether Dora was clean all over but he never stayed conscious long enough to find out. Gloria and I took our time and Dora learnt a few things she'd thought about but never actually tried. I discovered as I had done in the past that I got a real turn on from watching Gloria as much as being with her. Gloria was in her element. Thinking back I suppose she hadn't really had an opportunity to enjoy herself like this since she came home from London. What I didn't realise was that the evening rekindled an old idea inside Gloria's pretty head. Teaching Dora new tricks and entertaining the three of us before Freddie passed out helped Gloria think a little bit more about her future. I suppose we all went home that night with new ideas.

Two out-of-town people came to the village for the weekend the following Friday evening. Daniel Lord slowly drove the Estate Landrover through the main street bringing Katya from the Oxford train.

'All I need now Daniel are results. Now I've got to sit and bite my nails.'

'But you're not like that Katya. Hi Gloria,' Daniel shouted and waved as he passed Gloria on her way to work at the George.

'Who's the good-looking girl Daniel, or should I say woman?'

'You met her earlier this year Katya, down by the pool. That's Gloria Manson and she works in the George. She's got your fan who thinks you are a "smashing bird" teaching her life-saving.'

Katya chuckled. 'I assume you mean Tony Daniel. My Spurs fan who like smashing birds. He's still swimming is he?'

'He's dedicated Katya. He swims most evenings and then on Sunday mornings he has Gloria there learning life-saving. What was it she said last Sunday in the pub? I was there with Samantha and Terence.'

'Playing gooseberry?'

'No Katya. I get on well with Terence now. He is a friend rather than a policeman.'

'Daniel he is supposed to be Samantha's friend I think. You should ask your sister. If you dare,' she added and she laughed. 'Samantha doesn't take kindly to impertinent questions from her little brother does she?'

'You're combative this evening Katya Howard,' Daniel said. 'We'll have to see about special red engines.'

'Red engines Daniel?' asked Katya unsuspectingly.

'Yes little lady. They are the ones with tender behinds!'

'Daniel Lord!!' and the pair of them laughed as Daniel steered the Landrover through the gates and up his dad's beloved stately gravelled drive. Fotheringham Manor appeared like a scenic charm before them.

'It is a splendid house Daniel, it really is.'

Daniel stopped and turned off the engine. The pair of them just sat and looked at the house and the surrounding lawns and mature trees. Bright green tassels on the larch trees fluttered in the dying evening breeze. 'In some ways it is a forester's little paradise,' muttered Katya. 'In such a small area you really do have a wonderful variety of woodlands. Fotheringham Manor Daniel, diverse environments to enjoy. You should add that as a one-liner as part of your brochure on the Education Centre. How is that coming on Daniel? I thought that was a brilliant idea for my green revenues.'

Katya turned and looked at Daniel. 'You've gone quiet again Daniel Lord. Should I be concerned?'

Daniel gently folded his arms around Katya and pulled her closer. Looking into her eyes he softly pressed his lips against hers and they kissed. 'I love you Katya Howard,' he said with warmth and affection. 'I hope you get the results you worked so hard for and I hope I get my results too.'

'Your results Daniel? Now what have you done?'

'Hoped you would marry me,' Daniel said very simply.

'Daniel?' said Katya as a question and then again 'Daniel Daniel!!' as an exclamation and she returned the kiss with passion.

When they gently pulled apart Daniel asked 'Is that a yes?'

'Why don't we both wait and get our results at the same time?' teased Katya.

Daniel turned the ignition key and smiling within himself he drove on to the stables with his prospective bride by his side.

Toby Dobbs was driving by himself but he too was smiling as he slowly coasted down in to the village and came to a stop in the George parking lot. Collecting his overnight bag from the boot he was still smiling as he walked into the bar and greeted George.

'Evening landlord, George. Good to see you again. Am I in the same room or do you have other guests tonight?'

'Mr Dobbs, it's good to see you too sir. Comfortable trip? Nice dry summer evening and so the roads should be okay.'

'Traffic George, lots of traffic. That motorway is a blessing for sure but then everyone has a motor now. But, as you say it's a nice evening and I wasn't in any hurry. Slow and safe that's me George. Suppose it goes with the job now. Wasn't always that way. Used to be fast and furious but those days are long gone. Now I listen a lot and think before we speak. Slow, calm, and try and bring peace and harmony to the two parties.'

'Negotiator our Gloria said,' said George. 'Funny business. Suppose I've never heard that term before although I can understand the need when Gloria explained it to me. Let me take your bag up to your room and get you settled. Then you'll have a bite to eat? I've a simple menu mind but we can fix something. If you want anything fancy there's a good restaurant about five miles back towards town.'

'No George something simple is fine. I heard there's a local pie-maker in the village who everyone says is champion. They say she started off with fruit pies but now she has expanded and makes savoury ones too. I'd like to try one of those if you have them?'

'Gloria will fix that for you when she comes in Mr. Dobbs. Well, bless me, how about that for timing. Gloria love your friend from London has come back and was asking after one of Betty Ferris's savoury pies for his supper. Can you look after that while I run his bag upstairs? Then I'd better open up or I'll have them pounding on the door on a warm evening like this.'

As George predicted several thirsty souls crowded into the pub that night. Toby sat quietly in a corner and watched the village world swirl around him. Our darts team led by George Crawford practised for tomorrow night's match. Daniel Lord came in with his American bird. I heard her asking about the darts match and she rambled on with several scientific questions like why they only had three darts and what was the penalty for having your toe past the line? Then I heard them go into a complicated story about one of the rules in golf if you hit the ball from the wrong place and as I had never played or understood golf I tuned out. Lester Rainer spent a lot of time aggressively grilling Freddie over what happened with his sister on the Wednesday night. Danny and Don chimed in whenever they could and they would all turn and look at me on occasions as if I was to blame. Gloria worked hard pulling pints and collecting glasses but she still managed to find time for a quick flirt and a chat with everyone in the room. Wearing one of her usual blouses she also managed to bend over and let the males enjoy the view which led to tongues hanging out and the need for another drink to wet the throat. George stood behind the bar and beamed. A good Friday night and this was only the start of the weekend. I was about to walk over and sit down next to Gloria's city gent when the door opened and in came two ladies who would knock anyone's eyes out. It's funny really because there was a gradual hush in the bar as people noticed and it was almost silent when Gloria's voice cried 'Lola, Gina, geez girls you're a sight for sore eyes. Come in come in.' Everyone else was saying the same thing of course but under their breath whereas Gloria's voice broke the silence and there was an instant buzz around the room.

I must admit I looked, after a quick glance at Gloria of course. Lola Martinez, whose name I found out later from Gloria was tall, slender and moved like a bull-fighter. Her friend, Gina Totti was a lovely piece of totty if you know the expression. As her name suggested the voluptuous Gina hailed from Italy via the back streets of Wapping Gloria told me. Her parents had come from somewhere in Sicily. They owned and operated a café in the back streets of Wapping where the walls were painted with scenes of dry rolling countrysides, little whitewashed villages and well-armed bandits. That was the closest Gina had ever got to Italy and the voice said Londoner as plain as day but then it wasn't the voice that caught the eye now was it? As it was a warm evening the lovely Gina wore a blue summer frock which swayed provocatively as she walked in from the door to greet Gloria. However, every male eye in the room was focussed on the cleavage. Harry Biggins, our retired postman was throwing darts at the time and he nearly speared one of his team mates as his eyes refocused from the double ten to the split two. The two girls reached the bar and each gave Gloria a big hug and their excited chatter rose over the hubbub in the room. Everyone was looking and everyone was talking. George became very business-like and wanted to know whether the ladies wanted a drink and could he offer them something special? Gloria turned to George and fixed him with a piercing eye.

'How about we find them rooms first George so they can freshen up a little. I know I'd want to straighten my clothes and clean my face before I wash the dust out of my throat. Come on girls I'll show you a room. You are staying the night I take it? Come on then. Let's get you both settled and then George here can fawn all over you.'

When Gloria wheeled the two ladies out of the room the noise level rose along with the male excitement level. The darts team stopped practising for a moment which was just as well as the concentration seemed to have changed target. Then I noticed Toby Dobbs. He hadn't moved when Lola and Gina came in but his face now wore an even wider smile than before. I wondered what he was up to.

'Mr. Dobbs isn't it? Mind if I sit here? Wondered whether you know those two ladies seeing as you're also a friend of Gloria's from the city like? Just listening to the voices they both sound foreign.'

'Surprised you heard the voices Gary. Most of the people here were looking rather than listening I noticed. But yes, in answer to your question I do know both Miss Lola and Miss Gina. They both worked in the same Club as Gloria up in the West End. Yes Gary I know both the ladies.' Toby leant back in his chair and supped on his pint.

'So how come they're down here then?' I asked.

'I imagine they've come to see Gloria,' he said watching me. 'She seemed pleased to see them don't you think?'

It turned out that Gloria was so pleased to see her two friends that I didn't get a look in that night. Mark you I had tried to get a quiet moment with Gloria when she went into the back room for something for George but all she said was later Gary, later. Later came and Gloria was all giggles, laughter and chitty chat with the two girls and I went home hot and bothered. Little was I to know that Saturday night wouldn't be any improvement. In fact the Saturday night was an absolute bummer.

CONFLICTS

SATURDAY, THE DAY AND NIGHT of conflicts yet the morning started bright and sunny and full of promise. Rupert Oldshaw led his band of eco warriors over the edge of the Mendip Hills and they started to drop into the Fotheringham Manor Estate.

'Hold up here Ted and let's look at that map of yours again. We've got a good viewpoint from up here before we descend into that mass of trees down below. Can you identify on that old drovers' map where we are on the Ordnance Survey one?'

Philippa and Margaret flopped themselves down and looked over the view. 'Behold the hand of God,' proclaimed Philippa.

'All I can see is the hand of man,' complained Arnold. 'Looks like God and the original wilderness has been cast aside to worship the almighty coin of the realm. I'll bet those coniferous plantations down there aren't on Ted's precious tatty map. Man has tamed the wild and probably banished any animals in the process. Now we have sterile rows of pines where we used to have habitats for a diverse population of wildlife.'

'They look like Douglas fir to me,' corrected Rory, 'and be patient Arnold. Nature will re-assert itself my friend. The rows down there will open up into mature trees and birds will sing again. Nature is dynamic my wilderness friend. Go with the flow. Hear some melody and think poetic.'

'Where's that Education Centre from here?' demanded Doris. 'I want to find out more about that controversial preacher. Think he's teaching today? I think we should tell the public about this hot-bed of creation. Instant humans versus Arnold's evolution indeed,' she snorted.

'Have a care Doris Lyon,' said Philippa aggressively. 'I too believe in the word of God I'll have you know but I just think it is a private thing. It's a bond between me and my God, not some subject for public debate or airing in your litigations courtroom.'

'Peace my children,' said Rory laughing. 'Enjoy the view, the air, the welcoming sun in the sky and feel the vibes of life within you. Lighten up Doris. Lighten up.'

'So we could scramble down the edge of this escarpment about here Ted?' suggested Rupert, 'and then head south. That Education Centre is probably too recent to even show on your OS map. Still it has to be along one of those rides through the plantations and there are two other small buildings marked on the map.'

'Makes sense to me,' added Mavis as she put her arm around Rupert and peered at the map. 'Maybe we should break up into smaller groups and explore? I'll come with you Rupert,' she said quickly.

'No Mavis, we'll stick together. The hike is the objective and whether we find the Education Centre or not doesn't matter. We should probably steer clear of the big house though.'

'Why Rupert? Why should we? If Ted's old road goes through the middle of the house we should just march through and proclaim our rights. Show them the map. I'll lead if you don't have the balls.'

'Christ Doris, you should have been born last century and been a suffragette or perhaps born just thirty years earlier than you were and been a ban-the-bomb marcher. You're all in your face girl. Where's the peace and goodwill? Let Margaret here walk with you and explain Christianity. Can you spare Margaret Philippa? Can your bosom buddy walk with Doris here and explain peace and goodwill to all mankind before she starts some civil liberties action? Are you sure you're not Irish Doris?'

'Rory Flanagan you're a perfect example of why the English walked all over your country. You've no backbone. It's all soft words, poetry and romantic songs with you. Stand up and be counted like a man.'

'Yes Rupert, perhaps we should all stand up and venture down there into the sterile green desert. I for one want to see whether there is any wildlife at all in that man-made tree farm below us. Let's go.'

Arnold's request motivated all of them to stand, dust off the clinging grass and dirt and start the careful descent off the escarpment. They reached the northern edge of the estate and walked down one of the clean forest rides bypassing the cliff, Michael's memorial plaque on the old oak tree and the cave of no treasure. Not far below them in the Big House that Doris wanted to invade Anthony Lord sat quietly in the first-floor library gazing out at the view down his stately drive and then turning his attention back to the large book on the table in front of him. He slowly leafed through a couple of pages and reread the words that explained a map in the book.

'Daniel this is not the map I thought I had seen when my grandfather showed me that map about the cave but this does explain some more about that cave and an old drovers' road just along from there. Apparently, well according to this book there was some agreement between the then owner of the estate and the cattlemen about rights of passage. Long before the estate was ever here and that is eons ago there used to be a droving road through here. Back in the seventeen hundreds or so when the estate got established much as it is today there was an agreement. There was some local land right's court that decided to permit the droving through the estate. I suppose our title deeds have some reference to this although they all rest down in the solicitor's office in the village. I'm not even sure when I last read them. What do you say Daniel?'

'It's all a bit passé now dad. There isn't any more cattle droving now. They all go in lorries from the farm to the slaughterhouse. It's quicker on the road. Cheaper too.'

Anthony laughed. 'You're quite like your mother son. Thinking of the bottom line with little or no romance.'

'Anthony I would be interested though,' said Katya quickly. 'There's another historical facet to add to the Education Centre, another green revenue dollar. That will please you and Sylvia.'

'What will please Sylvia?' asked Sylvia Lord as she swept into the library, 'and why are you people all stuck up here in this dusty library when you could be outside enjoying the bright sunshine this beautiful morning. We should be out riding Anthony.'

'Yes my dear, you're so right. We'll ride and we'll go and find my recent library discovery in the flesh so to speak. We'll protect our heritage before young Katya here leases it all off to the uneducated and probably unwashed youth of today. Come my love and let's exercise the horses and enjoy your beautiful sunshine.'

Katya stood in the centre of the library and watched Anthony sweep his wife up in his arms and wheel her out of the room. She laughed as she turned to Daniel. 'Your father is such a romantic Daniel. He really is a people person. Perhaps I could train you.'

'Train, trains, yes trains Katya. Red engines, blue engines, engines with tender behinds,' cried James as he exploded into the quiet room with his mouth spouting words and arms flailing like disjointed engine connecting rods. Katya collected young James in her arms and spun him round and round like a merry-go-round.

'Faster faster on the turntable,' demanded James.

157

'I'd wind him down Katya if I was you,' suggested Samantha as she too entered the library. 'He's full of umpteen bowls of oatmeal laced with maple syrup. Daniel, where is dad chasing off to dragging our mother? He was waxing eloquently about defending the domain and ensuring mum's chastity from the hordes. When I asked him he just continued rushing down the stairs and all mum did was laugh and cry "My saviour".'

While James demanded to show Katya how steam engines worked Daniel quietly explained to Samantha that 'Dad had found something about old rights of way on the estate. When mum wondered why they were all indoors dad reacted like you just saw him. He romantically decided to ride the horses out into the estate and defend Fotheringham for his bride. End of story' said Daniel.

Toby Dobbs took a reflective bite out of his toast and slowly lifted a small spoonful of sugar into his tea. As he munched he stirred. Warm sunlight streamed in through the lounge windows of the George and Toby could see people strolling down the street. Wiping the crumbs off his lips he sliced his fresh apple and scraped out the core. His neat little teeth bit into the firm fruit and the tartness livened his throat. A quick sniff he told himself and all the senses are go-go-go. Ready to negotiate.

'That all you need Mr. Dobbs?'

'Call me Toby George and yes that's fine. A little of this and a little of that is what makes the world go round they say. A nice cuppa sets me up for the morning and now I'm ready to see the sights.'

'Ain't a lot to see Toby but its pretty in its own way. We like to keep the village neat and tidy 'cos we get a few visitors during the summer. There's nothing special goes on here like in some other places. We don't have no dances or festivals but we do have more people now with that Education Centre. Sir Anthony opened that up on their Estate just earlier this year. Quite popular it is with schools and the like. Different place to learn you know. Not quite the schoolrooms we knew Toby but then times are different now. Several groups come to the Centre and Sir Anthony's son has organised some other attraction. What did he call it now? Outgoing, Outsomething. No, Orienteering that was it. Never knew anything about it until Daniel Lord came and explained it. Have to run from flag to flag in the forest until you get completely lost. Still, good for the kids I suppose and given everyone is overweight these days perhaps it'll be good for them. The Estate is further up the street. Not far I suppose and you can't miss the gates. Sir Anthony put a new road in that bypasses the Big House and you can drive right to the Centre now. Signposted they say but I've never been up there myself.'

Toby tidied up in his room and thought on a plan of action. Perhaps a call on Gloria first of all and maybe a talk with her mother. Might be able to help and Gloria would appreciate that. Told me a lot about her mother she did, and her dad and all of that worried her.

'George, I'd like to call on Gloria. Actually I'd like to call on her mother really as she and I go way back but I don't know where they live. I'll do that first and then maybe go and see this new Education Centre.'

'Mrs. Manson, how are you this morning? It's good to see you again. George at the pub was good enough to tell me where you live. I hope you don't think it too presumptuous of me but I thought we might share some old times together. Gloria told me a lot about you when we used to meet up in London. She always thought you were a live young woman who got overwhelmed by her dad. Now he's has passed on she hoped you would come alive again.'

At Tilley's front porch Toby smiled as he recalled Gloria's words. 'She said you were like a butterfly and you needed to spread your wings again and look beautiful to the world. Oh Gloria, you weren't supposed to be listening to that. I didn't see you quietly walk up behind your mum. How are you this lovely morning?'

Tilley stood in the doorway still holding the door and looked at Toby. Toby the Fixer she remembered and now look at him. Neat, tidy, quiet and soft-spoken and not at all the man she had seen as a teenager. Then he was flashy, loud, with hands and mouth going non-stop as he harangued musicians, dancers and roadies all at the same time. Tried to keep the groupies out of the dressing rooms too she recalled.

'Invite him in Mum. Let's have a chat. I've never heard about Toby the Fixer as you call him. I just know him as a really good friend from London. Actually, talking of friends I should go and see Gina and Lola. I don't suppose they were up Toby when you had breakfast?'

Toby laughed. 'No Gloria, I wouldn't expect they were up either knowing those two. You should go round there and roust them out. Quite like old times with those two appearing the way they did last night. Opened a few eyes in your pub they did I can tell you.'

'Good for business though Toby. Earned George a few extra drinks they did putting in that appearance. I should tell him to give them a discount rate for the room, or perhaps a freebie. How about that Toby? Think George will let them stay for free if they do a little number each evening? Think our locals could stand an hour or so of our Lola and Gina?'

'Spread the word Gloria and you'd pack the place.'

'Mum I'm off out of here and check whether the girls are up for a giggle. You listen to my Toby here and he'll recall nights for you that you have forgotten but wish you'd remembered. Good is Toby for that. He'll bring you back together with your old past mum. When you lived a little. Kicked off your shoes. Bye.'

Gloria left her mum still holding the door and looking at Toby. She knew Toby would win her mum over. He was good at what he did.

Suppose once a fixer always a fixer thought Gloria as she smiled to herself and considered the opportunities with Lola and Gina.

'Do you know where you are?' asked Anthony as he walked his horse up to the band of eight hikers.

'Of course we do,' answered Doris rather belligerently. 'We're walking on a public right of way. Says so on our map.'

'Of course it does,' said Sylvia as she lightly vaulted off Sir Galahad and strode up to the group. 'And as the owner of this Estate I should know that shouldn't I? But my OS map and my Estate ownership records don't show any right of way so maybe you can show me your real, authenticated and dated map which does? Nice day isn't it,' she added as she held out her hand. Ted, who was clutching the photocopy of the old map looked at Rupert as if to say now what do I do. Rupert looked at Ted and said, 'You're the historian Ted. You've got the map. Show the lady.'

Anthony dismounted and he too walked slowly over to his wife leading Temptress who snorted and tugged at her reins. Several of the hikers backed away alarmed as Temptress kicked her heels. Anthony just turned and spoke quietly to her and she calmed down.

'Photocopy of some undated document. No mention of author or authority', stated Sylvia, 'but then no harm done. Where were you going?' she asked, 'on this supposed drovers' road.'

'Where the road goes of course,' retorted Doris sharply. 'Obvious isn't it? We were going along the right of way, just as the map shows.'

Sylvia smiled and handed the map back to Ted. She slowly surveyed the group and asked whether they knew where they were.

'On the right of way lady, like I said.'

'Do you know where you are?' Sylvia deliberately asked Ted looking straight at him and ignoring Doris and her belligerent tone.

'Yes Madam,' stuttered Ted and he unfolded the Ordnance Survey map and ran his finger across the sheet to finally point to where they were.

'Close,' said Sylvia, 'but actually one forest ride too far west. And you were going to where?' she politely asked.

'To that Education Centre,' snapped Doris who was now quite pissed off at being ignored.

'Well carry straight on then,' said Sylvia. 'Just keep going south on this ride and you'll see it. There's a large sign which says Education Centre so you're not likely to miss it. Have a nice day.'

Sylvia easily vaulted back up onto her horse and wheeled it sharply around. 'This is Fotheringham Manor Estate by the way,' she added. 'We welcome visitors but we do run a commercial operation and so we like to keep guests away from any dangerous forestry machinery. We also run an intensive breeding programme for sheep and the study of genetics so we would ask you not to leave gates open or damage fences. They are valuable animals. Apart from that our Forester welcomes people to view and understand what we have here.'

As Sylvia spoke Anthony too had mounted Temptress and he rode alongside Sylvia as they both trotted away.

'You're more of a people person than you think my dear. That was very positively yet diplomatically stated. I'm impressed Sylvia love.' Sylvia laughed as she looked at her husband. 'I thought I should act like the lady of the manor Anthony dear and not stir up too many unnecessary conflicts. Perhaps having Samantha home has mellowed me.'

This time it was Anthony who laughed. 'Samantha and mellow approaches shouldn't be mentioned in the same sentence Sylvia love. That's like an oxymoron. Still, apart from that sharp-tongued barrack lawyer they seemed a docile enough group. Actually, I was looking at a

162

book in the library this morning and found something about old rights of way you know?'

'Yes Anthony dear and that is why we are out here riding the bounds my love. Making sure that the old rights of way are honoured and we don't have people wandering willy nilly all over the place. It's bad enough when Daniel gets those Orienteering fanatics here for one of their meets or whatever. Daniel is never quite sure whether we lose the odd one or two. Some of the running options pass through some pretty rough ground Anthony. Daniel is much better at counting trees than people.'

'He needs more friends Sylvia. He needs more friends to help with some of those meets.'

More friends thought Gloria. Yes, that's a good idea. With Lola and Gina down we should talk about having more friends come to visit. Bet those two haven't got up yet. They won't be used to conventional hours. Gosh, just look at the time. I'm almost late for work. Gloria walked into the George through the back yard and on into the kitchen.

'George, I'm here a little early 'cos I wanted to chat to my mates for a moment. We aren't open yet are we? Another fifteen minutes or so?'

'They're in the snug Gloria, but we do open in fifteen minutes love so you be ready.'

'Sure George.'

Gloria walked on through to find Gina and Lola. 'Did my Toby contact you two?' Gloria asked. The two girls giggled and looked up at Gloria standing in the doorway.

'What do you think then Gloria love?' asked Lola. 'Toby thought you could do with a little action down here. When he phoned we weren't doing anything special this weekend and so we said we'd see him down here. You looked pleased to see us but you were rather busy last night.'

'Be the same again tonight too. Actually it'll be worse 'cos there's a darts match here tonight and the place will be packed. I'll be run off my feet. Should I ask George to put you two on casual staff and help? Trade the cost of your room for a couple of hours of keeping the bar hopping. Anyway it's a treat to see the pair of you. Look, why don't we plan a get-together tonight after the bar's closed? We could invite Toby, just like old times. That a deal or what?'

'I'm opening up Gloria girl so get your cute little bum in here love. There's work to be done.'

'Look around you two and see whether there's anything down here that catches your fancy. We'll all meet up later. Gotta go. Tata.'

Because it was busy in summertime over the weekends George had two other girls in to help Gloria and they worked shifts. It was close to three o'clock when the eight hikers ambled into the bar and plonked themselves down rather tired around a couple of tables.

'So what will it be folks?' asked Tina.

The order came back around the table as diverse as the backgrounds of the eight people. Tina had to check as a couple of the requests were rather unusual for a small village pub but she managed to get it right. Gloria was on a break and having a quiet drink and a bite to eat with Gina and Lola. As usual Gloria was enjoying one of Betty's pies and explaining to her two friends how the success of these pies was helping put the village on the map.

'So you'd recommend I try one of those pies then darling?' asked Rory as he overheard the conversation.

'You know what they say love. Try it you'll like it. My two friends here think they're smashing and they ain't local. Well girls, think this gent should give it a try. Hey Tina, give silver tongue here a look at the choices. Make his mouth water. He'll thank you for ever.' Gina and Lola both laughed at Gloria's sales pitch.

Rupert stood up and came over to Gloria's table. 'Think they'll suit me too?' he asked and he beamed at Gina. In a flash Mavis Taylor was by Rupert's side and pulling possessively on his arm she asked Rupert whether he would share a pie with her.

'Are you sure it's pie you want my love?' inquired Gina as she put her head on one side and leant earnestly across the table. When she saw that several of the buttons on Gina's blouse were undone Mavis pulled harder on Rupert's arm. 'You haven't finished your pint Rupert and we should be thinking of going pretty soon.'

'Shame,' said Gina, 'just when I was thinking we could share a little pie together.'

Back at their own table Doris loudly said, 'There's a law about solicitation.' On hearing this Gloria watched with a smile on her face because she knew what would likely happen next. Skinny bespectacled Doris was about to be pressured and by an expert. She heard Lola push back her chair and majestically stand up. Moving with measured but firm steps Lola walked over to the hiker's table and slowly lowered her face until it was inches from that of Doris. 'And you my lovely would be the first to be attracted to such a law just as I am attracted to you. I could make you feel over-whelmed with such a law. Make you feel absolute subjugation.' And then quickly standing up tall Lola cracked her little whip which Doris had not seen and everyone jumped out of their skins.

'Jesus, now isn't that a magic number?' said Rory.

'Wash your mouth out Rory and don't take the Lord's name in vain,' cried Philippa. 'We should leave Margaret. Rupert, we're leaving. This place has too many devils in it. There is an air of heathens and ungodly spells about this domain.' Margaret stood up quickly and joined her friend as they both left the bar.

'Seems we have broken up the party,' giggled Gina. 'Lola you come on too strong my love. Perhaps a softer more sensual approach is called for, along with the fruit pie of course. You're right Gloria love, those pies are a real treat. Come again my lovelies when you have more time to sample the local wares.' Gloria laughed at the performance of her two friends as the remaining six hikers followed Philippa and Margaret outside.

'I told you two to help George attract customers, not drive them away,' she laughed. 'Don't try that line this evening Lola.'

'Well the little darling was just looking for a strong dominating touch. She's all mouth but I'll bet she gets excited when someone comes back forceful. She'd be putty in my hands Gloria.'

As Gloria predicted that Saturday evening the pub was packed. The George's darts team played really well and the locals got behind their team and cheered them on lustily. For once the players from the Crown were having an off night.

'Bert, those two youngsters on our team aren't pulling their weight tonight for sure.'

'Seaun I tell you every Saturday night man it's just a game. Dennis and Jack here are doing the best they can. It's one of those nights.'

'Sure Bert and I can tell that from my winnings. Still, hold on there darling and can I have another pint my lovely. I may not be winning much but I do have this thirst. Will it be another one for you Bert or do you need the steady hand?'

'I'm fine Seaun. Just let the lady get on with her job. You've a full house tonight love,' Bert said to Gloria as Seaun wasn't letting go of her arm.

'Long as they're all happy,' replied Gloria cheerfully, 'and yours will be a pint then my Irish leprechaun?'

'When you've the moment my love.'

Gloria bustled back to the bar and fixed her orders. She looked around at the jostling mass of humanity. Although some of the fans could see the darts match sitting down there was a fair number standing near the back of the room. Gina and Lola were sitting in a corner with Toby Dobbs and sharing some old stories Gloria noticed. Freddie and his usual mates were following the darts match but their language was more constrained than usual and then Gloria noticed why. She hadn't seen them come in but over on the far side of the room was Samantha MacRae with that copper friend and Daniel Lord with his American bird, Katya or somesuch. So that is why Freddie is speaking proper for a change thought Gloria. A hand stroking across her buttocks and a slight squeeze made her jump and she nearly dropped the tray of drinks. Turning she found herself looking into my eyes.

'Christ you gave me a shock Gary. I bloody nearly dropped all these drinks with you doing that. Would have cost you a fortune mate. Where'd you come anyway? I never saw you come in. Anyway, I'm busy. I ain't got no time for hanky panky right now Gary. Go and sit over there with Gina and Lola. They'll entertain you I'm sure. You can gaze down Gina's cleavage for a while before Lola cracks her whip and keeps you in order. The pair of them can handle you all right Gary Templeton. Now, away from under my feet while I sort out these orders.'

I had come in quietly and gone up the corridor for a quick piss in the gents before coming to look for a drink. Gloria hadn't seen me sidle up behind her and give her a thrill. Looking around I saw that Gloria's friends were sitting chatting to that old bloke who had been in here last weekend.

'Gina isn't it? We met sometime around last Christmas. You were in here with some red-headed Irish girl. Sheena, yes that was it. Gloria sent me over to keep you ladies entertained. She thought you might want to know some things about the village and how's she doing. You were Toby

167

weren't you mate? Gloria said you were some old friend, some old bloke she knew when she was working up in London. We met last Saturday I think. You were down here last weekend weren't you?'

Toby had sat quietly listening to me prattle on. Suppose I get a bit excited when there are pretty birds in view. When I eventually dried up he smiled and offered me his hand.

'You're right son. We've met. I am Toby, and yes I am an old friend of Gloria's.'

As I turned from shaking the little old man's hand I saw Gina looking me up and down. It was like being undressed and I must have blushed. The other girl put out her hand and laid it on my arm.

'Don't you worry pet. Lola here will look after you and protect you from Gina's paws and claws. I'll keep you safe love. Think I can look after him Gina?'

Swivelling my eyes from Lola to Gina I saw a glance pass between them and felt I had been put in my place.

'Yes Gary, Lola here will certainly protect you. When she puts on her bull-fighting costume, picks up her whip and stands astride you you are protected for all time. Mark you, when she's destroyed all the competition she'll turn her dominating personality onto you and you'd better fess up or you'll end up being tickled to death.'

At this point Gina couldn't continue as she rolled about with laughing. Lola tried to look stern and dominating but she in turn was pissing her pants. I noticed Toby sat back there quietly with a bemused expression on his face as if to tell me he had seen all this pantomime before.

'You three all know each other?' I asked and this question caused all three of them to laugh. Gina actually fell off her chair. Being the gentleman that I like to think I am I bent down and tried to help Gina to her feet. Standing up holding her waist I felt her hands travel smoothly up the length of my body and I had to sit down quickly before my embarrassment became obvious. Jesus, what a turn on. Gina devoured me with her eyes and I desperately looked around for Gloria and the chance of a drink.

'White wine ladies, and a pint for you Toby is it? We're dying of thirst over her Gloria. You need to look after your friends you know.'

'So you remember Sheena do you Gary? She sticks in your mind does she? Gloria said your mind wandered a little, or was that your father she was talking about? What was it she was telling us Lola? Your dad's Brian eh? Was it Brian or Gary with the wandering you know what Lola?'

'Stop teasing Gina. Anybody would remember Sheena. She's a great dancer and nobody's likely to forget her. That right Toby?'

Toby sat up a little straighter and appeared to ponder on Lola's question. Before he could answer Gloria appeared with a tray of drinks. 'Here you go then my friends. Back before you knew it aren't I? Two white wines and two pints. Bill to you Gary. Enjoy' and she was gone.

'Thank you Gary,' said Toby as he lifted his glass, 'and yes, Sheena is a memorable dancer and a lady with several other memorable talents too. But then you all had memorable talents girls, every one of you.'

'There are more of you?' I asked. 'Did you all work together? Is that how come you all know each other, from up in London somewhere?'

Gina and Lola thanked me as they lifted their glasses and sipped.

'Gloria's never told you Gary? Your Gloria's never told you about us and her life up in the big city, the big sinful city Gary? I suppose there were five of us who did a lot of things together. That right Toby?'

'Yes Lola, although there were six of you when I first met you all.'

'You're right but then that silly cow Phoebe got homesick and buggered off back to Newcastle or somewhere wild. Shame that 'cos she was a right laugh, when you could understand her that is. Half the time I needed a bloody translator and I thought that I knew English proper like but some of her words were foreign to me. She was happy though as long as I called her pet.'

'Girl could sing though Lola.'

'Funny that 'cos she spoke clearly when she sang. Still, wrapping herself around that pole the way she did would make anyone sing clearly. You ever do a duet with her Gina?'

'No, strictly a one girl action show was our Phoebe. She never did duets for punters. They always went away happy though so she must have been good.'

'So who were the other two?' I asked as I managed to break into this reminiscing.

'Sheena you've met Gary, your Gloria was one and then there was Belle Katz. Yes, young little schoolgirl Belle Katz. You ever go to school with Belle Toby?' asked Lola.

Toby grinned and to help him think what he was going to say he took another sup on his pint. He looked at Lola and then at Gina.

'I had the odd lesson or two,' he laughed. 'She could be a naughty little girl when the mood took her.'

'And needed a good spanking,' added Gina.

The two girls looked at me. 'This all doing your head in Gary? Did you think your Gloria was waiting on tables in Joe Lyons then? Didn't she tell you about the Club?'

'Sure, the Oasis wasn't it?' I said quickly, wanting to show that I knew what Gloria had been doing in London. 'She told me all about it. She just never mentioned all the people she worked with that's all. So I never knew who you were before you and Sheena came down here last Christmas. Then last weekend Toby here makes a surprise appearance. Quite a shock that was Toby mate. You really surprised our Gloria.'

'No Gary, it takes a lot more than that to surprise your Gloria,' and the three of them laughed as they lifted their glasses.

170

After the darts match, after that lot from Fotheringham departed, and after we finally moved Freddie and his mates out of the bar door I watched Gloria round up the last of the glasses and close up shop.

'You too Gary love. I know it's Saturday night but Gina, Lola and I have some serious catching up to do.'

'I'll just sit and listen Gloria,' I said. 'You know me, quiet as a mouse.'

'Gary this is girl to girl talk mate and you don't qualify. You're not built right.'

'Don't know about that Gloria,' said Lola as she advanced towards me. 'A little redesign with my whip and we might be able to turn him into a girl. Fancy that Gary?'

'Tomorrow then Gloria. We'll make up another foursome. I'll talk with Freddie.'

'Is Freddie that noisy wanker with the wally mates? He was yapping about he should be on the darts team. Then he was bragging he was all over you Gloria.'

'In his dreams,' Gloria added as she started to clean up the glasses. 'No Freddie's a front Gina. He might sound like a useless git, which I suppose he is really but Gary and I use him to avoid upsetting my mum. She has some real hangup about Gary so we arrange this foursome where Freddie's with me and Gary here is with some other young thing.'

'And what does Gary do with this other young thing? What do you do Gary? Would I like this other young thing?' Lola asked.

'Lola leave off love or you'll bugger up our Gary's mind. The foursome is complicated enough without you adding spice to the mix.'

'Maybe we all should stay and make it a sixsome or something Gloria,' suggested Gina.

'No love, we've commitments remember,' said Lola. 'Maybe another time though. Think you could handle us Gary, after that other young thing that is?'

'Out Gary, out. It's time you left. We might give you nightmares. We'll see about tomorrow. It's my night off from here and I've got my date at the river in the afternoon remember. Can't miss my sessions with that gorgeous Tony now can I? He and I have got that mouth to mouth technique just fine. He's teaching me to crawl too, as well as breast stroke.'

I watched Gina and Lola sitting on their chairs listening intently to Gloria. By the time she had finished the pair of them were rolling around again with laughter.

'Jesus Gloria, you had us going for a moment there. Then Toby whispered that this Tony is ten and he is teaching you swimming. We weren't sure whether this was a windup or you had someone on the side you hadn't told us about. Tony eh? Competition all over around here Gary. Conflicts and challenges everywhere you look. You had better go and lie down Gary and have a good night's kip. Sounds like you'll need your strength for tomorrow. Nighty night.'

It was too much. The three of them were determined to drive me out and all this time the quiet and dapper Toby sat in the corner with twinkling eyes and listening ears. Wonder what they are up to I thought but I would find out. Tomorrow I'll find out. Gloria will tell me.

'Night,' I said and walked out of the bar hearing Gloria slam the bolt behind me. I could hear them giggling as I walked back to my car. Tomorrow, I'll find out tomorrow.

I found out tomorrow, well that next Sunday all right. So did most of the village too before that Sunday was finished. As she had said Gloria had a lot of catching up to do with Gina and Lola. Seems that included

Toby and they all spent most of the night in Toby's room. All sorts of rumours ran around the village about three women and one man for the night in the George. It took me a while to eventually find out the whole story, well as much of it as Gloria was prepared to tell me.

The four of them had taken some booze back to Toby's room and before long they were re-enacting old times and old tricks. Apparently Toby had always been a good customer at the Oasis. In his former life managing music groups he had established contacts with all sorts of people especially the Club life lot. As the girls had hinted at before they all knew each other very well. Toby might have been past it in my books but he still could play his part explained Gloria. I asked what part and Gloria just looked at me. Sometime in the early hours Gina and Lola must have tiptoed out back to their room 'cos it was Toby and Gloria George woke up around eight with a cup of tea. Funny it was Gloria told me. Bloody hilarious really but George didn't think so.

'Imagine Gary. I'll run through the scenario. Knock, knock, "your morning tea Toby. Thought you'd like a cuppa before breakfast," and in comes George bearing a tray complete with cup, saucer, teapot, milk jug and a couple of those sugar packets. He's about to put it down on the dresser when Toby woke up and looked at George.'

'So, nothing special,' I said.

'But there was Gary, something very special, 'cos I woke up too and in my usual sleepy self I threw back the covers and George got an eyeful.'

'Of tea?'

'No you stupid prat. Fortunately he'd put the tea-tray down by this time or Toby and I would have got an eyeful of tea. No, George got an eyeful of Toby.'

'Didn't he see you? Didn't you just say you threw back the covers? You wouldn't have had pyjamas or a nightie or anything.'

At this point Gloria curled up in a ball and giggled. 'Jesus Christ Gary, you are a laugh a minute you are at times. Of course I didn't have pyjamas or any bloody nightie. I was starkers and when I sat up George did a double take. He'd just had a shock with Toby though and that was the real knockout.'

'Why?'

'No you had to be there to understand. Earlier in the evening the four of us had been remembering old times. We'd had some laughs and I suppose Toby started one of his routines with dressing up like a woman. Lola had a wig, a gorgeous wig it is too. Toby was wearing this plus a beautiful expensive padded bra and a pair of really frivolous panties although George never saw those. He'd left by the time Toby started to explain.'

'So what did you do?'

'We shared the cup of tea you silly bugger. After a night's drinking we were both quite thirsty. I thought of calling down and asking George for more but Toby reckoned that might not be too wise, even though it was a Sunday and a day of forgiveness and Christian charity.'

'But then George went ballistic I heard. Everyone says he threw you out onto the street. Called you all sorts of names and told you you were fired. I saw Harry Biggins earlier today when he and his missus were going to church and they told me all about the commotion. Almost told me word for word Harry did but then his wife told him to wash his mouth out and not use such language on a Sunday, even though she would pray for the retrieval of his soul.'

'Look Gary I can't stop. It's a lovely sunny afternoon and I'm supposed to be in the river with young Tony. He's expecting me. I'll see you later. Did you talk with Freddie or with Dora? You were dead keen last night to see me today you know. I'll make it up to you tonight if you like but now I've got to dash.'

I suppose I stood there beside my car with my mouth open. I'd woken up late and messed about the house in the morning. When I went over to Freddie's house he was still in bed but I left a message with his mum about a foursome for this evening. Mrs. Dunster told me she'd tell him when the lazy bum finally got up and so I left. It was when I knocked on Dora Rainer's door that I heard about the goings on at the George. Seems Mrs. Rainer heard about it at church and the word was going round like wildfire. When I knocked on the door around one it was Dora who opened it. She grabbed hold of my shirt and pushed me round the corner of the house. Before I had a chance to speak and tell her about this evening she had her mouth clamped on mine and wriggling against me like there was no tomorrow. When I finally came up for air all she could do was giggle and then explode with the story of Gloria and the great chucking out.

'Gary you should have heard,' she said. 'Apparently the entire main street could have heard George and the language. Called her all sorts he did.'

'What happened to Toby?'

'Who's Toby?' asked Dora but before I could reply she was back at my mouth again with arms and tongue and hips all going at the same time. I managed to slow the pace down and ask her about this evening as a foursome.

'Like before?' she asked. 'That was cool. We had some fun didn't we Gary? That Gloria is some girl but then you told me she learnt a lot of that up in London. Fab though. Can't wait. About six then? You'll come here?' and she giggled and wriggled at the double entendre.

Wonder what really happened I thought. George won't tell me that's for sure and it sounds like he wouldn't know the half of it anyway. Wonder what happened to Toby and the two girls though? Quite a wild bunch that lot. Wonder whether they'll come down here again,

175

although I can't see them staying at the George? Old George will have banned them for life. Still, if the rumour spreads around the reputation will bring in some new punters that's for sure. Gloria love you do cause some fireworks wherever you go. Seems like we should have some more this evening, especially as that young Dora seems to be on fire already. Wonder where Gloria's other two friends are, that Sheena the dancer and Belle something. Sounds young though. What was it Gloria was saying to Toby about going to school? Can never tell with that lot 'cos they talk in riddles half of the time.

That Sunday morning there were several other incidents in the village and some of these gave rise to new conflicts. The Reverend Gabriel Godschild, who had been born and christened Alan Briggs, led the service in the local church where Harry Biggins and his praying missus were in the congregation and the Reverend preached a powerful sermon. Quite by chance, no, come to think about it probably by design Anthony and Sylvia Lord were also in the congregation that morning although I never knew all this. However, the sermon was of concern to Sir Anthony and his good lady as well as several other people in the congregation. The preacher was firm, thunderous even in his proclamation of the special place on earth for us humans. Apparently we were all God's children, like he was obviously from his name, and we were special. We were the chosen ones. Our place on this earth was God's explicit purpose and we were to rule accordingly. All other living things on earth were ours to convert, and that included any other humans who had not yet got this clear and fundamental message. He extorted the congregation to go forth, talk the talk to use the modern vernacular and bring everyone in to God's fold. I could almost hear him adding under his breath and bring gifts too but apparently that wasn't in the script. According to the Rev. Gabriel God had sent a flash of light and the world was populated with man as God's instant messenger on this earth. Now I'm not holy, certainly not a church goer. Back several generations the Templetons probably went to church but in those days everyone did. The Lord said so. That's the Lord of the Estate and not the Lord God I mean. I'm not even sure that I'm Christian and when I remember I'll ask mum whether I was ever baptised. But, instant people, no Rev. Gabriel whoever I don't buy that. It turned out that half the congregation didn't either and when they all trooped out that morning there was a lot of muttering going on.

'Anthony, that's the man who is teaching occasionally up at our Education Centre. You think we should do something? I mean that's a whole pile of codswallop. I'm not religious Anthony but that's heresy or some such word. We're offering an education opportunity for young people in a semi-natural setting where evolution is obviously all around you and that man is spouting such drivel. Instant world indeed! Perhaps we should have your aunt Stephanie give him a tour of her sheep.'

'Sylvia that's controversial. That's more like Samantha and in your face.'

Sylvia laughed and tucked her arm into her husband's. She grinned. 'Right,' she said.

'Still, your comment does bear thinking about. We want to make that place a success. We don't need to make it notorious in the process. Do we have any controls on who we let book the Centre? I suppose we naively presumed that it would be put to good use although the Reverend Gabriel blowing his horn would think his use was good use.'

About the same time as the church service George Doone cleaned house, but only after his guests had paid for their rooms and their drinks. Gina, Lola and Toby had a good laugh as they all got into Toby's car.

'You were still wearing that wig Toby?' asked Lola.

'And the bra?' added Gina and both girls rolled over in the back seat.

Toby smiled to himself as he settled comfortably in the driver's seat and turned the ignition. 'Place needed a little livening up don't you think?' he suggested over his shoulder.

'Toby you'll have the Sunday tabloids down here if this gets out. You'll end up with the place on the map. Gloria was telling us about the new activities up at Fotheringham and then about those pies which were helping bring in the tourists but this will give it five star billing. You're a naughty man Toby Dobbs,' and Lola wagged her finger so that Toby could see in the rear-view mirror and they all laughed again.

'Okay girls. Change of pace. How about we go and see whether Gloria has any scars from George and see about any more excitement? No, not excitement because you two talk with Gloria and I'll talk with Gloria's mum, and that's more slow and serious. Tilley Manson needs some salvation and as today is Sunday it will be appropriate to offer some.'

Later that evening, with Freddie having passed out again and Dora tucked under my chin I looked at Gloria and asked her what she was going to do next.

'I thought you were just about finished Gary,' Gloria said. 'Dora doesn't realise you're not a teenager any more and don't having the stamina like you used to. Do you love?' and Gloria ran her fingers down Dora's back.

'No Gloria, not right now but tomorrow, next week, now that George has thrown you out?'

'I'll have more time for swimming lessons with Tony now won't I Gary?' Gloria teased.

'Give over girl. Be serious for just a moment.'

'Could come and work with us Gloria,' offered Dora. 'Betty's always got more work than she can handle. Now she's expanded the business has taken off. Sells all over she does and we're run off our feet.'

Gloria curled up closer to Dora's smooth back and wrapped her arm across Dora's shoulders and ran her fingers over my lips. 'That's sweet love and I thank you for the offer but if I was there alongside you do you think we'd get much work done?' and she cuddled close to Dora.

Dora giggled and I could feel her body pressed up against mine. 'Think we'd get much done Gary?' Gloria asked as she stroked my face with her fingers.

'Getting up early wouldn't suit you Gloria,' I said. You're not a morning person, as was obvious this morning I hear.'

'Actually Gina and I did a little talking later this morning back at our house. Toby came over and spent a couple of hours with mum before he took off back to London. He's a big help and mum seems quite different after he has visited. She seems more alive if you know what I mean. What was it Gina said? He was bringing salvation Gina said, part of the great resurrection. Trying to get mum to be a born-again living person as opposed to a born-again Christian which she is now.'

'What else did the voluptuous Gina say?' I asked.

'Am I voluptuous Gary?' Dora asked as she looked up at me. 'Look at me. Look at me Gary,' and she rolled away from me and let me see her charms.'

'You're gorgeous love,' I said and I pulled her against me and gave her a kiss. 'Delightfully voluptuous Dora you are,' and I heard her little chuckle as she wriggled against me.

'We were talking about livening the place up down here Gary. We were talking about Gina, Lola, Sheena and Belle bringing some action to this place. Toby thought it had potential. He likes George and despite this morning's differences of opinion he thinks any action could help the pub.'

'Toby thinking of some kind of floor show? Bringing singing and dancing to the George?' I asked. 'Now there's a clash of cultures Gloria. Late night or early morning West End entertainment takes over village pub life. I can see the headline.'

'No you dumb bugger. We wouldn't entertain in the pub Gary. Christ you're thick at times.'

'And other times he's not thick,' giggled Dora.

'So where?'

'We got to talk about that. The girls don't know the area but they thought you might be interested in any such idea and you could scout around for some possibilities.'

'You going to put up posters?' I asked sarcastically.

'No, going modern, going to use the Internet. We'll put up a website. Belle knows all about such things. She's been working that way for a while and says it's the best way she knows, away from the big cities that is. Lola is going to talk to Belle and we're going to look at setting this up but we need a venue Gary. We need a place. Somewhere quiet, somewhere accessible but off the beaten track and somewhere comfortable.'

'Then it can't be Betty's bakery,' said Dora. 'That don't have nowhere comfortable. But I'm comfortable right now Gary. What you going to do on this website then?'

'Interested Gary? Toby thought it might appeal to you. He knows we get on okay.'

'And me, and me,' said Dora. 'We all get on okay don't we Gloria? Even Freddie gets it on okay when he's awake or sober.' Freddie stirred and opened a bleary eye.

'Where did I go? Christ I'm thirsty. Do we have any more to drink Gary? Hi Gloria and hello that's my Dora I see. Where you been girl? You look good.'

'Voluptuous?' asked Dora.

'Absolutely,' said Freddie and the four of us came back to life again as a foursome.

Later that night as I lay in bed I thought about Gloria's talk. She might decide to go back to London if she's got no job. But no, now she's got Toby working on her mother she'll want to stay. Still, if there's no place for the girls to liven this place up they may decide to go elsewhere. Shit, there's got to be somewhere around here. I thought about the Education Centre and had a good laugh over that idea. What an education I chuckled. Not quite what Daniel Lord and little Miss Katya had in mind I'm sure. Dedicated to the memory of all those dead Lord folk it wouldn't quite be suitable for Gloria and her friends. Too like a morgue for them. Still turning thoughts over in my mind and wondering how long Tony Lord was going to teach mouth to mouth I fell asleep.

Gloria's past and
Gloria's future

For some unknown reason I wasn't feeling myself on the Monday of that last week in May. Perhaps I had a touch of the flu or perhaps I was just shagged out after the Sunday night. Anyway, I skived off work for the Monday and Tuesday and it was Wednesday when Freddie told me what Gloria had done.

'Doesn't let the grass grow under her feet that one,' said Freddie. 'Where you been anyway? Bob Edwards was asking on Monday morning and I told him you were fine on the Sunday night.'

'So what did Bob say?'

'He laughed actually and said he understood.'

'Understood what?'

'That if you were fine on the Sunday night it explained why you were poorly on Monday. Said he could remember being young and what Sunday nights could do to you.'

'What about Gloria? You said she had done something. She went back and bought the pub and fired George I suppose?'

'Christ mate, you have been sick. No, now she's got two jobs.'

'Two jobs?' and I thought back to her last conversation about wanting to liven this place up a bit. Then I thought back to her wanting to find some place to do this so I asked the obvious question, 'Where?'

'At Darlene's Tea Shop of course, where else? Then she's persuaded old Mrs. Digby to let her help as an assistant in the hair-dressers too. Mrs. Digby does men's haircuts as well as ladies you know and Ray Salter had his done on the Monday evening. Well, who was there helping but Gloria.'

'So she's staying?'

'Of course she's staying Gary you berk. Where's she going to go? Where do any of us go? We've got it all here mate. You know, the job, the home, the pub and your mates. What else is there? No Gary, Gloria ain't going anywhere. Why did you think she was?'

'Freddie, think a little mate. Use that brain of yours for once. Last time things got a bit stressful our Gloria did leave if you remember. She went to London and she was there a long time mate. Just this past weekend she's had several of her old mates down from London. People she worked with. People she had a laugh with. Who's to say she won't go back with them?'

Gloria carefully swept the fallen hair away from the chair and into her pan. She looked around the little salon and wondered whether she had done the right thing. She smiled to herself. Shit, it had been a bit of a giggle though. In fact the whole of that Saturday night had been great, just like old times. Fun days they were she thought. Sure there was a job to do and the normal bits of living with shopping, eating, laundry and the rest of life's crap but they were fun times.

'You have a break now Gloria,' said Mrs. Digby. 'I don't have another client until eleven love and so unless someone walks in off the street we've a little time for ourselves. Do you want a coffee dear? All the fixings are out back you know. I'm just going to pop out for a minute 'cos I need to talk with Mrs. Telford in the Post Office. You watch the shop for me Gloria.'

Sitting down in one of the customer's chairs Gloria took her break. They'd sure brought back some good memories that Saturday night with Gina and Lola. Toby was his usual playful self and it was amazing what that man had done with his life. Amazing what Lola can do with anyone's life she said to herself and smiled. Lola Martinez, Spanish, slender and dressed in her matador outfit with a whip and cape rather than a sword was a dominatrix. She loved to play the part of dominating, chastising, beating her partner. Very often Gloria remembered there was no sex involved. The delight came in the chase rather than the kill. If there was any sex involved it was most often when the partner was a woman and there Lola could "kill" in any number of ways. As with all of the girls Gloria had watched and participated. All of them could "entertain" in a variety of couplings. Gina Totti was taller than Lola and she had a wonderful and exciting wardrobe of dresses. You could take Gina out looking elegant to the poshest of restaurants Gloria remembered and then again she could look and act like some slut in the back streets of Naples. You pick my friend and Gina will entertain. What's your fancy for tonight then?

The shop door opened and Brian Templeton walked in.

'Good morning Gloria,' he said. 'You're looking lovely this morning. Working in a hair-dressing salon suits you you know. With your hair and good looks you are a lovely advertisement. Should help bring some more custom in for Mrs. Digby. Breathe new life in the place you do. George's loss I'd say. Now, I was looking for two things really, well maybe three,' and he smiled.

'Yes Mr. Templeton but Mrs. Digby's out at the moment. She'll be back soon. Would you like to make an appointment? I'm assuming you're here for a haircut?'

'No Gloria, I'm here for you,' and Brian Templeton laughed.

'For me? I don't understand.'

'Oh but you do Gloria, you understand very well. I know Mrs. Digby's not here. She's up the street chatting with Dora Telford. And no, I wasn't looking for a haircut. I was looking for you, for some information, and maybe some future commitment.'

'Mr. Templeton I'm........'

'Gloria, we're alone, it's Brian and I could do with some TLC like my poor sick son. After last Sunday night poor little Gary was so exhausted he had to stay at home in bed. Apparently he was with you and that little minx Dora Rainer on Sunday and you were giving our Gary some TLC and I thought I might like it too. The odd dash of TLC is good for a man Gloria and believe me I'm a man.'

'You asked about information,' Gloria said, trying to think how best to handle this situation.

'Now should we have TLC before or after the information?' asked Brian as he advanced further into the shop. 'If the information is really upsetting I will need lots of TLC. If the TLC is before the information I will be in a better frame of mind, and maybe body to bear the bad news,' he smirked.'

'What bad news?' asked Gloria.

'That you're leaving us again,' replied Brian.

'But I'm not Mr. Templeton. Not that it's any of your business but I'm not leaving. I've just changed positions.'

'It was because of your last position, horizontal I hear that you had to leave your last place of employment.'

'Mr. Templeton if you're not here for an appointment can you please leave? I'll tell Mrs. Digby you were in looking for a hair-cut shall I? No, I've no need as here she is now. You can explain yourself.'

Mrs. Digby walked slowly into her salon and looked at Gloria and Brian Templeton. She frowned. 'Gloria, what is going on dear? I heard rumours about you in that public house down the road but I chose to ignore them. I don't care for village tittle tattle. Your mother is a fine woman and much given to worshipping God. I like that. I hired you because I thought you would bring some younger customers into my salon with your wonderful hair and good looks. You are an excellent example of what a good hair-dresser can do for someone but now I see Mr. Templeton in here and I know he does not come here for any hair-cut. You get your hair done somewhere else don't you Mr. Templeton? You don't patronise village services. You're almost an outsider with your sales activities. What are you doing here Mr. Templeton?'

Brian Templeton had not been a silver-tongued salesman all his life without learning a thing or two. He walked over to Mrs. Digby and took one of her hands in the pair of his and looking her straight in the eye with a smile on his face he quietly said, 'Good morning Mrs. Digby. It's a delight to see you so bright and lively this sunny morning. You're absolutely right I'm not here for a haircut although maybe I should come here next time as you suggest but I just popped in to ask Gloria something. She was out with our Gary last Sunday and he was poorly the Monday and Tuesday. My wife Catherine, who does come here for her hairdressing and her pedicure I understand, asked me to check with Gloria and find out whether they ate anything that might have been off. Gary is usually a fit and healthy young man and Catherine was quite concerned.'

Gloria stood there and listened to this well-spun tale. If you're going to lie she thought keep as close to the truth as you can and just bend parts

186

of the story. Smooth move Mr. Brian Templeton. Mrs. Digby looked at Gloria. 'Were you out with Gary Gloria? I thought I had heard you had some friends down from London.'

'They went back in the afternoon Mrs. Digby,' Gloria said. 'Gary, Freddie Dunster, Dora Rainer and I were all out together the Sunday night. We went for a burger up at the café off the Motorway. We all had the same thing so I don't know why Gary got sick. Just as I was telling Mr. Templeton here and then I offered to let him make an appointment for his hair. I told him that he could do with a trim and that you would be only too pleased to service him. I told him it would be good business 'cos his wife comes in, and if he did as well then maybe we could persuade some of the other younger men to come here too.'

Mrs. Digby, bless her Christian heart bought all of this old cobblers and smiled. 'Well,' she said looking at her appointment book, 'shall we say this Friday Mr. Templeton? I can fit you in early on Friday morning my dear. Gloria's right you know, your hair is rather long at the back. That's too young a style for you Mr. Templeton. You need to look more your age, more mature you know. Yes, yes, the more I look the more I see a need to trim those long parts quite severely. You've a good eye Gloria, a good assessment of what needs to be done. So Friday morning then Mr. Templeton - we'll see you Friday?'

Brian Templeton swept out of the salon and managed a glare back at Gloria before he left. Gloria tried hard not to giggle.

'Well done Gloria. You've got the idea how to attract customers love. Now, we'll get ready for Mrs. Ralston. She takes two sugars in her tea dear if you'll get that organised and I need to find that special light brown rinse she likes.'

Daniel Lord stood on the tee box of the sixteenth hole and looked out across the water.

'The water's not there Daniel. I've told you before,' said Katya holding Daniel's bag. Now that she had finished at University and was awaiting her results she had time to come down during the week and be with Daniel. As it was the same foursome who Katya had met on her Sunday visits there was a welcoming familiarity with the three other men. They all joked with Katya about helping them when she realised she had to give up on Daniel. 'A firm five iron and hit it with your usual draw. I would sooner play a four iron fade but you always tell me you'll come over the top so go with the five but hit it firm. That flag's back up the green again today and I've seen you four putt here remember. No, forget that Daniel. Positive thought. Hit the five. You can't go over the back with that.'

Daniel listened to his caddie. He liked listening to his caddie. If it wasn't for the three other players waiting their turn he would stand there and listen longer.

'Hit it Daniel' and Katya gave Daniel his five iron.

Just like he saw it in his mind before the stroke Daniel hit the five iron and successfully landed the ball five feet from the flag. It jumped forwards two feet and then spun quickly to a stop. Katya smiled as she took the trusty five iron and wiped the dirt off the face from the divot. Larry Sykes stepped up onto the tee box and looked back at Katya.

'Think I've got the right club too?'

'Larry you know you shouldn't do that and I'm not going to hear you, otherwise we would know you've just broken one of the rules. I can tell you it is two hundred and ten yards but that's all, legally that is.'

The rest of the foursome smiled at this diplomatic rebuke from Katya. Walking down beside the lake that is not there according to Katya Daniel asked whether Katya heard what had happened out in the forest last Saturday.

'You know dad had found this old book about rights of way in the forest?'

'Yes Daniel, I was there in the library when your father was explaining it and then he swept your mother off her feet so I never did hear the end of the story. We were out playing golf on the Sunday and it never got mentioned again. What did happen out in the forest?'

'It was funny really, well a typical life coincidence I suppose but I'm glad I heard about it.'

'What?' cried Katya in exasperation. 'No, wait up, you've a good birdie putt coming up so let's wait until we're walking down the seventeenth. That's a par five with lots of opportunity to talk. Get your head around the next shot partner. We need birdies Daniel, and not the smashing bird kind either,' and she giggled.

Daniel smiled too when he remembered his nephew Tony's exclamation when he first met Katya. Who's the smashing bird Tony had asked and Katya had laughed.

'Birdies Daniel. Breaks left to right and it's downhill so gently and delicately. Like caressing.'

Daniel wasn't sure the analogy would let him concentrate on the right topic but he did look and think on the shot. He played it in his mind and saw the ball drop in the cup. Fine, so just caress it he muttered under his breath and he watched the ball trickle positively across the smooth green and drop convincingly into the cup. 'Birdie,' he said and he heard Katya say the same word in harmony.

'So, what happened out in the forest that was this earth-shattering coincidence? Don't tell me it is a long story like all the other Lord family explanations Daniel either. This might be a par five but you will have to hit the ball soon so give me the two-pager rather than the whole thesis.'

'Dad and mum found this group of hikers walking through the estate. When mum asked were they lost and where were they going one of the group demanded to exert her rights. Quite a little firecracker she was mum said. Apparently they had some old map showing a drovers' path across our land.'

'What are drovers Daniel?'

'I suppose an American equivalent might be a cattle drive. In the old days in England people use to drive cattle to market and it might be a long way to go. Land was owned by a variety of people and often there were no real long roads to market or to any port so some land court authority issued rights for the movement of livestock. Before this landowners would charge for the right of passage across their land. This court authority took away that charge and made it profitable to move stock long distances. I'm sure America would have had similar fees and land rights. Anyway, this young firecracker was shouting the odds about her God-given right to walk along this supposed road.'

'And did she Daniel?'

'Mum looked at the photocopy of an old map they had but there was no date, no authority named and so it could have been anything. Could be just a bunch of students seeing whether they could put one over the landowner; kind of a prank or a college challenge. You must have seen this kind of thing? Students get up to all sorts of authority challenges. It goes with the territory.'

'Daniel, you've walked past your ball old man. You still playing with us or with your caddie?'

'Sorry Alan, we were talking about an incident at Fotheringham.'

'Well just for a wee moment Daniel close the mouth and hit the ball son.'

For the next thirty seconds Daniel refocused his mind and managed to hit an excellent second shot which found the front edge of the green some two hundred and thirty yards away.

'After that shot I'll not interrupt a second time,' said Alan. 'I'll let you walk right past your ball all the way into the Club House.'

Daniel and Katya both laughed somewhat sheepishly and Katya put the three metal back in the bag and slung it over her shoulder.

'So what did your mother do Daniel?'

'According to dad mum read them the riot act, very politely of course and told them they were welcome etc., but typical mum she pointed out they were not where they thought they were and the position of the road on their map was another kilometre or so away but never mind.'

'Where were they going?'

'They said they were looking for the Education Centre.'

'Why Daniel? Doesn't sound like they were teachers or anything, just hikers with some legal guardian.'

'They'd heard about the Reverend Godschild. Two of the group were quite excited about his preaching. They'd heard he was talking to school groups and wanted to find out more. Wanted to know where and when.'

'And the others?'

'Mum and dad weren't sure who all the others were. There was some bespectacled serious bloke who had the map but mum didn't think he was the leader. There was an older chap with them, about thirty mum thought. They had this little legal firecracker, two young women in rather drab clothing who got excited about the Reverend, and three others I suppose as there were eight in total. Oh yes, one of them must have been some kind of wildlife person because he got agitated when mum said she talked about Stephanie's sheep. She was explaining the need to keep gates closed and not to damage fences as we had some very expensive breeding programme and didn't want any wandering sheep and wildlife mixtures. Somewhere in that explanation this wildlife bloke must have made a comment or something about leaving nature alone and not trying

191

to play God. Mum remembered this because the two plain girls got very annoyed that Arnold or whoever he was should suggest mankind wasn't God's messenger on earth. We were here to do God's bidding according to these ladies.'

'But didn't your mother go to church the next day and hear this Revered Godschild?'

'Yes Katya, while we were out here communing with nature.'

'Daniel, can we leave the communing my friend until after the round. Your distracting Katya from tending the flag for us and it's you to putt my friend. There is something in the rules of golf that furthest from the flag goes first and you my friend are the furthest. So shut up and putt up!'

'Nicely put Larry. I couldn't have said it better myself.'

Daniel waited until Katya was holding the flag and as he was furthest from the hole, and as he was seventy feet away and couldn't see the hole he had Katya stand there with her hand on the stick ready to pull it should he come close. Looks good he thought, Katya that is not the putt. Daniel putted and the other three men appropriately tut-tutted as Daniel was still the furthest from the cup when his ball came to rest fifteen feet short. Katya lifted the flag out of the cup and walked away from the line of sight. Two more putts and Daniel lifted the ball out of the cup. He glanced at Katya and his caddie smiled and positively said 'Par'.

'And the Reverend Godschild speaks in tongues Daniel? The word of the Lord God is about to descend on Fotheringham and the Lord family is about to realise its surname brings great responsibility to the forest, the farm, the inhabitants and all the peasants in the surrounding villages?'

'Katya Howard you heathen, you blasphemous Yankee!'

'Daniel, one thing I'm not is a Yankee. Get your history and/or geography right. I'm from the South and I'm definitely not a Yankee. Plus, for your information my Lord my family is deep south Baptist although father is not too enthused about complete ducking in the river for washing away his sins. He knows where the river comes from and what his mill empties into it.'

'Am I your Lord?' asked Daniel who had listened carefully to Katya's words and heard at least one that caught his attention. 'Am I?'

'Eighteenth hole Daniel. Play as usual?'

In the car on the way home Daniel told Katya about his parents' concerns over the words of the Reverend Gabriel Godschild and the fact that he was preaching to youngsters at the Education Centre. Katya also wanted to know about the hikers and where else they might wander for whatever mapped or unmapped reason and Daniel said they had been advised that the forest was operational especially during the work week. When his mother had talked about safety and liability the firecracker had up and spouted words about owner's obligations to ensure everything was safe and if any of them got hurt they would sue.

'Is there any risk of damage Daniel? Would this group think of vandalising anything given its list of controversial thoughts and ideas? What sort of conflict is likely to happen? We thought this Education Centre was a positive longterm contribution. Peter and Tony certainly thought so. In fact all your family accepted it made sense, complete with the family memorial room. I thought that was a particularly nice touch to bring all those family members' memories together in one place which was a more natural part of the estate. It was like bringing them all home in a place for the future and letting them be a part of that future.'

'Let's hope so,' said Daniel. 'Dad was mentioning the cottages too now that they are both unoccupied.'

'What is the family going to do with those Daniel? We've talked about converting them into residences for people wanting to stay longer at the Education Centre. There really isn't any other place to stay in the village apart from the few rooms in the George.'

'Talking about the George did you hear what happened there Saturday night, or perhaps I should say Sunday morning?' asked Daniel turning in the car seat. 'No, before I mention that you should know that we had an application the other day from a family in Yorkshire who had heard of us through some friend and wanted to know whether we had any vacancies on the work crew.'

'Yorkshire is up north isn't it Daniel?'

'Yes and the context is weird.'

'Why weird? No, I can see a long story coming on. I can see it from the expression on your face. I'm right aren't I Daniel? I know you.'

'Yes you do my love and I'm glad. I know you too and I really like what I know.'

'Daniel are we going to play I know and I know that you know and so on because that could take us all the way home and I'd never hear about this other long story?'

The pair of them laughed and Daniel took a quick glance at Katya beside him and then back down the twisting road.

'Okay, two-page version to use your expression. My brother Michael used to go to Bristol House School.'

'As did you, as did your brother Geoffrey, as did your dad and so on. Yes, another long story Daniel but go on.'

'At Bristol House Michael had a fag called Aubrey Worthing and Michael terrorised poor Aubrey.'

'What's a fag?'

'Someone who fetches and carries for you. Who cleans your shoes, gets your tea and generally acts as a dogsbody.'

'Dogsbody?'

'Forget that Katya. Coming from the south I suppose I could say a fag is like a slave. At an all boys' school senior boys, well the prefects at least have young pupils who are their fags. There's not normally any sexual connotation in all this but for your first year you will likely end up being a prefect's fag. You serve.'

'That's awful Daniel. That's bullying.'

'Not necessarily Katya. Depending who is the prefect it can also be mentoring. The prefect may be able to help the youngster settle in and belong. It all depends on who is who. Anyway, it's been a tradition in England since forever. We all go through it, both as a fag and as a prefect. It's part of our growing up.'

'Barbaric. No wonder you're weird at times.'

'Am I weird at times Katya? Is it good weird or not so good weird? No, don't answer it's just part of growing up to be a typical eccentric Englishman and I've always told you we are an eccentric family.'

'Aubrey Worthing, the poor little fag whom your brother terrorised?'

'Yes, well the Worthing family has large estates in Yorkshire and they run a very successful lock-smithing security company too, Worthing Securities. They are longterm landed gentry and the head of the family sits in the House of Lords.'

'Another barbaric institution,' muttered Katya.

'Michael caused all kinds of upset with that family and they never did business with dad like we did with Cohen and Townsend. Anyway, after Michael died there seemed to be some kind of truce with the Worthings and my dad is ever one to bring people back together. Over time the Worthing family thought we could be tolerated and so we did still keep in touch with common business interests. Mum and dad went up there once to Yorkshire. Massive house mum said and some interesting property. They too manage forests and farmland plus they have shooting moors so it is an extensive and diverse estate. Michael was never mentioned mum said when she came back. It was as if the entire confrontation had been taken care of. Mark you, Vanessa Worthing was there too and mum said she should have taken Samantha. It would have been love or hate on sight as they are both alike and there could have been sparks flying.'

'So now we have this real groovy bond between these two old decadent and eccentric English houses Daniel Lord and can we leave page one, which has been an excessively long page one and turn over. We're nearly home and we haven't yet reached page two.'

'Groovy bond!! You've been listening to your mother or someone else of that era,' joshed Daniel. 'How about positive pact?'

'How about page two?'

'Colin Entwhistle and family live and work for the Worthings. His wife wanted to move south and be closer to her mother who is poorly. Through the Worthings the Entwhistles heard we might have a vacancy. The Worthings wrote. The Entwhistles wrote. My mother replied. The Entwhistles are moving south next month. End of page.'

'That's more like it,' said Katya. 'Just in time for a happy ending because we are home Daniel.'

'Are we home?' asked Daniel as he turned off the engine and wrapped an arm over Katya's shoulders. Katya kissed Daniel and the pair were still kissing when a loud rapping on the side of the car disturbed them and they heard Sylvia say, 'Get a room for God's sake.'

Daniel and Katya unravelled themselves and got out of the car both laughing. Sylvia wrapped her arms around the pair of them and kissed them both. 'You've obviously had a good afternoon Daniel. Did he have a good afternoon Katya?'

'Fine Sylvia, when he concentrates.'

'We work well together mum. We make it work.'

'So how do we make this work Belle?' asked Gina. 'You've done this before?'

'Yes Gina, one of my teachers showed me.'

'And spanked your bottom in the process?'

'No, a proper teacher. When I was at school for real you know. He taught me all sorts of things.'

'That's as maybe Belle but what we want now is some web site thing, for callers.'

'Lenny showed us how to do that. He was ever so clever and he liked me. He said I was special. He said I had potential and would go far.'

'And did you go far?' asked Gina.

'No,' giggled Belle, 'just round to his flat and we did the web thing. Look, I'll explain but then I'll let Lenny actually do it for real 'cos he's good and there will be no comeback on us. You have to be smart and keep it anon......, anony....something or other. So no-one can find you.'

'But we want to be found Belle. That's the whole point. We want people to find us and call us so we can entertain.'

'I know that Gina love but you need to be careful about the Bill. We need to be able to screen and ....look I know what we want and I'll get Lenny to set it up and show you all. It won't take him long. 'bout a couple of days.'

'Gloria talked with Toby and we thought it would be best if we only took cash. That way we don't have to worry about any business set-up for credit card processing and the punters wouldn't have to pass on their numbers over the internet.'

'And their wives wouldn't see anything on their statements,' added Lola as she came into the room.

'What about prices and faces?' asked Gina. 'How do we handle that?'

'We can do full-length photos wearing whatever dress or costume suits the service,' said Belle. 'Lenny does those too. They're not a problem.'

'Fees?' asked Lola.

'Could do those two ways,' suggested Belle. 'We quote a flat cover charge and an entertainment fee as extra, plus we suggest enhanced opportunities after negotiations. We did it that way at the Club and everyone understood.'

'Yes but there we talked face to face,' said Gina. 'We could explain.'

'Same thing,' said Belle. 'Bait the 'ook and pull 'em in. Show them a picture and talk. Look, we can have a second salesman too. Once they show we can give them a more detailed list of goodies. You know. Tell them the real menu of what's on offer. You said Gloria's thinking of having some go-between, some gopher to screen the punters and then guide them to the show.'

'That's right,' said Gina. 'To start with we want to keep it low key. We don't want anyone local to know where. So, we plan to meet up with the customers somewhere public and have this gopher bring them to us in secret. Gloria thinks that is the best way to start and might even excite some of the customers even more. She's still not sure exactly where to put on the show so to speak. She's got someone working on that. Toby thought it was for the best as well. He's been down there a couple of times and the village itself shuts up tight around eleven.'

'Not quite the West End then?' said Belle. 'You sure they got the 'lectric down there yet?'

'Belle it's a winner. Blokes will have their tongues out and this will be a kinky deal. We'll all have a giggle. The five of us will be together again and we can see how it goes. Still, we do need you to set it all up for us, with teacher Lenny. He's cool Belle, knows what this is about does he?'

'Lenny's fine Lola. I'll keep him sweet. We might give him a ride in the country now and again. He thinks my little girl routine is a charmer. Says he has to watch himself when he's really teaching in a class and one or two of the girls make eyes at him.'

'Get him to keep his fingers on the keyboard or whatever for a couple of days darling and let's get this show on the road. Gloria's dead keen. Did you hear what happened last weekend, when we all got together?'

'And we all got a bit carried away,' added Gina.

'Before we explain that,' added Lola, 'have you talked to Sheena?'

'Sure, yesterday and she wants in. She thinks a holiday in the country will do her good.'

'She realises that this is not a regular every night thing Belle? This might start off slow and be once a week for the first little while. You know, until the trade builds up.'

'Yea, I explained all that but Sheena said she wanted to breathe fresh air again and the city was doing her lungs in. She jogs you know? The silly cow actually goes out and runs. Says it's good for her legs or something. Anyway, what has Gloria been up to now? Never a dull moment with her is there but she's a hell of a laugh at times? Be good to work with her again. We had some great times together. Could turn blokes inside out could Gloria. Treat to watch.'

'Fine. We'll leave you Belle and be in touch. Give us Sheena's number and we'll try and catch her before she's out running round the houses. I prefer the confines of the bull-ring personally for my training. How about you Gina?'

'I don't need to do any training sweetheart. I just need to go shopping.'

Later that afternoon Sylvia Lord decided to take Daniel and Katya out with her before they followed up on her suggestion about "getting a room".

'Daniel, we should check on the cottages and see which we think would be best for the Entwhistles. Katya you come too love. You might be able to decide better than Daniel as he used to tell me he could live in a tree-house and I don't think that is what the Entwhistles have in mind. There is a young wife and a five-year old as well as the husband himself. According to his letter Daniel this Colin Entwhistle is quite a mechanic, a craftsman as well as a good forestry worker. Lady Diana Worthing added in her letter that the wife is one of these old hippie earth mother types given to long dresses and organic foods. Mark you, Lady Worthing had some other descriptions but I'll skip those. She really is quite a character Daniel. She's another very eccentric English person Katya and will charm you one minute and shoot your head off the second. They say she used to hunt a lot in her youth, out in the Middle East somewhere.'

'There's no game in the Middle East mother, just sand, rocks and oil.'

'Seems Diana Worthing used to hunt bandits Daniel. She was on some archaeological dig or something in Turkey or maybe Syria and the camp got raided. This annoyed her so much she took off after the intruders and hunted them down. The British Consul had to keep it all very hush hush but Lady Diana will tell you all about it, with relish too as if she would do the same today given half the chance. Lives up to her name does Lady Diana Worthing. The more I learn about her the more I'm surprised Michael ever challenged her. Still, I suppose it was her son that Michael took advantage of although we never did learn the whole story. Anyway, come on you two we've work to do. Come and look at cottages.'

Daniel opened the door to Enrico's cottage and sighed.

'Not quite like old times eh Daniel?' asked Katya and she put her arm around him.

'Work you two,' said Sylvia briskly. 'This is not a search for "rooms" Daniel, well not for you and Katya. Could a family live here do you think?'

'A family did live here Mum, for many years.'

'Yes son I know and I also know that you, Samantha, Michael and even Geoffrey spent hours down here with Antonio and Enrico. Yes, a family did live here and I see no reason why a new family doesn't live here next month.'

'Sure Mum, ever the romantic you are.'

'Daniel, the bottom line my boy. Katya, talk to your man here about real life, moving on and what's for dinner tomorrow. Bit bare isn't it? Suppose we could furnish it although the Entwhistles might have some things of their own. I should phone and ask. Daniel, are you with me. Look in the other rooms and see what's there. No Katya, don't you go with him or the pair of you will go into a clinch or something. You look around the kitchen with me and think of this earth mother living here. Enrico always kept a garden and so that would be a bonus. Stove's fine. The electricity works. Anthony checked and upgraded the insulation in the walls and ceiling when we refurbished both cottages back in the eighties. There's the two bedrooms so they've room for their son. How's that bathroom Daniel? Let me come and look.'

Sylvia bustled around the cottage in her usual no-nonsense style and Katya smiled. Daniel came back into the kitchen and Katya held his hand. He looked at her and she smiled and rested her head on his shoulder. 'Love you,' she whispered. Daniel was about to respond when his mother came whirling back into the kitchen.

'Fine, clean, tidy and nearly empty. After some dusting, sweeping and perhaps a question about paint colours and furniture this would do nicely. What do you think Daniel?'

'Ask Enrico,' said Daniel.

'Yes, good point Daniel. In fact that is a very good point. That's just the sort of thing your father would have suggested. A people thing. We'll go and talk with Enrico on the way home. He'll understand. He's quite settled now at Home Farm you know. Christina loves it. She was telling me the other day and of course she got quite emotional about it, about family and having people around her. I think Enrico is settled Daniel but we will ask him and make sure he understands.'

'Mum I think he'll be delighted. There will be another family here and a new youngster for Enrico to make toys for. But, I would like us to ask.'

Katya squeezed Daniel's hand in agreement.

'So, let's go and look at Betty's old cottage. I'm not so sure about having anyone there Daniel. There is too much history associated with that place. In some ways I'd think of tearing it down but then you and Katya were talking of converting the cottages into residences for people at the Education Centre weren't you?'

'Yes Mum we were but you've "moved on" with this one as you so pointedly put it. You're right though, the Ferris cottage does have a lot of baggage that goes with the place. Wouldn't be so bad if only we knew about it, the family I mean but the whole village knows what went on in there. Anyone new living there would soon get to hear the stories and that could frighten anyone. Still, we can look but I think you're right choosing this one.'

Sylvia got back in the Landrover and drove the three of them down to the Ferris cottage. She stopped outside and didn't get out for a moment. Daniel sat there too beside Katya and recalled the whole series of events that had taken place here. Norton Ferris and his two sons had lived here, Idwal and John. Nine year ago now Daniel thought. Norton got killed in the forest, not far from here and just around that time Idwal finds those twin cousins of Freddie Dunster. The treasure in the tree by the cave, the murder of the twins and burying them in the cottage, Idwal and John fired, John's return and him marrying Betty Travers and all their happy family with Katey and Paul living here for six or seven years and then Idwal returns. Christ and did he return thought Daniel. Back to avenge his dad's death who he thought Enrico killed, then assaulting John's wife, burning the stables and finally ending up with his throat slashed in this cottage. Blood everywhere with a shot dead girl friend, a raped Betty Travers and his brother John still holding the knife in his hands. Yes thought Daniel, a lot of baggage goes with this cottage. There might have been happy family years when John and Betty lived here with their young kids but that all ended with Idwal Ferris.

'You going to get out Daniel?'

'Yes Mum. I was just remembering.'

'True. I think I understand Daniel. This place has a lot of unpleasant memories for you whereas Enrico's cottage is home.'

'Yes Mum. Still, we've come down here so let's go and look. I'll try and see today and tomorrow as you suggested rather than see the past. Come on Katya let's see whether Betty's garden has anything to offer. We filled in the soil pit Mum. You know, the one Peter and Tony dug last October for their school project. When they found those old clothes belonging to Freddie.'

'Looking forwards Daniel, forwards not backwards. Let's go in.'

They didn't take long to inspect the cottage. As Betty was still living with her parents the cottage looked much like she had just left it. True enough most of the children's books and toys had gone and all the little things. Betty had taken her precious pots and pans especially anything to do with her pie-making. Otherwise it was a comfortably furnished cottage. Even the infamous hidey hole was covered over and the closet filled with brushes and brooms.

'You'd never know would you?'

'Daniel, forwards. Could do with a wash and a dust,' said Sylvia practically. 'Could be converted I suppose. Wouldn't it be easier to knock it down and start again? Build something more suitable as a residence, closer to the Centre? This is a long way from anywhere Daniel. What do you think Katya?'

'You're right Sylvia. It's a fair distance for anyone to walk to the Centre from here. It is rather remote but I suppose that was part of its charm when it was a forest cottage. It is a lovely setting and it does fit in to the forest so well. It looks like it belongs here. I wouldn't want to see it destroyed and we could think of building residences closer to the Centre if we ever wanted to go that far.'

'I like the we,' added Daniel and he put his arm around Katya. 'Let's leave it Mum. I think you're right. Enrico's cottage would be for the best. Let's leave this place to some peace and quiet. It could do with a healing period. The surroundings will help.'

'Not if we have to thin that plantation there Daniel, right next door. Those trees look a little dense and you need to check on the Operating Plan to see when they are due for a thinning. The healing period maybe a little noisy for a while.'

'Ever practical my mum Katya,' said Daniel.

'Revenues Katya,' said Sylvia and she turned and grinned at the pair of them. 'Come on then. Home and let me phone the Entwhistles. How does one talk to an earth mother Daniel? Are there special expressions?'

'Should I make this call?' asked Daniel teasing his mother. 'I mean to say Katya and I know all about getting rooms and so on. Don't we Katya?'

'Get in you two and I'll make the call Daniel and you can take Katya into the library with James and explain about steam engines or something. He was telling me the other day that when he's five, which is right soon he pointed out he was going to take me on a trip on a real engine so I could see how they work. He went on at length about steam and cylinders and valves and whistles and why the steam wasn't blue even though the engine was.'

'Sounds like James Mum. Mouth going a mile a minute.'

'We'll find him Sylvia and I'll take him into the library and he can tell me all about anything. I think he's sweet.'

'Fine Katya and my sister will love you for it. I think Samantha is finding her juggling act of Heritage Adventures, her son and her tryst with Terence quite demanding at the moment. How is the tryst going Mum?'

'They're both mature adults Daniel and both have demanding routines. I think they are finding it hard to get time together, unlike you two I should mention. Terence's job can be all times of the day and night and interruptions and cancellations are part of the routine. I hope things work out for Samantha. She needs a man Daniel.'

'And what Samantha needs she usually gets Mum so stop worrying and we'll go and find James to be our chaperone.'

Sylvia laughed and put the Landrover into gear. Back at the Big House she phoned Yorkshire and managed to talk with the earth mother quite successfully.

I had found Wednesday hard graft after being off sick for a couple of days but Thursday turned out to be a different day altogether. Bob Edwards didn't send us out with the rest of the gang but had Freddie and I wait behind.

'Got a special job for you two useless buggers,' he said. 'You weren't actually being that productive working with the gang and so Mr. Daniel wanted something done he thought you might be able to manage. Come with me and remember this ain't no holiday and I want the job well done.'

Bob took us in his truck down to Enrico's old cottage. He hadn't lived here since last September if I remembered right and it was rather bare and empty. Inside Bob led us through all the rooms so we knew where everything was.

'Right, you've got your lunch and your gear and so you're here for the day. I'll come by periodically and check, and quite likely Mr. Daniel will be around so no slacking off. When it's time to finish I'll come by and pick you up. Is that clear?'

'Yes Bob,' said Freddie.

'And what special job does Mr. Daniel want done here then?' I asked. 'It's pretty clean and empty. What does he want done?'

'Dust, sweep, wash to clean, let dry and then paint some of the walls. We'll get to the painting tomorrow probably but we need the place clean first. Enrico and his brother kept the place in pretty good shape and there's no repairs need doing. Move what little furniture there is from room to room or outside if necessary as you work. In the closet there are brooms, brushes, dustpans, mops, pails, cloths, extension handles for reaching cobwebs in ceilings. Get it really clean before we start painting. Wash all the windows inside and out and there's window cleaner fluids for that plus squeegees. There's a tap in the yard as well as in the kitchen so it's easy to fill buckets. Take it steady and do a good job.'

'And after this one we go and do the Ferris cottage?' asked Freddie. 'I ain't going in there Bob. Not after what I know about my cousins I ain't. I don't care who asks but I won't go in there.'

'No Freddie, no-one's asking son. We're cleaning and painting this one for a new family coming to work on the estate. They'll be here in a couple of weeks and Mr. Daniel wants it ready and clean for them to move in. Mrs. Lord has talked with the new family and they decided on colours so we can go ahead with the painting when it's clean.'

'What about the Ferris cottage then?' I asked.

'The family are leaving that the way it is Gary as far as I know,' answered Bob. 'Mr. Daniel didn't say anything about the other cottage so you needn't worry Freddie. Just get the job done here. Any questions? Good. I'll be off then but I'll come around later in the morning so make sure you've got something to show me.'

'Jesus, why us?' asked Freddie when Bob had left. 'This is girls' work,' he added. 'We should go and get Gloria. She's only working part-time today and that's this afternoon. She's probably sitting down somewhere cozy painting her nails or something Gary. Gary, you listening to me? Am I talking to myself or the bloody trees? How did Enrico ever live out here for so long? Work out here is fine 'cos then you can leave and go somewhere civilised but out here on your own all the time I'd go bonkers.'

'You can talk Freddie. How about John Ferris then? Poor bugger worked out here all day, went home every night to his cottage just like this one and then on the only night he went into the village you were there giving him a bollocking. Is it any wonder he went bonkers?'

'But he didn't go bonkers,' chuckled Freddie, 'he went without his bonkers, or his bollocks anyway. I heard that silly little Australian tart cut his balls off before she bled him to death. Bonkers is off your 'ead Gary and John Ferris went off his balls.'

'You're a vindictive little cunt you are at times Freddie. You've got one mean vicious streak you have. You like to twist the knife you do, especially when someone's down or got something to hide.'

'So what,' said Freddie, 'that ain't your concern. Anyway, how we going play this special job thing? We'd better make a start or we'll have Daniel Lord down here prancing about or that flaky American bird of his full of ideas of turning the forest green. Christ the girl must be colour blind. It's green all around us.' Freddie waved his arms about expansively and I thought of clocking him one but then I was still feeling weak from having the flu or something so I restrained myself.

'Let's open some windows and move the dust about,' I suggested. 'We'll damp everything down a little beforehand and sweep it all through into the kitchen and out into the yard. You take one back room and I'll take the other.'

'And I'll be in Scotland before you,' sang Freddie and we both grabbed buckets and brooms.

Gloria sat in her mum's living room and slowly painted her nails as Freddie had guessed. She stretched the fingers and looked. Her nails were clean, well cut and shapely and her hands looked smooth and ladylike. Just right for working in the tea-shop she thought: Miss prim and proper with the correct tone of voice, the right offer of specialities and the efficient bustling to and fro amongst the customers. Not quite the same crowd as in the George but I can do service said Gloria to herself.

'You say something dear?'

'No Mum. Well maybe yes Mum. How do you get on with Toby?'

'The Fixer dear? He's changed Gloria you know. He's a different man from my younger days.'

Gloria thought that we've all changed mum but she didn't say so.

'But he still fixes things Mum. He still listens, organises, talks and makes things happen you know. They may not be the same things like when you were young but he's still very good at what he does. Don't you think so? You had a good chat with him last Sunday I saw. When I talked with Gina and Lola they said Toby talked a lot about you in the car on the way back to London. He took them back and most of the way Gina told me Toby had talked about how concerned he was and that he would come down and bring you back.'

'Bring me back Gloria? Whatever did he mean?'

'We all want you back Mum. I certainly want you back. Why do you think I'm staying? George sacked me but I didn't run off back to London with Gina and Lola now did I? No, I went looking for something else to do down here so I could help bring you back. Got me a small job helping

Mrs. Digby but there's not a lot to do there and then I'm working at the tea-shop. Well, I'll will be all summer and we'll find something else when the season closes down. By then George will have calmed down and be losing trade 'cos I've gone and I'll go back to working in the pub. You'll see Mum, but I'm here for you you know. Toby said he'd help. Always has been a helper for me has Toby Mum. He was good to me in London.'

'That's nice dear. I'm glad he helped you. He's a fine man is the Fixer. Now, where did I put my bible? There's a passage for today that I must read and understand Gloria. It's something to do with repentance if I remember and we all must repent Gloria love. All of us have sinned you know.'

'Yes Mum,' Gloria agreed and she wondered whether Toby could really help. She genuinely did want her mum back. Walter was gone and Wendell could go as far away as he liked thought Gloria but I would like to have mum back.

'Mum I've got to go. I'm due in the tea-shop in ten minutes and Darlene Roberts doesn't take kindly to lateness. Do I look the part?'

'You look lovely my dear. You'd look just right in the choir, along with all the other angels. Now you sing nicely Gloria and I'll pray for you. I'll see you when your service is over.'

Gloria walked over and held her mum's hands. 'Sure Mum, we'll see you later. You have a little rest and read a bit of the good book. I'll sing for you if you pray for me.' Gloria turned away with a sad look on her face and walked to work. Smarten up girl she told herself. Toby will come through and I've got to smile and be waiting on tables. Maybe I should suggest a special on Betty Ferris's fruit pies. They are always a winner.

Lunch-time extended into the early afternoon and the bright warm sunshine had brought out the tourists. While the George did a brisk trade down the road as Gloria well knew the tee-total crowd flocked to the tea-shop. They were the only two eateries in the village itself and the restaurant out on the Motorway was rather impersonal and commonplace. Darlene's Tea Shop offered lunch and afternoon teas. The latter meal spread itself into an early dinner as the shop closed at seven. Although the menu wasn't extensive Darlene prided herself on quality food without being ostentatious. Simple country fare she offered but it was tasty and served on tables with crisp white tablecloths, sparkling cutlery and china crockery in a refined fashion. There were three waitresses in plain black skirts, clean white blouses and low comfortable heeled shoes. Even on a weekday the place was crowded from eleven when it opened until they shooed the last customer out of the door around seven. Darlene took charge at the till and oversaw the whole operation. A young girl cleaned away empty plates and helped a second girl in the kitchen with the washing up. It was a neat, tidy, cost-effective seasonal business and Darlene had managed her little empire for fifteen years now. Depending on the weather she would typically close down after Christmas and for January and February Darlene would take the sun in the south of Spain and leave the pub as the sole place for eating out in the village. In many ways Darlene and George did not compete as there were two quite distinct client groups. Nevertheless they both offered and served Betty Ferris's pies, although now Betty preferred to label them as Betty Traver's pies. Darlene had thought of offering the entire packaged pie but Betty said her mum already did that and so did her dad through the off-licence so she didn't think they would want the competition. Darlene agreed but only after some discounting on the price from Betty. Gloria sat in a small back corner of the kitchen and rested her feet on her break.

'That's the lunch-time rush over then,' she said. 'Suppose we'll get a breather before tea-time starts and extends into dinner?'

'Same as the pub surely Gloria?' asked Rachael as she put the plates into the dish-washer.

'Yes and no love,' said Gloria. 'Different clientele and so different tone of voice, and language too I suppose,' and she giggled. 'Had a bloke in here this morning who wanted gunpowder tea. Of course I had to ask who was he thinking of blowing up and he didn't think it was funny. He explained that he grew up with it in India, although it sounded like Inger and I didn't twig at first. When I just stood there looking a little quizzical he asked to see the manageress.'

'What did you say? Couldn't have been your usual reply from the pub days or you wouldn't still be here. Mrs. Roberts won't have any bad language. She is always going on about manners. So, what did you do Gloria?'

'I politely asked if he would wait just a moment and I'd get the manageress for him. Walked slowly over to Darlene didn't I and explained that the customer was asking for her special. Didn't say what the geezer wanted did I? Let her sort out Mr. Gunpowder. Jesus, this is England not the bleeding colonies. Earl Grey in the morning and Orange Pekoe ever after. Next thing you know we'll have the bloody chinks in here wanting green tea or something. It's our bloody country.'

'So, you retired gracefully and then what happened?'

'My feet are killing me in these shoes. Must have been easier carrying pints. Perhaps George has different floors or something. Them tiles in there might look smart but you sure have to watch no-one spilt anything on the floor. Slippery they are. Bloody nearly dropped a pie and cream in some poor ladies lap I did. That would have been a giggle. Mark you she was so blind she wouldn't have noticed. I almost had to stand beside her and help lift the fork into her mouth. She would have put it in her ear otherwise.'

'Give over Gloria. Did the bloke get his gunpowder?'

'No, Darlene politely explained what we had and he resorted to coffee. Freshly ground I trust he asked.'

'Didn't some of the clients at the George get up your nose the same way? I would have thought that after a few pints some of the crowd down there get a bit lippy, and a bit handy,' Rachael added with a laugh.

'True,' said Gloria, 'but you can give as good as you get down there. A bar-maid's expected to take a bit of this and that and give it back too. It's free and easy and not so stiff upper lip as here. Still, it's work I suppose and I'm off back to the trenches. Smile Gloria and look like you want their business. Hi Darlene, I'm just back off my break and ready to keep them smiling. Ready with the thank you for dropping by and come again please. We're here to serve.'

That Thursday evening Gloria phoned London to get an update from Lola.

'Belle's on board Gloria and she'll have this website thing up and running by the weekend she says. She's quite familiar with the process and she'll show us how it works when its operational. The guy who is doing it is good she says.'

'How good and what's he want?' asked Gloria.

Lola laughed down the telephone. 'Belle is smart Gloria and she's a young kid who learnt a lot at school. She just thinks there are smarter ways to earn a living than going to any office or whatever. The guy is an old teacher of hers, a real live school-instructor type teacher with qualifications: Teacher Training College qualifications that is. A professional Gloria and he doesn't want anything special. Belle says he's well looked after and we needn't worry. The way she said it she assumed we all knew what she meant. So, that's underway. Also, I talked with Sheena and she says she desperately wants to visit the country. She remembers your pub and the area although it was winter and she didn't see a lot when she came down with Gina. How about your end?'

'I haven't heard back from my scout yet Lola. The rumour running around the village is that he was sick for two days after our last Sunday night so I haven't seen him.'

'Gloria you're not supposed to knock them flat for days kiddo,' laughed Lola. 'We all know men haven't got much stamina and that's one reason I prefer women but take it easy or you'll lay low the western counties. Still, we do need a place so prop your scout back up and make him work for his pleasures.'

'Sure Lola. I'll chase him up tomorrow and phone you with an update. This is starting to look good. Bye.'

'Who was that dear?'

'Lola from London Mum. One of the girls who was here last Sunday with Toby.'

'The Spanish girl? She must be Catholic. I'm not sure I like you going out with Catholic girls Gloria. They have some funny ideas about the Pope coming between poor sinners like myself and my God. Throw a lot of incense about I've heard. That would irritate my throat. Nice girl though Gloria and very pretty in a thin way. Perhaps she goes on these fasts and scourges herself. Do you think so Gloria?'

Gloria thought of all the things she knew that Lola did and somehow that didn't include fasting or scourging. Well maybe on the customers but certainly not self-inflicted. Where was Gary she thought? Sick maybe but he must be back at work by now. I'll find him tomorrow she told herself.

'She's a fine lady Mum and a good friend of Toby. He helped her too Mum, just like he can help you. And Lola is not Catholic Mum. I'm sure she's never been to a church that throws incense about.'

'That's good then dear. I'll pray for her tonight. So she can stop fasting,' added Tilley.

Freddie and I had worked on and off all that day and actually had something to show Daniel Lord when he drove down that afternoon with Bob Edwards. They both seemed pleased and told us we would continue on the Friday. Laying in bed that night and still feeling weak and achy from the flu and all that scrubbing I was thinking about new people in the cottage. Another family moving in Bob had said, from somewhere up north. Christ, I wonder whether we'll understand them? Still, better to move into Enrico's old cottage than the other one. Suddenly I sat up in bed. Bull's-eye I almost shouted and then lay back flat again and smiled at the ceiling in my room. Cottage, the Ferris cottage, remote, quiet, spooky because of all that has happened there. Freddie didn't want to go there and clean it now did he? Everyone else in the village will steer clear and it's well away from any other buildings. Sits peacefully quiet deep in the remote forest and yet it is neatly accessible from the main road without going anywhere near the Big House or that new Education Centre. Wonder what the inside is like? Did it ever get cleared up after that bloodbath last year? Must have because Betty Ferris went back for some things. Then Daniel Lord did his cleaning thing and his nephew knocked down that urn with the other gold coins. So, it is clean and tidy. I'll look. I'll take Gloria there on the weekend and we'll look. Sunday morning would be good as Daniel Lord takes his bird and plays golf or something so he won't be around. Good thinking Gary. Absolutely bloody brilliant. You're a real winner. Hey, Gloria will be chuffed. Perhaps this will earn me some real loving although last Sunday was good. That Dora is a handful but she fits right into the group real good. Surprise that is but it would surprise her useless brother Lester even more if he knew. I fell asleep dreaming of big stars, Gloria, Dora and an answer for everything.

TRIAL RUN

FRIDAY AT LAST I THOUGHT as Freddie and I continued working at Enrico's. Everything was clean and rubbed down and Bob Edwards had given us the paint, rollers and brushes. Daniel Lord had been thoughtful enough to give us some old dustsheets to spread about or else we would have had paint all over the floor as Freddie paints worse than Lester Rainer. Sensibly we hadn't cleaned the windows yet because we had to remove some paint from those too after our taping job wasn't so hot. Not forestry work I thought, not at all.

Gloria worked in the salon with Mrs. Digby and there was a steady procession of customers all getting themselves primped up for the weekend. Cut, curled, set, tinted, streaked, blow-dried and everything else but Mrs. Digby had been a hairdresser for many years and had kept up with the times and the requests of her clientele. She let Gloria handle the less skilled tasks of washing and rinsing hair, sweeping up the split ends, making and supplying tea, but she shared that most important task of chit-chat. Mrs. Digby believed that she could out-gossip Mrs. Larkin down at the grocers and Dora Telford who ran the Post Office. Of course she had good competition from Mary Travers who ran the greengrocers and who had other information from her daughter Betty at Marples the

215

baker. Mrs. Digby thought she might have an inside track with Gloria as that way she might hear more about the younger set and their antics. Still, it was an important part of the business in the village and you had to know what was happening and keep your customers wanting to return to hear the latest you know. She only had half her mind on the job and the chatter when the salon door opened and in walked Katya Howard.

'Hi Gloria,' Katya said cheerfully. 'I should have telephoned but as Daniel was driving through the village I thought I'd pop in and try and make an appointment. Good morning Mrs. Digby. I'm Katya Howard, a friend of Daniel Lord. I came in to see whether I can make an appointment for a little attention to my hair. There's no rush and I'm still here next week if you have any openings.'

'Look in the book for me will you Gloria dear. I'm rather involved with Mrs. Beaston here at the moment. I'm sure we can fit you in ... Katya was it?'

'Good to see you Katya and let's look in the book. Here, how about next Wednesday?'

'No, not Wednesday thanks. That day I do have another commitment but any other day would be fine.'

'Tuesday afternoon, at two? Would that suit?'

'Fine, splendid. Thanks Gloria. Thanks Mrs. Digby. Must dash, Daniel's waiting.'

Katya left and as soon as the door had closed Mrs. Digby looked around and said, 'Now there's a fine young lady for Mr. Daniel. About time he settled down. Sir Anthony will be looking for more grandchildren knowing him.'

'Well he's got young Peter Lord who is a fine lad, and then that little walking talking monster of Miss Samantha's who is full of life like his mother.'

'Wonder whether she'll have another?' mentioned Mrs. Beaston.

'Not with Mr. careful do-it-by-the-book Terence Field she won't,' answered Mrs. Digby.

'Going out together though aren't they?' added Mrs. Beaston.

'What do know about them Gloria? They're all about your age dear.'

'Not a lot I suppose,' said Gloria. 'They all used to come in the pub occasionally but I can't say I know any of them well. Daniel Lord's been with that Katya since what, last September. That was soon after Samantha came back from Canada with her son. She came home and got involved in rape, murder, arson when all she was looking for was peace and quiet after her husband got killed.'

'Killed in Canada was he dear? Was he Canadian?'

'No Mrs. Beaston he was a Scot I think. He'd studied forestry or something and met Miss Samantha at University. Well she was a mad young thing as we all know in the village and to spite her mother she married this Scot, had little James and they all went to Canada. I heard Sir Anthony was quite upset but then I was away in London at that time so I don't know all the details. Seems her husband fought forest fires or something. Anyway, he was out one day and got caught or so I heard. Burnt his truck and burnt him too.'

'Yes, that's right dear. Towards the end of last summer it was and Sir Anthony and Lady Sylvia rushed over to Canada to bring her home, her and her son. She seems to have settled though. Got her son James into school here. Heard she's got herself a job too. What was it Mrs. Masters was saying? Oh yes, Miss Samantha is bringing foreign folk here into the village to find their long lost cousins or something. Real shock it was for Mrs. Masters.'

'I remember that,' said Gloria. 'I was working in the pub when Samantha brought these folk in and cornered poor Danny. Frightened the life out of him that did. She had some people from Canada who thought they had the same great grandparents or something as Danny. Every time he came into the pub after that he looked about to see whether Miss Samantha was there with some other new folk. Like a frightened rabbit is Danny Masters.'

'Yes yes Gloria but what about Terence Field and Miss Samantha? How is that going?'

'I only worked in the pub Mrs. Beaston. I only saw them there. I'm not exactly in the same social crowd as the Lords you know. I see them around and they seem to be an item but you never know these days. I might find out some more from my swimming instructor. He might know.'

'Swimming instructor Gloria? Who is that then dear?'

'Young Tony Lord.'

'You mean that coloured boy?'

'That's as maybe Mrs. Digby but Tony's a fine lad and a good instructor.'

'But wasn't his mother that little black lady who rented the caravan up the hill above the quarry? Years ago now it was. You know, where they tried to tip Michael Lord over the edge. She was a sweet lady and ever so polite. Mrs. Larkin thought she was a real black treasure and her son Tony was only a baby then.'

'You're right Mrs. Digby,' said Mrs. Beaston. 'She disappeared and then we had those two accidents up at the Manor.'

'Tony was the love child between the black girl and Michael Lord I thought,' suggested Gloria. 'She was trying to get him to marry her and then ran away.'

'And Sir Anthony went and found them after Michael Lord was killed and eventually that Danielle, yes that was her name came back down here last September with Tony. Surprise that was after all those years her coming back here,' said Mrs. Digby.

218

'But then she got killed didn't she?' asked Mrs. Beaston. 'There was some break-in up at the Manor and Tony was hurt and his mother got killed. I heard part of this from Rosemary Dunster as her Freddie works up at the Manor. For a couple of days there was police all over Freddie said.'

'Well I don't know about all of that,' said Gloria. 'I only came home after those events but Tony is real good at teaching me life-saving and such. That kid's a good swimmer but he does miss his mum on occasions. We talk a bit and he loves being here with his cousin Peter and he likes his Italian aunt, Christina isn't it? He thinks his other aunt Miss Samantha is a bit of a nut case. The person he really likes in that house is Enrico of course.'

'He's a lovely man,' agreed Mrs. Digby. 'There Mrs. Beaston, how does that look dear? I've waved the sides around just like you asked and straightened out the front curls. I think you look a charmer.'

'Go on Mrs. Digby. That's a line for all your customers. What do you think Gloria?'

'You'll knock 'em off their feet Mrs. Beaston,' added Gloria supportively.

'I doubt whether my Sid will even notice,' said Mrs. Beaston. 'Still, thanks Mrs. Digby. I feel good and that's what matters.'

The door opened and in walked a pretty little girl with blond curls, a clean summer dress and a bright smile.

'Good morning Mrs. Digby,' she said, 'and good morning to you Mrs. Beaston and to you Miss Gloria.'

'Yes it is my dear, a very good morning and what can we do for you Katey Ferris?'

'Mummy says we're going to change it back to Travers.'

'Does she now? Well then Katey Travers, what can we do for you?'

'Mummy asks whether you can fit her in later this afternoon Mrs. Digby?'

'For your mummy darling we will look and see. I'm sure we can find time for the champion pie-maker in the village. Your mummy is somebody special love. Yes, you just tell your mother that I can look after her at four o'clock this afternoon poppet. But, I must say you yourself look very special this morning. Doesn't she look a picture Mrs. Beaston?'

'Are you going somewhere special Katey?'

'We're going to look at a house mummy says. We're going later this evening.'

'So you're not going back to live in the forest?' Mrs. Digby asked. 'Your brother and you used to like living there didn't you? Little Paul would tell me all about the birds you saw and the rabbits playing by your garden.'

'No, mummy says we need to find a bigger house than grandma's but she's going to stay in the village. She needs to be close to the bakery now as the business has expanded. She says she has to earn some money.'

'But she sold the cottage didn't she Katey? That gave her some money surely?'

'I think so. I don't know really. Anyway, I know we're not going back to the cottage but I've got to go. Thank you Mrs. Digby for mummy's appointment. She'll be here at four. Bye. Bye all.'

'She's a fine lass is Katey. Takes after her mother I hear and soon we'll have another champion pie-maker in this village. Brings in the tourists you know. Folk are starting to talk about Betty's pies. Had a lady in here just the other day from way up near Birmingham she was. I had difficulty understanding her part of the time as she sounded as if she had a head cold but she'd heard of our Betty's pies. Came down special she said 'cos her husband had a sweet tooth.'

'Not surprised she isn't going back to that cottage though,' said Mrs. Beaston. 'After all that happened up there I wouldn't go anywhere near the place. That Idwal Ferris was an evil man. His father, old Norton was pretty useless but he was only a small time thief. That son of his Idwal was a real nasty man. Good riddance I say. I'd have given John Ferris a medal, even though he was his brother. Still, dangerous place that cottage. It's a wonder that Lady Sylvia doesn't pull it down. She must know how people think in the village.'

'Talking of Lady Sylvia I hear she was in church last Sunday. Now there's a first. I don't think she's seen inside a church since she was married. Maybe not even then.'

'Go on Mrs. Digby. Sylvia Lord in church? Whatever was she doing?'

'With Sir Anthony too I hear. When I saw them I was so surprised I had to look twice to be sure.'

'Well why Mrs. Digby? Why were they there?'

'Listening to that new preacher weren't they now. You should hear the right Reverend Gabriel Godschild. Speaks a strong sermon that man.'

Again the salon door opened and Tilley Manson walked in and then paused and looked about her in a rather uncertain fashion.

'He's a god-fearing man but he's not giving God's message,' she said very clearly as she slowly looked at everyone in the room. 'Hello Gloria dear. I didn't expect to see you here. I've come for my usual manicure Mrs. Digby. I need fine hands when praying to my God. Good, clean and pure hands. You are ready for me?' she asked as she looked pointedly at Mrs. Beaston.

'I was just going Mrs. Manson,' said Mrs. Beaston. 'Thanks Mrs. Digby and I'll book again within the month. Bye Gloria. Thanks for the chat Mrs. Digby.'

During the long dialogue between Mrs. Beaston and Mrs. Digby Gloria had stood there half listening and half thinking. Several thoughts rolled around in her head but before she could put them in any order she heard Mrs. Digby ask, 'Gloria, could you put the kettle on for me love? I'll need some warm water if I'm going to clean your mother's hands. Sit you down Mrs. Manson and we'll have a little talk while the water warms.'

Gloria finished work for Mrs. Digby soon after four thirty when the last customer had been Betty Travers. Betty had elaborated on her Katey's story about looking for a house and that they were going to see a possibility this evening. All the family were excited and her dad Toby was going to come too. She was anxious to have a place of her own and not crowd her mum and dad any longer. It had been nearly nine months now and it was time she should get her life back together. Gloria didn't say anything special or ask any questions but she did listen to Betty and Mrs. Digby talk about this and that. Some of the words confirmed an idea already twirling around in her head.

From there Gloria went and did a couple of hours on a Friday evening at Darlene's. It was a busy evening and several tourists came through the village, some especially looking for the tea-shop where they sold those special pies. Lots of people Gloria noticed; lots of visitors and non-locals. There were even people who lived separately in the village but came down here to meet up and gossip while having tea together. More ideas gathered in Gloria's head. She went through her waitress routine almost on automatic pilot that Friday evening and she was startled when she got home.

'What were you doing at Mrs. Digby's Gloria dear? I didn't expect to see you there. Were you having your hair-cut? It does look so nice dear. She does a good job that Mrs. Digby but she has no idea about the right God. She was telling me that the Reverend Godschild spoke of divine creation, of divine revelation and of divine salvation. Now I know that isn't true Gloria. I know we are all God's creatures and that we came here slowly over millions of years and eventually God decided to make someone like him after he had tried with all sorts of other animals and they hadn't learnt his message well. He tried and tried Gloria and you see all kinds of animals who had the opportunity to spread his message. The Reverend Godschild is wrong Gloria, wrong. I must stop him.'

Gloria walked over to her mother and knelt by her chair. She reached out and held her mother's hand.

'Mum,' she said gently, 'why don't you rest a little before you pray with those clean hands from Mrs. Digby. I'm sure she means well even if she has heard the wrong message. Let me make you a cup of tea and we'll talk about tomorrow. You know who is coming to see you tomorrow Mum?'

Tilley leant back in her chair as if her speech had tired her. She looked at Gloria.

'You're a good girl Gloria. You're a good daughter and I'm glad you came home my love. It wasn't good when you went away. I know it wasn't good. I told Walter he shouldn't but he said you liked it. He said that was why you ran away. He told me you didn't want to hurt me but I was already hurt Gloria. Walter hurt me Gloria, really hurt me. Sometimes he wouldn't stop,' and Tilley burst into tears. Sobs racked her body and Gloria just knelt there and held her mum's hand. She didn't know what to say or what to do.

'Toby will listen Mum. Toby will come and he'll explain about dad. He'll help you fix everything in your mind. He'll bring you back. I know he can. He brought me back Mum. Well, he persuaded me to come back here to you. He can fix things Mum. He'll be here tomorrow for you.'

Slowly standing Gloria slipped her hand away. 'I'll fix you some tea Mum. Then I've got to go out.'

'Where Gloria?' asked Tilley sharply suddenly raising her head.

'Tea Mum and then I'll change.'

'Where?' said Tilley again, 'with who?'

'Gary Templeton was looking for something for me and I haven't seen him all week. I'd heard he'd been sick but I need to know what he has found.'

'No Gloria, not Gary Templeton. You shouldn't go out with Gary Templeton. That family is trouble. Catherine never does anything, doesn't care and Brian is real trouble. He's the devil Gloria. Look what they've got between them, that son Gary. All slippery, bendy, with no beliefs and only worried about themselves. Not Gary Gloria.'

'Mum I'm only going to ask him something. Remember it's Freddie I go out with when we're a group.'

'Will Toby go to church and hear the Reverend Godschild?' Tilley asked completely out of the blue.

'Ask him Mum when he comes tomorrow. I'll go and make tea.'

'Make me one too,' demanded Wendell as he walked into the living room. 'Mum I need five quid. Where's yer purse?' Wendell looked around the living room. 'Two sugars sis,' he shouted, 'and a couple of chocolate biscuits too. Gotta go soon. Where's your purse Mum? I need that five quid. More would be better though.'

'I'll pray for you Wendell,' said Tilley.

'Sure Mum, whatever. Where's that tea Gloria? Christ you're slow. You this slow at that slop shop where you work? Work, now there's a laugh. Don't do bugger all do you except flash those tits of yours around. Still, that probably got more response in the pub though didn't it? Where's the biscuits? Shit, this tastes like soup. You put any sugar in? Purse Mum? You gone and lost it again? Christ, you should put it on your altar and then you'd always see it.'

'Wendell what do you want five pounds for?'

'Nothing to do with you Miss nosey parker so piss off. Where's your purse Mum for Christ sake?'

'With my Bible Wendell.'

'I ain't got time for this. Gloria, give us five quid and be quick about it.'

Gloria came close to giving her brother a knuckle sandwich but thought better of it with her mother in the room. She looked at him. Wendell now stood six feet tall, coarse-faced, abusive and broad-shouldered like Walter had been. Being a bully went with the appearance Gloria thought. Slowly she looked him up and down and she put down her cup.

'Piss off Wendell,' she hissed through her teeth. 'Get lost little brother before I think of something to do other than give you five quid. Go and play with your faggoty friend with the grass-reeking clothing. Go and play on your wanking keyboard, or perhaps his wanking keyboard. Just get out of my sight.'

Wendell deliberately dropped the mug of half-drunk tea on the floor.

'Oops,' he said smirking. 'I'll fix you sister dear,' he muttered and walked out of the room.

Looking back at her mother Gloria saw that Tilley's eyes were closed. Probably her ears too Gloria imagined. Had that boy really been conceived out of that wild loud night? She had lain in her bed that night. She must have been about ten she thought. Even at that young age she had known enough about men and women, men and women and babies. Her mum had screamed and then she had heard the scream cut off. There were thumps, thuds, moans, beds moving and then loud shouts from her dad. Night of the devil she wondered or just happy families? Mum was already quiet by then and not happy but after that night things really changed. The first thing Gloria had seen was the altar in her mum's bedroom and her dad sleeping in the spare room. Dad was away more often and when he was home the mood was tense, about to explode some nights. Wendell slept in our mum's room for a long time, long after he was a baby. It became his room as much as mums and still dad slept in the spare room. The room that is now Wendell's with his magazines, computer and secrets. Then came the night that dad came to her room. Gloria shuddered and looked at her mum.

'I'll fix the mess Mum and then I'll go and change. I won't be home late Mum. We'll talk about Toby later.'

Gloria tidied up the broken mug and mopped up the spilt tea. She changed out of her tea-shop "uniform" into something more frivolous. A quick wash around the gnarly parts she thought and a dash of this or that around the this and that and she felt a lot better. Time to nail down Gary and see whether he's found out anything useful. He's had all week to think the useless tosser. At least the girls up in London have been doing something constructive. Wonder who will come down with Toby if anyone?

'Not barred am I George?' asked Gloria as she walked into the bar at the George.

George Doone looked Gloria up and down and thought he remembered her better when she was half under the covers and naked but he didn't say so. He smiled.

'No Gloria. I couldn't bar you love. Half the village would stay away if I tried to bar you. Gary was asking after you earlier. Said he'd had a brainwave which I think is highly dangerous but he told me he would come in here later and that you would be over the moon. Yes, that's the expression he used. When I told him that the cow jumped over the moon he told me to wash my mouth out and not be so rude.'

'I get the message George,' said Gloria. 'I'll have a pint please and wait. I'll sit quietly and not jump over any moon either.'

Halfway through her pint I walked in through the open doorway and up to the bar.

226

'Pint please George. Jesus but it's warm out there. Freddie and I have had this poxy job of cleaning out Enrico's old cottage and the dust was something else. Spent the day breathing paint fumes today didn't we. Bob Edwards says there are some new folks moving in and that Daniel Lord wants the place looking clean and tidy for them. So, expert Freddie and me got lumbered with the job 'cos we can turn a hand to anything. Dry work though, dry.......hey, hello there Gloria. Didn't see you sitting there quietly. Good to see you. Haven't seen you all week. Missed you. I was just telling George here about my special project.'

'Gary, shut it. Your throat is dry and you are thirsty. Stop the yap. Drink the beer and think what you have to tell me. And that's nothing to do with cleaning and painting Enrico's cottage so think about the other thing you are supposed to have done this week all the while you have been missing me. Understand?' and Gloria lifted my pint up to my lips and started to tip.

'Yes but....'

'Drink Gary.'

George laughed. 'There's times Gloria when you're a right charmer. This how you act with the customers at Darlene's? Must be a hell of a place with you holding up cups of tea for customers to slurp and stuffing pieces of pie down their throats. I'll bet Darlene thinks that's a real polite and refined approach.'

When I held my pint glass Gloria took her hands away and looked at George. 'If I remember the nursery rhyme George "the little dog laughed", just like you did.'

'I found it!' I said and plonked my glass back on the bar.

'The dish or the spoon?' asked Gloria.

'What?' I said, 'what dish or what spoon?'

'Never mind Gary. Your mother obviously never sat you upon her knee and told you nursery rhymes. How about old Mother Hubbard or Jack and Jill?'

'Jesus, what's with you tonight Gloria?'

'I suppose I've just been shouting at my stupid brother and wondering how my mum really brought him up. Wondering what she told him when he was small because now he's a bloody monster. He's a big bullying git and he gets up my nose. He abuses mum something awful and I could do with seeing a lot less of him. Perhaps I should teach him about Humpty Dumpty and how he fell and they couldn't put him back together again. What do you say Gary?'

'I found it,' I said, quieter this time. 'Come over in the corner and I'll tell you all about my brainwave.'

'Yes, the cow over the moon brainwave Gary.'

'Give over with this weird shit and listen. Before I start I'd better get another pint. You too?'

'Sure Gary and we'll sit here quietly supping and jumping over the moon while your brain waves all around the room like a magic carpet.'

'Christ, working with that old bird Mrs. Digby has done something to your head girl. You've been around the blue rinse crowd too long. That or the tourists in that tea-shop are getter weirder by the day. They packing them in from the Old Folks Homes now are they? Special Tour today old folks – piece of pie and baby talk from the local fortune teller.'

'Gary give over and get the pints in. We both sound like Friday night after a week we'd sooner forget. Go and get some drinks.'

Gloria and I compared notes and decided to look on Sunday morning.

On that last Saturday in May Toby Dobbs drove his little black sedan down the Motorway with Lola sitting beside him. Belle had spoken nice with Lenny and Lola had seen what he had done.

'That's coming along nicely,' said Lola to Toby. 'Gloria will be pleased. Wonder how she's making out? Said she was worried about her mum though Toby. Think you can help there?'

Toby looked at the road and drove safely along the inside lane while other people chasing yesterday and future salvation sped past. He thought.

'Bit of a challenge Lola darling,' he said. 'Still thinking on the best approach. She was a groupie you know. Wild they were. Young screamers and full of tricks. Hide everywhere and try and make out with the blokes in the band. Anything for a kiss and cuddle. Wild those days Lola.'

'Sure Toby, and then you found us and settled down!!'

Toby laughed and corrected his slight jiggle of the steering wheel. A heavy articulated lorry sounded his horn and overtook him as he came back into the inside lane.

'I found you dear lady and your special friends when I was still juggling the bands, the theatre owners, the groupies, and the money, plus being in every part of the country all at once. I didn't earn the moniker of "The Fixer" by chance Lola love. It became a badge of honour for me you know.'

'Well mate, Gloria is expecting you to earn the right to carry on wearing it. She's real worried about her mum. She loves her Toby. She may have a thick skin and be a real hard case when she needs to but she loves her mum. If it wasn't for her she'd be back up in the city. She loved that life. Gloria and I had some good times together Toby. You know, you've been there. You've seen us, and felt us,' and Lola laughed as she remembered some of the times with Gloria, and with Toby too.

'We'll work something out Lola. Need a coffee or anything? This old man needs a leak. The body doesn't have quite the same capacity any more.'

'You did all right last Saturday night though didn't you?' said Lola. 'Right through until that wonderful Sunday morning. Shit, Gina and I should have stayed but your bed wouldn't have held all four of us. I would have loved to have seen George's face though when he brought you that cup of tea. Gloria nearly pissed herself when she told me the story. She thought it was so funny.'

'Aye,' grunted Toby pressing his knees together. 'Here, I won't be a moment.'

'Toby darling you take your time. I'd come and help you love but I'm not sure we'd be allowed back on the Motorway.' Lola laughed and leant back in her seat as Toby hurriedly rushed into the toilets. Gloria girl, what are you up to now?

Saturday morning was busy in Darlene's tea-shop. Some English people, well those who thought they were with it, had weaned themselves away from the inevitable cuppa and graduated some might say to coffee. Only now it wasn't just coffee but café leche, expresso, and a variety of other possible combinations. Darlene sat at her cash register and looked over her domain. Gloria and Penelope moved quickly and efficiently between the tables and served her steady customers. The cash rung up and her smile widened. Morning coffee and tea graduated into lunch-time and the busloads started to arrive. Visitors flocked in through the door and Darlene added Gretchen, a Dutch au pair girl who worked part-time to her serving team. She wondered whether she should think of expanding but the problem was how or where. Perhaps tables and chairs out on the pavement; artistic settings with umbrellas; almost a continental flavour? But then would it fit in with the village country style of inside? Ching ching, another happy customer.

'Please come again. Nice to serve you. Enjoy the village.'

'That's ham and spinach pie, two veg., and a slice of peach pie for dessert then? Coffee to follow? You prefer tea? Fine, I'll be right back.' Gloria carefully placed the four glasses of water and a thermos jug on the table and went back to the kitchen to place the order. Noticing that number five was done she picked that up and delivered the four pie and chips to the young students who had left their bicycles outside.

'Four teas too lads?' she asked. 'Just water? Yea, I know what you mean with money's tight. Been there meself. Enjoy the pies anyway. Betty's specials they are.'

Soon after two Gloria hung up her apron and washed her hands in the sink. The number of customers had dropped a little and Penelope and Gretchen carried on while Gloria had finished for the day.

'Monday then Darlene?' called Gloria as she went out of the door.

'Yes please Gloria, for the morning love and remember we open at eleven sharp.'

Once again the hiking group came over the brow of the escarpment only a little further east this time. Rupert still led the group with his eager follower Mavis Taylor almost on his heels ready to wrap herself around Rupert if he looked like falling anywhere, preferably on top of her Mavis hoped. Ted walked looking intently at the two maps in his hands and would have walked off the edge of the cliff if Rory hadn't seen the potential disaster and caught his flapping shirt-tails.

'Professor, you'll blind yourself with all this reading. Give a look to the world for a moment and breathe the sweetness of the air about you. Feel the joy of freedom from your dusty historical tomes, your archival attitude and stop trying to fall off the bloody cliff because it is a long way to carry you home you useless sod.'

'Rory Flanagan you're a heathen, a fallen Catholic, a speaker of evil tongues, a......'

'Saviour of brother Ted here who is trying hard to martyr himself on the drovers' road. Ted give over with all this map reading. We know where we're going.'

'Yes we do,' asserted Doris as she adjusted the spectacles on her pert little nose. 'We're off to hear that Reverend speak words of controversy. Rouse the rabble and the unconverted and set fire to the minds of the ill-informed youth. He is speaking today isn't he Rupert? That's what you said.'

'But they are not words of controversy Doris. They are God's words, God's truth. The Reverend speaks of God's wonders, his creation.'

'And he was drummed out of his last parish I heard,' said Rory. 'I think the message was too blunt for the strong-minded people of Yorkshire wasn't it? I think your good Reverend's creativity was a little too creative for country folk who deliver calves, lambs, piglets on a regular basis and have trouble with instant animals.'

'You're a heathen and a blasphemer Rory. We are God's special creatures and not at all like cows or sheep,' exclaimed Philippa.

'Well said,' added Margaret. 'You should listen to Philippa Rory and perhaps to the Reverend Godschild. Just look at his name. How can you not believe when the man telling you these wonderful things is named Gabriel Godschild?'

The little group was missing Arnold Church but that didn't really matter as Arnold would have been looking for wilderness and the group was looking for salvation. They descended the cliff and this time they were close to the cave and the ancient oak tree. Rory saw it first.

'Hey, there's something on that old tree up there. Look, the tree that Arnold would have hugged and then cried as he saw the young conifers crowding around it like predatory sharks looking to attack a dying source of nutrients.'

'That's rather a mix of wildlife there Rory. Some sort of poetic licence I believe,' said Rupert as he turned the group to walk along the foot of the escarpment and towards the old oak tree.

'Disgusting,' exclaimed Doris, 'littering the area with trash like that plaque. We should tear it down.'

'And do you think the parents of Michael Lord might take offence little lawyer? Do you think that Lady Sylvia, who was mighty polite to you last week you may remember would take kindly to you defacing the memory of her son?' said Ted. 'Historical artefacts are protected you know. This is their land you may recall. You were told you were welcome to walk here but that doesn't give you the right to deface the property.'

'Well said Ted,' cried Rory as he clapped his hands together. 'Let's have a little civility Doris dear. Let's show a little human consideration for heroes past who should be remembered with dignity and respect. Such a plaque adorning such a magnificent and longlasting oak which shows great courage and resistance to events all around it with a worthy flourish of fresh foliage and the signs of a full crop of acorns should command a modicum of decorum.'

'Rory you are Irish to the hilt with words flowing out of you like the Guinness flows in.'

Rory laughed and reached out for Mavis's hand. 'And you fair maiden should dance and sing for Rupert's dad and end up in motion pictures to beguile us all with your wit and charm while us poor mortals ooh and aah in our plush theatre seats watching you soar to stardom.'

'Crap,' announced Doris.

'Now is that an order, a suggestion, a discovery, a confession or just a four-letter word?' asked Rory.

'Time to go I think,' said Rupert.

'We're further east than last time so we have to cut back somewhere along here to reach that Education Centre. You said that Reverend was talking about three Rupert and it's getting on for that now. We'd better cut across this open field. I think that will be quicker according to the map.'

'You sure Ted? We'll have to go over the fence then,' said Rupert. 'Look for a stile chaps or someway over this fence. It's high.'

'Doesn't look like they've planted any trees in there although I can see fresh stumps so it must have been a plantation or forest compartment just lately,' added Rory.

'There's no stile Rupert. We'll climb over,' said Doris.

'But it's so high,' said Philippa rather obviously as they all could see the fence was eight feet high in front of them.

'High to keep deer out,' suggested Rory as he was a wildlife biologist after all and did know something about the forest.

'Fine, but not us,' said Doris and she promptly swung up onto the fence to reach the top.

'It's getting closer to three o'clock,' urged Philippa, 'and I do want to hear the Reverend. Come on Margaret. Climb up alongside me here next to Doris.'

The fence was designed to deter deer. It was high but made of open webbing on top of three feet of conventional fencing and netting to deter rabbits and other smaller creatures. It was also important to keep the rather special sheep inside from any extraneous outside influences. However, it was not designed to support four swinging adult females as Mavis joined the group. The staples opened, the netting peeled away from the tall fenceposts and the four girls fell to the ground leaving a large hole in the fence and four bruised backsides.

'Shit,' exclaimed Doris and she looked angrily at the fence and felt her tender derriere.

'Another order, suggestion, discovery, etc. like last time?' asked Rory laughing. 'Are you considering suing Doris dear?'

'I might,' came a new voice.

Turning from the disarray at the fence the group found themselves looking at Sylvia Lord again only this time she was not smiling and not accompanied by her husband. Instead she had a young lad on a smaller horse with her.

'They tore it down Grandma. They ripped the fence. Now they've got tender behinds,' and the little lad laughed. His horse turned her head to look at her rider. He leant forwards and stroked her neck. 'Hush now Dainty. Don't frighten the people when they're hurt.'

'But I might frighten the people,' said Sylvia, 'whether you are hurt or not. I thought we understood each other last week? Did I not make myself clear enough?'

'You should put in a stile,' exclaimed Doris standing up tall. 'Anybody with any sense of decency and public spirit would have put in a stile. It's required, as you can now see. If there had been a stile this wouldn't have happened. It's obvious who is to blame.'

Sylvia sat on Sir Galahad impassively. Her horse also turned his head and looked at Sylvia as if to say, 'Well your ladyship. Shall I stomp on her or will you?'

'What was wrong with the forest ride?' Sylvia asked looking at Rupert.

'Nothing mam,' replied Rupert.

'It's a charming ride,' added Rory, 'and quite in keeping with the beauty of the forest. This beautiful day it is a sight to behold it is.'

'Rory shut it!' shouted Doris. 'This is serious you fool. We could have been hurt. We could have been killed. Philippa you sure you haven't hurt that ankle? Mavis you cried out. What damage did you do?'

'A lot,' said Sylvia, 'quite unnecessarily I might add. Damage to my property.'

'They broke it Grandma. They pulled it down. Things will get in. Auntie Stephanie's sheep can get out. She'll be cross Grandma.'

'Yes James, Stephanie will be cross and so am I. Right now I should add. And disappointed. We made an offer of friendship and trust last week I seem to remember.'

'We were trying to take a short-cut to the Education Centre,' blurted out Ted. 'We were late to hear that Reverend whatshisname.'

'One hundred yards further down this ride you would have found a path leading to the Education Centre,' said Sylvia loftily from her saddle. 'A little effort and thought might have avoided this contretemps.'

'They broke it Grandma. Dainty hold up. Stop nuzzling into that bag. Grandma Dainty won't stop.'

Sylvia moved Sir Galahad over towards James and made Dainty get her nose out of Margaret's rucksack which was lying on the ground. She had dropped it when she started to climb the fence.

'Fine. Here's what we do. You walk down the ride, through the beeches and you'll come to another ride which will take you to the Education Centre if you turn right. I do not want to see any of you at Fotheringham again. I don't think you are to be trusted.'

'What about the fence Grandma? Aunt Stephanie's sheep will get out.'

'We'll sort that out James, don't worry. Off the lot of you. Off and out of here.'

'You can't do that. We've got rights. We've....' but Doris stopped as Sylvia took photograph after photograph. She clicked at the fence, at the group and back at the fence again. 'You were saying?' Doris's mouth clicked shut like Sylvia's camera.

Without a word the group turned south and headed down the ride as Sylvia suggested.

'The fence Grandma?'

Sylvia swung down off Sir Galahad lightly onto her feet. She looked in the saddle bag she had and extracted some tools. Looking back at the fence she eased her horse up close and remounted. Carefully, just like a rock climb, she delicately stood up on the saddle and after speaking with her horse she repaired the torn fencing. James watched.

'Be prepared James. Always be prepared. That will hold until Monday when we can get it fixed properly. Your Auntie Stephanie's sheep will be fine now. So will we. Is Dainty ready? Good, we'll walk first, then canter and finally if you feel like it we will gallop. How about that?'

'Smashing Grandma. Like the fence was,' and the pair of them walked the two horses up the forest ride away from the Education Centre and the Reverend Godschild's exhortations to seek God and be his messenger on this earth.

'Toby Dobbs, but it is good to see you again. Gloria told me you would come calling. Would you like to come in? You too dear,' Tilley added looking at Lola. Gloria will be home soon from her morning at the tea-shop. I've just been saying a few prayers for her you know.'

Toby and Lola walked in and sat with Tilley in the living room. Wendell came crashing down the stairs and poked his head into the room.

'Who's the old geezer Mum, and the tarty bird?'

'Wendell dear, come in and be introduced properly. You really must learn some better manners. All that time you spend in your room and on your computer. You never speak to real people now do you?'

'So who are they then? Ain't they got tongues? Little prissy mouths on both of 'em. Oy, you, Mister, I'm talking to you. Who are you sitting in my house then?'

Toby rose and his full five feet six didn't come too high on Wendell's frame. 'I'm a friend of your mother's son, an old friend. And the lady is a friend of mine and a friend of your sisters. I'm Toby Dobbs,' and Toby held out his hand.

'Load of old bollocks,' Wendell said. 'My mum ain't got any friends, though you are old as you say. As for 'er, she's a tart and no mistake. Can see that a mile off. Ain't you love? A real tart, just like my sister. Tarts the pair of you. I'm off. Don't be here when I'm back though 'cos I've things to do.'

Wendell walked out and the three of them heard the front door slam.

'You lock the car Toby?' Lola asked suspiciously. 'Want to go and look at the tyres or for key marks down your bonnet?' Lola looked at Tilley Manson but she seemed to have gone inside herself. 'Jesus Toby, what are you going to do here?'

They heard the door open again and Lola went into a defence position thinking it was Wendell returning. The door to the living room opened and Gloria walked in.

'Why you all looking at me like that?' she asked. 'You look like you're expecting an attack or something.'

'Your charming little brother Wendell just met us and wasn't impressed Gloria. I could do things to that boy. Things he might remember for a while and would help him improve his manners,' Lola said with vengeance in her voice.

'Look,' Toby said, 'why don't we let Gloria get changed into something relaxing and then as it is such a nice day why don't we take Tilley here out for a drive? Take the four of us out and we can show her some fun places, see some people and let her see a bit more than just the village. What do you say Gloria? How about a quick trip down to the sea? Say, you two both swim. Why don't we go down to the sea-side and while Tilley and I reminisce you two can go for a dip? You said you swim Gloria and I know that Lola does. Be a nice change for all of us. Bet you haven't been in the ocean for a while Lola? Bet your mother hasn't been out of the village for a while Gloria? You go and change Gloria and sort out some costume for Lola. I know you two exchange clothes so that's not a problem. I'll talk with Tilley here while you two get changed.'

Slowly swirling around in his brain Toby the Fixer had the glimmerings of a plan. He thought it might work given Tilley's state of mind. Somehow, through God he thought we can bring this woman back and that will please Gloria. Like a daughter she is to me thought Toby. I like all the other girls too but Gloria I always thought of as someone special. It didn't take long for Gloria and Lola to get fixed up with clothes and costumes and the four of them packed themselves into the car, which still had four firm tyres and didn't boast any keymarks.

The water on the Somerset coast is not warm even in the height of summer and this was still the end of May. It had been a sunny week and so the sand was quite hot underfoot but the edge of the Bristol Channel was cool on the body. Gloria and Lola stripped down to their costumes and ran shrieking into the ocean. Toby slowly walked Tilley down to the water's edge and taking off their shoes and socks he gently held Tilley's arm as they paddled. Washing away any sins he said. The two young women swam about vigorously, dunked each other, splashed and shouted around for some ten minutes or more before they both ran strongly up the beach to grab towels.

'Jesus Gloria but I haven't done that for a while.'

'Neither have I, well not in salt water. Easier to swim in though, just tastes bloody awful. Look, grab a towel and rub my back. Then I'll do yours.'

'Anything you want sweetheart,' murmured Lola and wrapped her arms around Gloria.

'Right now Lola I want a dry back and then I'll towel you. Once that's done we'll walk with the towels and dry off in this warm sunshine. We can go and walk with Toby and my mum. He's got some plan going on. I can sense it.'

Very gradually Toby moved with Tilley deeper and deeper into the water. He talked about the use of water to help people. He even talked about some of the Groups he used to manage that came over from the States.

'Some of them had funny ways you know Tilley. Even though they played wild music with crazy words some of those kids were church-going, some very tied to Sunday and the washing away of sins. Funny world and you were there as part of that Tilley,' said Toby. 'You were there and it was part of your life. You remember those days?'

Tilley muttered something and Toby asked, 'What's that Tilley? No, we can't go back to those days darling. We can never go back love but we can move on. Look at me? I've moved on. I'd like to see you move on. Think about washing away the ties on you. Think about washing away the barriers to moving on. Some of the Groups used to wash away their sins and go back out on stage and be great, be fantastic, be wild and girls like you would go wild too. They've all moved on now Tilley. We've all moved on love. Move with us. Let a little of the water cast off the shackles and move forwards with us.'

Gloria and Lola walked quietly behind listening mesmerised to Toby's slow but firm voice. It almost lulled you into belief Gloria thought afterwards. Toby the Fixer is going to move my mum. Tilley walked alongside Toby holding his arm as the waves surged in and out around her legs. He held her firmly so there was no lack of balance. Like a rock he was as the water surged around his knees and sometimes higher as he was outside of her and he wasn't tall. The voice and the water soothed her. She felt emotions drain away and she felt more at peace within herself. Now and then she heard Gloria or Lola say something but mostly all she heard was Toby and his quiet persuasive voice. After half an hour or so they all turned round and started walking back the same way. It was a productive afternoon and the journey home in the car was low key yet somehow victorious. Although Toby suggested it Tilley wasn't keen on going to the pub with them and so after she had cooked a meal Toby decided to stay at home with Tilley while Gloria and Lola walked down to the George.

'He's smooth Gloria. I'll say that for him. I think he's halfway there. What did he say about tomorrow?'

'He's interested in what Gary and I have found and we'll all go and look tomorrow morning. There is less likelihood of anyone being around at that time in the weekend and I know Daniel Lord and that Katya will be away. He always plays golf on Sunday mornings and she goes too.'

'Twiddles his club does she?' asked Lola and she giggled. 'Didn't know American girls did that,' she added.

'I reckon. Hell, they've been going out now since I came back here and that's ages ago. He's not a very passionate bloke if he hasn't had his leg over by now. Still, that Lord family is a funny lot. They're all different. The parents as well as the kids that is. Anyway, she's stayed around and she's a typical American in some ways.'

'What about your mum?'

'Toby reckons that the answer is in the water. Leastways, that is what he said. I asked him what water? In fact I asked him what the hell he was on about?'

'And he said?'

'How did I enjoy this afternoon?'

'And how did you enjoy this afternoon?'

'Jesus Lola don't you start going weird on me. I'm having enough problem with my mum and then Toby starts talking in riddles about bloody water and now you've gone off your nut.'

Lola held Gloria's arm and slid her hand down into Gloria's. She squeezed and pulled Gloria around to face her standing there on the pavement. Slowly holding Gloria's chin in her hand she gently kissed Gloria on the lips. 'You're special you know Gloria love. You're special to me and special to Toby in his own way. Toby wants to wash away your mother's supposed sins. He thinks she has some enormous hang-up over something. He doesn't think he needs to find out what it is but he thinks he can use your mother's love of God and the symbolism of washing away sins to help move your mother forwards. That was partly what he did this afternoon. He started the process and your mother reacted favourably. He wants to continue tomorrow.'

'Tomorrow afternoon you mean, after we've done our tour of the forest in the morning?'

'Exactly.'

'But I swim with Tony on Sunday afternoons.'

'Exactly, and Toby wants you both there, holding hands in the water with him. He's going to exorcise your sins and free your mother.'

'Jesus Christ,' Gloria said.

'Well not quite,' said Lola, 'but a small present-day approximation. A sort of stand-in performance as the main act couldn't show. Toby Dobbs back as Toby the Fixer. Always with a trick or two up his sleeve to cover contingencies.'

When Lola and Gloria walked into the bar there was an animated discussion going on. Seeing who was involved Gloria continued on towards George.

'You didn't bar my friend Lola here now did you George? She was nicely tucked up in her own bed last Sunday morning. Two pints George please. What's all the aggro over in the corner?'

'Don't ask me,' said George as he drew two pints and passed them across the counter.

'But I am asking you George. I don't like pitching into fights until I know the rules, or at least know the cause.'

'Seems some hikers were walking through Fotheringham looking for that Education Centre and they did a bit of damage. Knocked down one of the fences or something. Sylvia Lord caught them in the act.'

'Christ, and they're still walking. Lady Sylvia doesn't take no bull-shit from anyone. So who's shouting the odds?'

'Well there's Daniel over there along with his sister. And they've also got that American lass and then Samantha has Terence Field in tow again. Wonder about those two. Would make a good couple if they ever had time for anything other than work. That little lad James needs a sensible parent along with his crazy mother.'

'Why, what has Samantha gone and done now?'

'When she's not out up to London dragging folk all around the country she's off rock climbing with young Beverley Nichols.'

'But she's another copper,' exclaimed Gloria.

'WPC Nichols is a fine girl Gloria. She's smart, good-looking and apparently does her job real good. Toby and Mary Traver's praise her and of course Betty won't hear a word said against her.'

'Hell fire George, since I left you've gone all holy or something praising coppers. Who are the other people 'cos I know all the ones you mentioned?'

'The tall good-looking blond lad is Rupert Oldshaw. When I heard his name I thought it rang a bell and then I remembered.'

'What George?'

'Isn't Magnus Oldshaw a big name in films? Isn't he some hot shot director or something? Famous he is. I'm sure that's his son. He's got the bearing and the attitude.'

'And who else 'cos there are two other girls over there in the corner that I don't know? I remember the faces 'cos they were in here a week or so ago. Lola here sorted out that little bossy bird with the glasses.'

'Don't know their names but they are with Rupert. One is all over him like a bloody limpet and the other has a mouth on her you can hear all the way around the village. She's sharp-tongued that one. The little bird with the glasses.'

Gloria supped on her pint and looked over the rim of the glass at Lola. 'Are you up for a little village entertainment? Think we should join the party and see how we can liven things up a little?' Lola smiled at Gloria and ran her tongue cheekily over her lips. She turned to look at George. 'We won't do anything naughty,' she promised and she winked at him. The two girls lifted their glasses and walked over to the corner.

'But we didn't realise it was so lightly stapled,' Rupert was saying.

'Should be a stile,' insisted Doris. 'Absolutely obvious to anyone sensible. That fence needs a stile.'

'And you would have gone through the stile not knowing what was inside the fence?' asked Daniel. 'There could have been dangerous animals in there.'

'There had better not be or I'll really come down heavy.'

'But I thought you did come down heavy,' retorted Samantha, 'on your behind I hear.'

'Keep out of this lady. This fight is the people versus the hoi polloi.'

244

'You need to get your facts right then,' stated Katya deciding to join in. 'The lady as you rightly say is Lady Sylvia's daughter and if you take on Samantha here you've less sense than I credit you with.'

'Keep out of this Yank,' snarled Doris. 'This is the English downtrodden versus the high and mighty. Typical class fight and your lot don't understand that. You're all the same, robotically useless and interfering into things you don't understand.'

Daniel stood up quickly and looked bloody angry. 'Slander is against the law lady. Being rude is just bad manners. Being ignorant is no excuse. An apology please or I will consider action.'

Rupert decided things had gone far enough which was just as well as Samantha could feel Terence stirring beside her. She gently laid her hand on his arm.

'Back off Doris and apologise. There is no need for any of this. Please say you're sorry as you don't know these people. We did damage the fence and I didn't realise how it was constructed. Doris, I don't hear an apology.' Rupert looked very directly at Doris and Mavis moved towards her.

'Sure, should be a bloody stile though. Here, Yank, here's my hand. I take back my remarks, well kind of.'

'Doris!' exclaimed Rupert. 'We would like to return to this part of the world and we don't need an armed barricade every time we set foot here. Apologise properly.'

Doris grudgingly held out her hand towards Katya. Katya stood up and smiled at Doris. 'I accept your apology. Actually, I'm not a Yank but then you don't understand us Americans either now do you?'

'Can we join in the apologies?' asked Gloria as she walked up to the group. 'Hi Daniel, hi Katya, Samantha and it's Detective Inspector Field isn't it?' Gloria quickly turned and walked straight up to Rupert. 'And you dear boy must be the son of that gorgeous and talented Magnus. You look so like your handsome father. May I shake your hand?' and of course

Gloria has to come up close as she does so which caused an immediate response from Mavis. Gloria swung round quickly, still holding Rupert's hand. 'Didn't you know Detective Inspector Field was here my dear?' Her eyes flicked between Mavis and Doris as she said this trying to see who was the most embarrassed. Letting go of Rupert's hands she turned again and spoke to Lola. 'I'm forgetting my manners Lola. This is Daniel Lord and his friend Katya. This is Samantha MacRae, Daniel's sister and her friend Detective Inspector Terence Field. Folks this is my friend Lola Martinez from London.' Quickly Gloria spun around one more time 'And I was right about your dear daddy?' she asked. 'So you are….?'

The whole group had been somewhat mesmerised by this spinning twirl of words from Gloria including Rupert. He was taken aback for a moment before Mavis spoke, 'He's Rupert Oldshaw of course, and I'm Mavis Taylor, Rupert's best friend and this is Doris Lyon. We're all from Bristol and a group of us hike. Well we hiked today and we were looking for the Education Centre at Fotheringham but we got a little lost. We wanted to hear the Reverend Godschild. No, not all of us I suppose but two of our group did, didn't they Rupert? But they're not with us now. They drove home earlier. That's Philippa and Margaret and they're awfully Christian but don't believe in evolution unlike two other members of our group. And they're…..'

Mavis tailed off and sat down. She'd quite run out of things to say.

'And did this Revered Godschild convert the other members of your group Mavis or just convince this Philippa and Margaret who are not here that they were holier than the rest of you and so their sins would be forgiven? Because, if I heard correctly when Lola and I came in, the group of you did sin today. Whether there was a stile or not it surely is a sin to pull down the Lord fence, especially as it was the Lord's fence if you see my point? Doesn't the good book say thou shall not trespass? Did they trespass Daniel?'

'Gloria it's sorted thanks very much,' said Daniel. 'My mother sorted it on the spot.'

'But little Miss four eyes here is still ranting and raving I hear.'

'Yes, no, yes Gloria but she apologised,' said Rupert.

Gloria moved smoothly but quickly to Rupert's side and looked into his eyes. 'But did she mean it Rupert dear?' and she slid her hand down over his chest. 'Can I call you bear?' she suddenly asked. 'Rupert Bear sounds much better than Rupert Oldshaw. I shall call you bear. I think that suits. Don't you Lola?'

'You take the bear Gloria and I'll take the bear's best friend,' said Lola as she walked towards Mavis.

It was about this time that I walked into the George, right on the heels of Freddie and his usual three cronies. While the four of them went straight up to the bar I did a quick look around. Saturday night but the darts team was playing away tonight so it was a little quieter. I noticed Gloria over in the corner with Daniel Lord and his sister plus their usual friends and three other folk I didn't know. Lola was there too and it looked like Gloria and Lola were putting on some kind of show because the rest of them were just sitting there watching Gloria and Lola.

'Gary, you're just in time to rescue Gloria here and her friend,' called out Daniel. I watched Gloria peel herself off the tall blond bloke with the white frightened face and Lola turned to me with a mischievous smile. 'Why Gary, where have you been all my life?' and she walked over towards me with her arms outstretched. What the fuck was going on was all I could think about when Freddie's voice cut through the sudden quiet.

'Gloria love, leave the blond ponce alone and join us real people. Evening all,' and Freddie raised his glass.

Whatever tension there might have been at that time was shattered by Freddie's inane remark and Gloria and Lola came towards me while Freddie and his mates went to play darts. I looked at the people behind

Gloria and Lola. I nodded to Daniel Lord and his sister and made eye contact with that Katya and Terence Field. I didn't know the other three, including the blond ponce who hadn't understood or risen to Freddie's comment.

'What was that all about?' I asked Gloria.

'Just Lola and I stirring up the locals Gary. Never you mind your pretty little head my love. Come and tell Auntie Gloria and Auntie Lola all about your new over the moon discovery. We're all set to go and see tomorrow morning.'

'So what you doing this evening?' I asked looking at both of them.

'Gary you don't have the stamina darling for tonight and tomorrow morning and tomorrow is more important. So this evening we'll just have a quiet drink and talk about our options tomorrow.'

Well it would have been a quiet evening but of course Freddie got lathered pretty quick for a Saturday night. He must have won at darts or something because it wasn't long before he wanted to join us and show his mates how much he and Gloria were an item. I could hear them egging him on and teasing him that he was losing his touch. Course that just made it worse and Freddie became all touch until even Gloria stopped his pawing all over her. George got in the act and told Freddie to cool it. When Terence Field came up to the bar to order some more drinks Freddie pushed too hard and Terence told him to sober up or ship out. He could ring PC Meadows without too much trouble but he didn't want to do that. Freddie caught the drift of the tone of voice and managed to stagger back to his mates. Terence looked at the three of us but he was mostly interested in Lola. He didn't say anything but I could hear the wheels going round in his head.

'Gary we're off mate. I've got to get back and check my mum's okay with Toby. He's been a big help Gary. He's really got my mum on the road back.'

'Sure sure,' I muttered although I was pissed off about going home alone. I looked at Lola and she winked. 'Think we should let Gloria go off alone Gary do you? Think you can look after me? Walk me home afterwards?'

'Where you staying anyway Lola? Don't expect George is letting you stay here again after last weekend.'

'Why ever not Gary? Gina and I slept in our own beds, not like some people we know eh?' and she giggled as she looked at Gloria and put her arm around her. 'Come on love. Let's check our Toby hasn't washed too many sins away from your mother. Probably find that prat of a brother has come back to queer the pitch. Someone needs to teach that bugger a good lesson but Toby's not the one. We need to find another way to straighten out your bloody brother. More food for thought Gary, unless you can't handle more than one thought at a time love. Right now your thoughts are wasted though 'cos Gloria and I are going home together. Just us love,' and Lola linked her arm through Gloria's and walked her to the door. 'Night all,' she said and the pair of them walked out.

I hadn't noticed but the three strangers had left too and the Lord family foursome was still chatting in the corner. I caught the fact that Daniel would be out on the golf course tomorrow morning along with Katya and that confirmed my first thoughts. Wasn't sure where madcap Samantha would be though although there was some talk about climbing somewhere but I didn't know where or with whom. Just have to be careful tomorrow I thought. Good practice though if the idea works out. I drove home thinking that Lola was a handful but Gloria had told me she was more inclined to make ladies happy. Looking at her though I thought she could keep anyone happy. We'll have to see whether I can make her and Gloria happy tomorrow.

RESCUE, REBIRTH AND REFURBISHMENTS

THAT LAST SUNDAY IN MAY was hot. As I sit in this cold damp cell I imagine I can still feel the warmth and excitement of that day. Sitting here it doesn't feel real but then again a good part of that early summer wasn't real now was it? However, telling you this story as I'm waiting here I try to remember that most fairy stories have happy endings. I'll think positive on that one 'cos for the moment I don't think that's likely to be true.

Once again, early on a Sunday morning Daniel found that he could play the first hole well. Now it might have been that his caddie looked particularly lovely that morning but then again he told himself if you've got the talent flaunt it. The usual other three members of Larry, Peter and Alan had all bogied the first hole and Daniel looked at Katya as he stood on the second tee box with the honour.

'Straight Daniel,' was all Katya said and Daniel listened and executed perfectly. He handed her back the driver and smiled as she dutifully slid it into the bag.

'Good teamwork,' he whispered as Alan practised his swing before launching his ball down the fairway. The bright sunshine continued as the five happy people walked their way around the golf course. Well, some of them were happy now and again but then that is golf so they tell me.

Closer to Fotheringham Manor three other people were walking around in the bright sunshine. Lola had borrowed Toby's car and with Gloria and me she had carefully and quietly driven out of the village and down the main road. Following my instructions she pulled off the road onto a shadowy forest ride and into the depths of the forest. At a leisurely pace Lola steered the car between the rows of trees and over a slight rise before the ride dipped gently into a hollow and the trees opened up around a sunlit clearing. There stood the infamous Ferris cottage.

'We're not going to Enrico's to look at that first?' asked Gloria. 'I thought you said you and Freddie had painted that one. That would look smarter Gary.'

'I also told you we painted that one for some new workers Gloria. You should listen more. Open the ears rather than other things.'

'Cool it you two,' said Lola. 'Park out of sight Gary or don't it matter?'

'Here'll do,' I said. 'You two can walk that far can't you?' I asked as I looked at the hundred yards or so to the cottage.

'Cheeky sod you are at times Gary,' said Lola and she switched off the engine. Opening the door Lola noticed how peaceful it was. 'This is lovely Gary. It isn't what I expected.'

'Yes love, we aim to please,' I said and we closed the car doors and walked towards the cottage.

'You thinking of coming in the way we did?' asked Gloria.

'Yes. The main road's got bends in it so it's not obvious where and when you turn. The actual turnoff isn't that easy to see unless you know what you're looking for and this forest ride is well away from any of the other buildings on the estate. Best of all the cottage itself is down in this little hollow so you can't see any lights from any road or house. I think this is just what you are after.'

'Simple yes would have done Gary,' Gloria said and she held Lola's arm as they walked across the flagged backyard past an old pump to the backdoor.

'Who's been digging?' Lola asked as she stopped on the edge of the yard and looked at the patch of ground that had been Betty's garden.

'That's last October,' I said. 'Young Peter Lord and your Tony Gloria were out here doing some school project or other. That Daniel Lord had them digging a soil pit.'

'What for?'

'So they could see what kind of dirt we've got. It's all different underneath. Some sort of layers like a cake and the trees like some layers and not others. Christ, I don't know Lola. I ain't no forester. I just work here. Something for school.'

'Just asking Gary. Thought you said this place was full of bodies. Don't fancy people finding any more on our doorstep. Do we Gloria?'

Gloria had already opened the back door and was prowling around the kitchen inspecting.

'This place could do with a brush and pan Gary. Get Daniel Lord to ask you to clean this one up too.'

'No way. Freddie freaked out when Bob Edwards told him to tidy Enrico's and Freddie thought we might have to clean this one too. Were his cousins that were buried in this cottage you know. Here, I'll show you.'

'Fuck off Gary. We don't need the gory details mate. We're here for business not a Jack the Ripper tour. Rooms got potential. How about the bedrooms? They're more important. Ain't they Lola?' Lola laughed and pushed me towards the back of the cottage.

'Come on Gary,' she said. 'Let me lead you to my boudoir and Gloria can watch you jump while I crack my little whip.'

Stone me if she didn't open up her bag and pull out a black short-handled whip and start flicking it around. 'Jump baby, jump for me,' she laughed and prodded me with the handle. Gloria and Lola checked out the bedrooms and looked around the bathroom, the closet (where Freddie's cousins had finally rested for all those years) and came back into the kitchen come living room.

'Gary my love we may have struck pay dirt or some such appropriate expression. With a little bit of this and that and a couple of additions in the furniture line we may have ourselves a new place to play. What do you think Lola?'

'Good place to start,' she said. 'We'll see how it goes. We need Belle down here 'cos she's a dab hand at electricity and lighting. Don't know where she learnt all that but she knows which is the red wire and which is the green. You're right about the furniture though Gloria. We need a couple of professional additions but we've got those back in London. I'll fix all that. Can you change those curtains in the bedroom?'

Gloria said she could fix those and I sat down at the kitchen table and looked around. Never would believe what happened here last September. Of course I personally never saw it, all the blood I mean. There was Idwal Ferris bollock-naked shooting this silly tart he had brought down here with him and having his end away with Betty Ferris. She had been waving a knife around apparently and had cut Idwal a few times so he was mad. In storms John Ferris and before his brother could stop fucking and reach the gun John ups and cuts his brother's throat. Bob Edwards said it was like a slaughter-house. Looking at the walls and floor I couldn't see any blood. I suddenly started back and sat upright. I had had my elbows on the table. The same table where Idwal had his throat slashed. I must have been peering rather wildly about me 'cos Gloria looked real close at me when she asked, 'You look like you've seen a ghost Gary. Snap out of it mate. That's all past. House of fun and frolics this is, or it soon will be, eh Lola?'

'You've never seen the likes young Gary. Be your special education the next couple of weeks. You'll see things you've never even imagined. Well, you will if you do your bit the way we see it. You explained anything yet Gloria?'

Explained anything I thought. What was there to explain? The girls wanted a quiet place to kip when they came down from London, away from the George. Sure they might have a few parties out here with it being so hidden and quiet. That's what Gloria had asked for. Somewhere out of the way where they couldn't be seen. Bring in some beer, maybe some vodka or scotch if you like that stuff. Even end up back in bed if you were lucky. Great place.

'Gary you seen the web?'

'Of course,' I said, 'but we can clean those out. Sweep them out the corners you know. Freddie and I had to do that at Enrico's before we painted. Found a few but then you expect them in the forest now don't you?'

'No Gary, not spider's webs, the web, the internet, the computer world of tying us all together and communicating.'

'No Gloria, not my thing. I don't have time. That's Tom Daley's world and he's a bloody pervert. Might have some good grass but I don't do that a lot either. Makes me sleepy. Doesn't your wanker of a brother bury his head in all that shit? Isn't he some kind of computer nerd?'

'It's like the telephone Gary, although better than the telephone. Suppose you don't know what a cell phone is either?'

'Give over, 'cos I do. Seen that Samantha Lord with the stupid thing pressed to her head. She seems to have it fixed there all the time. Don't know what she finds to yip yap about but I rarely see her without it. What's that got to do with this web thing?'

'No worry Gary. It's not important. Look, here's what we've got in mind. We'll fix this place up a bit and then the girls will have a place to stay when they come down. Our house is not big enough for any party so we can use this place for that as well. Now we've got a few friends of the girls who will want to come down too Gary and we want you to be the guide. We don't want other people knowing about this. You said and I've also heard that no-one in the village wants to come out to this place. It has too many memories for most folk here in the village so we're not likely to be disturbed. Right now I've heard Daniel Lord say his family is just going to leave it while they decide what to do but that might be ages so for the while we'll have it. We won't do any damage and no-one will be any the wiser. You understand all that?'

Made sense to me. Seemed a bloody brilliant idea but then I thought of this cottage in the first place and so it seemed I was right on track with Gloria's idea.

'So what's this guiding thing then? Why can't you tell the blokes where to go?'

'The girls like to keep the blokes guessing Gary. Makes it more exciting for a john if he's not sure where he'll end up. Bit of an adventure and a turn on. So, we'll arrange for you to meet them somewhere obvious in the village. There's lots of visitors, tourists and such in the village right now and so the extra car and warm body isn't going to raise any eyebrows. It'll be an evening meet so we thought the pub was probably the best. We'll arrange it for the car park so they needn't even show their faces in the George itself. That way old sticky-beak George won't see them come and go and wonder who they are. You pick 'em up in the car park and bring 'em out here.'

'But then they'll know where,' I said. 'Any bloke with half a brain could find his way out here again. Once you've found the turning you follow your nose. Can't miss this place. Only place out here. Shit, even dumbass Freddie could manage that, or even his more stupid mate Lester. Think Dora will want to join in the parties? She'd fit in Gloria. She'd think it a right giggle. Jesus, wouldn't brother Lester do his nut if he knew half of what she gets up to now?'

'Gary, we're keeping this out-of-town mate. This is not a village party and that's why we've picked here. No-one in the village will come and that includes Dora. You and I can play with Dora elsewhere. You're right, she's a great kid but we'll keep that game going somewhere else. Understood? Lola and I don't want to hear you and her have been teaching each other things to blow her brother's mind out here. Lots of other open space for that Gary.'

'Sure Gloria, I hear you. So what's this pickup thing then? How we going to fix it so the blokes don't know where they're going?'

'Same way as up in London Gary. It's all part of the wind up and when the bloke gets here he's already in the party mood and excited. The girls get a great charge out of the bloke already in the mood and he can't wait to see the action. It's like a stage show where they eventually draw the curtains and you get to see what you've been waiting for. You explain Lola while I go and have one more look.'

Lola walked over to me sitting on a kitchen table chair. 'Here Gary. Let me sit on your lap love and little Lola will whisper in your ear. I'll tell you a trade secret sweetheart and you'll be on the team. Special you are Gary Templeton, very special.'

Of course I didn't know it at the time but now I know how special I am. When Lola came and sat on my lap she didn't know how special but she thought it was a right giggle later when she did find out. She and her friends helped Gloria like they always did in the last act before the grand finale but we'll come to that later.

'Now Gary, you sitting comfortably love? I'm only a little girl and I'll whisper sweet nothings in your ear. When our friends come down and meet you in the parking lot we'll arrange a special code, like a spy story or something dead exciting. You meet them and make sure they're the real thing. We don't want no surprises and we don't want to see the Bill so you've an important job Gary out there. You understand darling?'

Lola settled more comfortably on my lap and wriggled her tits in my face. She leant her head over until her tongue tickled in my ear. 'You hear me Gary?' she whispered and she wriggled her bum. I couldn't help it. I know she was a lesbian, well that's what Gloria told me she preferred but shit she wriggled and I responded.

'I can feel you listening to me Gary,' she purred in my ear and she wriggled some more.

'Now darling, the blokes will be expecting you to check out the passwords and accept the blindfold.'

Like a thick shit I asked, 'What blindfold?' but my mind was distracted by Lola's body which was making me think of all sorts of things and not about blokes in cars either.

'Gary, pay attention love. After you've checked them out with the magic words you tell 'em to let you blindfold them as a special part of the trip. Heightens the excitement you say and so you wrap a blindfold around their head. We'll give you the gear so don't worry. We know what works. I know what works Gary,' and Lola ran her tongue around my ear and her hands slipped inside my shirt. I certainly wasn't cold but my little nipples were hard when Lola nipped them with her fingers.

'Good to see you're paying attention Gary,' she said. 'Now, once they are blindfolded and sitting in your car you drive out of the village and around a few of these wonderful twisty laneways. After a while, when everyone is hopelessly confused you slowly drive up here but again you go on past and circle around a little before coasting back to the cottage. We'll check where best to park but it maybe where I did this morning. Then, after you have stopped you come round and help the blokes out of the car. You all hold hands and you walk slowly in a series of loops and turns as if navigating a series of corridors until you come to the back door and we'll all troop in. We may have the girls outside to hold their hands for the last bit. We'll think about that but once inside and the door closed then curtain time.'

'And I pull open the curtains?' I asked now quite aroused with the vision and the feeling of Lola.

'No love you have another special job. Your work isn't finished yet. Once we are all nicely inside we need a guard. We need a patrol to check all is nice and quiet outside. We don't want any gate-crashers or any forest spooks to come without paying for the show so to speak. You listening to me Gary? I can feel you love but I'm not hearing you.'

'So I make sure everything is safe?'

'Yes love. Walk about a bit and do a lot of listening.'

'But won't the blokes know where they are at the end, when they get taken back? Who takes them back?'

'Our trusty guide Gary, you love. We'll call it a night sometime before it's light and you run them quietly back to the George, blindfolded again of course. Back at their own cars it's been another night of surprise and success. Should work a treat, just like London but with a nicer atmosphere.'

Thinking back there were a million and one questions I should have asked but Lola was occupying my mind and making sure I heard her words. 'Blindfolded,' she whispered as she slid off my lap and placed her hands over my eyes. Suddenly I felt another pair of hands on my knees, sliding up my thighs and feeling my response to Lola's wriggling. Lips moistly ran over mine and a tongue flicked at my lips. Gloria I realised. Both girls let go and giggled.

'You little hussies,' I said and stood up to catch one of them.

'My Gary, I can see how well you listened to my friend here. She obviously explains things so they are as plain as a pikestaff and what a pikestaff!'

The two of them curled over with laughing. I reached out and caught Gloria's arm. She let herself be caught and I pulled her hard against me. She wrapped her arms around my neck and opening her mouth she kissed me hard and long. Lola came over and wrapped her arms around the pair of us. We stood there switching mouths and tongues.

'Deal Gary? Think we can manage this?'

I signed my life away with a kiss and my hands on her and Lola's buttocks.

Although I might have been a major player in the morning's action I wasn't there that afternoon at the river. Gloria told me afterwards how she and Lola continued their playacting but this time the other players were Toby Dobbs and Tilley Manson. In his own way Tony Lord was involved too although he never knew all the dialogue that went on between Toby and Tilley. Sunday afternoon, warm and sunny and the pool of the river was fresh but certainly not cold. Tony Lord swam slowly and steadily lap after lap up and down his uncle's line of anchored bottles.

'Water's fine again Gloria,' he called as he rolled over into back stroke and saw Gloria appear on the bank. 'That new?' he asked as he looked at Gloria's costume. 'Looks real good,' he said but he blushed and promptly sank under the water so she wouldn't notice.

True enough Gloria had bought a new costume and she had worn it yesterday when out with Lola in the ocean. She'd rinsed the salt water out and let it dry. The material had shrunk just a little and now it fitted like a glove and Gloria enjoyed the sensation of what was covered and what wasn't. Far sexier than being naked she thought. She slid into the water and relished the cool feel over her body. Walking just behind Gloria were Lola, Toby and Tilley. As usual Toby was holding Tilley's arm and talking quietly but directly with Tilley.

'Just like yesterday Tilley remember. We walked in the water yesterday and we washed some of the old stuff away. I was telling you about Gloria and Lola and you watched. Right under they went and you could hear the old sins pour out. Shouting they were and releasing the devil. We all heard them. I heard you trying to shout too. Walking along in the water we could feel the pull of stuff floating away, being washed away. Gloria and Lola are here again today and that young Tony is teaching Gloria how to really get the feeling of forgiveness. See how he holds her. See how he breathes fresh life into her. Then see how he carefully tows her to shore. Life-saving Tilley. All done in the water. Come, we should paddle a little like yesterday. You told me you enjoyed yesterday. You said how much better you felt when we came home. Lets take off our shoes and walk in the water. It's Sunday. It's the Lord's Day. Watch Gloria and Lola feel the benefit of the water.'

Lola was wearing her costume under a blouse and skirt and she too walked into the water. 'Come Tilley,' she said. 'Come with me and Toby here. We helped Gloria and look how well she is doing. Young Tony is working wonders with her but she needed help. When she came to London we all helped her Tilley. Gloria was so thankful she wanted us to come and help you.'

'Come Tilley. Feel the water,' and Toby held Tilley's arm as he walked further into the pool. The bottom was sandy and the river quite clear of weeds so it was easy to gradually move into the deeper water. Toby was now waist deep in the pool and not at all worried that he was normally dressed in trousers and shirt. Lola walked alongside Tilley and she held her other arm.

'We're washing it all away Tilley. I can feel the troubles washing away. Just like the Lord as he washed his people's sins away Tilley. He's here with us and helping as we help you. Gone is Tilley of today and when we walk out it will be the new Tilley. Gloria's mother will return along with life and happiness.'

Tony and Gloria had changed roles and Gloria was now pushing Tony as he placed his hands on her shoulders and leant back and she swam breast-stroke to move him across the pool. Gloria could hear most of this dialogue but she had agreed with Toby not to interfere. She wanted her mum back and she was prepared to go to any lengths to have it happen. When Toby explained what he and Lola had thought up she went along with it. Tony looked at Gloria and raised an inquiring eyebrow.

'I'm trying to help my mother Tony,' Gloria whispered. 'Just like you did I heard. I'm fighting to have people help her like your Auntie Samantha did. My friend Toby and Lola are trying to help my mother feel better.'

'I tried too Gloria,' said Tony, 'but I wasn't strong enough.'

Gloria gave him a hug and held her face close to his. 'I'm sure you did everything you could Tony. I'm lucky 'cos I've got two strong friends to help me and you didn't have anyone did you?'

'No,' said Tony, 'but I understand Gloria, I really do. I think you're brave to try so hard.'

'And I think you're sweet Tony,' and Gloria kissed him. Tony blushed and wriggled and feeling Gloria's body pressed against him he blushed even pinker.

'Race you,' he shouted when he was far enough away and he turned and swam as fast as he could. Gloria almost turned to wink at Lola but then she realised that might spoil the moment as she saw her mum nearly immersed now in the pool and short Toby trying hard to keep his feet. Lola stood the other side of her mum and was helping Toby hold Tilley.

'Born again Tilley, born again,' softly intoned Toby. 'Not back as my friend of old but back as my new friend, my new Tilley and her new life. Come Lola, let's walk our new friend to the side of the pool and sit and enjoy the warmth of the sun. We are like caterpillars to butterflies that have shed our old coats and are ready to spread our wings in a new lifestyle.'

Tilley slowly walked with Toby and Lola to the side of the pool. Lola collected a couple of the towels she had brought and sat beside Tilley and slowly and thoughtfully dried her hands, her arms, her hair. Toby took the other towel and knelt at Tilley's feet to dry them too. No words were spoken and it was quiet and peaceful: a baptism, a kind of resurrection, an allaying of old conflicts.

Gloria swam strongly after Tony who had gone beyond the buoys and was close to the current in the river itself. He turned and saw her close behind.

'Have a care here Gloria. The current is strong in the river itself. Keep back in the water of the pool where it is calmer.'

The current tugged and Gloria turned to swim back towards the pool. She didn't seem to be making any progress. She pulled hard with her arms but still she seemed to be standing still.

'Turn on your back,' shouted Tony, 'onto your back and kick like a frog. I'll get you. Remember what we learnt. Don't panic and we'll be fine.'

Gloria didn't feel fine. She felt frightened. She rolled on her back and kicked hard, frenziedly and thrashed her arms about. Suddenly Tony was in front of her and his determined face looked straight at her. He smiled and said, 'Fine, just like the lessons now Gloria. You lie back and kick. Hold your arms straight and hands on my shoulders and I do all the work. Remember?' and he smiled again. Gloria relaxed a little and felt less frightened but the current still tugged and she could feel it.

'Just like the lessons Gloria. You know how we do it. We both do this together. Kick and I'll push. Slowly now. No rush and we come through together. Keep kicking those legs and let me push you backwards. We're doing fine, we're making progress, we're nearly there.' The soft quiet voice, the gentle smile and the strong swimming of Tony all convinced Gloria to do as she was told for once. She lay back with her ears under water, her arms out straight to reach Tony's shoulders and she kicked. She felt her head pushing backwards through the water and she looked up at the blue sky and helped Tony. It seemed to go on and on and all the time Tony's quiet voice helped her do her part.

'You okay now? We're back in the safe part of the pool. It's still deep but there's no current now.'

Gloria let her arms fold and Tony's forward motion carried him into her arms. 'You saved me Tony,' she exclaimed. 'You really and truly saved me. That was not a lesson but you really saved me.' Gloria tightened her arms and hugged him. She wrapped her legs around him and kissed him. As Tony said the water was still deep and both of them promptly went under. With a flurry of arms and legs they separated and rose to the surface. 'Tony I'm sorry love. You were marvellous. It was real. You saved me.'

'Yes,' said Tony as he swam a little further away nervously. 'I know.'

'And I thanked you,' said Gloria.

'Yes,' said Tony, 'I know that too.'

'Tony it was a hug and a kiss of thank you. People get happy when you save their lives. I got happy when you saved my life. I thanked you.'

'I know,' said Tony for the third time but he still swam a little way away from Gloria. 'We should go in now. You will be tired and a little in

263

shock. People always go into shock when they think they are drowning. We were taught about shock. You need to get warm and dry. You should wrap up and feel safe. We should go in. I'll follow and make sure you are safe.'

Tony trod water until he saw Gloria roll over and swim towards the bank and the other three. Only then did he leisurely crawl through the water after Gloria, but still keeping his distance from the lips and legs. They sat towelling off on the bank of the pool. Tony rather quickly pulled on his clothes and saying goodbye to everyone he sped off on his bicycle.

'See you next Sunday Tony?'

'Yes, no, yes, well maybe Gloria,' came spluttering out as Tony raced away.

'Helpful lad that,' said Toby. 'Saw him helping you there Gloria.'

'He just saved my life Toby. No, seriously, I mean it. We were practising before when you first came but just then he really saved my life.'

'Me too,' said Tilley. 'Gloria, I too feel saved. Toby and Lola here helped me wash my sins away just like you. I too had my life saved today. Thank you my friends,' and Tilley held both Toby's and Lola's hands in hers. 'Come on, let's all go home and set about cleaning the house now that I've cleaned my life. A new life Gloria and we'll clean house.'

Back at Tilley's house they all managed to change into dry clothing and quite quickly Toby and Lola said their goodbyes and set off for their drive back to London. Lola arranged with Gloria for a return trip next weekend and said she would bring Belle and probably Gina. They talked about a computer and Lola said Belle would sort all that out.

Once Toby and Lola had gone Tilley turned to Gloria and held her hands.

'Come daughter. You and I have one or two things to do and we'll start with the first and that is the house. Upstairs I think and we'll make a beginning in my bedroom. Once we've done my room I will tell you about the second.'

Gloria's head was a real swirl of swimming, life-saving (hers), her mother's apparent conversion, the visit with Gary and Lola this morning to the cottage and now house-cleaning. She followed her mother up the stairs and wondered what might happen next. The following hour was a revelation for Gloria. Her mother swept virtually everything out of her bedroom. Gone were the pictures, gone the altar, gone the crucifix, gone the candles, gone the praying knee-rest. Down with the drab dark curtains and in with the light. The pile of rejected materials on the landing grew. Tilley looked around the room. The sombre lamp came out, the mournful bedspread was pulled off and all the little saints arrayed on the dressing table were respectfully put in a box but definitely placed in the reject pile.

'I'll make some new bright curtains Gloria. I'll buy a smart modern lamp. I'll find a new colourful bedspread to go with a new carpet for this room. We'll change the light bulb for starters,' and Tilley promptly ran downstairs which was something Gloria hadn't seen her mother do for years. She came up with a new bulb. Standing on a chair she quickly changed the bulb and tried the switch.

'There Gloria, let there be light my love. There's one more thing to do before we look at your room but I'm not sure where they are. In the cupboard I think although it's a long time since I saw them.' Gloria was astonished at the change. She had wanted her mum back but she hadn't realised what that really meant. Toby had certainly done something and Gloria wasn't quite sure what. She watched her mother rummage around in the cupboard and come out looking frustrated.

'I'm sure they are there. I need that chair Gloria,' and her mum was now up on the chair and digging higher up in the cupboard. 'Now look at these Gloria. Feast your eyes on something treasured and rare. These are part of my new celebrations. Toby the Fixer has fixed things again.'

Gloria didn't know what her mum was going on about but she moved forward and held out her hands for the rolls her mum had found. Tilley moved down off the chair and eagerly took the rolls. She spread them on the bed and used brushes and boxes to hold down the rolled-up corners.

'One, two, three and even four Gloria. All signed, all mint copies and all fabulous. A bit of my youth these Gloria. A bit of my life before you were born love. Days of peace and happiness. Days of fun and joy.'

'What are they Mum?' Gloria asked.

'Posters my love. Posters of the four great bands of that time. Signed by the blokes in the band and all for me. Fabulous and all through my Toby, my saviour.'

Christ thought Gloria, Toby has changed her from praising the Lord to praising Toby the Fixer: out of the frying pan and into the fire.

'I'll frame them Gloria. We used to fix them up on the wall but these are too good for that. Now I'm older and can look at them as days gone by, good days gone by and so I will frame them. They are warm happy reminders Gloria. They will help me look forwards with warm and happy thoughts.'

'Sure Mum, I'll help. Say, how about a bite to eat before we start on my room. After this afternoon and the great life-saving I'm hungry. I'll go down and see what I can put together in the kitchen. Come down with me Mum and we'll do it together.'

'Yes Gloria my love, we'll do it together.'

On the Monday Bob Edwards had Freddie and me back at Enrico's cottage working away with brushes and rollers. It wasn't hard graft and I had time to think about the visit to the Ferris cottage yesterday. The girls seemed to think that was a good idea of mine. Wonder how I can get in on the act. Gloria doesn't seem to mind if I wander and share a little. Lola's keen on other birds but that Sheena now she was something else. Gina too and I wonder what this Belle lady is like.

'Okay girls, gather round and we'll all go back to school.'

'Can I be the teacher this time Belle?' giggled Sheena. 'I'll spank your bottom any time.'

'Later Sheena, but only after you've passed the test here. Look, Lenny has set up this website. We thought for a long time what to call the site. We needed a name that caught the eye but didn't attract the wrong types. It also couldn't let on where we were or be too suggestive so we dismissed "Forestry frolics", "West Coast Adventures" and several others. The name can be changed but we thought of "Maiden Venture" with the site adorned with photographs of each of us suitably dressed in our one or more specialities. Tapping any one of the photos leads you into a more detailed description of the lady in question and the kind of entertainment offered while still keeping it within the law. You can hop back to and fro between the pages like most websites and then we have contact routines.'

'What about fees, prices?'

'Always a problem love aren't they. We all know it depends on the time, place, service, even the kind of client. Lenny and I discussed this at length. We thought there should be a base cover charge which we could state in absolute terms and then talk of a final fee to be negotiated depending on the details. We aren't sure of the wording yet but we can all think about that.'

'And the contact routine?'

'Telephone number of an answering call centre to start with,' said Belle. 'Client identifies more specifically who or what they want. Response is an email address. We need a way to screen before the next step which is making contact down with Gloria and Gary. By the time there is contact down there we need to be pretty clear what they are looking for and they are clean.'

'Or something else,' giggled Sheena. 'I do a wonderful dance routine with a brush or mop.'

'Sheena, concentrate love for Christ sake,' said Belle. 'This is easy but you need to think through exactly how to set it up. We want business not balls-ups.'

'Oh I don't know Belle. Balls up can be a real turn on. Not for Lola of course but for the rest of us it's a bonus.'

'Shit, you people serious or not? Lenny's put some time into this. I want it to work. I want some fresh air and action all at one time. This is a real chance for something different: away from the scum and stink of the city.'

'Okay Belle, you've made your point.'

The girls settled in for a long yet worthwhile session of how to make the web gateway work for them in a safe and convenient way. At the end of the lesson even Belle was pleased with her schoolmates.

Gloria's week was certainly a change. True enough there was the routine of Mrs. Digby and the salon and there were several shifts at Darlene's keeping the coffee and tea-drinkers happy but it was the evenings that were so different. First of all her mother continued with her house cleaning. Out went lots of pious and sombre clothing, furniture, accessories and in came light, bright and lively curtains, clothes, fabrics and attitude. Just as she said Tilley got her autographed and precious posters framed and hung two in her bedroom and two in the living room. Gloria was amazed when her mother unearthed some very old records from a box in the loft. There were no 78s but some 45s and a few special LPs. Unfortunately there was no record-player in the house but Gloria thought they should ask Toby about turning the records into CDs or even downloading some of the music from the internet. Gloria guessed both of these things could be done but she didn't know how. What really amazed her though as she explained to me later in the week was what happened next. Sometime mid-week Gloria came home from Darlene's and her mother was there all excited about something.

'Jesus Gary, I thought she'd won the lottery or something,' Gloria said, and she explained the evening's chit-chat.

'Gloria love we've something special to do tonight and I want to do it with you.'

'Can I wash and get changed first mum or is the house on fire?'

Tilley laughed. 'You're a good girl helping your mum you are Gloria and now I want to do something for you.'

'Well Gary, I washed and got changed into some comfortable clothes and mum and I had a bite to eat. She didn't rush me but let me unwind from work.'

'And then what did she do Gloria?' I asked.

'We went upstairs and we took everything out of my room and she offered a change of paint, of wallpaper, of furniture, everything Gary. She said she wanted me to feel at home and really understand the room belonged to the here and now Gloria. She and my dad had never done anything to my room the whole time I was away. I'd left a kid's room Gary, well a teenager's room at least. Mum wanted me to feel this was the new me, just like she had done with her room.'

'So, what did you do?'

'We talked about it and I decided. We both knew it would take time and so we threw a few old things away and put the rest back until we had time to change it. It was after that though that I got a bigger shock.'

'How come?'

'Well mum didn't stop there now did she? No, she decided to do the same to Wendell's room. Well that started a mini-riot.'

'Wendell objected?'

'My brother went ballistic Gary. He threatened mum and you know he's not a small kid any more. He pushed her out. Shouted that she could never go into his room and locked the door. Christ he's a pain. He inherited all of dad's bad points and none of the good.'

'How did your mum take it?'

'She was surprised I suppose. Toby's change seems permanent and there was no going back to her old ways of wandering off and praying. She shrugged and told me he would come round in the end. Wanted us all to be happy she said and started on some new curtains. Then I had a bigger shock when I told her about the coming weekend.'

'What kind of shock?' I asked.

Gloria explained that the conversation carried on and she asked her mother, 'Mum, you know that Toby and a couple of the girls are coming down again this weekend?'

'Yes Gloria and they'll all stay here. I'm going to offer Toby my bed. We came to a beautiful understanding last Sunday and he's coming to stay with me. I'll have my room looking beautiful by then with the new curtains and bedspread. It will be light, fragrant, nostalgic with the framed posters and just fine for an old friendly couple. It will be like old times Gloria although as you said a new me and a new Toby.'

Gloria looked hard at her mother and nearly swallowed her tongue. A multitude of thoughts ran around in her mind and then she smiled and said, 'Smashing Mum. It's so good to have you back and I'm so happy to be home. Toby is a real friend and he's so happy to be with you again. We talked a lot when I was in London Mum, about the village, the people and our family. I'll love having him here to stay with you.'

'And the girls can sleep in your room. How many are coming Gloria? That Lola is a beautiful girl and the friend you had down here before, Gina is such a looker. Does she model up in London?'

'Yes Mum but I think it will be Lola and Belle who are coming down with Toby. I'll fix everyone up in my room though, no problem.'

That first Saturday in June the sky was wild and a strong series of gusts chased in from the southwest and tore apart the rolling clouds. Once again Rupert had brought his energetic troop of fellow hikers through the area but this time they had tried to approach the Education Centre from the other direction. Philippa and Margaret were as keen as ever to hear the Reverend Godschild and the rest of the group thought that Fotheringham offered a good series of hikes along with a diverse array of woodlands. That particular weekend there was an orienteering meet going on too which had its start and finish at the Education Centre. Daniel was out with Katya and they were checking on the progress of the orienteering teams and looking at other aspects of the forest as they walked along one of the forest rides.

'That's Enrico's cottage Daniel. The one I didn't see in the fog that first time we came here. Did you and your mother do anything after our visit a week or so ago?'

'We've been sprucing it up,' said Daniel. 'We've hired a new worker starting later this month actually. Remember me telling you that he and his family are from Yorkshire and his wife wanted to move south and be closer to her parents? Quite by chance his current employer knows our family, through the software business actually and so we talked it over. Colin Entwhistle and his wife, who I think is called Ophelia and their son Adam are moving in here. We've talked to Enrico like I suggested and he's happy to stay at Home Farm. I think that is good for all concerned, for Enrico, for Christina, for Peter and for young Tony.'

'Sounds like a happy next step Daniel. Wonder what my happy next step will be? Wonder when my results will finally be released? Daddy and mummy are planning to come over in a couple of week's time, for my hopeful successful graduation.'

'You'll be fine Katya love. I'll predict a First or a strong Second if not a First.'

'And then James will really be confused if I am First and his mother is First,' said Katya as she smiled at Daniel. 'Hey Daniel, who are those people cutting through that new plantation? I thought the orienteering teams all had clear bright yellow colours? Who are they?'

'I don't know,' said Daniel, 'but we'll go and find out. We can cut across over there and head them off. It's hard to see who they are from here.'

When Daniel got closer he could see who was traipsing through the new young trees. Suddenly the group stopped and he could hear some comments.

'I'll just jump over. Here, let me hold the wire down for you. Yes, I know it's high but I'll pull it down. There, that low enough.'

'Hey, that fence is there for a purpose you know,' said Daniel with some strength in his voice. 'Oh, it's you lot again. Why can't you stick to the rides?'

'Wanted to see some of the flowers you have in here. They'll all disappear in a couple of years when these sterile conifers block out the light. Changes the wildlife into a nothing desert.'

'And you knocking down the fence doesn't help now does it?' said Daniel.

'Fences, gates, stiles chum. Ever think of putting in gates do you? Ever think of helping people so they don't get hurt falling over your fences? Some of us nearly got seriously hurt last week you may remember and now Margaret here has ripped her shorts on your fence, and Ted, who never sees anything close up anyway, got his fingers caught in the wire and is bleeding. Thought about damages? I've told Ted he should think about damages, and Margaret's shorts. Just look. Stiles help mate. You know stiles? Funny little things to get over fences. They come in all shapes and sizes. Do you ever think.....?'

'Lady, do you ever shut up?'

'Not a problem though?' asked Rupert as he walked down the line of trees and looked intently at Katya. Mavis came hovering at his elbow. 'Stile over any fence what? Not hard to put in. Saves any damage. What do you think young lady? You look like an outdoors type. Must hike a bit. Don't you think a neat stile just here would suit?' Rupert came up close to Katya and held out his hand. 'We met last weekend I believe. I'm Rupert Oldshaw but then you must have heard of my father Magnus. Everyone's heard of my father, haven't they Mavis?' Rupert took Katya's hand and held it in his. He turned the hand over. 'Stiles and gates my dear. You agree with me surely?'

'Of course she does Rupert. Stands to reason. Legal requirement in any fence,' Doris continued her harangue.

'Stile or no stile, gate or no gate,' said Daniel emphatically, 'all of that doesn't condone breaking fences or trampling through young plantations. This is private property. The law of trespass talks about damage – damage to the landowner's property and the liability of people who trespass and do damage. Walking over the land is one thing although walking through a young plantation could do unseen damage but deliberately damaging the fence is quite another.'

'I say old boy,' said Rupert, still holding Katya's hand. 'Steady on. This young lady definitely thinks that's a little strong. Don't you my dear?'

Katya snatched her hand away when she suddenly realised that Rupert was still holding it and Mavis was advancing with a non-friendly look on her face.

'What, yes, yes stiles are elegant. Yes Daniel, stiles could be quite a good thing here. We should consider them. If we want more people to come in here and not damage the fence we definitely should consider them.'

'Absolutely right little darling,' endorsed Rory. 'Young Arnold here is a fanatic about wild life and wilderness. He just has to see and photograph things before they disappear. Couldn't do that from the forest ride now could he? So, over the fence we go and off to grandma's house so to speak and let's look at the wee flowers. If you want people to appreciate the woods here young feller you have to let us in if you know what I mean.'

'And the plants in here are precious,' added Arnold looking earnest. 'They have some special relationships with a rather rare species of butterfly I think. Yes, I'm right, or no maybe it's not that flower. Anyway, very important to look and check you know.'

'So you see old man, we all think that the stiles are an important feature. Definitely should be included somewhere along here.'

'Rupert, we have to get on. Just look at the time. We've stood here so long arguing I quite forgot about the time and it's getting on for three. You know Margaret and I have to be at the Education Centre before three and Margaret has to mend her shorts now after climbing over that dreadful fence. Quite sharp some of those wires are Rupert. Come along Margaret, we'll have to hurry. Which way Ted? You've got the map remember?'

'Yes, fine, we'll all be off then old man. Remember about the stiles though. Good idea from this charming young lady. Perhaps we'll meet again fair maiden,' Rupert said looking at Katya and they all set off through the woods following Ted who had the map remember.

'What a bloody shower,' said Daniel, 'and what a bloody attitude. The cheek of that devil. Coming on to you, holding your hand and going on about a bloody stile. They don't realise that one: they shouldn't be traipsing through a young plantations and two it's no simple job to put in a stile anywhere you feel like it. Who does he think he is?'

'Rupert Oldshaw I think he said Daniel,' said Katya, 'but I agree. If we're going to open up Fotheringham for people to appreciate we do need to accommodate their requirements.'

'At an expense to us and free to them?' retorted Daniel angrily. 'Green operates two ways Katya. Costs to the producer get passed onto the consumer; that's standard business procedures. What's the American saying, "there's no free ride"? Yes, that's it. Well, any extra cost we incur like a stile or a gate should be reflected in the price for entry and that lot just walk in as if they own the place. Look at this fence. Dam, and I didn't bring any tools with me. I'll just have to get it fixed on Monday, like we had to do with that deer fence last weekend. Wonder what else that lot might do. We'd better put locks on the doors of the cottages and check on the security of the Education Centre. I don't know what you were thinking about Katya when you agreed with them. Gave them completely the wrong impression.'

'But I do agree with them Daniel. I think you should put stiles in.'

'You're wrong Katya, very wrong,' and Daniel tried to reset some of the wires in the fence and do a temporary repair. When he straightened up he looked around. Katya had walked off down the forest ride back towards the Big House.

'I'll be right there,' he shouted but Katya kept straight on.

'Dam and blast,' said Daniel to the fence, the trees and the empty air but there was no reaction to his outburst. After five minutes he thought he had done all he could to keep varmints out of the plantation and he set off after Katya. However Katya had been quite upset over Daniel's reaction and she wasn't going let Daniel catch up with her. It wasn't until the evening that there was a truce.

Samantha had detected an air of friction at the dinner table and she suggested an evening down at the pub after she had packed James off to bed. To assess the situation in a more diplomatic fashion than she usually did Samantha had Katya come up with James and read him a bedtime story.

'Something happen?' Samantha asked quietly when James had finally shut his mouth, closed his eyes and drifted off into the land of polo-playing ponies and jumping fences ahead of his mother. 'Go Dainty go' whispered into the pillow and Samantha smiled as she looked down at her son.

'No Samantha, no not really. Daniel and I met that same crowd of hikers in the forest this afternoon. The same crowd that James and your mother met last weekend I think. They'd wanted to see and photograph some unusual flowers in a plantation and to reach them they had climbed over the fence. Well, some of the members are not quite so agile and one of the girls had snagged her shorts and ripped them. Then one of the men who is some fanatic about wildlife caught his fingers in the wire and was dripping blood. On top of all that the group included that lawyer lady with the non-stop mouth and then there was the film-star leader. No, it's his father who is some big shot in the movies although I don't know the name. Out of all this confrontation Daniel was annoyed at the damage to the fence and I agreed with them that a stile would have been a good idea. Somehow this minor argument developed into some really bad vibes between Daniel and me. I walked off hurt and Daniel mended the fence. We came home separately.'

Samantha held Katya's hand. 'Sounds like what we English call a "storm in a teacup",' she said. 'Perhaps Shakespeare said it best with "much ado about nothing" although my brother will not think of the broken fence as nothing if I know him. Very conscientious is my brother Katya when it comes to Fotheringham's forests. He always believed in doing things right whereas I just believed in doing them. Still, an evening with a pint and watching the locals might be good for a giggle. We might get a chance to watch some more darts. There's probably a match on tonight and the place will be crowded. Just the place to ease the tension.'

'Where's Terence? No, sorry, I shouldn't pry.'

'Nonsense Katya, you're family. Terence, bless his heart is working on some case up in Bristol. There's some trouble with illegal workers in the Night Club scene apparently although Terence is not supposed to tell me too much. Still I miss him.'

'You do don't you Samantha?'

'Yes Katya I do. I might miss Andrew, in fact I do miss Andrew but I also want my life to go forwards and I believe that Terence should be part of that life. If I really look inside myself I love him. I can feel it is right and I can feel it will be good. We go well together. James likes him because Terence has a talent which most of us don't often see because Terence listens rather than talks when he's working but with James he talks. Now you know James loves to talk but with Terence it's quite amusing to watch. James is quite quiet and he loves to listen to Terence tell stories and Terence has a wonderful knack of telling stories. Even I can sit and listen and you know I'm not one for sitting about and just listening. I'm your go-go-go girl, on wheels sometimes.'

Katya laughed and gave Samantha a hug. 'This is surely one crazy family,' she said, 'and you're right. Daniel and I need to laugh a little more and not be so serious. I suppose I'm tense waiting for my results from Oxford. My parents are flying over from Florida and I do want to do well for them, especially my dad.'

'Both your parents will be proud of you Katya. I know mine think you are a really good influence on my baby brother. Still, I suppose we had better go and haul him out of his dungeon and get him to lighten up. Come on, we can leave sleeping beauty here to his galloping over fences with Dainty.'

The two girls went downstairs and collected a suspicious Daniel who was never sure what his sister was up to and was equally concerned when he asked and Katya just winked at him. As Samantha surmised the pub was crowded. There was a darts match going on and the noise level was high. Samantha managed to get her brother sitting next to Katya and have him explain the strategy of playing darts. Rupert Oldshaw had stayed in the village again and when he saw Katya he started towards her. Samantha laid a hand on Rupert's arm.

'I would leave alone if I were you. My brother has already talked with his workers and there is a new policy with regards to trespass. This includes any thoughts you might have on personal trespass. The Lord family is strongly protective about personal property. We had two attempts last September, attacks on personal property that is. The man who set fires to our stables ended up with his throat slashed from ear to ear,' and Samantha dramatically drew her fingers across Rupert's throat. 'Died quite horribly he did,' she added, 'blood everywhere. And then the two men who came to kidnap my nephew were shot at. We know that one escaped from England but we are not sure where the other one died. He's probably gasping for breath somewhere but he wasn't at all happy after being trussed up naked and had knife marks made in appropriate places. Lost a lot of his good looks he did. No longer the pretty boy he was when he came if you know what I mean?' and Samantha stroked her finger down the side of Rupert's cheek. Rupert turned a pale colour and beat a retreat. Out of the bar, out of the door Samantha noted and if that is his car I can hear out of the village too. Samantha smiled and went back to put her arm around Daniel and Katya. 'Good to see you two explaining things to each other,' she said. 'Always thought clever people could talk and listen well. Wasn't always my thing of course but then I'm the hard-driven, won't be beaten, in your face, got to be first do it kind of girl. Just like our mum Daniel.'

Daniel laughed and looked up at his sister. 'Samantha you're a real nut case and mum's nothing like that.'

'That's all you know Daniel. Actually, talking seriously for a moment, now that there's a lull in the darts match, what do you think about dad?'

'Dad?' asked Daniel. 'What do you mean? He's not hard driven in your face. He's happy, hand held forwards, how can I help, will you join us? He's a team player. Actually he's a team builder is dad.'

'Yes brother dear and right now there isn't a lot left to build. We sold Brainware, which was a brilliant move I thought, even if it was my idea. There is a lot less stress for both mum and dad. You run the estate and you do a bloody good job despite your protestations and occasional side trips out on the golf course with little Miss forestry/golf pro here.'

'Samantha!' exclaimed Katya, but she laughed too.

'What's dad got to do?'

'Relax,' said Daniel. 'Enjoy being with mum. Enjoy seeing Christina, Peter, Tony, James and Enrico. Seeing you you know. He always was your champion. You could never do any wrong and even when you did dad would always come and fix it. And he did. You don't realise how happy he was when he brought you home. He was full of it.'

'Sure, then he went away to play golf or something and all hell broke loose.'

'But you handled all of that and he and you talked. He understood your point of view and even if he didn't he had James home too. What's the concern?'

'Something mum said actually. She said she had mentioned it to you towards the end of last year. Sometime before your birthday I think. I'd just come home and mum said she was worried about dad and told you.'

'You're right Samantha. I remember now. There was some trouble over John Ferris and his coming back to work for us. Then we had that meeting with Betty and John. Mum didn't want dad to have to deal with all that. I suppose I didn't think anything of it and I just got on with the job. I dealt with it and that all went pear-shaped too remember.'

'But that all ended happily really Daniel,' said Katya. 'We found the treasure, the gold, and that beautiful necklace for your mother. Betty Ferris sold the cottage and now she is successfully making pies for everyone. Her kids are happy. When I was in the village the other day that talkative Mrs. Larkin, who always asks after Enrico you know, said that Katey and Paul were fine and that Betty was looking at a new house. So that ended up just fine Daniel. You did a good job.'

'We did a good job,' added Daniel and he squeezed Katya's hand gently and smiled at her. 'So what about dad Samantha?'

'I'm not sure Daniel but mum's worried. Dad has slowed down but that's to be expected. I think mum's worried he has too little to do now. He has no people to bring together any more. She thinks he misses people but she also thinks he's not so well. She thinks he can't take stress any more. When that confrontation took place last weekend she said she was glad it was her and not dad Daniel. Got any ideas?'

'Not immediately Samantha. Katya, can you see anything we can't see because we're too close?'

'I think he looks a little older Daniel. I think he looks a little more tired than when I first came. There's not quite the same wild charm that used to make me wonder about this family when I didn't know you so well.'

'And now you realise we are all eccentric and so that's acceptable?'

'Not quite Daniel, although I can remember that friend of your dad's telling my mother about how lovely you all were even if you all were crazy English Lords. My mother wasn't quite sure who to believe. She enjoyed coming to visit though.'

'And we'll enjoy having her and your father in a couple of weeks time,' said Daniel. 'Samantha perhaps we need a project for dad. We need something that is his and where he can pull in other people for special parts. An alternative is to take him out to the golf course more often because that game relieves stress, brings people together and lets you feel ten years younger.'

'Daniel, stop pulling Samantha's leg. She doesn't play and doesn't realise how full of it you are. Relieves stress indeed!'

'You haven't seen how dad plays Katya. Remember him telling you that the score doesn't matter: that the camaraderie is the thing, the great outdoors, the fellow players.'

'Yes Daniel, and the jokes and tall stories afterwards on the nineteenth hole.'

'I thought there were only eighteen holes Daniel. What's this nineteenth?'

'See Daniel, I told you Samantha doesn't play. The nineteenth Samantha is the bar or the Golf Clubhouse where players brag about the one that got away and all the "maybes" and "if onlys". It's probably where your father learnt all those jokes your mother thinks are pathetic or dangerous.'

'Actually Daniel you have just mentioned two possible ideas that might work. Look, dad plays golf with people and it is people he needs. Talk him into going out there more often. Take time out and go out there with him. Get him into some crowd and he's like a fish in water. Fantastic idea the more I think about it. Great. Knew you two could help. Now, the other idea, a project. How about dad spends time writing up some history of Fotheringham? We caught him in the library the other day looking at old tomes and he was interested, quite interested in fact. So, we suggest he produce a history of Fotheringham and the book will have a place of honour in the library and a copy in the Education Centre. Perhaps it will be the book of reference for any student wanting to know more about the estate. In this project dad will have to go and visit all the relatives, talk with Enrico, perhaps some of the other workers, and he can ask for help from Peter and Tony as school holidays are fast approaching. Christina would love to have some time to herself and not have the two boys around her kitchen all summer. Better and better Daniel. You're a genius brother. Dad would also have to tour the estate and both boys would like that as would Enrico. Solved it. Daniel you and Katya have solved it. I'll tell mum we have it all in hand and not to worry. Time for another drink after that. I'll get them in. Thanks.'

Away Samantha went at speed to the bar. The locals who knew all about Miss Samantha and her errands of mercy stepped aside because there was this reputation about Samantha bowling over anyone in her path, and that included poor PC Meadows at one time they all remembered. 'Three pints please George. Hello Gloria. You're looking very happy. See you've got some friends down again. They from London? Hi, I'm Samantha MacRae. Pleased to meet you. Thanks George. Enjoy your stay. Bye.'

'Non-stop that one Gloria. Tell your friends about our lovely Miss Samantha. Tell them why the locals all stand aside in a hurry. Notice that did they? Knocks over coppers she does. Let's see whether I can get this straight. She knocks over some, she climbs with others and she goes out to dinner with another one. Explain all that Gloria.'

'Sure George, easy.'

'Anyway Gloria, why are you looking so happy? Perhaps I should chuck you out more often. Actually, I've had punters asking about that. Several people have asked where you are.'

'Working for the competition aren't I George? Serving them tea and crumpets and Betty's pies at Darlene's, just like you do, and sharing gossip at Mrs. Digby's just like you do. So we're really in competition George. You making me an offer?'

'I'm still thinking about it Gloria.'

'See how popular I am around here girls? Centre of attraction. George my love, I'm happy because I've got me mum back. Toby the Fixer has fixed it. The Toby who you so rudely offered a cup of tea to at the ungodly hour of eight has come up trumps. He's pulled my mum back into real time. She's happy, laughing, cleaning the house, and when we left she was singing along with Toby some song they both knew from the sixties. Like a new woman she says. Something about being born again and she looked at Toby and they both burst a gut laughing. I'm happy George to be home with my old mum again, although now she's a new mum. So girls, let me get them in and we'll celebrate a new beginning.'

There's a first time for everything

That Sunday's round of golf was a mixture in several ways. Daniel was erratic and his mind kept swinging from his golf, to Katya, to the argument, to his dad, to trespass and possible damage and back to golf just when the damage was done and he'd three-putted again. Katya kept quiet and wondered what was troubling her player. The other three members of the group were usually pretty placid and so it was a rather sombre five people who walked off the eighteenth green after the traditional handshake. Daniel excused Katya and himself from the usual Sunday lunch explaining that there were a couple of things on the estate that were troubling his parents and he needed to be there to help. Katya put Daniel's clubs in the boot of the car and slid into the passenger seat. As he climbed in Katya put her hand out to catch Daniel's arm.

'What's wrong Daniel? You're not your self today. We didn't work as a team. I suppose I'm still anxious about my results and not always paying attention. I'm sorry.'

Daniel sat in the driving seat staring ahead of him and it was almost as if he hadn't heard her. 'Daniel, I love you,' she said softly and there was almost a sob in her voice. Daniel turned and smiled and folded his arms around Katya and gently pulled her towards him. 'And I love you, and I'm sorry for being a bear with a sore head for the last two days. I've no excuse Katya and my game reflected my self-centred attitude. Come on, it's still a bright and sunny day. Let's go and find some mutually professional excitement in our forests. Come and show me how to convert badger gates into badger and people stiles. We'll design a new fence model with access for animals and people with a very selective mechanism to keep out the unwanted. We'll do it together,' and he kissed her before she could answer. Laughing he put the car in gear and drove smoothly away.

Meanwhile, in the same forest another car was slowly driving that fine bright morning. I piloted the car through the sunlit woodlands to the Ferris cottage. Sitting in the car with me were Gloria, Lola and Belle and it was Belle who was so excited. 'This is heavenly. This is fabulous. It's neat. It's is so clean and free of fumes. Gary you work in heaven mate. You must be a bloomin' angel.'

Gloria laughed and turned round to talk to Belle. 'He ain't no angel Belle love and I think he's only up here on probation. In a couple of weeks they'll probably send him back down again. Proper little devil he is usually, ain't you Gary?' and Gloria turned back again and lightly punched me on the shoulder. Once again I parked under the trees and the four of us walked across the clearing to the cottage. Lola continued through to one of the bedrooms and started pacing and counting. She took out her little whip and cracked it a few times and then softly drew it over one of the beds. Belle walked in behind her and looked around.

'See what you mean about some of the lighting. You going to keep those curtains or get something denser? We could use some heavier darker-coloured stuff. Would look better from inside as well as keep any light from getting out. I can fix some temporary lighting in here. It'll be okay if that Lola doesn't get too wild with that whip of hers. What do you say Lola?'

'You know best Belle love. You sort it and I'll restrain myself,' and Lola laughed and goosed Belle with the whip handle.

'Toby's got some gear for the other room,' Belle said. 'Got a better bed and a couple of couches. What about the main living room? Change the curtains again, find a cover for that kitchen table and bring down some form of drinks cabinet. I see they've got a fridge and I assume the electric is still on. Yes fine. Let me make a couple of notes and that's great. This is real neat Gloria. Gary you on side mate? This will be some place. You wait and see and we'll all have a ball.'

I stood in the kitchen come living room and watched the three girls going from room to room. They seemed to know what they wanted and how they were going to do it. Didn't seem to matter to them that it wasn't theirs. They had this carefree attitude of finders-keepers and obviously had thought through what they had in mind much more than Gloria was telling me. I told myself I needed to find out what Miss happy face was really up to. Better watch yourself Gary I told myself. These women were all good fun and great to be with but what was coming down the line. Think about it, I work here. I work all around here. Sooner or later someone is going to come looking. That new family is going to move in and sure enough they will start to wander around and see what is what. It isn't more than a kilometre or so between the two cottages. Wonder if I should have a word with Gloria.

'Gloria, do you realise….'

'Gary you're brilliant darling. This is perfect. We'll fix this up so you'll never be able to tell we've been here 'cos everything can be shifted real easy. You guide 'em down here and we'll have a ball. You run 'em back and no-one's any the wiser. You're the key Gary my love. You keep 'em honest and just bring us the real goods and we'll do the rest. We'll start this real slow for a couple of weeks and then see about later.'

I asked whether they wanted to see any more of the forest thinking I could show them what I did and how neat and tidy I was but only Belle had any real interest because it was all new to her.

'I've never seen the likes Gary. I've never been in a forest before. Never seen so many bleedin' trees. Of course we have a few in the local park but not like this. This is amazing. Look at all of them. Do you have to sweep up the leaves or something? Do that in our park they do, in the autumn you know. Makes a mess otherwise and the dog shit gets stuck everywhere. Gets on your shoes. Be lots of leaves here Gary.'

Belle rabbited on but Gloria and Lola were still checking out some details in the cottage. They decided to curtain off the closet area with all the cleaning things. I didn't explain that the closet covered Norton Ferris's hidey hole complete with buried dogs, buried twin cousins of Freddie and part of John Ferris's nightmare. I suppose I was excited about what was going on and anticipating some future activities too. I still had a small idea going round in my head about my involvement. Guide and protector yes, I could handle that but what about some pictures, some photographs or video perhaps of what might happen inside the cottage. Gloria said to wait outside and patrol. Keep everyone safe she said. Sure Gloria love and miss all the action. Well maybe Gary old son you should think about a sideline, a number that is yours that might even pull in the odd quid or two if you could find the right contact. Food for thought Gary Templeton. I didn't realise it at the time but I was thinking just like my old man. Look out for number one and enjoy whatever you got offered and maybe now and again take something to be one up on people. Always good to have a little leverage. Dad used to tell me that about sales but I never really listened although some of it must have stuck.

By late in the morning the girls had done everything they wanted and I drove them all back to Gloria's house. I noticed that Toby was down here again and it seemed that he and Mrs. Manson were looking very happy together. In fact Tilley Manson didn't look her old self at all. She was wearing a bright quite short summer dress and was livelier than I'd seen her in years. I looked at Gloria and she just beamed at me.

'My mum's come back to life again Gary thanks to Toby here. Works miracles he does, don't you Toby love? He's a real angel,' and Gloria went over and gave him a great big hug. 'Anyway Gary, thanks for the tour my love and we'll see you later in the week. The girls and I have some things to discuss and Toby needs to check some things out in the house with my mum so I'll catch you Tuesday or Wednesday. Thanks.'

That was that then I thought. I'm in and I'm special but I'm not right in. Well bugger that. How can I get more in than they think I am? Who knows what I need to know? Who was the bloke that dad was going on about with all that video stuff? Some mate of his in town. Dad I think I need a favour. Just for once I believe we're going to have to talk and I took myself off to make sure I could benefit from this little caper of Gloria's. Belle was impressed with what she had seen and thought she could fix things up her end. Lola talked with Toby and they both thought the transformation of Tilley was quite something, especially as Toby had shared Tilley's double bed and she was more than happy Toby said. Belle just hoped that Lenny had done his homework with or without any double bed. That Sunday afternoon Toby drove the girls back to London, Daniel went investigating in the forest with Katya, Gloria went for her swimming lessons with Tony and I went to find my dad and information about cameras and photography.

'I want to check on the property in the forest Katya. After the last two weekends and those hikers I'd like to be sure that we've everything under control and we can prevent any vandalism or further damage.'

'Makes sense to me Daniel. Let's start at the Centre although I think that's the most secure anyway.'

There was an afternoon session going on at the Education Centre with a local naturalist explaining to a group where and how to conserve deer habitat. Following the discussion they were scheduled to tour parts of the forest for the rest of the afternoon. Daniel managed to catch the group leader as the discussion wound down and was assured that the key would be returned to Fotheringham as they left and all would be locked up safe and sound.

'Where next Daniel?'

'Let's check the Ferris cottage and then finish up at Enrico's. I'd like to see that Enrico's cottage is virtually ready for the Entwhistles at the end.'

At the Ferris cottage Daniel drove up to the edge of the yard and parked. He and Katya walked across the flagged backyard and in through the kitchen door which Gloria had closed only three hours earlier. Everything looked neat and tidy and much like Betty had left it last year. Daniel had been down here a couple of times and had one of the forestry crew do a sweep and tidy up quite recently. He walked through and checked the windows were closed. The fridge was empty and the place looked ready to be lived in.

'Just a pity that the place carries all that baggage,' said Katya. 'Almost seems a shame to think of tearing it down. Still, I suppose if anyone ever knew what had happened here they would need to be pretty strong to want to stay here. What was it Daniel, two rapes, two kidnappings or confinement, one shooting death and one knife slashing death and all on top of two murdered young men and two dogs? Quite a little house of horrors this is.'

'And yet for five or six years it was the happy home of John and Betty Ferris with Katey and little Paul, one very happy family. Strange but true. Let's shut the door and leave the cottage to its memories. Over time it will change again and a new set of things will happen here. I suppose I should see about a lock on this door. The front door is bolted as usual but I will have to see about a lock for the kitchen door. Shame really as we never had to even think about locking doors out here. We're so far away from anyone else and the only people ever out here were the workers or our family. Times change I suppose. Let's go and look at a happier cottage.'

'Come and see all the rooms this time Katya,' said Daniel as he stopped outside Enrico's cottage. 'That first time you thought I was too upset to show you all of this cottage, just after Idwal's rampage. Then you saw it rather rapidly with mum in her speedy inspection just last week. It's been cleaned and tidied up now and the crew have done some repainting. Mum talked to Mrs. Entwhistle and they decided on the paint. When the family comes down we may still do a few more things for them. Anyway, come and see.'

Katya walked slowly into the kitchen behind Daniel and then she stopped.

'Daniel, it's changed. It's light, airy and still empty but it looks younger somehow. It is a young family that is coming isn't it?'

'I think so,' said Daniel. 'I think mum said Colin's about thirty and his wife a bit younger. Their son is around James's age. Come and see what they did to the bedrooms?' One bedroom was clearly meant for the son with the bright wall colours of brown along the bottom, green on top of this and the top half of the wall in light blue.

'Like the forest outside his window,' exclaimed Katya. 'With drapes and pictures it will delight a little boy. Something is missing though Daniel, something little boys like, well the ones I know do.'

'Which is?'

'Trains Daniel, well engines, carriages, wagons, and tender behinds,' she said and giggled. Daniel wrapped his arms around her and hugged her tight. 'I'll give you a tender behind young lady,' he said.

'Will you Daniel, will you?' and Katya wriggled out of Daniel's arms and ran into the next room. Daniel caught her just as she started to turn and they fell across the remaining bed in the place. For the next little while the forest hummed along quietly in the June warmth and Daniel and Katya made up their disagreement, their maybe argument, their anxieties about results and security and shared each others love and affection.

Tony was all set to ride his bicycle to the river and the pool that afternoon. Rather protectively he had asked Peter to come with him, and his aunt Christina.

'Yes, come on Mum,' Peter had said. 'It's a lovely afternoon. Enrico will enjoy a little nap and you can watch us swim. Tony says I'm improving although not as fast as Gloria.'

'How will I get there Tony?' asked Christina. 'I don't ride a bicycle.'

'Come in the car Mum. In fact we can all go in the car. That will be easier Tony than us riding our bikes. We can park off the road by the edge of the trees. It's sheltered there and the car won't get too hot out in the heat if it's under the trees. I'll get my costume and a towel. Super idea Tony, especially as it's hot this afternoon.'

'Hi Gloria. Wow, that swimming costume looks......well, looks good. What do you say Tony? What did you call Katya? I remember, a smashing bird. That's it. Tony just thinks you look good Gloria. It's a nice expression and you lived in London so you know it means you look.....'

'Smashing Peter? Do I look smashing Tony?'

Tony tried not to blush but even with his darker skin the pink flush crept up his cheeks. He quickly waded into the pool and dived under to swim vigorously up and down his line of markers.

'Well Peter,' and Gloria walked slowly over towards the young heir to the Fotheringham Estate. Peter looked down for a moment but then proudly raised up his head and looked Gloria straight in the face. 'I think you look smashing Gloria and I think you know you are and Tony and I are happy for you. I'm glad you've come back to the village and helped with my cousin here. He needed to feel at home after all his sadness from London and your swimming has helped him.'

'And he's helped me too Peter,' said Gloria and she held Peter's hand. 'We've all helped each other and I'm happy for Tony too. He's a fine young man, just like you are. So, shall we swim before our teacher gets upset and thinks we're skipping classes? Race you to where Tony is,' and Gloria waded in and swam strongly towards the blushing Tony. Peter jumped in afterwards and splashed furiously trying to catch up. The lessons were a success and Gloria didn't try and take advantage. Tony felt safer but they didn't practice mouth to mouth that afternoon. Christina sat on the pool side with an umbrella shading her from the sun and watched her son and her nephew. Happy families she thought and she smiled to herself. Enrico will be napping now and we will have an interesting discussion at dinner and the two boys will be excited with this afternoon's activities. We will all be happy this evening.

On Monday Bob Edwards told me Mr. Daniel wanted the finishing touches done to the cottage. Just scrape any unwanted paint off the frames, clean the windows, one last sweep and dust and everything should look fine. Bob said that Lady Sylvia would likely be down some time this afternoon to make a final inspection so look lively lad and do it right. Sure enough Sylvia Lord came by with her son about three and by then I had just about finished.

'You've done a good job here Gary. I'll tell Bob I'm happy. What do you think Mum?'

'Daniel you're right. Thank you Gary. I'm sure the new occupants will be really pleased when they arrive. Did you get Enrico's key Daniel?'

'Mum there never was a key to any doors here. The front door has a bolt but that is never used. The back door has a latch. There never was any key. There's never been any need for a key.'

'You're right Daniel but I'll ask the Entwhistles when they get settled whether they think there's a need. With more people on the estate now what with the Education Centre, your orienteering people and those hikers like the last two weekends we may need to think about that. We'll see. The family are moving down here next Monday and we'll talk with them on the Tuesday or so. How's the other cottage Daniel, Betty and John's?'

'Come and look Mum. It's clean, tidy but still carrying a reputation in the village. When Freddie Dunster was working here with Gary he was worried we were going to have him clean up that cottage too. That's right Gary isn't it?'

'Yes Mr. Daniel. Freddie said he wouldn't go there for any reason. Real spooked out he was. Talked about his cousins and away he went. No Mr. Daniel, folk in the village won't go there. Too many ghosts and too many horror stories.'

Gloria had obviously had a trying Monday or else she was still working with her mother revamping the house because it wasn't until

293

Tuesday night that I saw her. Even then she was full of amazement at her mum.

'You'll never believe Gary. I was shocked but in she went and out everything came. Wendell must have been at school 'cos she stripped everything out that Monday. I was late home Monday because Darlene had us doing some cleaning that evening. When I came home there was a battle royal taking place. Mum was adamant. The room gets cleaned. Wendell was shouting his head off about his stuff, his computer, his magazines. I thought he was going to hit mum. In the end he stormed out and said it had better be sorted by the time he returned. When mum asked where he was going he told her to fuck off.'

'What did your mum do?'

'Well she'd already swept and washed everything down in the room. She must have scrubbed after she'd taken all Wendell's posters, pictures and diagrams off the walls. She told me she was thinking of painting the walls light blue and what did I think. Clouds she thought, clouds dancing on the light blue walls and she asked whether it would look right.'

'So what happened?'

'We put the bed back so Wendell could sleep there when he returned but mum was going to take it out again and buy some paint. When I asked what she thought Wendell would do all she said was it was her house and she'd look after him like the good mother she was. I don't know Gary, Toby's changes have been pretty dramatic.'

'Well you wanted your mum back Gloria. That's what you said. Perhaps you never realised what she was like before she went away.'

'Cottages Gary, cottages for the use of. What's new?'

'Nothing much,' I said.

'We need a dry run or something. We need to practice the routine.'

'How about you explain a little more about what's going to happen? I understand you and the girls want to use the cottage on the quiet. You want to entertain some friends and you want to keep it a secret. So you want me to guide these people there so they don't know where they are. I understand all that but who are these friends?'

'Sit down Gary. Look, I'll get a pint in and we can sit here quietly and I'll explain. It's a variation on the work up in London. Pint right?'

'Sure, yes a pint please,' I said and I wondered what Gloria was talking about. London was night life, Clubs, and illegal dancers. Was Gloria going to bring foreign girls down here? Was that why they mustn't know where they were? If they got caught they couldn't tell who or where?'

'Okay. Up in London I worked with Lola, Gina, Sheena and Belle. There were a couple of other girls but they moved on. We were together for a while. I told you I worked at the Oasis?'

'Yea, and that other place you said. The place where you...'

'Yes, right, but we're talking about the Oasis now Gary. We used to wait tables. Sheena and Lola danced. Belle could sing and we all worked behind the scenes with special guests. In fact most of the action and the money was made behind the scenes. Toby helped a lot with that part of the business.'

'What business, what's this behind the scenes stuff? What could Toby do?'

'Toby knew people Gary, knew some cool people who liked acting, special performances, one on ones, one on twos. You know.'

'Know what Gloria? I work down here in the forest girl. I plant trees, prune trees, cut trees down, put up fences and all that sort of shit. The great outdoors and the smell of resin you know. I don't know nothing about acting although Freddie sometimes acts up like the prat he is. What's one on ones or whatever?'

Gloria sat and looked at me. She took a long pull on her pint and lowered the glass onto the table.

'You get turned on watching?' she said. 'When we were kids with Freddie and Sandra you used to get turned on just watching. You were excited and it didn't matter who was with who. We had one on one, two on one and sometimes you were involved and sometimes you watched. Performances Gary, acting, one on ones, remember all that do you? When you were young Gary, like last year or something?'

'Okay okay,' I said, 'there's no need to get snarky and smart. I get the picture.'

'Good. I was beginning to wonder. Well, up in London that was part of the job. In fact that was the best part of the job. Toby acted as a neat screening device and most if not all of the punters were straight blokes looking for a good time. No, they weren't all straight come to think about it but it was safe and we all had a ball. Each of us had one or more special personal routines and most of us could swing any which way. What we did depended on the desires of our customers. You know Lola has her whip?'

'Yes,' I said, unsure what was coming next.

'That's only a small part of her special routine. She has this bull-fighting costume that looks fantastic on her and she can use a cape but most of all she uses a series of whips. There are some blokes who really get a charge out of being tied up and dominated. They like to be teased, stroked, taunted, whipped and so on. Some like to charge around like pretend bulls until Lola exhausts them and some like to be bonded in an elaborate process. That's Lola's trademark. She's a dominatrix.'

'A what?'

'She likes to dominate Gary. She likes to make you her prisoner, her slave. Actually she works best with women. Even I get turned on watching her with a woman. They've usually got more stamina and the whole scene lasts longer.'

'So you're thinking of performing at the cottage?'

'Right on. Want another pint? All this talking and imagining how this will work is making me thirsty.'

'My shout,' I said and I carried the glasses over to the bar. 'Two pints George. Just the regulars in tonight?'

'There's a couple of tourists in Gary lad. Upstairs getting settled in at the moment. How's that cottage coming on? The one you and young Freddie were painting? He was coming in here looking more like Lester Rainer every day last week. Could tell what colours he was using just looking at his clothes. New folk moving in I hear?'

'Apparently George. That Mr. Daniel said they were moving in after next weekend. Some bloke from up in Yorkshire. Be a job to understand the bugger I expect. Supposed to be good with motors so Danny Masters better watch out or old Taffy Evans will be thinking about a new mechanic.'

George laughed as he handed me the two pints and I carried them back to Gloria. 'Here you go love. So how do you and I fit into this cottage caper? What's in it for me like?'

'Gary you and me's the main bit love. We're the management as well as the operations. You'll be like Toby and do the screening. Also you'll do the guiding and the protection. Hell Gary, you'll be able to quit your day job,' Gloria said and she laughed.

'How do these blokes know where to find me?' I asked, 'and how do I know they're safe or straight like you said?'

'I told you young Belle knew a lot? She's a smart kid.'

'Yes, she was all over the place looking at lighting and fixing the electrics. Seemed to know what wires were all about.'

'As well as that Gary she also knows a lot about computers and the internet. You know, the thing that my bully brother Wendell is in to, along with Tom Daley.'

'Tom Daley's into drugs.'

'Right, and computers Gary. He's the know-it-all in the village with regards computers, the internet, the web and all sorts of illegal hacking, pornography, you name it.'

'I don't know shit about all that,' I said. I was about to brag that I knew a lot about photography and video and then realised that I'd better shut my gob. Gloria didn't need to know that yet, maybe not at all but it was good to learn what else Tom Daley might be useful for.

'Belle has a friend who has set up a web site. People go looking on the net and find this web site and what they read and see interests them. They decide that they would like a little of this and a little of that, just like they did in London. Instead of asking Toby they ask the web and it tells them a bit more about this and that. It also tells them who to call. Once we've come to some form of agreement on the basics we pick a time and place. I'll tell you the time and place and who to expect. When they arrive you check them out. Are they who they should be and do they understand how this works? Then we go through your blindfold routine, the disorienting car ride, the party greeting, the fun and games followed by back to square one blindfolded again. Everyone goes home happy and content. As I said, just like London. Us girls get to enjoy ourselves in a location that is far healthier than up in London, healthier in a lot of ways Gary my love. Give us a kiss and seal the deal?'

I suppose I sat there somewhat stunned. I was with it enough to kiss Gloria and make it linger but my mind was whirling around every which way. At Fotheringham, in the forest, my forest, in that cottage, that ex Ferris murder and mayhem cottage. Jesus the stories that place can tell I thought and look what's to come. I've got to get that video deal sorted. If what Gloria is describing is for real it should be fantastic. Watching Gloria and Sandra was a turn on. Watching Gloria with Dora just recently excited me more than ever. Christ, this was Christmas every day of the week. If I do this right Gloria I thought you're right. I might be able to give up my day job. Looking at Gloria I saw her watching me. 'Excites you don't it? Makes you hot and horny just thinking about it Gary Templeton?' she said and she smiled at me with a funny look on her face. 'Bit like your dad you are you know. He likes to wander but he's a doer not a looker ain't he? In out and thank you mam although with the silver tongue of course. You're a little different. You think a bit more. Like to look a bit more. More concerned with what people think but in the end you like the action too. Right aren't I? You're partly ashamed of your dad and then again not. What was it you told me all those years ago? Must have been with Freddie and Sandra when we had all fucked each others brains out and you were lying there looking up at the ceiling and almost out of it. You were proud to be a Templeton and yet ashamed of your father having that name. Don't know what you were looking at but you went on about your grandfather and great grandfather and long traditions at Fotheringham. Said how you were proud and now with your dad your family name had been dragged through the mud and you'd lost face and were the bottom of the pile at Fotheringham. Pissed off you were about Bob Edwards or something. His family used to be nothing and Templetons were in charge and now your dad had tipped it arse over teakettle. Bottom of the pile again. But then you got real wound up about getting the name back again, getting on top again. When Bob Edwards finished you told me that you'd take over. Bugger your dad and his besmirching your name. Bugger all his illegitimate offspring, all your brothers and sisters you never knew and that you'd put it right. Funny that night. I suppose all of us were pretty fucked up that night. That was almost the last time before your party and Sandra topping herself poor cow.'

'Christ Gloria, don't bring that up again. That was my dad again. A pox on him and his fucking offspring. Drink up and let's get pissed. Perhaps your new deal will change things around. If I'm the main man then I'll get some respect back. Perhaps I will become the main man in the forest before Bob Edwards quits,' I laughed. 'I'll be in charge and they won't even know about it. Now that would be a gas Gloria. Yes, let's drink on the deal and make it happen darling. We're onto a winner. You and me girl. You and your singing dancing friends who perform for kicks are onto a winner with us.'

Well of course I got pissed that night and as we both had to work the next day I dropped Gloria off at her house and went home. I wasn't prepared to stumble all over Wendell's bedroom shit lying around Gloria's house and went home late bouncing from kerb to kerb until I staggered into my bed. Wednesday was a day when I worked with my eyes shut, my head pounding and lacking in conversation. Fortunately Bob Edwards was quiet too and he had Freddie working somewhere else in the forest so I didn't have to put up with his yapping at me all day.

Wednesday at Fotheringham Manor Big House was a day of great excitement which certainly wouldn't have done my head any good. It turned out it was the day that the news came.

'I've done it, I've done it,' cried Katya as she excitedly waved the letter about. 'Look Daniel, at last I've heard and it's fabulous, it's wonderful, it's better than I hoped,' and she hopped from one foot to the other. Suddenly Katya realised that Daniel wasn't there because he was out in the forest with the crew and Anthony and Sylvia were looking at her with big smiles on their faces. She blushed and then she ran over to Sylvia and gave her a big hug.

'So you've done well I can assume Katya. Brilliant love. We always thought you'd do well but obviously you've done better than you expected. Your parents will be delighted and so proud of you. I know your father will be and I expect your mother will have just assumed that you would do so well. Well done.'

'Katya my dear I'll share a hug and I don't doubt that you've got a First with all your excitement,' added Anthony getting up from his chair at the breakfast table. He folded his arms around her. 'Congratulations. I know you have been on tenterhooks waiting for that magic piece of paper. With your parents coming this weekend we should have a celebration party. What do you say Sylvia?'

'I think you miss the office and all its parties Anthony, or all its hustle and bustle but yes dear. We'll do it Sunday and that way Deidre and Delaney might have recovered a little from their jet lag. You are going to meet them at Heathrow Anthony? They're coming in early you remember?'

'Yes Sylvia, I remembered. I've talked with Katya here and we decided that I'd take the car and go alone so we would have room for all the luggage. Katya will stay here to greet them when I return. She had something special to do with Daniel I think. That right Katya?'

'Yes Anthony, if that's okay. Mum will want to gush all over me and that will be easier down here than in the car for four hours. I'll meet them down here.'

'So Katya, you never said,' said Sylvia quietly.

'It's a First Sylvia, a First, a First, a First. It's great. I can't wait to tell Daniel.'

'He'll be so excited for you he won't be able to concentrate on his golf game this afternoon. Aren't you playing too this afternoon? Didn't Daniel say you were playing now and practising for his Open Championship or something? When is that?'

'The Open's sometime in mid July, weekend of the 24/25 I think.'

'And your graduation ceremony at Oxford is July when?'

'July 12 Sylvia so Daniel and I will have time to recover from Oxford and concentrate on golf before that next big day.'

'And the next big day?' asked Sylvia.

'That's still work in progress Sylvia,' laughed Katya. 'You know Daniel. He's not given to wild impulsive decisions. He'll want to talk with my father and understand the right etiquette and protocol. He's a sensitive man is your son Sylvia and I love him dearly.'

Gloria knew that Wednesday was the day that Daniel Lord played golf and as it was her half day away from the hair-dressers and the tea-shop she caught me as I was driving home through the village. I must have had my eyes open by then 'cos I saw her waving wildly near the George.

'Gary love, Gina wanted to know something and I told her I would find out as soon as possible. Drive me out to the cottage Gary. Daniel's playing golf or something with Katya so they won't be around and I heard that Samantha is off somewhere away from home on her leading old strays about. There'll be no-one about right now. I need to check straight away. We're close to ready to go.'

So I turned the car around and off we went. True enough it didn't take long and while Gloria was in the cottage she told me to look around and see where and how were the best places to patrol. Look for where people might come Gary she said. Think of how best to deter them. Bollocks to that I thought. More important to me at that time was seeing where best to put some video cameras. After I learnt a little more from dad's friend and bought some gear I'd come out here myself and fix a few things. Should go into town tomorrow I thought and get a move on. If Gloria thinks she's close to starting I should be one jump ahead. Once back in the village we both said we had things to do but Gloria wanted to do a dry run tomorrow evening like the real thing. Some dress rehearsal or something she said. I told her I had a commitment tomorrow night and could we do it Friday? She looked at me for a moment and I could see things going through her head so I pulled her to me and kissed her.

'We're fine darling. Tomorrow I'll be busy and I'll go with you on Friday. Talk to the girls and sort out how they want to play it. You said Gina needed something and Belle has still got to get some lights fixed. Toby talked, or rather you talked about Toby having some other gear you said you wanted. What's the rush? We ain't got everything fixed up yet. Let's get it right love. I want this to work for us. You and me Gloria, this will be a winner. See you Friday night in the George.'

Gloria gave me another look and then leaned over and slipped her tongue in my mouth. After some time she wriggled free and jumped out of the car. 'Friday night,' she said and walked away.

Gloria's next two days were busy what with her two jobs and I didn't get to see her until the Friday night. Then, after a couple of pints in the pub Gloria and I sat in my car in the parking lot and went over a possible routine.

'Right Gary. The bloke or blokes know to meet here in the parking lot. Pull in like some other customer for the pub. They know what you drive and they'll know what you look like. We'll tell 'em that. They come over and ask for the Belle of the Ball. Got that? Belle of the Ball. And you say..'

'Don't you mean Belle on the ball?'

'Cut it out Gary. This is business. Don't fuck about. You say Belle who? If they're legit they say Belle from Hackney Wick.'

'Jesus Gloria, this is like a fucking book. We'll be here all night just gassing.'

Gloria got out of the car and walked away. She turned and walked back to the driver's side window. I had it open 'cos it was a warm evening.

'Hi, you look like just the bloke I need. I'm looking for Belle of the Ball?'

'Belle who?'

'Belle from Bethnal Green.'

303

'Right mate. You hop in and we'll find you a blindfold. Remember that is part of the entry fee. In the other side.'

'Gary Gary Gary, get it right for Christ sake. Belle who?'

'Belle from …. I don't know where Gloria. Where's Bethnal Green anyway?'

'That doesn't matter Gary and it's not Bethnal Green you silly bugger it's Hackney Wick. You're starting to get on my wick Gary. Now pull yer finger out and listen. It's Belle who? And the answer is Belle from Hackney Wick. After that you need to look at the silly sod and make sure he looks like the description we'll give you. If he's not tell him to piss off or something. If you think he's kosher you need to ask whether he's got the basic price and some spare change for any extras. Remind him that this is a cash deal. There's no paper or plastic floating about anywhere in this deal Gary. I don't want no paper trails or any other traceable items. We had enough problems with irate spouses reading credit card statements they shouldn't have seen. Some of the punters get careless and sloppy with their own personal security. Cash Gary and the right bloke. After all that then you can play the blindfold game. You got all that? It ain't rocket science even for a bloke who's a tree chopper or whatever.'

We went through the routine a couple of times before Gloria was satisfied I had got it right. After that we drove out towards the cottage. Even there Gloria wasn't satisfied until we did several loops through the local lanes and then went into the forest. I had to drive past the cottage, around a couple of compartments and back to the clearing before Gloria felt comfortable.

'Okay, now pretend I'm the client and I'm blindfolded. Come round my side and walk me over. Slow Gary, I can't see remember. In a circle or loop you silly bugger not dead straight. Talk so I can't count steps or anything daft. Talk Gary for Christ's sake. Hold my hand or I'll stumble in the blindfold. Jesus you are a piss poor guide Gary. I'll get the girls outside I think and let them take over halfway there. Okay, so you've handed the customer over and now what do you do?'

'Go out and patrol,' I said. 'I check around the area, back down the forest ride will be the most likely. If anyone has seen the lights like,' I added.

'Good, good idea,' said Gloria. 'We'll do this again this weekend and I'll get one of the girls to be the customer. We'll get ladies too you know Gary. We'll get ladies as well as blokes love.'

After this we had a quick pint because she was going shopping with her mother for all sorts of new curtains, furniture and Christ knows what. Seems they had already redecorated most of the house but they were still working on Wendell's room. As we left Gloria gave me strict instructions to be in the pub on Saturday night 'cos she wanted to do another run through with the girls.

Toby had organised a small van as well as his car for the weekend and Lola had driven the van down with Belle. They had all left London really early Saturday morning and it was soon after nine that Toby arrived with Gina and Sheena.

'Toby love, come in come in,' welcomed Tilley. 'Come and see what we've done to the rooms. Gloria and I have been shopping and we've got some real bright curtains. The girls aren't coming in then?'

'Not at first Tilley dear. They've got some things to do with Gloria. You know where then Gloria?'

'Sure Toby. I'll go with Sheena and Gina and we'll be back later. I'm working this afternoon Toby, or later this morning I suppose at Darlene's and so we'll sort our stuff out first thing. We won't be long Mum. Give our Toby here a guided tour. Show him what we've done. All his doing if you think about it. Thanks Toby,' and Gloria gave Toby a big hug and ran her lips across his cheek. 'Come on then Gina. We've work to do girl.'

That Saturday morning Gloria directed Gina driving Toby's car out of the village to the rendezvous with Lola and the van. The two vehicles slowly moved past the edge of Fotheringham until Gloria was satisfied there was no-one else in sight on the road. They turned down the forest ride and moved slowly and quietly through to the cottage. Lola moved the van up as close to the back door as she could. The girls spent an hour moving stuff from the van and then Gina ran Gloria back into the village to go to work at Darlene's.

'I may change all this,' said Gloria.

'Change what Gloria?'

'When we get started I think I'll drop one or maybe both jobs. In fact I may go back to the George. We'll see what kind of routine we can work out.'

'Is Gary on for tonight?'

'Yes, I told him yesterday Gina. He can probably remember from then, provided he doesn't do anything stupid this morning. Anyway, I've got to work until seven and then we'll all get together and do a dry run. You going back to Lola?'

'I'll be discreet Gloria. I'll make sure no-one sees me turn off, but yes, Belle said she wanted a hand with some of the wiring. Lola and Sheena don't know bugger all about that and Sheena wanted to see about space for any dancing routine. We'll see you later. By the way, is Toby safe with your mum now she's found herself again?'

Gloria laughed. 'He slept last weekend in her bed Gina love. Well, let's say he spent the night in her bedroom. Don't know about any sleep. No Toby's fine Gina and my mum is a new lady. I really am happy about that. After all these years I've got my mum back and that's thanks to Toby. I think the two of them are safe Gina.'

While Gloria spent the afternoon looking after customer's tea requests, 'and with a slice of that pie love?', Gina and her friends were working at the cottage. They re-arranged a few things and wired up a few lights. I didn't know this until later but they had some removable screens to change the appearance of the cottage, especially the kitchen area and these could be easily folded away when the cottage was supposed to be empty. Gloria reckoned that Daniel Lord wasn't likely to remember what things looked like exactly and she was sure that Betty Travers wouldn't be going out there any more.

Gloria's friends were all back with Toby and Tilley when Rupert's merry band walked into the clearing around the Ferris cottage. Arnold was quite fascinated with Fotheringham and it was he this time who had insisted they return. Philippa and Margaret had heard the right Reverend Gabriel Godschild speak three times now and although they believed in his message he wasn't saying anything new or intellectually challenging. There was no rush to hear him again but Arnold and Rory were both anxious to see more of the area because there was a wide variety of wildlife here. Ted, the historian still hadn't managed to convince himself that the drovers' road was truthful although Doris was quite emphatic that it was obvious and that they had every right to be here.

'And in the cottage Doris? That public property too?' asked Rory with a smile on his face.

'Don't be cute Rory Flanagan. I don't break the law, I uphold the law,' Doris said with a toss of her head. Meanwhile Arnold was waxing eloquently about the broken edges of the clearing and the juxtaposition of habitats which explained the quite diverse array of bird species he could hear.

'That's more than I can hear,' said Rory, 'with Doris rattling on about human rights. Wonder whether your laws offer rights to the wildlife Doris? Shouldn't we be quiet so that Arnold's birds can hear each other?'

'Peasant,' muttered Doris.

The group moved on and Rupert led down the forest ride. Within another twenty minutes, just about the time Rupert was going to call a halt for lunch the group came into another clearing with another cottage and here stood a Landrover. The cottage door opened and Daniel Lord walked out talking with Katya.

'So it looks all ready for the Entwhistles,' he said.

'Daniel I think the wife will really like the painting job that was done in the little boy's room. Oh hello, I didn't see you in the sunshine. How are you all this morning?'

Daniel too looked up and held his hand across his forehead to shut out the bright glare after coming out of the cool and dimmer light of the cottage.

'I'm happy to see you walking on the forest ride this morning.'

'Do you just have the two cottages in the forest?' asked Arnold. 'They would be neat places to stay if I was really to study the wildlife in this forest. I would be right in the heart of the area and would hear everything all around me. Although you pretend this is a commercial forest and such it is still quite wild in places. Did you ever think of turning it into a wildlife sanctuary?'

'Hold up there Arnold. They have commercial logging going on here and artificial planting. It's hardly wildlife and certainly not wilderness like you're always pining for.'

'No Rupert, I realise that but it has potential don't you see.'

'Do you think so?' asked Katya stepping forwards. 'We're trying to find ways of making the forest more "green" as part of the Education Centre experience. Daniel here has already changed a few of the plans to broaden the array of habitats and we're thinking of letting the straight edges of the forest rides become more fragmented with more edges.'

'But that's what it is all about,' cried Arnold enthusiastically, 'it's all about edges. It's all about change from one place to the next. It's the inter-zone areas that are important.'

'Could we talk sometime?' asked Katya. 'Daniel, maybe we've found someone to help with our thoughts and ideas.'

'We might do a trade,' offered Daniel, 'a non-paid consultant in exchange for access to the Estate. Overall we're trying to manage the Estate from a tree farm back towards a more diverse and perhaps more natural area of woodland in the widest sense. Over one hundred years ago we did manage the Estate along those lines, primarily for hunting but then my great grandmother changed the emphasis towards commercial forestry.'

'But that's great,' said Arnold, 'a great idea. Rory, you're a wildlife biologist, you can see the benefits from their idea. We could help you know.'

'Why no pay?' demanded Doris. 'You cheap or just trying to exploit the proletariat as usual? Make the peasants pay again, and again, and again!'

'Doris, just for once button it,' said Rupert.

'Look,' Katya said, 'we should arrange to meet sometime and talk about this. Right now we've got other things we have to do and Daniel here is just making sure this cottage is all ready for some new employees who are moving in this weekend. If you are around here next Saturday we should arrange to meet up in the Education Centre and discuss what we might do. You could become our occasional forest wardens if you're going to be here for some time. We use the Estate as a course for competitive orienteering too so we have a fair number of people through the Estate but it is always good to have other sets of eyes watching for things, especially as you have some wildlife knowledge. Daniel and I are both professional foresters so we are very familiar with most of the plant life but we would welcome some ideas on the animal kingdom.'

'From some other members of the animal kingdom,' suggested Rory with a smile on his face.

'So this cottage will have people in it?' asked Arnold somewhat sadly.

'As of this weekend,' said Daniel. 'We've a new family moving in, a new employee with his wife and son.'

'But didn't you say she was organically minded Daniel? What did your mother call her? An earth-mother, that was it, so she would also be interested in any ideas about a greener more natural forest.'

'It's still got to pay for itself Katya,' reminded Daniel. He turned to Rupert and the other folk. 'Sorry we all seemed to have got off on the wrong foot but as you can imagine we don't take kindly to broken fences and do appreciate people respecting the forest. As Katya here explained we are trying to slowly move the Estate to producing what Katya calls green revenues, environmentally sensitive revenues. It won't happen overnight and starting the Education Centre was an idea that appealed to the young heir, my nephew Peter Lord. I'm Daniel Lord by the way and this is Katya Howard.' Daniel held out his hand and slowly the group shook hands and exchanged names.

'Will you be back here next Saturday? It is only Saturday that you hike isn't it?' asked Katya quite eagerly.

'Yes,' said Arnold, 'that's right isn't it Rupert? We could come back here? Actually Daniel, Philippa and Margaret here are also quite interested in your preacher. They come here to hear him too. Didn't you Philippa?'

Philippa looked at Arnold and it wasn't a very Christian expression on her face Daniel noted. Perhaps Philippa's creation beliefs didn't coincide with Arnold's naturalist and no-doubt evolutionary beliefs thought Daniel. Takes all sorts.

'Say three o'clock at the Centre?' suggested Katya. 'If you're there we'll talk and if not no problem. We can catch you later sometime. There really is no rush as nature moves slowly. Come on Daniel. We're late already.'

'Soft you are Arnold Church. Soft. Free advice. No fees. No wonder you're still a poor nature freak.'

'Whereas you Doris my love are a hard-shelled, tough as nails, in your face, love 'em and charge 'em legal freak. Takes all sorts.'

'Go sing a song Rory. We going to lunch here Rupert? Good as anywhere. If we're back here we might get some herbal tea from the new earth-mother next week.'

Back in the Landrover Katya was quite excited about her new find. 'A wildlife expert Daniel, someone who could help us with that part of the plan. He's keen too and the Irishman is supposed to be a wildlife biologist as well. Perhaps their coming here wasn't too bad after all. You got the fences fixed pretty easily and so that wasn't so bad and now we have a new source of ideas plus additional sets of eyes about what is happening out here. Cool eh?'

'Maybe Katya, maybe,' said Daniel. 'We'll see but remember this is an operational forest and we don't need people interfering with any of the commercial operations. If they only hike on the Saturdays that is not so bad as we typically just work weekdays. Still, I'll make mum and dad aware so we don't have any more meetings with mixed signals.'

'Mother, father, it's so good to see you both. Did you have a good trip?'

'My darling little girl,' cried Deidre as she rose from the sofa. 'Doesn't she look a picture Delaney dear? Quite the grown up lady and looking so workman-like in those breeches and shirt. You look like the lady of the manor. No disrespect Sylvia but she does look good don't you think?'

Katya gave her mother an all-embracing hug and managed to smile and wink at her father at the same time. She kissed her mother on both cheeks and slowly let go with her arms as she turned to Delaney. 'Hello dad,' she said quietly and folded herself into his arms as Delaney held his little girl.

'I hear you've done well my daughter.'

'Of course she did Delaney. Whatever did you expect? Mark you that manager of yours wasn't so happy with her work I heard. Still, what does he know? He's never been to Oxford. Come and sit by me treasure and tell me all about it. When are we going to Oxford? Will I need a gown or will a summer dress be appropriate? Does your father need his tails and is this a top hat or just a Fedora? It is outdoors I suppose and they will have those nicely-cut triangular sandwiches with the crusts cut off? I do like those my dear. Do you speak Katya? Do you all have to speak? Is it in Latin? I'm sure I won't understand half of it if it's in Latin. Do you have your tails Delaney? I can't remember whether we packed them or not. Go and look dear in the bags. Upstairs Delaney.'

'Mother, mother slow down please. It's Saturday. We aren't going to Oxford until next Friday and it's Saturday afternoon. You've just had a tiring flight and a long car drive and it's time to relax. Fotheringham is a wonderful place to relax mother believe me.'

'Queen Deidre, Queen Deidre and King Delaney,' cried James as he interrupted Katya's attempt at peace, quiet and relaxation and came charging into the drawing room with his mother in tow a good step behind.

'My little English Guide and Interpreter,' cried Deidre as she accepted James with arms, legs and mouth all going at the same time.

'Hello Deidre, hi Delaney,' said Samantha. 'Please excuse my little Canadian Sault warrior. I'm still trying to civilise him but it is good to see you.'

Gradually the group of people in the drawing room quietened down and a happy peace fell over the house. Katya Howard's parents had come over from Florida and the entire household was scheduled to go up to Oxford next week for the graduation ceremony. Another professional forester would be in residence at Fotheringham.

Not so very far away another group of people were also fairly happy and peaceful as Gloria set about training me for my new position of authority and responsibility. We'd all been to the George for a couple of pints and now we were crowded around Belle's magic box of tricks in Tilley's newly decorated front room. Belle sat in front of her computer and slowly explained what she was doing. I didn't know all this but when Wendell the wanker had wanted a computer the technician had put four outlets in the house as it was the same price as one he said. So Belle could plug her machine into whatever special cables let her talk to this web thing. The more I heard about it the more it sounded like a spider's web but then I didn't know bugger all about computers anyway. Belle was operating in another world as far as I was concerned.

'So you see, the customer can look here and if he sees something he likes he can go to this tab and lo and behold he gets more detail. He can easily flip back and check out another scene, or another hostess, whatever. It's easy.'

'Okay Belle, we've hooked our lovely fish who's looking for an evening of fun and laughter. What does he or she do next?'

'Contact numbers are here Lola. The screen tells you what to do and where to go. Phone here, follow the instructions and remember the words. Just like a treasure hunt darling and we're the treasure.'

'He tells us a little about himself, so Gary here can check him out like?'

'See here,' said Belle and she tapped a couple of times with her fingers and another screen appeared. She typed something and letters appeared telling me she was tall dark and handsome. Bullshit I thought.

'Gary you watching this mate? You'll get this description so you know the punters are for real. No match no deal Gary. We ain't picking up strays.'

'Sure sure,' I said, 'I'm watching. I understand.'

'And we handle the money Gary but you check he's got cash. We don't want no tossers coming out there waving plastic about. Cash Gary, you got that?'

'Jesus Lola, I ain't that thick. Gloria's told me one hundred times now. No pennies either I hear, just notes.'

'Very funny Gary. This ain't no charity either love. This is business.'

'Okay Belle, as long as the punters find it easy we needn't worry. Let's go and sort out our end girls.'

Belle did something and pretty soon the magic box shut up shop and I was being hustled out of the door and into my car. Toby appeared from the back of the house with Tilley in tow.

'We're just off for a last drink Toby. Don't you go doing anything we wouldn't do,' laughed Sheena. 'Don't wait up mum,' said Gloria. 'Keep Toby happy.'

'I'm slowly remembering all about that Gloria love,' said Tilley, 'aren't I Toby?'

Toby wrapped his arms around Tilley and gave her a hug. 'You're my million dollar baby,' he sang and we all trooped out of the house laughing.

'Right Gary, show time. Got your gear? You're sitting here in the car and along comes Mister Plod. Evening Gary. What you doing here mate? Shouldn't you be home lad? Pubs closed you know. George has shut up shop. So Gary, what you going to say?'

'Shit, I don't know Gloria. I ain't thought about that. We never talked about that.'

'Get your head out of your arsehole then Gary and think.'

'I'm checking whether I'm okay to drive home or maybe walk,' I suggested.

'Not bad for starters Gary.'

'I'm waiting for Freddie who has taken Gloria home and said he'd be back in five minutes.'

'Don't take the piss Gary.'

'No Gloria, no girl, that's not bad either,' said Gina.

'Okay Gary. I've just driven in and I'm parked over there in the shadows. I get out and walk over to you and knock on your window or look in, whatever. Hi I say. I'm looking for the London Road?'

'Just up to the top of the road there mate and turn left.'

'No you stupid prat that's a meeting call.'

'That's not what you said last night. You wanted to talk about Belle on the ball and she came from Hackney Wick.'

'We changed all that Gary. Weren't you listening back there to Belle? Don't want no names too close you know.'

'Yes well, anyone could be asking for the London Road for real you know.'

'Not if you ask them do they mean London Street?'

'And now what do they say? You mean Hackney Wick?'

'No Gary, you're getting on my wick again you dumb bugger. They say they mean Forest Street but I need a blindfold. You got that? London Road, no London Street, no Forest Street and need a blindfold. Easy.

Check the face, check the cash, get the blindfold. Right, we'll give it a try. Lola, you look just the part as an eager beaver out for a night's fun.'

'That's me darling, an eager beaver. Aren't I always Gloria?' said Lola and she gave Gloria a sensual hug.

'Cut it out Lola and let's get Gary here half-trained at least.'

After three or four times the girls were relatively happy that I knew enough to screen out any losers and had the blindfold routine down okay. Using the two cars we quietly drove out to the cottage and Gloria made me go through the routine out there two or three times. Eventually we all ended up inside the cottage and I saw what they had done. It was neat and looked quite different. Belle had done quite a clever job with the lighting. Gloria told me to go outside and walk around the cottage.

'See if you can see any lights Gary? We think we've got the place fairly dark but we haven't checked in the night time. Listen for noise too. Go to the edge of the clearing, out on that road and see whether you can hear us.'

Yes sir, no sir, three bags full sir I thought but I went and did what Gloria asked. I'd get my share I thought now I've got that camera gear. Come back on Monday and fix that up. Dad's mate said I'd got the right idea how to use it and so I just need to look around and fix a few things. I'll bring a drill, a few more tools and give it a dry run on Monday. Shit I muttered as I fell over a root. There were no lights from the cottage and I couldn't hear fuck all either. I turned on my torch and nearly fell in a hole on the edge of the clearing. Fuck it that's young Peter Lord's other soil pit from last year where he found Freddie's old clothing. At least they could have filled it in properly. A bloke could get killed out here if he wasn't careful. I chuckled to myself when I thought of the number of people who had been killed out here. Jesus, I wonder whether that bothers Gloria at all. I pushed open the cottage door and suddenly I heard the soft music, the giggles and the sound of glasses.

'Come in Gary. Come in and shut the door love. Time to party. Grab a glass and have a drink. Watch Sheena here dance and then we'll let Lola walk all over you in her high heels. How long do you think he'll last Gloria?'

I suppose I lasted about an hour before I was overwhelmed. I dreamt about making videos; amazing, exotic, exciting, and cock-stiffening videos. I awoke to peace, quiet, snoring and a sour taste in my mouth. The girls was scattered around the cottage and I remembered last night. Smiling about my future enterprise I put the kettle on.

Parents, who'd have them?

As I boiled the kettle I managed to look around more seriously in the kitchen. I found some tea, some sugar and even some mugs but obviously there was no milk. The girls gradually woke and sorted themselves out in a slow, quiet and dreamy sort of way. Everyone talked in a low voice and it was a lethargic group of people who put the cottage back the way we found it for appearance's sake. There was a discreet discussion and agreement that we had a possible future and this could really be a blast. With our two vehicles we peacefully trundled back to the main road with lots of yawns and sleepy bodies. Taking care not to be seen by any other vehicles as we left the forest ride we drove the few kilometres back into a slumbering Sunday morning village and pulled up at Gloria's house. Somewhat surprisingly Gloria found both her mum and Toby up, dressed, breakfasted and full of life which was more than could be said for us lot I thought. After some last-minute words from Gloria and instructions to be in the George tonight I left for home, my bed and a chance to rest up. I also had some other organising to do I thought as I closed my eyes and crashed.

Despite jet lag Deidre Howard was up quite early at Fotheringham Manor and button-holed her daughter early on. Daniel managed to escape with Delaney as Delaney wanted to see some of the forest operations and the changes being made in the forest. Katya had tried to escape too but Deidre needed a mother to daughter chat. Samantha cleverly unloaded James with her brother and Delaney so that she too could catch up on some business associated with Heritage Adventures. Anthony wasn't quick enough to go out with Daniel and Sylvia made sure that she told Anthony they both had to be available to help the Entwhistles who were coming today. Activity abounded in and around Fotheringham.

Gloria told me later that she didn't want all of her girl friends showing up en masse at the pub in the village and so the girls spent lunchtime huddled over the computer with Belle while Gloria took Tilley and Toby into the George. These three all ganged up on landlord George to re-instate Gloria working back behind the bar. Gloria had already told me she thought working in the pub would be better than either the hair-dressers or Darlene's. Secretly she had explained that she was more likely to find some punters in the bar than at the tea-shop and certainly more likely than at Mrs. Digby's. For all that though she wanted to negotiate with George which times she worked. Already Gloria was thinking of using the cottage on Wednesday and Saturday nights initially so working those two nights was out for starters. She reckoned she might want to skip Sunday lunchtime and maybe Sunday evening too but she wanted to wait and see. It was Tilley who was the most vocal with George and this was a new Tilley Manson as George soon found out.

'George, you know my Gloria pulls in the punters for you. Just look at her. I heard you had all sorts of questions when you let her go. People have discovered she is an attractive reason for coming in here. You might think you're the only pub in town but folk will go out to that roadhouse on the highway you know unless there's a special attraction like my Gloria. Toby here recognised that, didn't you Toby love? You recognised that when my Gloria was working up in London and you thought she was special up there too. You used to go to that Club she was working at didn't you Toby? Told me she was a big favourite there. Stands to reason George: great personality, fully experienced, talks friendly with the customers and often knows what you want before you've even asked.' George collapsed. He couldn't withstand the arguments and suggestions. He held up his hands in surrender.

'Okay Tilley, okay. I accept. I'll re-instate her. I'll give her her job back. Gloria, you're back on this side of the bar darling. How about right now?'

'There George, that looks much better, much more natural and mine's a pink gin darling.'

Gloria worked a shift until three when she went home with Toby and her mum and the girls all left with Toby and went back to London. A constructive weekend they all agreed. Gloria explained all this to me that evening in the pub. In between times she sorted out with George times and conditions that suited her. Seems the word quickly spread in the village and there were lots of people in the pub that night congratulating Gloria on getting her job back and praising George for eventually seeing sense.

With the Howards coming Daniel knew that he and Katya wouldn't be playing golf that Sunday morning but at lunchtime Daniel did explain that he and Katya both had to play on the Wednesday as his Club's Open Tournament was coming up soon and they both had to practice.

'Daniel that's all very fine but you have some commitments this afternoon son. The Entwhistles said they would be here just after lunch and I've told your dad that we will all help them get settled.'

'Can I ride Dainty grandma? I'm sure they'd love to see Dainty. I could make her stop and turn. We don't have any jumps down there Mummy. Why don't we take some hurdles down in the lorry Uncle Daniel? I could show them jumping too.'

'Samantha dear, can you gently explain to your son that the Entwhistles are just moving house and unfortunately they will be very busy this afternoon despite the entertainment your son is offering?'

'Sure Mum,' said Samantha, 'but we could come down and help. Didn't I hear the family had a son about James's age?'

'Sylvia I know you're all busy with this new family so I told Delaney we would take ourselves off this afternoon and let Katya show us a little more of the countryside here. Now she knows the area she can be our guide and that way you'll not have us under your feet. Delaney can drive, Katya can navigate and I can enjoy the delights of this wonderful little country. Give us the grand tour Katya. There, that's settled then.'

Katya glanced across at Daniel. Parents she mouthed. Daniel smiled and winked. James was in a quandary. Should he go with his special friend and show them where to go and explain it all to Queen Deidre, or, should he go with his mother, on Dainty for sure and show this new boy all about horses and his forest? I mean to say, it had been Enrico's cottage and James knew all about that place as he had been there at least twice before. The decision for James got made for him as an old dusty dormobile slowly drove up the driveway and stopped in the forecourt. A man rang the front door bell.

James had heard the van coming and he was out of his chair and halfway down the hall before any of the adults responded to the bell. Samantha however was hot on his heels.

'Afternoon Miss,' said Colin Entwhistle and he took off his flat cap with his left hand. His other hand was firmly held by a young boy with tousled hair, rough clothing and a big grin who in turn was firmly holding the lead of a young Labrador puppy.

'A puppy,' exclaimed James.

'I'm Colin Entwhistle Miss. I'm looking for her ladyship or Sir Anthony. I'm expected.'

'A puppy Mummy, a real black puppy,' and James excitedly ran forwards to greet his new friend. The young boy with Colin Entwhistle wasn't sure whether to get closer to his dad, protect his puppy from the charging James or take a pro-active and possessive stand against the mad charger. In the end the two young boys crouched down and shared the excited licks and nips from the lively puppy.

'This 'ere is Adam Miss, me son,' added Colin.

'Colin Entwhistle is it?' Sylvia asked as she came through to the front door, 'And I see our James has found a new friend, two new friends it seems. Good afternoon, I'm Sylvia Lord and have you had a good journey?' Sylvia stepped forwards and offered her hand and Colin let go of Adam and shook Sylvia's hand.

'Mrs. Lord mam, your ladyship,' said Colin. 'Pleased to meet you. The wife's in't van and we're set to find the cottage. Just thought I'd drop by and tell you we're 'ere. Lady Worthing sends her regards. I won't disturb you and we'll find our way. Got a map from Lady Worthing so we're fine. Come Adam son.'

'Mummy can I go with them? I could show them the way. I needn't ride Dainty. I could go in their van and be with the puppy. We won't be long.'

Sylvia laughed and she turned to Colin Entwhistle. 'Colin you had better meet some of the others while you're here because this one you will see all too often I expect,' and Sylvia took James by his hand and gently eased him up away from the roly-poly puppy.

'James MacRae meet Mr. Entwhistle and his son, Adam isn't it? This is Samantha MacRae, my daughter and mother of the energetic James. And you are Adam young man?' Sylvia asked as she too squatted down beside the young lad and his puppy.

'Aye missus, and this is Storm me dog.'

'And a fine looking dog he is too Adam,' said Sylvia and she straightened up just as Daniel and Katya came out of the doorway.

'Daniel, this is Colin Entwhistle down from Worthing Hall, plus his son Adam and fearsome hound Storm.'

'He's not fearsome Grandma, he's cute.'

'Good afternoon, I'm Daniel Lord the Estate Manager here as you know. It's good to see you and I'm pleased to see you've arrived safely. We thought we'd all give you a hand getting settled in and make sure you know where everything is. If you can hang on for a second I'll get my Landrover and we'll show you the way.'

Sylvia smiled at Colin and suggested she meet his wife. Together they walked back to the minivan. As they approached the front door opened and a young lady in her early twenties wriggled herself out from the van. Ophelia Entwhistle had never been slim and after one child and obviously expecting another she was close to being round but she was all smiles, long blond hair and chubby hands as she stood there to greet the Lords.

'Mam,' she said and Samantha thought she almost curtsied. 'We're pleased to meet you. Lady Worthing herself said you'd be out to meet us. Her ladyship told me you'd see us right. My Colin's a good worker mam. Knows his business and a dab 'and at motors. We'll do right for you. I can work too, in the nursery perhaps after the young 'uns born,' and Ophelia patted her swollen belly. 'Another couple of months I reckon.'

Samantha felt a twinge of jealousy. A second child and their son Adam only just a little older than James. She stepped forwards and held her son's hand. The grip was so strong that James looked up at his mother and wondered. 'Can we go Mummy? We could go with Uncle Daniel when he shows them the way. I could play with the puppy. Can we can we?' and James tugged on the tightly-held hand.

'Mrs. Entwhistle might like someone for her son to be with while they're moving in Samantha,' suggested Sylvia. 'You could have James and Adam away from the hustle and bustle of moving in and let the adults get organised without the little ones under their feet.' James was already away from his mother's tight grip and playing with Adam and the roly-poly puppy. 'Can we?' he pleaded again.

'Sylvia why don't I take James and young Adam here with his friend Storm for a walk around their new home while you make sure Daniel gets them settled. Samantha might be able to handle ultra-demanding rock climbs but taking on young dynamos like these two takes an older more mature man.'

'Anthony, you really are full of it,' laughed Sylvia.

'Hello, I'm Anthony Lord,' said Anthony as he joined the group of people. He shook hands with Colin and then with Ophelia. 'Look, I know you're tired after the journey so let's get this show on the road. Daniel, you all set son? You take your mother and I'll take the small truck to bring these two plus Storm. Colin that okay, if I take your son? He'll be fine with that?'

Colin Entwhistle stood there somewhat overwhelmed. Lady Worthing had told him in her plain-speaking way that the Lord household contained some funny people. He remembered her snorting about new money people but some of the family are decent enough she had added. Have some weird ideas of course, and do some crazy things but then they are from the south she had said as if that explained everything. Seems she was right.

'Colin, that okay?'

Colin started. 'Aye aye that's fine, fine Sir Anthony. Adam will be fine. Go with the man Adam. The wee lad is James Adam, his Lordship's grandson mind. We'll meet at the cottage son.'

Colin turned to his wife. 'Adam's fine love. It'll help if he's not under yer feet. You rest up now back in't van and we'll take it slow over any bumps. Lead on Mr. Daniel sir. We're set.'

'Samantha you okay with this? You okay if I borrow James for a while?'

'Yes dad, sure. Look after him though. Look after him dad. He's precious you know.' Samantha stood there and watched as Colin and the pregnant Ophelia climbed back into their van. She watched as her mother climbed into the Landrover beside Daniel. She watched as her dad strode around the side of the house with James, Adam and a rolling bundle of black hair called Storm. Suddenly she felt a bit lonely.

'Quiet all of a sudden Samantha,' said Katya as she came and stood beside Samantha.

'Have children,' cried Samantha suddenly turning and gripping Katya's arms. 'Have lots of babies with Daniel Katya,' and just as quickly Samantha let go of Katya and ran indoors.

Katya stood there on the forecourt of Fotheringham Manor and looking down the stately gravelled driveway she wondered what in heavens was that all about. Samantha she wondered, what caused that reaction and those words. Daniel's sister was as tough as nails and did some death-defying rock climbs, cheerful in your face attitude to life and not worried with messing up murder crime scenes yet suddenly she looked like she was going to cry. Strange people some of these Lords she thought.

'Have they left you out here all alone sugar?'

'Yes mother, well no, not really as they have gone to help the new family settle in to Enrico's old cottage. Daniel had the men do a lovely job on it mother. They cleaned it out to look spotless and then they painted it such delightful colours. Sylvia had talked to the mother up in Yorkshire and they had chosen the colours. Daniel had them paint the walls and the ceiling and Sylvia organised some new curtains just as the family had asked. They think about their people Mum. Anthony especially is always thinking about people and bringing us all together. You should see him when the family are all here, like it was on Daniel's birthday last Fall. That cousin Henri wanted to start an argument about money but Anthony gently avoids any conflicts and binds them all back together again as one happy family.'

'You like it here dear, don't you?'

'Yes mother I do. I didn't expect to feel this way when I first came to England. I was all set to come back to Florida and see whether I could change dad's company. Make them see green you know.'

'Well you certainly made them see sense,' said Delaney as he too came out of the front doorway. 'That thesis of yours certainly made a few of them sit up a little straighter. Think a little more.'

'Yes dear, we know all about your company and its funny way of thinking. Those southern boys could never get it quite right now could they? Always needed one of us Yankees to help lead them back to common sense. Too many inbred families Delaney I say. I've told you I don't know how many times that you folk just need to find more Yankee girls to stir you all up a little. That plantation life seems to put you all to sleep. You might have nice manners and all, wear the right clothes and say the right things in company but you have some old-fashioned ideas when it comes to business. Our Katya did the right thing in coming over here and learning some of the new ways to think about the forest. We've got to move with the times now Delaney the IIIrd. We might even have to change the name of our sugar's first child. Change from Delaney to Adam as a guide to a new beginning. Make a fresh start with some new blood from this dear little country. What do you say Katya dear?'

Katya was about to remark that this was twice in the last five minutes that someone had suggested she have a baby but she caught herself and smiled as she said, 'Mother, Daniel and I do need to get married first before we think about having a baby let alone naming him.'

'There,' said Delaney pointedly, 'our daughter has learnt to be a southern lady and observe the proper procedures Deidre my dear. Courtship, engagement, marriage, establishment in life, and then progeny, successors for the line. Well spoken Katya my love. Your mother's impetuous Yankee ways will be the downfall of civilisation. Anthony here realises that.'

'Actually Daddy I think you're absolutely right. Daniel hasn't actually proposed as yet although we both know we love each other so much but I think he learnt from his father that he should talk with you first. I think he wants to ask you for my hand, in the proper style.'

'That's beautiful Katya sweetheart,' gushed Deidre and she gave her daughter an all-embracing motherly hug. 'I'm so happy for you. You deserve the best and this family can certainly offer you the best.'

'It is truly a great estate,' agreed Delaney. 'Anthony and Sylvia have done a wonderful job here and I hear they have successfully taken the money from the sale of their software company and invested part of it here back into the estate. I was hoping we could go out with Katya and see this new Education Centre. That sounds an exciting example coming out of our Katya's thesis Deidre. She's been finding some green revenues for Sylvia here.'

'Didn't you find some treasure too Katya, for Sylvia that is? I seem to remember you writing about some treasure. You were explaining it last Christmas when you came home to see us. Weren't there some hidden gold coins and then you found a necklace in an old tree. Amazing Delaney. I'm quite amazed at what these people do with their trees. You haven't got trees like that in your forest Delaney. They're all in straight rows and looking like southern soldiers all dressed up in the grey dust. Then they all sway about in the hurricanes and drop those big pine cones everywhere. Dangerous they are Delaney. I won't walk through your plantations but here the trees all seem softer, greener and more shapely. I feel more at home here Delaney. Would you like to live here Katya?'

Katya jerked herself back into the present. When her mother took off on one of her monologues she tended to let her mind wander and look about her. Trouble was she'd been away from home for so long she'd forgotten when to catch the winding down part and appear to have been listening.

'Deidre it is delightful and I'm so glad we came. In fact I'm so glad that young James found us nearly a year ago now. You remember Deidre, the train ride and young James falling all over our feet?'

'Of course I remember Delaney. I'm not likely to forget that lovely little boy explaining ever so many things and speaking with his different voice. And of course Daniel was so polite and apologetic, and then talking with you Delaney about your forestry as if he'd known you all his life. I always thought the English were aloof and rather unfriendly towards us Delaney but that day was a delight my dear. Gave me a completely different picture of England and the English. Look how we met Sylvia, right here in fact. I had expected the lady of the house to be dressed in a lovely gown standing in front of this magnificent house at the head of this truly stately drive but Sylvia got out of her car looking like one of those beach bums that Katya kept finding before she went to College.'

'And she swept you off your feet mother,' said Katya. 'She met you, charmed you and we all ended up as guests of this wonderful family and I'm so glad,' and Katya in turn gave her mother a hug.

'Come on,' she said. 'Father's car is just fine to go and see the Education Centre and I know he's bursting to get into the forest. I can drive and I'll show you what Daniel and I have been up to turning the forest green.'

The short convoy of Daniel leading the Entwhistles leading Anthony with the two young boys and the dog slowly moved through the forest to the clearing around Enrico's old cottage. As Daniel and Sylvia got out they turned to help the Entwhistles while Anthony held the two youngsters back and quietly explained where they were before James went into overdrive. Adam was fascinated. He had lived in a worker's cottage before but that was in a row of other worker's cottages and not all alone out in the forest. He'd spent a lot of time with his dad in the forest so that wasn't strange but the house being all alone was different.

'Okay Adam, while your mum and dad are moving in why don't we take Storm here and explore a little of your new world. We'll let James lead the way and you and I can make sure our leader stays on the path. While we are out here do you want to let Storm run or would you sooner hold him as it's new to him too you know?'

'I'll hold him to start with sir,' said Adam.

'I could hold him,' interjected James.

'Yes James but you're the leader and you need both hands free to fight off any possible strangers trespassing in your forest. You look forwards for us and we'll follow. Just like your mother, remember?'

'Yes grandfather. I'll be first, in front, just like mummy,' and the three humans and one small wriggling puppy ventured forth into the surrounds of Adam's new home.

'Did you have some more furniture coming tomorrow Ophelia?' Sylvia asked.

'Yes your ladyship,' Ophelia replied. 'Colin arranged for that to come tomorrow. He told the driver to come to the House mam. Colin said he'd ask when he got here how you wanted him to handle it from there.'

'We'll look after your driver Ophelia and make sure he finds his way. But you've got enough stuff for this evening and tonight? You've beds?'

'Colin said we'd be fine for the one night. We've all slept rough before mam. It's not a problem. We've bedding thanks.'

Sylvia moved round to where Daniel was helping Colin with a couple of larger items out of the van. That seemed to be taken care of so Sylvia came back to Ophelia.

'Come and see what we did with your ideas about painting. I think it looks delightful and we hope it is what you wanted. As you suggested Adam's room looks like earth below, with grass, trees and sky. Just like living with no walls yet still warm and safe in the forest. I hope he likes it.'

'Eee Colin, cum and loook luv. That's greet.'

'Reet champion that is missus. Our Adam will think he's died and gone't 'eaven.'

Sylvia smiled at Daniel and at the comments. 'Seems that Gary and Freddie did a good job here Daniel. You should pass back the comments, translated into the local language though Daniel else Freddie will never understand.'

Daniel laughed and slapped his hand lightly on Colin's shoulder. 'A couple of the young lads in the work crew did all this for you Colin. Actually they did a good job too and my mother and I hope you will be happy here. Now, you've another couple of heavy items to shift and then we'll let you sort yourselves out in peace. Mum we've got some things in the Landrover too, some milk, bread and groceries. If you'll bring those in for Ophelia I'll just finish off with Colin. I know the fridge is plugged in and working because Katya and I were here yesterday. I'll show Colin how to get from here to the Estate Office for work tomorrow morning and then I'll come down here and check if Ophelia and Adam have all they need for the day. I suppose they'll have to think about school for Adam too.'

'No no Mr. Lord sir,' said Ophelia. 'I teach our Adam. He don't go to no school. He learns at home with me. I teach the right things, about the earth and the sky, about water and fire, about the animals and the plants. We don't need no school. Not Adam and me.'

Sylvia and Daniel stood there and listened and Daniel could hear the strength in Ophelia's conviction. Old Lord Worthing, Aubrey Worthing's dad had told Daniel a little about this family before they moved down here. Good people he had said, dedicated workers and Colin was skilled with small motors. Given that Lord Worthing himself was a very deft and skilled locksmith Daniel had smiled. He could remember tales his brother Michael had told him about Aubrey Worthing and his father's skill at locksmithing and lockpicking. Skilled with his hands thought Daniel, like our Colin here, and then he remembered Lady Diana Worthing's warning with her rapier-like bony fingers emphasising the point. 'But they are a little strange Daniel Lord, a little strange when it comes to education. I'm not much for educating the workers at any time. Best if they don't know too much I always reckon but that plump partridge Ophelia is a little over the top at times. Perhaps her husband should use those deft hands his Lordship talks about for a little application of the whip now and then, keep her in line. Bit too weird for my taste but then I think her mother was a Romany, a Traveller so what can you expect?'

What did he expect Daniel thought? Dedicated workers would do for starters and we'll worry about other things if we can achieve the work.

'Fine Ophelia. I'll be by tomorrow and see whether there is anything else we can do to help you get started,' said Daniel and he went out with Colin to finish unpacking the van.

Katya drove her father's rental car with quiet assurance through the forest from the Manor House to the Education Centre. Since she had come to England Katya had mastered gear-shift transmissions and she smiled to herself as she watched her father critically watching her shift gears.

'Not many automatics over here dad,' she said. 'Standard here means standard. Most English people prefer stick shift anyway. They say they feel more in control than relying on some unseen and probably foreign computer. You should have heard the comments when some of those Japanese cars first came with voice reminders that your seat belt wasn't fastened or the doors weren't locked.' Katya laughed. 'Some of the comments were unrepeatable.'

'You know your way around here Katya I see,' said Delaney.

'Yes Dad. Daniel and I are out here a lot. He really cares for his forest you know. It may not be big by American standards but he knows his forest and he really cares. When Anthony and Sylvia finally managed to sell Brainware Daniel had a lot of ideas how to improve and diversify the forest.'

'Your ideas Katya surely love?' said Deidre from the back seat. 'You suggested them I'm sure as you were always thinking of new ways to change your father's forest back home. I can remember your father having to ask you to be quiet and then for nearly a month or more he wouldn't even take you into his office. What was it you said Delaney? Katya was going to get you fired? Nonsense, our little girl was just telling them how it should be done. Weren't you Katya?'

Katya watched her dad smile and she too smiled and caught her mother's serious and convinced expression in the rear-view mirror.

'They wouldn't have fired father mother,' Katya finally said. 'Here we are; the new Memorial Education Centre.'

'Why Memorial Katya? Who's buried here?'

'Mother come and see. Come and look inside and you'll see why.'

Katya held open the door and let her father and mother pass inside. There was a small discussion group meeting in one of the rooms and there was a guided party looking at some of the exhibits in one of the labs. Standing in front of the memorial display was an older couple.

'Henri isn't it? Henri Lord? We met at Daniel's birthday party last October. I'm Katya Howard and I'd like you to meet my parents. This is my father Delaney and....'

'I'm Deidre Howard, Katya's mother. Are you related to Anthony and Sylvia? I don't remember seeing you when we were here last time. We had a lovely time when we were here last September. We met Daniel and little James of course. That's how we all met in the first place.'

Delaney stepped forward to shake Henri's hand and try and stem the gushing flow from Deidre. 'We're pleased to meet you all,' he said. 'We're just visiting again from Florida but we're really here to attend Katya's graduation at Oxford next week.'

'I was just going to tell them that Delaney.'

'Yes dear.'

'Hello Katya, and you too Delaney and Deidre was it? Yes Katya I remember you. You had some ideas about green revenues I believe: trying to transform the trees into turnstiles for my aunt Sylvia.'

'Haven't seen your percentage of the cut yet Henri,' said Henri's companion. 'I'm Leslie Dauphin. I'm the lead reporter for the London Daily Crier. No doubt you've seen my stories? Well if you've been looking at the news you would have. Still, down here in this nether-nether world it's sometimes hard to believe you realise where you all are.'

Katya looked at the source of the voice and along with the unisex name she wondered whether she was looking and listening to a unisex human. Was it male or female?

'Memorial to who Katya?' demanded Deidre again, completely oblivious to any previous conversation. Henri and Leslie whatever drifted away chatting in an agitated fashion while Katya brought her focus back to her mother and the question of Memorial.

'Start on the left mother. It covers the Lord family from the present older generation so it starts with Charles, who was Anthony's brother. Charles and his wife Helene both died while mountaineering in France in 1966. They were Henri's parents by the way. Next we come to Jean Lord who died in April 1990 at the young age of nine while sailing on the East coast of England with Michael Lord.'

'Who died later Katya?'

'Yes father and we'll come to that in a moment. Bear with me. In June of 1990, while climbing in North Wales with Daniel and Michael, the eldest son Geoffrey was killed but Daniel told you all about that. That's how young Peter Lord, Geoffrey's son became the inheritor of the Lord Estate, much to brother Michael's disgust, and to Henri's too. That sharp comment about getting their percentage of the cut was that Leslie's dig about the entire Estate passing to Peter. Henri thinks like Michael did that the Estate should be divided up amongst all of the family.'

'And next Katya? That is not a Lord family name.'

'No dad but that family, or rather the two Branciaghlia brothers have been a part of the Lord family since the 1940s. Daniel wanted to include them and everyone agreed. The younger brother Enrico still lives here with Christina and Peter at Home Farm. I will take you to meet them because they are all delightful people and there is another young cousin living there too, Tony Lord who is Michael's son.'

'But I thought you told us Michael died Katya? I thought you said he died before he got married. Wasn't there some American girl involved? Wasn't she the daughter of that nice Californian we met here last September? What was his name Delaney, that nice tall Californian?'

'Stanley Rogers my dear,' said Delaney. 'In computer software, graphics I think like Anthony. Business friend I thought Sylvia said.'

'Right dad, and right mother. Michael never did get married before he died but he had a son with a young lady and that son Tony now lives at Home Farm with his aunt Christina and cousin Peter. Tony is a real charmer and I like him a lot. Now, after the sad death of Geoffrey we have the forestry accident that killed Antonio. That too was tragic and even today it is a sensitive memory for Enrico. Daniel talked a lot with Enrico before they both agreed that having Antonio's name here was right and proper.'

'Then you have Michael Lord,' said Delaney, 'and that was a mystery too Katya you were telling us.'

'Father, this is the land of the long stories and several mysteries. The Lord family seem to specialise in them but yes, even today that is still an unsolved mystery, murder actually.'

'Who is Andrew MacRae Katya?' asked Deidre.

'Remember the day we met James and Daniel mother? Do you remember what James explained to you? He wasn't with his father but with his Uncle Daniel.'

'Yes dear and his mother was out with her mother doing some rock something. Quite unexpected I can tell you. I wasn't sure all that day what we should do. James and Daniel seemed normal but listening to the stories that little lad was telling me I began to wonder about the rest of the family.'

Delaney smiled and put his arm around his wife. 'But you decided to put your best Yankee face forwards my dear, step boldly into battle and take on any challengers. You're my trooper Deidre, you really are.'

'Go on Delaney. You do talk nonsense at times you know.'

'Andrew MacRae was Samantha's husband and the father of little James,' said Katya. He'd only died about a month before we all met the Lords. Somewhere in Canada Daniel told me in a rather horrendous forest fire. He was working with his technician and they both got caught up in the fire.'

'And Danielle?'

'She was Tony's mother,' said Katya. 'Listening to Daniel she was quite some lady, courageous lady I should say. Her background is terrifying and she came to England and fought to get her life back again. Apparently she was quite short and slender but she could fight and in the end it cost her her life as she fought to protect her son. After Michael was killed Danielle lived up in London with little Tony and it was Anthony who went up to London to find her again. Danielle had wanted nothing to do with the family because she thought they had all turned on Michael. Anthony in his usual gentle and persuasive way managed to enfold her back into the family and when she was threatened in London she fled down here. Unfortunately she died here fighting to save her son. Samantha gets quite emotional over Danielle. Normally Samantha is as tough as nails but that is one subject where Samantha stops and looks different.' And there's another issue I saw today thought Katya that caused Samantha to suddenly not look as tough as nails. I wonder what that was all about.

'So Anthony and Sylvia decided to display this history of death?'

'Yes father. Originally Daniel and I thought up the idea for an Education Centre and Daniel took it further with the family, and young Peter and Tony thought the idea was smashing if I remember Tony correctly. Tony comes from London and many things are smashing according to Tony mother. The family liked the idea of the Centre and so we had a series of design options drawn up. While we were still in the early days it was Daniel's birthday party and when Daniel described the idea he talked about a memorial for his two brothers. He wanted a more positive outdoor place to remember them and he thought both brothers were interested in the future and young people. At the table Anthony suddenly thought wider, and as is typical of him wanted to include more people on the team, even on the passed over team so to speak. So he suggested why they don't include all of the Lord family members known to people in the room and that included spouses, hence Helene, Andrew and Danielle. It was Daniel who suggested they include Antonio and so we now have this tribute to all these good people who have unfortunately died. A few of the teachers actually include the thoughts and memories of some of the people shown here as part of their lessons. Antonio's accident needn't have happened dad. Andrew's death too was another forestry tragedy that perhaps could have been prevented so there are lessons to be learnt even from this display.'

'But I want a puppy Mummy, just like Adam.'

'We'll think about it James.'

'That's what you always say when you mean no.'

'James do you want to show Deidre your birthday gift to your uncle?'

'Yes Grandpa, that's a great idea. Come on Deidre. You too Uncle Daniel. We need a guard to blow the whistle and wave the green flag. We'll find Queen Deidre and King Delaney in miniature. We'll let the King pull the coaches.'

James slowly pulled an unsuspecting Deidre up the stairs while he explained about the people, the surprise birthday present, the railway, the model railway and why the engines were green. Anthony caught Samantha by the arm. 'I wanted to try and move James away from the idea of a puppy for the moment Samantha. We'll think about it for sure but there is a lot going on and he is a busy little lad at the moment. One step at a time and let's see how the Entwhistles settle in with their puppy.'

'Thanks dad. That helped. I was a bit stuck for a moment.'

'Something else on your mind love?'

'No dad, although yes dad I suppose so. I had a call from Janet while you were out. The Peter's family are back again in England and they wanted me to do a follow-up. Sounds as if there was a second part of their time capsule. Anyway, they want me to go up to London over the weekend and then come back down here next week. I explained to Janet about my commitment on Monday in Oxford but otherwise I think I can manage the timing. Can you and mum look after James to take him up to Oxford next weekend? I don't want to take him up to London with me.'

'Of course we can love. Don't you worry yourself about James. I'll keep him happy. Anything else worrying you? You look a little stressed. Missed your climbing today with Evelyn?'

'No dad, everything's fine. Sure I would have liked to have gone climbing. You know that it clears my head and gives me a real boost of adrenaline. Pumps me up for the next week.'

'Terence is okay?'

'Dad stop prying. I told mum no boyfriend vetting.'

Anthony laughed and put his arm around his daughter. 'You know me Samantha. I like people to get on together, be happy and productive together.' Anthony beat his chest with two arms and said, 'Me team builder' as if he was Tarzan. Samantha laughed and she too beat her fists on her father's chest. 'No dad, it's me Samantha and life is good. Terence is fine dad and so am I.'

Katya had seen and heard most of this exchange between Anthony and Samantha. She too thought Samantha seemed a little subdued, a little unsure which was not the usual Samantha. When Samantha left the room Katya walked over to Anthony and asked whether he had a minute.

'Sure Katya love. What can I do for you? It's good to have your parents here though. Did you show them around the forest this afternoon? I know your dad's eager to see more things and your mother just delights in seeing our part of the world. Anyway Katya, what can I do?'

Katya explained that she had taken her parents to the Education Centre and that they had thought that idea was a good one. 'But when we were there Anthony we met Henri and Leslie is it?'

'Did you now? And they never mentioned coming to visit. Samantha never mentioned them coming to the house and she was here when we were down at the Entwhistles.'

'Henri recognised me from Daniel's birthday party but Leslie was quite, well accusative. He/she was demanding their percentage of the money you raise from the use of the Education Centre, from the turnstiles she said. Is it a he or she? I wasn't sure.'

Anthony laughed and he held Katya's hand. 'Here we have another eccentric or perhaps non-standard Lord family member,' he said. 'Henri has always been a strange lad and man now I suppose. When he was younger he used to chase after Marie, Marcel's wife but that may just have been trying to annoy his brother. I know Marie didn't like the attention. She misses Marcel and she never really recovered from Jean's death. Then Henri did some supportive work climbing several times with Daniel both before and after Michael's death. Daniel told me that all that helped him. After that we didn't see Henri for a while and even Stephanie lost touch. Next thing we learn is that Henri is living with a man. That seems to have led to this "partner" of Leslie. And yes Katya, Leslie is a man although I agree it is hard to tell some days. Leslie Dauphin seems to be one of those vitriolic journalists. Almost like the paparazzi but in words rather than pictures. Actually he does work with another close friend who is a press photographer. Perhaps a male ménage a trois. So, Leslie was voicing off as usual?'

'Yes Anthony. I thought you should know. I hope it's nothing. Daniel and I want that Education Centre to be a success. We really think it is a piece of tomorrow for the Estate. As a last item Anthony that Leslie made some throwaway comment about the preacher Godschild and exposing his heretical teachings coming from such a conservative home as Fotheringham. He sounded vindictive when he said this. Fortunately they left and I explained the Memorial Display to my parents.'

'Food for thought,' said Anthony. 'More attackers on the horizon.'

'But we have some good news too Anthony,' said Katya. 'We have found some additional allies for our defence of Fotheringham.'

Anthony laughed. 'It's good to hear you joining in the fighting spirit of the Lord family my love. What new allies have you found us?'

Katya explained about meeting the hikers again and Daniel offering an alliance and a meeting of the minds over wildlife biology and possible "forest wardens" if the group is hiking through the Estate. Actually we are planning to meet them at the Education Centre next weekend.'

'But you'll be in Oxford Katya love, or had you forgotten that so important day, your important day?'

'Anthony what have we done? Daniel and I were so excited about the possible new thoughts and ideas for the Education Centre and the Estate that I completely forgot about my graduation. I must have moved past that event and be into future things to be done. Daniel and I really want to make this work and he had turned an initial confrontation over fences into a forward-looking alliance.'

'He had or you both had?' asked Anthony looking at Katya.

Katya blushed. 'We both work so well together Anthony. We both love working here.'

'So I should make sure that Daniel and your father get some time together should I? It sounds like it is time for my son to make the next move. What do you say Katya?'

'Yes Anthony.'

'Perhaps King Delaney should go and meet his namesake as it traverses the tracks in the Railway Room upstairs. I hear that James has renamed King Henry VIII into King Delaney and that engine is James's favourite. The fastest grandpa he tells me. First and out in front like his mother.' Anthony laughed and left a pensive Katya to find her father.

'Did I hear you bumped into Henri Katya?'

'Yes Sylvia. I was just telling Anthony and about the comments from that Leslie he/she.'

Sylvia laughed at the expression. 'That's good Katya. I like that, he/she, appropriate. I just hope this doesn't worry Anthony any more. He's taken to worrying of late. I need to banish him to the golf club. Didn't you have some project for him? I seem to remember you and Daniel had some ideas.'

'We did Sylvia,' and Katya took Sylvia over to the sofa and explained some of their ideas.

On the following Monday morning Deidre greeted everyone at the breakfast table with tales of patriotic embarrassment. 'We were so excited. We had so many things to do and see. It is so lovely being here and seeing you all that I completely forgot. Delaney completely forgot. He never forgets and we both forgot.'

The other members of the Lord family around the table listened and waited for the shoe to drop. What had Deidre forgotten?

'You had better explain my dear,' said Delaney as he noticed the rather puzzled looks around the table.

'July the fourth,' said Deidre. 'Independence Day. Our National holiday with parades, parties, fireworks, the whole shebang. We completely forgot.'

The expressions on the faces of most of the people there seemed to say "so what" but Katya thought she had better explain. 'Americans get very passionate about our National holidays. We don't have many of them compared to other countries and those we do have we celebrate in a typical American fashion. I suppose we are a new and passionately patriotic people and so days like Independence Day are special, really special. As my mother says the whole country goes party crazy and Americans everywhere in the world celebrate too. You could probably see the parades from space.'

Everyone understood, well they thought so and went back to bacon, eggs, toast, coffee or whatever. Katya looked around the room. We are different she thought, well not different but we do look at some things in different ways. We have different values for some things. Daniel was already out at the Forest Office and Katya looked across at her parents. Do I belong here she thought? Yes Katya Howard, yes you do and that's how it's going to be young lady. She looked at Samantha who as usual was juggling James with breakfast, words, arm-waving, shoes on the wrong feet, more words and trying to get to school on time. Yes she said to herself I belong here. Definitely time for Daniel to find my father.

After introducing Colin Entwhistle to Bob Edwards and the rest of the work crew Daniel took off to see Ophelia and Adam. All seemed to be under control there and so Daniel returned to the Big House to check on the rest of the family. Katya caught him as he came in from the backyard.

'Daniel, dad wants to see some of the other thoughts and ideas you have been introducing in the forest plus he said he'd like to see some of the conventional operations too. He was particularly interested in what you are thinking about with regards to the hardwoods as he doesn't have a lot of those back home. They are a novelty for him. You know Daniel, some of your ideas with interplanting with the conifer nurse crop. He's up in the library Daniel. Can you take him out love on your inspections?'

'Sure Katya. I'll go and find him. And your mother?'

'I think Sylvia was going to take mother into the village and perhaps into the local town. I might go too as I need to keep my eyes and ears on my mother Daniel. Dad is straightforward but my mother sometimes has these strange ideas. I'd like to keep tabs on her while she is here.'

'Understood. We share conventional fathers and mothers full of surprises. I'll handle the easy end of that equation. Best of luck with yours.'

Daniel found Delaney up in the library as Katya had said. Also there were Anthony and Samantha, both separately absorbed in large books. 'Looks like a hive of industry,' said Daniel. 'Delaney, Katya told me I should show you some of the things we've been doing out in the forest. She said you had been asking about the interplantings.'

'Yes my boy. Sounded interesting that. Suppose we have never done anything quite like that and I wanted to see what you had done and what you thought might happen, or what you wanted to happen. I'm ready when you are by the way.'

Anthony stayed engrossed in his book and half-abstractly waved his hand as they both left. 'Something to do with Janet and Heritage Adventures Samantha?' asked Anthony after Daniel and Delaney had left. Samantha looked up from her book and turned to face her father. 'No dad,' she said, 'it's a medical reference book.'

'You think we're all suffering from some genetic shortcoming or is it something the Templetons have? You had a call from Janet regarding the Peters or Templetons didn't you? They want to come back down here again?'

'Yes dad they do but that isn't what I was looking up. Perhaps if I want a more up-to-date explanation I should use the web.'

'Anything I can help with Samantha? Your mother wants me to get involved in some project about the history of Fotheringham but that is only to keep me out of the way. Fascinating it might be Samantha but I do better face to face with real live people as you well know. So, face to face with you is there anything I can do to help?'

'Only if you know something about women's internal sexual plumbing dad and I don't think that is your speciality, even if you did end up a doctor.'

Anthony thought about his daughter's comment and realised Samantha's joking tone covered something potentially more serious. 'Want to talk?' he said.

Samantha moved to sit beside her father and slowly explained about Andrew, STDs, PID, only children as in James and whether there was any chance of her circumstances being cured or reversed. Anthony listened and recommended Samantha go and see a specialised clinic at one of the London hospitals. When you're next up in the city Samantha go and find someone who knows best love. This is important for you and we're here for you. Your mother and I will do everything we can to help you have children again. James would love that I know and I'd guess Terence might too. I'm right in assuming that Terence is the likely man involved?'

'Yes dad, you assume correctly. I just want it to be right for us. No past but a new future. You understand that?'

'Yes Samantha dear I understand you wanting to look forwards to a new and exciting future. Meanwhile I suppose I had better dig back in time and find some answers to things past or your mother will think I have been sitting somewhere with my feet up.'

'Not you at all dad,' Samantha said, 'but thanks for listening and understanding.'

'So you want to give in your notice Gloria?' asked Mrs. Digby.

'Yes Mrs. Digby. Thanks for hiring me like you did. Actually I may have found you a replacement if you need someone. Lester Rainer, a friend of Freddie Dunster has two younger sisters. I've been out with the elder sister Dora and she already has a job but her younger sister Janis is still at school and could work afternoons. I think she'd be interested and many of your customers are afternoon bookings.'

'That's thoughtful Gloria and I thank you. If you see her, this Janis, ask her to pop in to see me would you dear? We'll talk and see whether anything comes out of it. So finishing at the end of this week then?'

'Yes Mrs. Digby, I'll work the week out.'

'You back in the George then I hear?'

'That's right Mrs. Digby and I think that suits me better. It's more in line with what I did up in London.'

'Well you know best dear. Your mother made a booking for her hair you know. Wants to come in this Wednesday. Now there's a first I must say. People say that she's a changed woman Gloria your mother. Seems you coming home has made a change love, for the better too I think. Always a struggle with parents isn't it Gloria? My old folks gave me a trying time too love, looking after them and making sure they got safely tucked away up in the churchyard in the end. Just sweep up there Gloria please and we'll expect Mrs Travers in any moment. Right on time she always is.'

Gloria had just tidied up the salon when the door opened and Mary Travers came in. There followed a detailed swapping of who had done what and who might be doing something else as the two village business women exchanged information. Gloria listened and learnt. So Betty Travers had bought that house and the family were moving at the end of July. More important, to Gloria that is, was the fact that Betty intended to refurnish the house with new stuff and not go back to their old cottage for anything she might have left there. Apparently Betty wanted to make a clean start and with the money from the sale of the cottage she could afford to leave the past behind her. Finally, Betty and her pie-making business were doing very well and she is seriously considering going into partnership with Mr. Marples the baker. Gloria filed away the information and wondered about her idea to change jobs. Would she have learnt that useful titbit in the pub?

By mid afternoon Freddie had had enough. It had been a hot and sultry day. The job was kicking up dust everywhere. His back ached from stooping over as the crew was cutting the competing vegetation away from a struggling new plantation. There was the new bloke Colin getting all the attention and Gary was rabbiting on about Gloria this and Gloria that.

'Fuck it,' he said. 'Ain't it time for a break Bob? Anything to shut up loud mouth here next to me.'

'You've just got back to work from lunch Freddie,' said Bob. 'These weeds aren't letting up son so why should you?'

'Too much shagging over the weekend then Freddie?' I suggested but Freddie looked daggers at me.

'That's part of the problem you thick shit,' Freddie said as he viciously swiped at some resistant bushes. 'You keep yer mouth flapping about Gloria and we ain't been out with Dora as a foursome for a while and its me who's supposed to be with Gloria you nonce.'

'You got a mouth Freddie. Get it done mate. Ask. Fix it. I'm on. Dora's fine.'

'How can I when you're always with her. Just leave her be Gary. I'm going out with Gloria. Dora's just a kid. You have her. I'm asking tonight so back off. Just a twosome too. None of your four's fun. I need a straightforward shag. I know what she did up in London. Christ, after all we did as kids she owes me.'

'She don't owe you anything Freddie you twisted prick,' I said. 'You're just a lazy bastard and you ain't prepared to work for anything. Look at you cutting them weeds. Bleeding useless you are Freddie. You should never have left the nursery mate.'

Suddenly Freddie stood up and looked at me. He was holding his bill-hook in his right hand. 'You say that again Gary fucking Templeton and I'll put you back in the nursery or somewhere, probably the fucking hospital that comes before the nursery. You'll be howling like the day your fucking mother opened her legs and popped you. Dunn your mum and yer dad done her too didn't he? Come to think about it your dad done everyone. Well everyone with a skirt on although they weren't on was they Gary? Pushed up, pulled off your dad didn't care did he? Slam bam thank you mam. You ain't got no brothers and sisters that show but I'll bet you've got lots. All around the fucking countryside Gary. Your dad with his cock rides again.'

'Shut the fuck up Freddie about my parents. You don't know squat. I never had no aunt who was on the game. I never had no mother who couldn't remember her own sister. Your dad didn't make fifty before your mum nagged him to death.' I was getting pretty riled up now and Freddie was really starting to piss me off. Colin Entwhistle must have heard us because he was working next to Freddie.

'Thought you two worked together? Didn't I hear Daniel Lord right when he said you two were responsible for the clean-up of our cottage? You obviously worked well together there. The place looked great. I was meaning to thank you, both of you.'

'You keep out of this Colin. I did most of the work there and had to clean up after Freddie's useless wanking his paint brush all over. He paints like he pisses by waving it all about,' I said.

'Like your dad waves it all about Gary. Your fucking dad. He should sell rubbers mate. He uses enough he needs the discount.'

Bob came over. 'Carry on Colin,' he said. 'Gary shut it, right now. Freddie you come with me. There's times son when all you want to do is annoy people. You're like a yapping little dog. Now John Ferris has gone you've lost your post to pee on. Fine, right now I want you to walk all the way around the fence on this plantation. I want you to check whether we've got any holes and how well the netting is fixed. This plantation's nearly free-to-grow and we can try and retrieve and re-use the netting. You walk round and check and maybe by the time you've done that you'll have spewed out all your frustrations just walking. At the moment you sure ain't working. Now go lad and check all this bloody fence.'

Rosemary Dunster had a surprise that same afternoon when Tilley Manson came to call. It was a new Tilley Manson, although afterwards Rosemary caught herself remembering that it really was an old Tilley Manson, like when they were both teenagers. She was still trying to get her head around the changes when Freddie clattered home from work.

'Tea's in thirty minutes Freddie. Gives you time to get some of the forest out of your hair love.'

'Right now Mum I want to get fucking Gary Templeton out of my hair, or out of my head. He's been doing my head in all afternoon. Jesus he's an annoying bugger.'

'Freddie go and wash up son and then come back here. I've something special to tell you. Something strange happened this afternoon.'

'As long as it's got nothing to do with Gary fucking Templeton,' Freddie said and he went off to wash and get changed.

'So Tilley Manson was round here this afternoon and talking and laughing like she was over twenty years ago Freddie. Of course I was still living with my parents then down at the old smithy but it was like she'd been reborn. She was so full of life talking about this and that. Told me how she'd found an old friend of ours, well an acquaintance really rather than a friend. Old Toby the Fixer we called him. You listening Freddie?'

'Why did Tilley go crazy Mum? She went all holy. I never knew her when she wasn't weird. She dressed in drab old clothes, was always praying and yet she always liked me. She never was keen on that tosser Gary. Christ he gets up my nose Mum.'

'She was such a livewire Freddie.'

'Gloria was telling us this Mum. She was telling us this just after she came back from London. She was talking about you and her and music and dancing and all sorts. Gloria was saying you two were a right pair, running off to rock concerts and such. You never play that music Mum. All you do is watch the tele. I seem to remember Gloria said she even came and talked to you Mum.'

'Yes, she did Freddie. When she came home Gloria was real worried about her mum. She knew a little about her mum when she was young.'

'So why'd her mum change? Perhaps when did her mum change? When did you and her stop going wild or whatever? Can't imagine you wild Mum?'

'Well thanks a lot Freddie. I was young I'll have you know you cheeky sod. Wild we was Tilley and I. Went to all the rock groups we could. Called groupies in those days. Fun Freddie, fun and outside the village. You never go anywhere son. You need to get out and see the world, well at least out of the village. Go to Bristol or even up to London. Gloria got out and she saw the world.'

'Yea but she came back fast enough,' said Freddie. 'Saw things in London she shouldn't have but she wouldn't tell us what. Said if we didn't know we couldn't tell or something. Did you know there were people came down here looking for her, soon after she left London? Bloody frightening that was Mum. George told me. Told me to find Gloria and warn her. That bloody copper Field saw him off though George said. One look and he scarpered back off to London. No Mum, life's too bloody wild up in London for me. Anyway, why did you stop going wild if it was so much fun?'

349

'Suppose I got married Freddie and your dad wasn't keen on that kind of music. Still, I continued going out with Tilley until she got married the following year and then it all stopped. Right like that Freddie. Over a month that Tilley changed. Went from wild fun party girl to clambed up tight. Her mother, my aunt mark you wouldn't let her go out and before I knew it she'd got married to Walter Manson who none of us knew by the way. Well he was a regular at dad and mum's B&B but I didn't really know him. She wouldn't speak to me. Wouldn't speak to anyone. When she married Walter they bought that little house where she is now and that was it. Goodbye Tilley Edwards and goodbye Tilley Manson too. Of course Gloria was born soon afterwards and she was a handful I heard.'

'So what happened Mum?'

'Not sure Freddie, not sure but here's your tea love. Eat up now while it's still hot. After the day you said you'd had perhaps it's good that it's your favourite.'

On the Tuesday Bob Edwards kept Freddie and me apart and as I was out to the cottage that evening fixing up some camera equipment I never knew about Freddie and his fumbles in the pub. Looking back I suppose he just got really pissed off about a lack of girl action and thought Gloria still owed him. Gloria had spent the Tuesday juggling three jobs. She'd started at Mrs. Digby's in the morning and gone from there for some five hours at Darlene's followed by a late evening session behind the bar. She'd arranged no other jobs on Wednesday because that was the day for the first customer at the cottage. Still, that Tuesday night she was feeling pretty tired and Freddie had been relatively quietly supping pints with his mates. Lester had been giving Freddie a hard time about being out with Dora and Freddie had patiently explained that it was me with Dora and him with Gloria. So pumped up a little from the beer, the taunts from Lester and overall Freddie frustration he decided to get his end away with Gloria. I heard a little about this the following evening, the Wednesday and its seems that Freddie had waited for Gloria to close up at the George. I don't know what actually happened because Gloria wouldn't tell me all the details but I know that Freddie was full of himself that Wednesday at work. Stupid wanker was crowing his head off most of that Wednesday and I came close to trying to clock him again. Then I remembered to play it cool 'cos tonight, that Wednesday night I had to be the selector, guide, guard and overall protector. That was for Gloria and the girls. For Gary I also had to be the videographer and that would be much more important I thought. I kept my cool and didn't thump cock-a-hoop Freddie.

With just two and a half weeks before the Club's Open championship Daniel reckoned he needed the practice. As Katya was all set for her graduation the following week she also could relax and concentrate on her golf too so Daniel had entered Katya in the competition. Daniel had changed his format this Wednesday and instead of playing with Larry, Alan and Peter he played with Katya and another married couple who were members. Daniel felt relaxed and he thought Katya did too. The forest was going well and so was the Education Centre. They had come to an agreement with that group of hikers and the Entwhistle family had settled in okay. Katya's parents were here and Katya was looking forward to the weekend in Oxford followed by her graduation. That would take next Sunday out of the golfing loop though realised Daniel. Just have to make the most of today he thought.

'You're away Daniel.'

Daniel started and brought his head back to the here and now. He had already lined up his putt and he took one more glance to confirm the weight. Steady, head still, breathe, swing in a neat triangle from the shoulders and keep that head still Daniel. Dam it, keep the eyes from peeking. He pulled the ball a little and trundled it past on the left about twelve inches. Next time just close the eyes and putt Daniel he told himself. You'll drive yourself nuts if you don't learn to putt sometime. He tapped in for par.

'You still mutter you know,' said Katya quietly after she had putted out. She picked up the flagstick and carefully replaced it in the hole. The four of them walked off the green to the next tee-box.

'So Daniel, is Katya here going to blow us all out of the water?' asked Dennis Thompson. 'Molly here reckons you've brought a ringer in. Is she one of those ladies who play on those mini-tours in the States? Well Katya, are you really a forestry student like Daniel says or is that just some disguise? We've learnt to be careful with your Daniel. He was away playing for a while as a youngster and then burst on the scene with a scratch handicap.'

'Honest Injun Dennis I'm going to my graduation ceremony next week at Oxford.'

'Yes Katya, that's as maybe, but is it for a forestry degree as Daniel asserts or for a blue in Sports, like golf maybe?'

'No Molly, it really is a forestry degree. When I'm not helping Daniel here on the golf course I'm helping him back at Fotheringham in the forest. We've done some good things there Daniel haven't we?'

'Yes, it's for real Molly. We took some of the family money from the sale of dad's company and built an Education Centre at Fotheringham.'

'And launched some crazy preacher I hear Daniel. Several people have been talking about it. He's who, the Reverend Gabriel Godschild I heard and with a name like that it has got to be a scam of some kind? Heard he has been preaching instant humans. Evolution and Darwin out of the window because all us humans are God's instant children. Just the sort of nonsense I don't want my children to hear.'

352

'Is he preaching in the village too Daniel? I can't imagine many of the locals are too taken with his version of God as the Creator, literally.'

'Mixed reaction actually Molly,' replied Daniel. 'You can never tell what people believe until you smack them in the face with a challenge.'

'And that's just the right comment Daniel as you're away son and this hole is always a challenge.'

Daniel and Katya finished the round with Dennis and Molly and shared a final drink before setting off to return to Fotheringham.

'Two under Daniel. You should be pleased. I am, especially as I haven't played seriously for quite a while. Still, it's great just to get out there Daniel. Clears the mind and today was really a fun day. I was quite concerned when you entered me in the tournament but now I'm really pleased you did. Thank you Daniel love.'

'Two under Katya and it should have been four under, or perhaps five under. Look at the twelfth? I should have birdied that hole. And then I missed a good opportunity on the fifteenth.'

'Daniel Daniel Daniel,' said Katya laughing. 'Lighten up a little love. You did well and it was a fine day. Dennis and Molly are fun to play with. Serious when they need to be and not too serious when it's time to relax. Fun people.'

'We will miss this coming Sunday you know Katya.'

'No Daniel wrong words. We will not miss it because we will be up in Oxford showing my parents all around the town. It will be a twenty-four day knowing my mother so we will not miss it but, and I hear you say it is a big but we will not be spending it on the golf course. No big deal. Next Wednesday my parents will have left for Florida, I will have that precious piece of paper with the funny writing, and I will have you all to myself with no other distractions. Then Daniel Lord we will be together concentrating on this funny funny game you love so much. And I will love being with you concentrating too. By the way did you talk with my father?'

'Sure Katya. He was very interested in that interplanting with the hardwoods. He thought that was truly cost-effective.'

'Daniel I'd thump you if you weren't driving or kiss you you obtuse man. You know what about?'

'Oh that, well yes I did mention it, ask you know.'

'And and and Daniel?'

Daniel did a quick check in his rear-view mirror and within a second he had braked and drawn up to the side of the empty road. He turned to Katya and took her hand in his.

'Tricky trying to get down on one knee from this position but Katya Howard will you marry me?'

'Yes yes yes Daniel Lord from any position tricky or otherwise. Yes I will marry you you crazy man. I don't even care whether you can putt or not but yes I will marry you.' Katya put her arms around Daniel's neck and kissed him hard. A passing lorry hooted loudly and flashed his lights at them after he had driven by.

'Seems the driver agrees Daniel. Take me home love and we'll share the news.'

'What about a ring? I haven't got round to going and buying a ring yet. I only talked with your father on Monday.'

'Whenever whatever Daniel. All that can come later. I just want to share the news with everyone.'

'What will we do about James? You are his special friend and he found you.'

'Perhaps I should persuade him to give me away,' giggled Katya. 'Don't worry Daniel I'll have a special blue engine red engine talk with James and sort out some answer in a book in the library,' and Katya collapsed back on her seat with a lengthy fit of the giggles. 'I'm so happy Daniel. I really do love you my Lord.'

GLORIA IS.........

WHEN I GOT HOME THAT afternoon my mum gave me an envelope.

'Popped in through the letter-box sometime this afternoon Gary,' she said. 'No stamp so it must be someone local.'

'Ta Mum. Tea in half an hour is it? I'll just go and wash up. Messy job today with all that weeding. Still, easy job really as the boss was away golfing or something and Bob Edwards had several things to show the new bloke Colin.'

'That's nice dear,' mum said. 'Oh Gary, your dad's away tonight. He had some sales go wrong somewhere up in Bath he said. And I'm out this evening at the Bingo.'

"Sfine Mum, I'm out all the evening anyway. Probably be late so don't wait up,' and I laughed as I said this. My mum has never stayed up late waiting for me or for dad for that matter. Easy going is my mum. Lets it all just slide over her head. I washed and changed. Tonight I thought as I read Gloria's note. Two blokes around eight, mid thirties, professional types Gloria says and looking for a good time for a couple of hours. Should be a piece of cake. Easy money. Not wanting to be too early and be sitting there like a berk I drove down to the parking lot of the George about a quarter to eight. I drove past the first time but there were no cars there that I didn't recognise. Coming back through the village I pulled in over to one side and waited. A couple of cars came in but the two couples headed right on into the pub. Just at eight a black saloon, a Jag I noticed pulled in to the parking lot and the driver slowed down looking. There were two blokes in the car. I opened my car door and got out so I was more obvious and when they saw me they drove over.

'Looking for me?' I asked, completely forgetting any routine.

'Looking for the London Road mate?'

'Oh yes, you must mean London Street. Yes, that's it, London Street.'

The driver turned back to his partner and I saw his partner look at something on his lap. He must have said something 'cos the driver came back with 'No, Forest Street which needs a blindfold.'

'Park your motor somewhere quiet then and hop in,' I said cheerfully. Piece of piss this is Gloria. Easy as taking sweets from a baby. I was about to say my name when I suddenly realised what we were supposed to be doing.

'Blindfolds guys,' I said. 'You've seen the procedure. Girls tell me it's a turn on. All the anticipation you know. You first mate. Just turn round and I'll fix it. Fine, you sit in the back then and now you mate. That's good. Got the cash have you? No, you can't see can you? Well, you know what you've brought 'cos it's cash only the girls tell me. We all set? Right, little tour around see just to get the throat dry with the expectations and a chance for the body to get eager if you know what I mean.'

I drove slowly out of the village and spent the next fifteen to twenty minutes wandering around the surrounding lanes in the gathering gloom. Watching the road I turned off down onto the forest ride and toured the forest for another ten minutes before circling to the edge of the cottage clearing around eight-thirty. It was still light when I turned off the engine and the forest was peaceful as most of the birds had got their roosting sorted for the night.

'I'll help your mate out of the back first,' I said, 'and then collect you chum' and I patted the arm of the customer next to me. I managed to get both of them organised and by this time the girls were outside and coming to help. No words got said and the girls held the hands of the two blokes and started slow caresses and squeezes. I folded into the background. Gloria caught my eye and I just gave her a silent thumbs up. She smiled and nodded her head. So far so good Gary she seemed to say. I went back to the car and waited. The girls slowly waltzed the two blokes around before easing them back into their web of the cottage. Spiders capturing their prey I thought and sucking the juices right out of them. Yes I thought, time for a little photo work, watching the spiders at prey, or is it play? Very quietly I eased myself back towards the cottage. After some instruction from that useful mate of dad's I had rigged up several cameras. I had three video cameras, one for each of the three main rooms and two still cameras but I wasn't so sure about those. I was concentrating on getting some good hot videos. That was what sells the bloke had said. You get the videos mate and I'll handle distribution. Money will come rolling in.

The girls had done a good job with the cottage. No light escaped and the sounds were muted. If I went to the edge of the clearing I couldn't hear or see anything. By ten o'clock when it was quite dark you wouldn't even know there was anything there. Cool I thought. I'd done some video early on as a test like and even checked a little of it in playback. Things looked okay although nothing much was happening, well nothing much that was saleable. Blokes having drinks with girls on their laps don't excite too much. I could hear the music and now and again caught glimpses of Sheena dancing. Now she looked a lot more exciting but the photo coverage was limited in the main room. I was more interested in whatever action took place in the other two rooms. Soon after ten I had gone back to a little tour of the surroundings which was just as well as Gloria popped out and quite unexpected that was. Suddenly this shaft of light splashed across the clearing and I started. Just as quickly she had shut the door and walked out onto the backyard. Quietly, but waving my torch about so I didn't startle her I walked towards her. I tried to fold her in my arms and start on a private session but Gloria wasn't having any part of that.

'Cool it Gary, I'm working love. Just checking everything out here is okay. We'll be about an hour and then you can run our two lover-boys back into the village. They'll be happy by then. Things good out here?'

'Yes Gloria, real good. Cottage is dark and the noise is real low. Belle did a good job there. Nothing out here that shouldn't be. Nice night actually. Give us a kiss then to keep the cold out.'

Gloria let herself wriggle into my arms and pressed herself up against me. I could feel the full length of her and it felt good, real good. Her soft moist lips found mine and we started a long sensuous dance with our tongues. Within seconds my body was responding to this activity and my hands started to explore.

'Gotta go Gary. There's only Sheena and Lola down tonight and the blokes wanted a special finale and that includes me. See you later.' She slipped away, flipped open the door and was gone. Jesus Christ woman, you can't leave me like this: hard on and hard up. Bugger you Gloria and I went over to concentrate on the cameras for a while. I'll get my money's worth darling you'll see. I'll get to watch, which I do enjoy as you said and I'll get to profit. Fuck the lot of you. And I did, well figuratively. I got some good scenes that night and felt right chuffed with myself. Seeing when things were coming to a climax helped know when to be ready by the motor and the door opened and the giggling girls led the two blindfolded blokes back towards me. The girls helped their two customers back into the car with a lot of hand action and then it was slowly round and round in circles before coming to a halt in the quiet parking lot.

'Right oh mates. End of the magic mystery tour. I'll take those blindfolds off and wish you a goodnight.'

The two blokes were fairly pissed by this time and pretty well shagged out too so I had to help them unfold themselves from my car. With a bit of a supporting arm I got the pair of them into their own powerful motor and checked that the driver felt good enough to drive. In a rather slurry voice he re-assured me he felt fucking marvellous and could drive anywhere. He tried to explain how good his precious Jaguar was but I just wished him goodnight and drive safely. Sitting back in my own car I thought about this evening. I thought about Gloria and what I had seen which caused me to get hard again and think about Gloria some more. I was about to drive round to Gloria's house when I realised she would have a house full with Sheena and Lola and I still wasn't sure how things stood with Tilley. I drove home planning a payment session with Gloria. I had learnt several things this evening and I might try some of them with Gloria tomorrow or the next night I thought.

Thursday was a day off for Gloria at the hairdressers but not at Darlene's. She moved about feeling tired and listless. Last night might have been a buzz at the time but the aftermath was something else. She managed not to drop anything and even kept the orders straight but the pace of play was decidedly slow and tropical.

'You're not your usual perky self Gloria,' observed Darlene. 'Smile love and keep them happy Gloria. They come here because they know we do a good tea and sympathy.'

'Sure Darlene, I'll get my face in gear. Still not sure about my mum I suppose. Still waiting for the roof to fall in. Bit worrying that is and then Wendell's gone and redesigned his room after mum spent time and money on it. Don't worry though. I'll put the smile back on Darlene.'

Gloria made the effort until seven when the door finally closed. She walked home to find her mum lamenting over Wendell's room.

'Look what he's done Gloria love? I'd had it painted so bright, so cheerful and now he's covered the walls in black paper. Talking about putting a new lock on the door he was Gloria. What's got into the lad? School seems okay 'cos I'm not hearing anything from there so that must be good. But he spends all his time hidden away in his room or down in the village. Where does he go Gloria? I was hearing the other day, from my brother actually that our Wendell has been beating up their Dennis. Bob was right upset about it. Told me I should be firm with Wendell. Said he was getting a bad name in the village. What should I do Gloria?'

'I don't know Mum, really I don't. I came home to help you and I'm glad that Toby seems to have helped and you're back with us but I never knew of any problems with Wendell. I could get Gary to have a word with him.'

'No Gloria, not Gary.'

'All right, Freddie then. Actually, why doesn't Uncle Bob have a word with him as well? If it's his Dennis Wendell's supposed to have bullied why doesn't Bob do something?'

'I'll have a word Gloria. Now, I'm going out to see Rosemary Dunster. I was over there briefly on Monday but I think it's about time I put some things right Gloria and talking with my cousin is one of them. I might mention it when I'm there for Freddie to have a word with Wendell. You going out dear?'

'No Mum, I feel knackered after working in that tea-shop. I'm going to have a bath, wash my hair and just relax Mum. You go and have a good chinwag with Rosemary. That'll shock her. Freddie too if he's there.'

I was sitting quietly in the pub supping on a beer and wondering where Gloria was when Freddie came rolling in and seeing me he brought his pint over.

'Well who'd have thought it?' he said.

'What Freddie? Didn't know you and I were speaking mate. You being such a tosser.'

'Guess who's at our house?'

'Father Christmas, Jack the Ripper, the Chief Constable of the County? How the fuck do I know Freddie? You've been such a drag of late with all your whining.'

'Gloria's mum that's who. Tilley Manson in the flesh and looking like a young woman again what with a summer dress and her hair done all different. You'd said that she'd changed but Christ this is a new woman. Chatting away nineteen to the dozen with my mum about old times, bands, groups, music all sorts. Couldn't understand half of what they were talking about. Then, right out of the blue Gloria's mum tells me to have a word with her Wendell. She asked me, and ever so polite she was about it too, to try and make him behave. Teach him to be grown up like me if you please. Of course I could have told her that the little shit was a bully, a faggot and a nerd but I don't think that was what she wanted to hear.'

'So you're going to beat the crap out of the stupid prat? He needs a lesson in humility.'

'Don't know about no humil… or whatever Gary but he's not at home apparently and so I'm going Wendell hunting. Want to come?'

'No mate. I've some business to attend to. Go and beat the shit out of the little bully.'

Freddie left and I sat and thought, although I didn't sit very long. Tilley's at Freddie's and Wendell's out waiting to be thumped by Freddie. Right Gloria girl, how about payback for prick-teasing last night then?

Ready or not here I come. Gloria opened the door wearing a towel and not much else as I found out a little later. Given what I had in mind that was good. Here was this bird, clean, polished and scrubbed up good with sexy wet hair, smelling gorgeous and I was remembering all the things I had seen last night. Tired or not Gloria was professional, although I didn't actually tell her that and she and I spent a pleasant hour or so trying out some of the things I had seen Lola try on her partner the previous evening. I didn't explain to Gloria where some of these ideas came from and tried to let the situation dictate what to try next but I felt a lot better when we were sitting having a cup of tea and the front door opened. Wendell came in. He was sporting a black eye and holding his arm. Gloria got up at the sight of him in the hallway.

'Wendell what's happened love?' she asked.

'Nothing,' retorted Wendell. 'Go back to your fucking,' and he turned to go upstairs.

'Wendell let me see whether you're hurt at least? Let's put something on that eye. Why are you holding your arm like that?'

'Bugger off. Go fuck yourself. I'm fine,' and he stomped up the stairs. We heard the bathroom door slam shut and the key turn in the lock. Water sounded. I didn't say anything but it looked like Freddie or someone else had found bully Wendell and decided to teach him a lesson. I just kept stum.

'What happened Gary? Mum was going to ask Freddie to have a word with him. She was worried. Apparently her brother had told her that Wendell had been bullying Dennis. Mum didn't know what to do.'

'Maybe somebody did Gloria,' was all I said and went back to my tea. Upstairs Wendell bathed his eye and looked at the bruises along his arm and shoulder. He gritted his teeth and vowed to get even somehow. No rush he thought. Revenge is a dish best served cold and he could wait. Useless bunch of sex maniacs. Fucking themselves and each other to death and his sister was the worst of the lot. Seen her website hadn't I? Corny software but Tom and I had soon sussed it out. Trolling for sex maniacs on the web. Bunch of over the hill bitches on heat and coining in the money. Wait my time I will. Jesus but that hurts and it will look like a bloody rainbow tomorrow. Still, badge of honour and I'll beat the shit out someone tomorrow just for the fun of it.

Tilley came home soon after Gary had left to find Gloria sitting in the kitchen nursing a mug of cocoa.

'Quiet evening love? My but Rosemary and I had a good chat talking about old times. Thinking of some new times too Gloria. Well neither of us have got husbands now and Toby knows some good mates. We might all meet up in London some time. Rosemary was quite excited about the idea. By the way Gloria I asked Freddie to have a word with our Wendell. He said he would.'

'Somebody had a word with Wendell Mum,' Gloria said. 'Don't try and disturb him now but in the morning you'll see that someone had a word with Wendell. Wouldn't talk to me. In fact he was bloody rude but you'll see in the morning. Got a shiner he has and a very bruised arm from the way he was holding it.'

'But he's all right Gloria?'

'He's probably asleep or murdering someone on his computer Mum. I'm not sure which I prefer. Go to bed and think on living it up with Rosemary. I'm going up too Mum.'

The three people in the Manson household slept but they all had different dreams that night.

Up in London on the Friday Janet Donaldson was working with Lewis and Shirley Peters – the long ago connection to the Templeton family. Lewis had been in email contact with his son Peter in Australia and Peter had found some interesting web sites.

'He has been investigating the name of Templeton Janet,' explained Shirley.

'And found some things that he wanted us to check. He wasn't sure whether he had got this right because he was into other family names and found a Templeton quite by chance,' added Lewis.

'What was the other name Lewis?' asked Janet. 'Should we get Samantha on the phone and we can have a conference call to discuss this? If she was involved at the start maybe she can help?'

'Sure, give her a call there Janet. Yes, let's get Samantha involved because she may be able to do some checking down there before we go down next week. Might clear up a few things before we revisit the village. Might avoid some embarrassments too.'

'Hi Samantha, James safely tucked away at Nursery School?'

'Hi Janet, yes the coast is clear so to speak. No violent interruptions expected from monster-mouth.'

'Good day Samantha. This is Shirley here. He's a right larrikin. A little charmer Samantha, really he is.'

'That's just your opinion Shirley but for the moment he is charming his teacher and good luck to her. Anyway, what's happening folks?'

'Lewis and Shirley's son Peter has been exploring the web Sam. He's found some things that weren't expected, well with regards to the Templeton family that is. Peter couldn't remember the names of all the other families in the village but he thought he had remembered this one.'

'Which one Janet?'

'Manson. Does that ring any bells?'

'Sure Janet and yes Shirley and Lewis. Peter is right, that is a village name. Actually it is a relatively new name because the husband Walter Manson married Tilley Edwards and the Edwards family have been here for generations. Walter though came from Devon I think.'

'That's it that's it,' said Shirley excitedly, 'it was Edwards that interested Peter.'

'Help me you lot,' said Samantha. 'I'm all confused. Who are we talking about and why any mystery? And why has this anything to do with the Templetons and hence the Peters family?'

'Patience Sam. Lewis is drawing me diagrams, like family trees you know. Okay Lewis I see Albert, with brother Reginald, down to Edward, down to Brian and down to Gary. Fine, that looks clear. Now Lewis is drawing another family Sam. This time it is the Edwards family. You following?'

'Kind of,' said Samantha holding the phone to her ear and trying to imagine what the diagrams looked like. 'When you've got the diagrams sorted fax them to me if it's that important so I can really understand.'

'Sure. Anyway Lewis has drawn the Edwards family tree. We have George down to Ernest and he married Gwen Biddle.'

'Yes Janet, that's another long time village family name. They used to be the village blacksmiths for yonks.'

'Well according to this chart Ernest and Gwen had two children. One was Tilley and her younger brother Bob.'

'Yes and Bob Edwards is our forest foreman. Works on the Estate. So?'

'It seems Tilley married this bloke Walter Manson in 1973 according to Peter's research and she has two children, Gloria and Wendell.'

'Yes Janet, yes yes yes, and they're all alive and well in the village. Well they were the last time I looked like yesterday. So what?'

'According to Peter the father of Tilley's two children is not the same man, well not the same name on the birth certificates of Gloria and Wendell.'

'How come? Some clerical error? Walter married in 1973 you say and Gloria is young enough to be their child. Wendell certainly must be?'

'Walter was not Gloria's father Sam, leastways not according to Peter's devious inquiries. Maybe we should hire Peter for our Australian office?'

Samantha heard Shirley and Lewis both laugh in Janet's office.

'Okay Janet, so where or how does all this fascinating and maybe devious investigation of Peter's tie in with Shirley and Lewis and so why am I listening to all this?'

'The father's name for Gloria is Brian Templeton, who is a second cousin several times removed from Lewis and Shirley here. That's why Sam. How about them apples?'

'So Gloria is half Templeton if I can draw diagrams as well as Lewis can?'

'And that Samantha love is the sixty-four thousand dollar question. Is Peter right?'

'All this is fascinating Janet but there is still my thick mind wrestling with the question of so what?'

'Samantha, Lewis here and it is important to us see. We've got this inheritance. Lazlo done good and Reginald tucked away something else with his time capsule surprise. We have some money, no a pile of money and we wanted to share within the family. We're all doing well out in Oz, better than we know. When we found out about this family back here in England we just wanted to come and see and share a little. We thought we'd give each family member some piece of the Oz riches. Old grandfather Reginald might have slunk away but he did good in the end and we thought we'd share with any Templetons we could find.'

Samantha sat in her parent's office at Fotheringham and thought about Lewis's comments. Christ she thought, from what I have learnt about Brian Templeton you might be handing out money to a good number of people my age scattered around the West Country. Best keep quiet about that or Lewis and Shirley will be going home broke and not be able to pay us. Quiet Samantha for a change: think first talk second. Samantha smiled to herself. Must be learning something she thought with all this business and people interfacing. Getting to be like dad.

'Samantha you still there? You've gone quiet. We still connected?'

'Yes sure Janet. I'm still here just thinking over your comment and Lewis's words. What do you want me to do? I could go and ask Tilley Manson. Actually she's suddenly changed. When I first came home she was all holy and dressed in nun's clothing. Used to pray a lot and never spoke to anyone. Then her daughter came home, soon after the death of her husband I hear, Tilley's that is, and Gloria has been all around the village doing various jobs. Lewis and Shirley may remember her because she was working in the pub when they were down here before Christmas. Anyway, according to gossip Gloria came down to try and get her mother back into the land of the living. Seems she has been successful because all of a sudden Tilley Manson is a new woman. Saw her yesterday in the village wearing new bright summer clothes and with a modern hair style. Suppose I could go and politely ask although I need a less blunt approach. Do you want me to check that out before I come up to London Lewis?'

'Sure Sam, you know us Aussies, in your face question. Heard that was your style too.'

This time Samantha could hear Janet chuckling in the background.

'I'll think of something guys. Leave it with me. Any other bombshells, although to be honest it is not that much of a bombshell. I'll try and find a polite way of asking who fathered who?'

'That's all for now Sam. When Shirley and Lewis came to see me we thought we should volunteer you for the pointed questions. Just like leading on those death-defying rock climbs you do. You always told me you liked to be first. Well go for it girl. Bye.'

Samantha heard Janet break the connection. She sat and wondered where and how to go first from here.

Upstairs, Deidre was trying to sort out the confusion in her life. Katya was engaged and so she was happy, as was Deidre. Katya was going to graduate on Monday and so was happy about that too, and so was Deidre. Katya sounded as if she was going to stay in England and Deidre wasn't happy about that at all.

'Delaney dear, what are we going to do?'

'Deidre my love, we are going to go to Oxford, stay the weekend and see our beautiful daughter attend her graduation ceremony on Monday and receive a First. A First my love from Oxford University.'

'And then what?' asked Deidre anxiously.

'Come back here Deidre and talk with Anthony and Sylvia. All will be discussed and arranged in a very civilised and Lordly fashion,' he added with a smile and a laugh in his voice.

'Be serious Delaney. Be serious for one minute. This is our Katya we are talking about.'

'One step at a time Deidre and all will be resolved my love. Now, are you packed for the trip to Oxford? Daniel wants to leave right after lunch and be there with plenty of time to settle in.'

'Mother are you ready yet?' asked Katya as she breezed in. 'Daniel wants to pack the car.'

Samantha listened to the hustle and bustle going on around her and decided to find her own peace and quiet to resolve her own particular problem. Dad might know but should she worry him. Mum had said he was feeling the stress of late and now that stupid incident with Henri had upset him when things were looking calm. It's not really mum's thing either thought Samantha. After nursery school and lunch Samantha decided to take James down to Christina, away from all the excitement going on at the Big House. Leaving Christina's Samantha eventually made up her mind. She had briefly asked Daniel where the work crew was and she went and found Bob Edwards.

'Bob do you have a minute please?'

'More bodies Miss Samantha?' asked Bob with a smile on his face. 'More errands of mercy? I suppose I shouldn't joke because my Frances tells me that Betty Travers still talks about you. She thinks you're partly responsible for her success with the expanded business. Mark you she can sure make a good pie can Betty.'

'Yes Bob but this is a little different. You know that I'm working with an old school friend up in London in a company called Heritage Adventures?'

'Yes Miss Samantha. I've heard some of the lads talking about your visits to see them in the George. Quite a shock you've provided for some I hear.'

'Yes Bob and I'm back with maybe some more shocks. Let's sit down and see whether I can sort this out for some new clients we've got. They were down late last year and blew Gary Templeton's mind.'

'Aye Miss, I remember that. Some relatives of old Albert Templeton wasn't it? My grandfather was of that generation although he was killed in '16 in France somewhere. Albert came back, along with your great grandfather Miss.'

'And Albert's son Edward carried on as the forest foreman?'

'Yes Miss, until he died way back in 1978 I suppose. You would have been a little girl then and Mr. Daniel himself just a wee lad.'

'But then my dad made your father the foreman, long before he hired that useless clown Norton Ferris. Do you know why the switch from the Templetons to your family?'

'There was no-one left on the Templeton side Miss Samantha. That Brian Templeton was off selling anything to anyone. My dad had worked here for ever and it must have made sense to your father. Why Miss, why the interest?'

Samantha looked at Bob and realised she was beating around the bush. She still wasn't sure how to line up the questions.

'Your mother came and talked with my mother sometime around the time I was born. Mum was telling me the other day. There was some question about your sister. Mum wouldn't tell me all the details but it had something to do with your dad becoming the foreman. Mum hinted it was something she did to help your sister. Something she promised your mother. I think it was something to do with Gloria. Tilley, your sister married quite young and mum said she had been a real tearaway. Quite like me in a way mum had said but something happened when Tilley got married. She changed mum said. I don't remember Bob 'cos I was just a baby but mum said Tilley suddenly went from a wild thing to a recluse. She went all quiet, wrapped up in herself and her baby and stayed at home with Walter away driving lorries. You would have been a teenager Bob but something happened to your sister.'

'Why do you ask Miss?' Bob said looking serious.

'Our clients up in London, who come from Australia Bob are trying to find out some more about their long lost relatives.'

'And you think one or more of them are Edwards, or even Biddles like my mum?'

'No Bob but we are having questions over Tilley and Gloria.'

'Yes Miss, my sister and her baby. Yes, I hear you Miss. You talked with my sister Miss Samantha?'

'No Bob, not yet. I'm going to later today. Tilley has changed and she seems so full of life at the moment. Everyone tells me Gloria is really happy too and that she has just gone back to working in the George. That seems to suit her Bob. She's a natural there. I don't want to go upsetting people over nothing but I thought I'd ask you if you know anything?'

Bob Edwards plucked a piece of grass from the forest ride bank he was sitting on and chewed reflectively. He looked at Samantha. 'Your people up in London are Templetons aren't they Miss?'

'Yes Bob, although their grandfather changed his name to Peters when he went to Australia. But yes the question is really about Templetons.'

'Aye the wanderings of Brian Templeton and how he messed up my sister's life. I'm right glad to see and hear what Gloria has done since she came back from London. She's helped my sister come back to life so to speak. Whatever happened all those years ago did something strange, something wrong to my sister. I can remember her as a wild thing. True I was only a youngster but she was so full of life. Used to drive mum crazy. Dad was always laid back and concerned with the forest but my mum used to worry so. She had tried to be strict but my sister wasn't having any of that. Used to crawl in to the house through my window she did. Middle of the night she'd come home and throw pebbles up at the window. Up over the shed roof and in over my bed. And the music Miss. Her record player used to be going non-stop with all her wild noisy music. Dad would go down the pub and mum would argue. Tilley would shut her bedroom door and sing along. She was a laugh Miss. She was a wild thing.'

'But then it all stopped Bob?'

'Yes. I never knew when or what happened but almost overnight it stopped. Mum became secretive and she would spend hours talking with Tilley. You're right though Miss because I'm sure my mother went to talk to Lady Sylvia. It was some women's thing and I was never sure what, leastways not then I wasn't, not when it all happened.'

'But later Bob?' Samantha asked.

'Aye Miss, later, much later mum told me. Probably about the time that I got married to Frances. Not long before my dad died and then mum died not so long after that. No-one else knew Miss, well apart from Tilley of course. Walter Manson never knew. That I'm sure.'

'Never knew what Bob?' Samantha asked gently looking at Bob.

'That Walter wasn't Gloria's dad. Someone else was Gloria's dad and my mum got Tilley married double quick to Walter and he loved the idea. Big man he was and friendly too. Used to take me for the odd ride in his lorry, until he started driving tankers that is. Strict they were about any passengers in those petrol tankers. It all started okay but pretty soon Tilley went weird, quiet, withdrawn and wouldn't talk to anyone. Even mum had difficulties some days seeing her and the baby.'

'If Walter wasn't the father Bob, even though he was obviously Wendell's father, who was Gloria's dad? Who really messed up your sister's life, although now she seems to be back to her old bright self? You must be glad to see that happen as you said, but who all those years ago now changed Tilley?'

'You asked how my dad got to be foreman Miss Samantha and I told you because we had worked here for generations. Also there were no more Templetons after Edward. My mum told your mum Miss and your mum promised to help as you said. So end of the Templeton era and perhaps you understand why I give that young Gary a hard time. He's not a bad lad and tries hard to be like his grandfather rather than his father but he is a Templeton god dam his eyes. Yes Miss Samantha, one night Brian Templeton took advantage of my wild sister and without him even thinking about it he changed my sister's life for nigh on twenty five years. A couple of minutes of slap and tickle for precious Brian Templeton took twenty odd years away from Tilley. So yes Miss, Brian Templeton is the father of Gloria Manson if that is what you are trying to ask.'

'Bob I will take your confidence away and think about it. I will go and see Tilley because she might tell me one other thing that I won't bother you with. All this stays with me Bob and I thank you for your time and confidence. My mother wouldn't tell me although I didn't know what questions to ask. I only got asked about this this morning and right now my mother is tied up with Katya, Daniel and the Howards. We're all going up to Oxford for Katya's graduation ceremony and of course my lovely brother has eventually popped the question. Being who he is Daniel had to wait until he could talk formally to Katya's dad and ask him before he asked Katya. Katya of course couldn't wait and told Daniel so but you know my brother Bob. He likes to do things taking all the affected people into account.'

'Bit like your father Miss Samantha. Sir Anthony thinks about people Miss. Always has thought about his people and tries to bring us together. Look what he tried to do for John Ferris, even after that night in the cottage?'

'True Bob but unfortunately fate took over and now we have an empty cottage.'

'But Betty is going great guns with her business and the little kiddies seem happy in their new house. Perhaps it will all work out in the end Miss. Go and see my sister but treat her gently. No bowling over people now.' Bob laughed and stood up. 'Must be getting on Miss Samantha and see what the gang's up to. It's Friday afternoon and given half a chance they will be looking to go home early. Take care Miss and be gentle with Tilley.'

'Bye Bob and thanks.'

Samantha got back into the Landrover and thought over what she had learnt; gently gently with Tilley. In a rather pensive mood Samantha drove back to the hopeful peace and quiet of the Big House now that Daniel had taken the Howards to Oxford.

Samantha found her mother sitting in the office looking over some estate papers.

'Mum can you spare a minute? Actually where is dad?'

'Your dad's resting love. He's feeling the strain of this past week what with the Howards, the encounter with Henri or rather with Leslie and then Daniel's announcement. I think events have rather overwhelmed him. Thinking about it I'm so glad Rosalind came through with the purchase of Brainware. All that would have been too much. Anyway Samantha, sorry love what did you want to talk about?'

'Tilley Manson Mum. Gloria's mother.'

'Ah yes, the wild and unfortunate Tilley Manson, tearaway daughter of thoughtful Gwen and quiet Ernest. It's funny Samantha because the parents were so different and then their two children were both different again. Look at Bob Edwards, hard-working yet clear-speaking and takes charge when needed but doesn't throw his weight around. Daniel thinks he is an excellent foreman. Gets the job done with a minimum of fuss and very little personnel problems. Bob sorts all that out before Daniel has to intervene.'

'Yes Mum sure, but what about the other child, the changed woman? Have you seen her recently? Wearing modern and young clothes and she's had her hair done to take years off her looks. I almost had to do a double take when I saw her in the village the other day. What about Tilley? By the way I've just been talking with her clear-speaking brother and Bob has told me a few things, about Tilley that is. I wanted to confirm a couple of things before I go and talk with Tilley herself.'

'Why Samantha? It's all done and sorted, especially if Tilley has put it all behind her. Sounds as if she has thrown off her sackcloth and ashes and buried the past. Leave it be can't you?'

'Wish I could Mum but we've got a client, the Peters actually who you might remember from before Christmas and they are looking for family to share some inheritance. Their son in Australia has been digging, or perhaps I should say hacking into some old records. He found some surprises, well surprises for his parents that is. They're trying to track

Templetons and it appears that Brian Templeton is the father of Gloria Manson and not Walter. Any comments Mum?'

'That's what Gwen Biddle told me all those years ago now Samantha. Came to me she did 'cos she thought I could help. Well I suppose we did in a way because we made Ernest foreman although he wasn't cut out for the job. Also we helped Gwen snare Walter as a husband pretty quickly.'

'No-one told Brian?'

'I didn't Samantha. There was no point. Catherine Dunn knew who she had married and that was another hurry-up marriage too.'

'Does Gloria know? If I am going to talk with Tilley I had better have all my facts straight before I do my usual routine of bull in a china shop.'

Sylvia laughed and held her daughter's hands. 'I can see that Janet is slowly training you Samantha. Your dad hoped that Janet would have some restraining influence. He always thought you two were a terrific pair but he sometimes despaired of your off the wall activities. Your dad might be a man of very innovative and forward-thinking ideas Samantha but he implemented them carefully for the most part.'

'What about the wild idea of marrying you Mum?' teased Samantha, 'and then the pair of you went even crazier and started Brainware almost straight away. Implemented carefully, sure! Guess where all us kids got our wild ideas from? Even Daniel is given to flights of fancy on occasions.'

'Will he and Katya be happy Samantha?' asked Sylvia going serious for a moment.

'I think she'll do an excellent job and Katya is just the sort of lady for Daniel Mum. They both really love each other and work so well together, whatever they are doing. I think my brother's going to be happier than you can imagine. No Mum, no worries there. Your precious baby will do fine.'

'And you my precious daughter, what about you?'

'Mum I'm fine. James is as happy as Larry. The job with Janet is interesting and demanding. I've a fine house to live in, family all around me, and ....'

'And Samantha, and?'

'Terence and I are still feeling our way Mum. His job gets in the way and it's hard to plan any social life. We like being together.'

'But you don't have a lot in common. Changing the subject your father mentioned you were going to do some inquiries at hospitals up in London. About children I assume?'

'Yes Mum. I want to find our for certain, one way or another. I need to know before I talk seriously with Terence. I want to be fair to him.'

'Go and talk with Tilley Samantha but tread lightly. Then you're off to London this evening aren't you? We'll see you in Oxford on the Sunday evening and we've got James looked after. He's at Christina's right now?'

'Yes Mum. I'll collect him after I've been in the village. Thanks Mum. I'll walk softly.'

Samantha stood in front of Tilley's house and knocked. There was no response. She knocked again, a little louder. More like Terence she thought and smiled. Footsteps clattered down the stairs and Wendell opened the door. Samantha took in the multi-coloured eye.

'Yes?' he asked. 'What do you want?' with the emphasis on the "you".

'Is your mother home Wendell?'

'Does it look like it?'

Samantha let an "in your face" thought go through her head before she answered. 'Do you know where she is please?'

'No.'

'Do you know when she will be coming home?'

'No.'

'And Gloria is where?'

'Fucked if I know.'

'How come you're not at school?'

'Piss off lady,' and Wendell slammed the door.

Obviously "manners maketh the man" was not Wendell's school motto thought Samantha with a wry smile on her face. She turned to get back in her car when she saw Tilley walking up the lane.

'Hello Miss Samantha, or should I say Mrs. MacRae now? I suppose I haven't seen you to talk with since you came home from Canada love. Were you looking for Gloria? She's still working at Darlene's but she'll be finished soon after seven dear. If it's important I'm sure Darlene wouldn't mind if you catch her on her break.'

'No Tilley, it's you I wanted to see. I knocked but Wendell didn't know where you were.'

'Yes he's a bit poorly today. Someone must have tried to teach him something yesterday that wasn't in the school curriculum. He'll recover. Boys bounce back don't they? How's your young lad, James isn't it? Goes to school already I hear. Grow up fast don't they?'

Samantha walked forward and held Tilley's arm. 'Tilley it's you I've come to see. I've been talking earlier this afternoon with your brother and then with my mum. It's private Tilley and I don't want to discuss it out here on the road. Can we go inside or would you sooner sit in my car?'

'We'll go inside Samantha. That'll be best dear.'

Sitting on the sofa Samantha turned to Tilley. 'You might have heard Tilley that I work with a friend of mine and we run a company out of London called Heritage Adventures. We help people look for their past, or their parents' and grandparents' pasts.'

'Yes Samantha, Freddie was telling me. Didn't you frighten poor Danny Masters last year with some people from Canada or somewhere? And then you had that Gary Templeton all hot and bothered over some folk from Australia. Well we don't have any surprises as far as I know Samantha. The Biddles and the Edwards have been in this village forever.'

'Yes Tilley and so I talked with Bob first and then with my mother as I said. Tilley, Bob told me about when you were a young woman, his older sister and how full of life you were. He laughed when he described how your mum used to despair. Your dad was always quiet and nothing seemed to faze him but Bob said your mum did get concerned. She loved you both so much Bob said that when you changed she had to do something and she went and saw my mother.'

Tilley went quiet and Samantha reached out and held her hands. 'Tilley I have a client, the family from Australia actually, who has found out something they didn't expect. They want to come down here next week and talk with some folk but they asked me to make sure of the facts first. They didn't want to embarrass or upset anyone. They actually want to help some people but we all very discreetly need to know who to help. I told Bob and my mum what these folks had found and both your brother and my mother confirmed the story. I told them both I would come and see you because I want you to know what might happen. Are you with me so far?'

'I think so Samantha. This is about Gloria isn't it?'

'Yes Tilley.'

'About Gloria and who her father really is?'

'Yes Tilley' and Samantha gently squeezed Tilley's hands and looked into her eyes. 'We learnt that the father's name on the birth certificate is Brian Templeton.'

'One wild silly night with thoughtless and worthless Brian Templeton and I end up with a beautiful lovely daughter. It changed me Miss Samantha, as you probably know. But my Gloria has come back and with some friends she has changed me back to my old self.'

Tilley sat up straight and shook her head. 'From now on it's the new me Samantha. No regrets, no recluse, new clothes and new outlook and to hell with the lot of them.'

'Tilley, does Gloria know?'

'No Samantha, leastways I never told her. My mother never told her and my brother never would. Dad never knew. Your mother never said a word to anyone and Brian Templeton never knew. Neither did poor Walter. Never had a chance did he poor Walter? He was a nice man but he never knew what had happened and then I couldn't take it anymore and shut up shop. Never had a real life did Walter and then he went up in smoke.'

'Tilley, the Australian folk want to give some of their inheritance money from their family to their relatives. This is what this is all about and that includes Gloria. If she doesn't know we have to think what to do for the best. I could tell my clients to forget it or you could tell her. That's why I've come to talk to you because it will be your decision. We'll just do what you want. Can I leave it with you over the weekend? I'm up to London tonight and then on to Oxford to attend Daniel's fiancées University graduation ceremony, but I'll be back with Lewis and Shirley Peters on Tuesday or Wednesday. I'll need to know by then what to tell them.'

Samantha looked at Tilley who was sitting up straight but obviously looking inwards rather than at the room. She flexed her hands inside Samantha's and turned the grip to squeeze Samantha's. 'Leave it with me love. I'll think on it. I'll not say now but I'll decide by the weekend. Bit of a shock and yet a bit of a relief. I don't intend to stand on the rooftops and shout mark you Samantha. Keep it quiet for the moment love.'

'Of course Tilley,' and Samantha stood up. 'I'll let myself out.' Samantha left Tilley sitting on the sofa and let herself out into the early evening sunshine.

'What's for tea Mum?' asked Wendell coming into the room as Samantha shut the front door. 'What's that Wendell? I was thinking on something love. I expect you'll want your tea pretty soon won't you son?' Tilley stirred herself and moved into the kitchen. Wendell smiled and thought over what he had heard. As good as a bastard he thought and that Gary Templeton is fucking his own sister. Absolutely beautiful. Won't Tom and I enjoy this little story?

Samantha drove back to Fotheringham and continued on down to Home Farm. There she collected the non-stop James and the pair of them parked in the back yard.

'Home sweet home James.'

'Why don't we have our own house Mummy? Auntie Christina has her house with Peter and Tony. Adam and his puppy with his mummy and daddy have their own house. Why don't we have our house any more? We did in Canada with daddy?'

'Yes James we did my love. Maybe we will have later. Don't you like living here? You have Dainty, you have your special friends Katya and Beverley Nicols, and you have grandpa and grandma. You also have your Uncle Daniel and his railway. What more could you want my love?'

'Cake and custard Mummy. We didn't have much cake at Auntie Christina's. We only had two each. Auntie Christina doesn't make custard Mummy. Why?'

'Come on then hollow-legs and let's see what we can find in cook's kitchen.'

'Whoopee!'

Gloria walked into her mother's house with a pensive look on her face. Last day at Darlene's she thought and thank God for that. Now a quick check on the computer and let's see what news Belle has for tomorrow.

'Hi Mum. You look smart in that frock. That really suits you you know, especially the way Mrs. Digby has done your hair. We'd be taken for sisters out on the street Mum.'

'Gloria don't you try and con me darling. I was the wild one Gloria before you were even a twinkle. I know who I am.'

'A moment Mum. I need to see what my mates in London have been up to. Toby say anything about this weekend? Is he coming down? Seems like Gina and Belle are coming down according to this email. They don't say anything about Toby.'

'I had a visitor today Gloria.'

'Nice Mum. Anyone I know, although I expect I've got up to date with who is who in the village now? Helped working at Mrs. Digby's that did. She's full of village gossip Mum but she's friendly with it you know.'

'It was Samantha Lord.'

'Christ, what's she want? Was she looking for me?'

'Let's sit down for a moment Gloria 'cos I need to ask you something.'

'Sure Mum. I'll be glad to take the weight off my feet. Waiting tables is a bloody sight harder than working at the George. I'll be glad to get back there behind that bar. What do you want to know Mum? How I met Toby? He's cool Mum. He's a good bloke. I'm glad you get on with him, even if you did know him before I ever did.'

'Gloria why did you run off to London love?'

'Jesus Mum that's a conversation stopper that is.'

'I know, or I think I know Gloria but I've never asked and now I need to know. I'll explain why in a moment.'

'It was Walter Mum. Or rather it was Walter and me Mum. We thought it would destroy you if you found out. Walter thought, no that's not right I thought it wasn't right for you. I ran away to stop it Mum.'

'Stop you and Walter being together Gloria, being together properly I mean? You know, in bed together? He used to go into your room didn't he? I didn't want to hear but that's what I think.'

'Mum he was hurt. You shut your bedroom door and Walter never meant any harm. He was kind, gentle and taught me Mum. At first I didn't know what to think because I was so young and later I didn't know what to do. I couldn't talk to you and Walter said to keep quiet. He never really threatened Mum but in the end I thought it would kill you if you found out so I ran away with Val Gordon.'

'You were happy Gloria. You weren't frightened or shy. You were going out with Freddie and that Sandra Porlock.'

'Yes Mum and Gary too.'

'Yes,' said Tilley, 'and with Gary Templeton too. Suppose you did all the things young people do?'

'Yes Mum. We had fun. We were careful, well we thought we were until Sandra killed herself. She was pregnant Mum. I never told you but she found out she was pregnant and that's why she committed suicide. Not long after that I ran away.'

'And Walter would come to you when he was home from his trips?'

'Mum don't beat yourself up over this. It's over, done. Walter's dead and I'm here with you. With Toby we're all back together again. Kind of happy family although Wendell is doing my head in.'

'Yes Wendell,' said Tilley. 'Child of Walter Manson and Tilley Edwards. In those last years before you ran away you liked it when Walter came to you Gloria. I'm right aren't I?'

Gloria hung her head. 'Mum that's why I ran away. It was good and it was wrong. If I hadn't run away something would have exploded in this house and I didn't want that. I suppose I loved you all too much for that so I ran. I'm sorry Mum, sleeping with Walter and all that but.....'

'That's what I thought Gloria. I suppose I knew about Walter coming to you. You never said and you didn't seem unhappy so I persuaded myself it was good. That you wouldn't get hurt. That it wasn't wrong.'

'But he was my dad Mum. That's incest.'

'Listen Gloria and listen good girl,' said Tilley suddenly sitting up straight and looking directly at her daughter. 'This will come as a shock but it's time you learnt and then you can have one less burden to carry. Gloria, all these years I've kept this secret. I didn't know how to tell you. I didn't know when to tell you. It changed me and I felt so ashamed. I tried to look after you and make sure nothing happened but then you started seeing Gary and I know Walter came to you. I couldn't help it Gloria. I couldn't help myself,' and Tilley sobbed.

Gloria was sitting with her mother on the sofa. They were sitting close together and Tilley was holding Gloria's hand but not looking at her daughter.

'Gloria love I've got to tell you now. Now Toby has brought me back to life I have to tell you the truth, about the real me and who you are.'

'Mum, what are you saying? I am the real me. You are who you are. What's changed?'

'Listen Gloria love, listen and let me tell you all in one go because if I stop I will not be able to continue and it's important you know, real important, especially now you came back and are seeing Gary again. You like him don't you Gloria?'

'He's all right Mum,' Gloria said. 'He's a bit of a laugh, good-looking, good with the words although not as smooth and smart as that dad of his. Do you know his dad came in the salon the other day and tried to come on to me? Cheeky sod he is Mum. Just because he thinks I might like his son doesn't give him any right to try it on now does it? Mum, Mum what's the matter?'

Tilley put her head against her daughter's chest and sobbed. Gloria gently lifted her mum's head up and looked at her. She held her hands tightly and looked straight at her mum. 'What is it Mum? I love you dearly and I'm glad I came home after all those years but I couldn't stay. I think dad and I would have broken your heart or driven you nuts or something. I'm sorry Mum and I suppose I was partly to blame.'

'No Gloria no. I did it. I was to blame. Listen and I'll tell you. Sit back as this will take a while daughter but you need to know love.'

Gloria looked at her mother. She held her hands tightly and she saw a mixture of happiness and sorrow in her mother's eyes. Very softly Gloria said, 'Okay Mum, confession time but remember I really love you,' and she squeezed her mother's hands.

'I was young, wild and full of fun: me and Rosemary Biddle. We were the best of friends, at school, at home, wherever. Music Gloria, music was everything. We'd sing, dance and imagine being in a band. Any money we had we'd spend on records when we were very young and then later, just as we turned into teenagers we started to go to concerts. Initially my mum took us. She is Rosemary's aunt you know and she'd take us to Weston-Super-Mare and then others in Bristol. That's where I first heard about Toby. He was managing bands and he stayed managing bands as we got older. Well, soon Rosemary and I were old enough to go on our own. We both worked part-time and earned some money. My dad didn't understand but my mum was okay. I think she was a flighty piece in her day. Her brother, my uncle Jack was the blacksmith and he always had a ready eye for girls but he was a good laugh and told us to go and enjoy ourselves while we were still young. Now this was the sixties Gloria and it was all peace marches, ban the bomb, long hair, wild music and a gentle drug scene. Yes Gloria, a drug scene, well marijuana and hashish I suppose. Smooth soft and gentle grass and no-one got hurt. I can understand Tom Daley, well his grass habit I suppose but I can't abide his other hobby. I think child pornography is completely perverted. Yes Gloria, I know all about Tom Daley and I know our Wendell goes there a lot. We'll sort Wendell out later don't you worry. Where was I, yes music, bands, Toby, Bristol and being young? Rosemary and I were smart with it though. We took care of ourselves. Wild yes but sensible. Well, when you're a groupie you have to be careful and that's what we became. We couldn't afford to chase all over the country after any of the bands but when they came down here we were there. We were right in there Gloria. After the show we were in the dressing rooms, with the blokes and I mean with the blokes Gloria. I didn't get all those autographs just from saying please love. But it was fun and it was wild and Rosemary and I were riding a wonderful roller-coaster until that one night when it changed. One night Gloria and it all changed, leastways for me it did. My mum was good though. Dad didn't know what to do when he found out but mum told him to back off. She said she'd sort it out.'

Tilley paused and looked closely at Gloria.

'My mum sorted it in a clever way but I couldn't handle it. It changed me. I don't know what really happened but something snapped or came unstuck but I wasn't the same any more.'

'What happened Mum?' Gloria whispered, not wanting to stop the flow and not sure what was going to come next. 'Wild music and fun times Mum, up in Bristol you said.'

'Yes Gloria until we went up to hear some new group. I can't even remember their names now but Rosemary and I felt good. We had some grass and got quite high. Toby knew us by then and he chased us out 'cos he thought this particular band was a bunch of wankers and we'd get hurt or something. He wasn't too keen on the gig but he had a job to do and he pulled it off. Told us to get lost before something happened that shouldn't. Rosemary was pretty far out by this time Gloria and I was sorting out the best way to get home. We used to catch the milk trains sometimes and get in at first light. I suppose we were walking to the station and I was propping Rosemary up when someone called my name. Well I stopped and checked out who it was and there in his car with his smiling face and smooth voice was Brian Templeton. He was about ten years older than us and he'd just got married at the beginning of that year. Rumour running around the village was that he'd had to 'cos he'd made a mistake and got a girl in the club. He already had a reputation did Brian Templeton but prided himself on never getting caught. Somehow, perhaps through an irate or threatening father because I never knew her family Brian married Catherine Dunn. Funny girl she is because she never seems upset that Brian is absolutely carefree with his favours. Smooth talker like you say Gloria.'

'So he called to you Mum.'

'Yes and offered us a lift home didn't he? Rosemary was becoming a dead weight and we would have had a long wait for the milk train and so I said thanks and paid the price.'

'What price Mum?'

'Being too tired, too excited, too stoned, too careless and too... I don't know Gloria love. Rosemary was out sleeping in the back. He had some great music on tapes for the car. He had a smooth tongue and I got flirty or something. Somewhere on the way home we stopped. He was hot and careless. Probably thought everyone was on the pill like his wife and the many other wives he pleasured. I wasn't thinking and a month or so later I realised what had happened. I was pregnant. It wasn't rape, it wasn't a mistake and my mum said she'd sort it. She got it out of me who it was and she knew Brian wasn't going to lose any sleep over it so she did a couple of things.'

'What Mum? I'm beginning to get some idea but what happened next?'

'My Mum told two people she thought could help. Mum and I agreed we would keep the baby and I'm ever so glad, no I'm delighted that I did. You were a wonderful baby Gloria and you've grown up into a beautiful and lovely woman.'

'Me Mum, I'm that baby. Brian Templeton is my dad, not my dad, not Walter?'

'Bear with me love and let me explain. You need to know all of the story. I need to tell you the entire story. Mum told Jack Biddle her brother and she told Sylvia Lord.'

'Sylvia Lord? Why? Why tell Sylvia Lord?'

'First things first Gloria. Uncle Jack Biddle and his wife ran a B&B and they had a regular customer in Walter Manson. They all got on very well and Walter was a young, handsome and energetic lorry driver but he was exceptionally shy with women. He was a big man as you know and strong. In fact he was frightened how strong and bad-tempered he could get and thought that turned women off. To make a long story short Jack and my mum brought Walter and me together. I understood what I was supposed to do and I was so annoyed, ashamed and desperate at that time I went along with the plan. I really wanted the baby but being a single mum in this village at that time would have been awful. No-one would have spoken to me, to us and I was the centre of the party. The wild one in the village and that would have been a disaster. Walter and I got married as fast as my mum could arrange it. Dad never said much but then dad never did until some five years later. He never knew what my mum had done and we all got some compensation from the Templetons for their mistake.'

'So Walter wasn't my dad Mum. All these years and I never knew. And all those years when…….'

'Yes Gloria love, all those years when Walter visited you. I knew he wasn't your dad. I knew what was happening and there was nothing I could do. Gloria I'm so sorry. I had gone inside myself and there was nothing I could do. Let me explain Gloria. Let me try now and tell you, please. I need to tell you Gloria.'

Gloria sat back on the sofa and looked at her mother. All those years when she thought she was with her father. Did it change anything? She had run away because she thought her mother would be hurt, be shocked, be disgusted because Walter was her father and she had liked it. Now, Walter wasn't her father: had never been her father, and all that time her mother had known. Had she let it happen because she knew Walter wasn't her dad? What had really happened to mum?

'Go on Mum. I'm really confused now. I suppose I'm relieved too but I need to know more.'

'I married Walter but everything overwhelmed me somehow. The wild fun collapsed into a sin, a mistake, a deceit, a break-up with Rosemary, pressure from my mum and a baby. I looked after you, with a lot of help from mum but otherwise I closed down. Walter couldn't understand it. He was away a lot on the road and still a handsome and active man. After being away for a week driving around England he would come home to his lovely and fun-loving wife who had changed somehow. I was good looking Gloria when I was young love. I had been full of life and Walter had met me a few times when I was over at uncle's Jacks and he was there. We had flirted, well I had flirted 'cos that was me and my uncle Jack would make suggestive comments 'cos he knew I liked the wild life and he had been young himself and a bit of a lad. Walter expected me to be keen, eager, loving, and full of life. I had you and me and that's all I wanted. That's all I cared about and I shut everything else out. Walter was strong and knew what he wanted so he took it. For three, four, maybe five years Gloria Walter took it and I shrunk up inside. Then Sylvia Lord honoured her part of the bargain.'

'What did she do?'

'It was 1973 Gloria and Sylvia had just had her daughter Samantha, the year before. She was finding her daughter a challenge and quite understanding about my situation. She had heard of Brian Templeton's reputation and knew that he or his family wouldn't be continuing the role of foreman on the estate. My mum went up and helped Sylvia Lord with Miss Samantha and Sylvia Lord made my dad the foreman when Edward Templeton died in 1978. My dad was the foreman from then up until he died in 1988 and my younger brother Bob took over. More money, more prestige in the village and recognition by the Lord family that the Biddles and Edwards were well respected folk by the family up at the Manor. She honoured her part of the bargain Gloria and that Miss Samantha was partly raised by my mum although I doubt whether she knows that.'

'And Wendell Mum?'

'You were growing up Gloria. You were such a sweet little girl and so full of life. Walter was good with you. He loved you and he would come home and pick you up and swing you all around the house. Knocked over a few lamps in his time did Walter but he thought you were special.'

'Wendell?'

'I'd turned inwards Gloria and I didn't know what to do. I felt I had debased myself, had sinned and I thought God had punished me for the life I had led. I had sinned and so I prayed for guidance and became a nun.'

Gloria almost giggled and translated "nun" into "none" as far as Walter was concerned but then she realised there was more to the story and she did want to hear the end. She squeezed her mum's hands and looked at her face questioningly.

'Walter was a man Gloria: a big strong man with healthy appetites. I knew he must have found some release on the road but something snapped that night. One of us must have said something and the other said something else and we had a fight and we had Wendell.'

'Mum I remember that night,' Gloria said. 'I'll always remember that night. I lay in bed and wondered what was happening. I was frightened and could hear all sorts of noises. There were crashes, thumps, screams and grunting. I lay in bed and shivered 'cos I didn't know what was happening. Next morning everything seemed normal. You were your quiet self like you always were in the morning and dad, Walter seemed cheerful, almost happy. I wondered whether this was a new kind of happiness and I went to school thinking I had worried over nothing but after that day it all changed again and Walter slept in the spare room. You often went into your bedroom and locked the door. Some nights when he came home he would knock on your door, talk to you, plead with you but you never answered. He was still good and kind with me and then, maybe a year later he came into my room.'

Gloria stopped and looked at her mum.

'Yes Gloria, I know what Walter did but I couldn't move. I couldn't stop praying. In fact I prayed more, mostly for you. I know Walter loved you as a daughter but I also knew that Walter wasn't your father. There was no incest love. He was kind, loving, and could be gentle. I watched and you looked happy. You didn't look worried or hurt. You didn't try and hide from either of us. I had the baby to look after and you ran around as happy as a lark. You changed from my little girl and I was happy for you as you blossomed into a pretty young lady and then into a wonderful young woman. You laughed, flirted, sang and danced around the house. You had friends, you even enjoyed school and all that time I knew Walter came to you. I was relieved. Part of me knew that learning about sex was important and that it was better to learn from someone who cared and someone who knew what to do and what not to do. Walter could be loving. He was tender and you seemed so full of life.'

'And I was Mum. I was but I thought Walter was my dad and part of me thought that was a giggle and part of me worried it would tip you over the edge. I ran away Mum because I enjoyed it so much. I ran away......'

'Because I tried to smother you Gloria. Because I tried to keep you away from Gary Templeton and you and he were having a ball. I guessed that your foursome with Freddie, Sandra and Gary was a group where anything could happen. I might have been shrivelled up inside Gloria and spent a lot of time on my knees but deep inside I remembered what it was like to be young. I guessed the four of you couldn't keep your hands off each other and I guessed that Gary Templeton was just like his father. Freddie Dunster might be your second cousin but Gary Templeton was your half-brother. I tried to keep you away from Gary but that of course didn't do any good. When Sandra committed suicide poor girl I imagined you consoling both Freddie and Gary so I tried again to keep you apart.'

'I never knew Mum. I ran away because of Walter and me and because you were trying to interfere with Gary but I never realised why. You're right though Mum, the four of us did all do things together. Suppose we did everything together. I'd learnt a lot from Walter and of course I had to show off with my friends. Try everything out like. Show that I knew it all and enjoyed it all the time.'

'I know Gloria. We're quite alike you and me daughter. We both grew up wild and full of fun. I don't think Walter ever knew he wasn't your dad. I don't think it ever really worried him 'cos you enjoyed it and he thought you were a loving couple. He probably died never knowing but he loved you Gloria, he really did.'

391

'And Brian Templeton, my dad? Does he know? Does Gary know? No Mum, Gary doesn't know. I'm quite sure that Gary doesn't know anything about this but what about his dad?'

'No Gloria, Brian silver-tongued Templeton doesn't know and probably wouldn't care. Knowing him he's probably got a whole troop of little Templetons running around the countryside. Women who weren't sure who was the father or never saw him again. No Gloria love, Brian Templeton and no-one else in the village ever knew. Mum knew, uncle Jack knew and Sylvia Lord knew but no-one else. I don't think my dad ever really understood but he's dead, as is my mum and uncle Jack. I can't see Sylvia Lord shouting it from the top of Fotheringham Manor either Gloria so the secret still stays with us.'

'What about Rosemary?' Gloria asked as she had a sudden thought. 'She must have known or even guessed? You said she had passed out that night but she might have heard something or wondered why you suddenly got married and then changed. Didn't she ever say anything?'

'Rosemary had got married the year before. Her husband William had some money and Rosemary had some weird ideas. Anyway, after she got married it didn't really change how we both went out together. William Dunster was a funny bloke and we wondered sometimes whether he was gay. Then there was some rumour about him and his son when Freddie grew up which made us wonder again. Anyway, back in '72/'73 Rosemary was married but she and I still went wild up to Bristol and such. She probably thought I was trying to keep up with her by getting married as quickly after she did. We always used to compete for blokes, for favours, for autographs, for anything really and the fact that she got married first probably made her think I was trying to keep up. I don't know whether she guessed or not. I certainly never told her and I know my mum wouldn't, even though Rosemary was her niece.'

'But you said you changed Mum, right after you got married to Walter. Rosemary would have noticed that surely. If she never changed after she got married what did she think when you suddenly put up the shutters so to speak? That's quite some change.'

'I don't know Gloria. We never talked. We still don't talk, well until this past week. I can talk to Freddie but I couldn't speak to his mother. Strange isn't it?'

'And Sylvia Lord, what about her?'

'Gloria we don't exactly move in the same circles love. I don't think I've seen Sylvia Lord for ages now, although funnily enough she was in church a couple of Sundays back. Strange that because I've never seen her in church before. She didn't see me. She was too intent talking with that husband of hers. Now that Sir Anthony is a fine man Gloria. Always looking after people he is. I'm not quite sure why my mother didn't go to him because he would have understood. Sylvia Lord is harder. It's funny she should help. Perhaps that Miss Samantha was more of a handful than we all know about. She's certainly got a reputation later in her life and now she's back frightening all the locals I hear with long-lost relatives from the past. No Gloria, Sylvia Lord is not a worry for us.'

Gloria sat holding her mother's hands and thinking all she had learnt. What a revelation: what an about-face of affairs. What she thought was incest wasn't and what she thought was good clean fun was incest, well sort of. And mum knew all this time. Knew who my real dad was: knew that Walter and I were…..: knew that Gary and I were together. Christ what a turn up for the books. Wonder what else there is I don't know about? And now what she thought? Toby Dobbs comes back into her life and suddenly I've got my mum back but a mum with secrets I never knew about. Hell fire Toby you've sure unlocked a real Pandora's box little man. You were my friend and mentor in London. You were my father figure and my lover. Now you're my mother's saviour and the possible key to

393

a new life for all of us. Tilley squeezed Gloria's hand and looked at her daughter. She continued, 'I suppose I knew about Walter coming to you. You never said and you didn't seem unhappy so I persuaded myself that it was good. Anyway, enough of that, but just realise you weren't sleeping with your father Gloria, just some bloke who's wife had shut her bedroom door love.'

'But I've been going out with Gary Mum. Is that why you tried to keep us apart all these years? You knew and you tried to stop me seeing Gary. Christ Mum I may not have been sleeping with my father but I've been fucking my brother and I never knew it.'

'Crazy old world Gloria isn't it?' said Tilley.

'Good job I don't have any morals Mum,' said Gloria and she sat back in her seat and laughed her head off. 'And he doesn't know either Mum?' and Gloria laughed even harder. 'Christ now I'll have to put poor Toby straight. He thinks I was shagging my dad. Well that's what I told him. He'll get a laugh out of this Mum. You tell him. He likes you Mum so you tell him. You can have a laugh about it together. Jesus Mum some of these home truths can be a bit of giggle can't they? That reminds me, I've got to get a message to my long-lost brother about something Belle said. I'll see him in the pub tonight but I'm not saying anything Mum. It's too good for words but I might change my bed partner.'

'Yes Gloria love, that might be a good idea. Just be discreet about it. When Miss Samantha came this afternoon I told her to keep it secret.'

'What did she want, and what did she know Mum?'

'I'll tell you later Gloria. I'd better check what Wendell is up to.'

Well what do you know thought Gloria when her mother had left the room. What I thought was incest wasn't for all those years and what I thought was teenage fun and games was illegal: ain't life one big giggle. Gloria remembered Belle's email and she had another giggle. Well tomorrow night will be all the sweeter she thought. Blow Gary's mind too she thought. I'll get changed and drop him a note for tomorrow's gig.

When I got home from work that Friday I was feeling good about the weekend coming up. I knew that Gloria would have something lined up and so I asked my mum whether she had heard anything from Gloria.

'Like what Gary?'

'Like a note or something Mum. No problem, I'll probably see her in the pub tonight anyway. Where's Dad or is that a silly question like always?'

'He phoned Gary. Said he was up in London and would be all weekend. There was a re-union or something with some old friends of his. Said he'd be away until Monday or maybe later.'

I only saw Gloria briefly in the pub on that Friday night because she said she was tired and needed to get organised for tomorrow. She was giggly but I didn't know what about and Freddie was banging in my ear asking for another foursome some time. Gloria told him to be patient and she handed me a note. The note said there would be three blokes and she had a brief description of them. Apparently they were all in their fifties and expecting to spend some time having fun so we would be home late that night. Start-up time wasn't until ten o'clock. After a couple of games of darts with Freddie, Lester and Danny I called it quits and went home. But tomorrow I thought, that should be good.

So Saturday evening I'm sitting in my car tucked away in a corner of the parking lot. It was crowded that night in the George and there was a lot of coming and going. I just hoped it wouldn't become a balls up because I knew the girls were counting on me delivering. A large Ford pulled into the parking lot and I did a double take. Coming towards me was my dad.

'You're in London,' I said.

'And you're the guide to Forest Street.'

'What, what did you say?'

'Gary son there are three of us, all looking for the London Road, or is that London Street, no it must be Forest Street? I'm assuming you're not going to sit there all night waiting for another three customers or are you usually this thick? Come on you two I've found our guide.' My dad told the other two to park the car somewhere out of the way and come back to our blindfold expert.

'Know what you're doing mate?' dad asked. 'New at the game eh? Suppose we've all got to learn sometime. Where are the blindfolds then?'

I pulled myself together and got the three of them blindfolded and sorted out who was sitting where. 'Is it far honourable guide?' my dad asked through his blindfold.

'Just far enough to get you all excited,' I said. 'Hope you've all got lots of cash gents 'cos this is a no plastic zone.' One of the blokes in the back laughed. Through his blindfold he explained in rather muffled tones that they were loaded and the other bloke laughed. Dad chuckled beside me. 'Night on the town honourable guide, well on something they tell me. Something special we've ordered and so we're ready for the royal treatment.'

Gloria I thought. Fuck, I wonder whether Gloria knows what is going to happen. Now what should I do? I drove around the dark lanes with several turns and even one un-necessary three-point turn backing up. Finally I turned off the road and through the forest. Following the plan I pissed around a little bit in the forest including passing the cottage. The girls would have seen and know when to expect me. I stopped on the edge of the clearing and I could see that the door was already open with only a dim light spilling out. I saw there were three girls walking towards the car and when they came closer I saw they were Lola, Gina and Belle.

Where was Gloria? How could I pass any message? The three girls helped the blokes out of the car with a lot of laughing and joking about magical mystery trips. I tried to catch Lola's eye and nod my head towards my dad but she didn't see me. Belle had my dad's hand and I darted round in front of her as she zigzagged a little. I made all sorts of hand actions but she wasn't interested. She shook her head and then jerked it as if to tell me to fuck off. I gave up. Shit I thought, it was their funeral. I had tried. Didn't they know who their customers were? I thought Belle was supposed to be smart. Still Gloria wasn't in sight so maybe all's well. They all went inside and the door shut cutting off any light. I nearly fell over in the instant darkness and banged my knee. I had left my torch back in the car. It was a dark and moonless night and the light cloud cover obscured most of the stars. Where had I left the car? I had been so intent on trying to warn the girls I hadn't paid attention to where I was. Eventually I had enough sense to stand still for five minutes until I got some night vision back again and could slowly move towards the car and the useful torch. Jesus what a bloody circus. Somewhat conscientiously I did a walk about around the perimeter of the clearing and then back-tracked towards the road. Once up the little rise you couldn't see the cottage and all was quiet and dark as it should be. Okay, so how about some video? Shit, but it's my dad. So what Gary I told myself. What's he ever done for you? Cheats on mum, cheats on everyone and now he's screwing my friends. No not really I realised. In fact it was more the other way round. I didn't know what Gloria and Toby had worked out in terms of charges for services rendered but I'd bet it wasn't cheap. So dad, perhaps it is you being screwed after all. Having sorted all that out in my head I decided it was time to pursue my side line and I quietly moved back to the cottage and my useful assortment of cameras. They'd had time to have a few drinks, seen Sheena do some dances and generally loosen up. Maybe we'll look in the back rooms first. Dad had said they had ordered something special. Let's see how special.

That evening I moved from camera to camera and got to be quite selective. After a couple of hours they were all in one of the back rooms. Belle had arranged enough lighting so everyone could see what was going on. Gloria had told me that some blokes just got turned on watching and other blokes really liked to see what they were doing. She told me this was entertainment and not some fumbling fuck in the dark. There was enough light for me to capture some of the specials. I nearly blew it though 'cos I dam near choked and cried out sometime near the end. Dad was flat on his back and Gina was straddling his head so he couldn't easily see and who should appear but Gloria. Christ she looked good and she was wearing a broad smile and very little else. The other two blokes came in to watch with Belle and Sheena, and then Gina and Gloria gave dad the ride of his life. I noticed that the two girls were nearly pissing themselves with laughter and it was Gloria who slipped away first and out of the room. I quickly shot back towards the perimeter of the clearing which was just as well as a minute or two later the door opened and Gloria slipped out.

'Shit Gary, that's a gas. This deal works a treat love.'

'Gloria I tried to tell Belle. I tried to tell her that one of the blokes is my dad. She wouldn't listen.'

Gloria put her hand on my chest and leaned against me. 'We knew Gary mate. Jesus but that Gina can keep a man quiet. Your dad never knew what hit him. They said they wanted something special. Well, I don't think they will forget tonight. Anyway, everything okay out here? We're nearly through. They might be able to walk right now but they'll be shattered tomorrow. What a giggle. I've got to go and hide somewhere before too many questions get asked. They'll be about fifteen or twenty minutes. Usual deal, round and round the houses before the drop off. See you later. No, I'll see you tomorrow Gary 'cos we've another deal lined up for tomorrow evening too.'

She spun round and slipped back into the cottage.

As I walked back to the car I thought about Gloria's last comment. I'd better check on those cameras tomorrow morning and make sure everything's fine for tomorrow night then. Hell, this was getting better and better. Within twenty minutes the girls led the three blokes out to the car and I spent fifteen minutes going round in circles until we arrived back at the George about one o'clock. Everything was locked up tight in the village.

Dad let the other two blokes walk over to their car. He leaned in across my window. 'You should try that sometime son. That young stuff is full of energy and kinky ideas. Takes years off me that does. Well, off back to London and my re-union. See you later Mr. Guide. Next time I'll ask for a family discount.' He laughed as he walked back to the car and the three of them drove off.

Just after Sunday lunchtime three things happened although perhaps only one was of catastrophic importance but they all three contributed in their own way. First there was a mass exodus of the Lord family to Oxford. Samantha had already gone up to London to see Shirley and Lewis Peters but Anthony took Sylvia, Christina and the three children up to stay until Tuesday to attend Katya's graduation. The result was a quieter or emptier forest. For some reason the Education Centre was vacant that next week and Bob Edwards managed the forest crew working on some weeding. Secondly, I got a new note from Gloria that there would be a pick up at eight that evening in the car park. This time it was a couple in their thirties the note said: driving a black minivan. This reminded me to get a move on and check the cameras that afternoon.

The third item caused me the greatest grief and as usual it was Freddie at the bottom of it. Seems he had been talking with his mum.

'Mum you know we've been going out with Gloria, Dora and Gary but I keep getting the feeling Gloria's mum's not keen on the idea. She's been over here now to talk with you and she's suddenly changed. You said so yourself the other day. Why am I getting the looks and why is she so down on Gary?'

'You're right Freddie. Tilley has changed and that is due to Gloria and an old friend. You've probably met him or seen him. Toby Dobbs he is.'

'That old bloke who came down from London claiming to be Gloria's friend, and then down again with a gaggle of girls, more friends of Gloria?'

'Yes Freddie. Toby Dobbs was Toby the Fixer when Tilley and I were young and we both knew Toby, well sort of.'

'Yes but so what Mum? What's that got to do with us? Why did Gloria's mum go so weird if she was as wild as you say? Gary was trying to tell me last autumn that you and Gloria's mum were a pair of wild things. What did Gary call you? Groupies or some such word. Anyway, Gary was inferring that Gloria's mum had to get married or something although he said, or perhaps Gloria said that Tilley was pissed off because you got married first. Why did Tilley marry Walter Manson anyway? He was from Devon and not even local. Gloria said she ran away because of her dad. It was all a bit confusing Mum and now Tilley's walking around trying to look like Gloria's sister.'

'So you say that Tilley's been trying to keep her Gloria away from Gary Templeton?'

'Yes Mum, it's strange 'cos she's always been that way. Right from the days when we were teenagers. What's she got against Gary? I know he's a thick shit on occasions and full of himself. He doesn't like to admit it but he's quite like his dad.'

'Yes Freddie, his precious dad, this village's prolific son. Gary is like his dad and his dad is a lot of people's dad around here.'

'What do you mean Mum?'

'I suppose now that Tilley's come back to us it's not so much a secret any more. She seems to have moved on, especially now that Walter's dead.'

'What secret? What was Tilley's secret. She was your friend but suddenly it all stopped you said. What did you do?'

'I fell asleep Freddie, although I was probably half-stoned too and that led to a problem for Tilley. We used to look after each other you know. Yes we were wild but together we were fine. We kept each other in check and made sure we both were safe. Oh sure we had a good time and kept a lot of blokes happy but together we felt we knew where we were. Great until that one night up in Bristol and I fell sick or something. Tilley was trying to get me to the train to come home and I was out of it. Got an offer of a lift didn't she and the silly cow said yes and that was the trouble. Freddie why didn't she say no?'

'Lift from who Mum, and what did it matter that you were asleep, stoned or whatever?'

'Couldn't help could I son? I was out of it. I never knew anything about it until long after, long after when it was too late and by then Tilley had virtually stopped talking to me. She changed and it was my fault Freddie.'

'What changed her Mum? What happened when you went to sleep, in this life or whatever?'

'It was who changed her Freddie. She couldn't stop him and he always had a silver tongue. Thoughtless, self-centred bastard he is and all he wanted was another notch on his totem pole. Marriage hadn't slowed him down. That poor Catherine Dunn but she's just closed her eyes and smiled silly cow. We got a lift at three or four in the morning Freddie from smiley pants Brian Templeton. I was out of it in the back and sometime on the trip home Brian Templeton just had to score didn't he? Perhaps I should be lucky that he didn't try and screw me even though I was asleep. Wouldn't have put it past him.'

'So Brian Templeton gave you this lift. Well, he lives here and that was easier than taking the train surely.'

'You listening Freddie? Did you hear what I said? Tilley was on her own and Brian stopped somewhere on the way home and screwed my friend. I wasn't there for her Freddie. She turned on me, she turned on everyone. She got married, had the baby and then went holy and God knows what. She led poor Walter a merry dance that's for sure. I'm always amazed that Wendell ever got born.'

'Shame he ever did,' said Freddie. 'Still, I punched his card last Friday. He's a bullying bastard and queer with it too. Tries to bugger the little kids. Can't stand that Mum. I can't stand queers. But, why did Tilley dump you if you were such mates?'

'Because the baby, her Gloria, her lovely Gloria wasn't expected. She loved Gloria Freddie, and she still does love her daughter and that's why it's so good to see Gloria back home and helping the way she has but she hated the father. She couldn't stand the father, never could and because I let it happen she turned on me.'

'But she married Walter.'

'And Walter my thick son wasn't the father though was he? He came on the scene later, but just in time though. My aunt got that all organized if I know her. Auntie Gwen was a good mum and she looked after her daughter. She picked up the pieces and got it all done proper. Tilley was married before the baby got born and I don't think Walter was ever the wiser. Don't think he ever knew.'

'That he wasn't the dad you mean, wasn't Gloria's dad?'

'Freddie for a man love you catch on real quick. Anyway, I've some baking to do this afternoon so out of my kitchen. Go and see your mates or something. Don't go singing all this around the village either. Tilley is my friend and I'm so pleased to have her back again but she isn't telling the world so don't you either. Out now, out son.'

Freddie sat with Danny, Lester and Don and all four of them were draining pints and lamenting on the fact that today was Sunday and it was work tomorrow.

'Your shout Lester,' said Freddie emptying his glass and thumping it on the table. The other two drained their glasses too and looked at Lester.

'Seems to come round to me pretty fast,' complained Lester. 'Anyway Freddie, I should be getting a discount seeing as it's your mate who's going out with our Dora. Looking at the smile on her face she must be getting it. You should know. You all go out as a foursome with Gloria. Say, where is Gloria tonight anyway?'

'Where is Gary too Freddie?' asked Don looking around the room. 'Perhaps Gary's got both of them smiling?' asked Don with a big smirk on his face.

'Silly prat won't be smiling after I've seen him on Monday though will he?'

'Why, think he'll be too shagged out to lift a chainsaw and old Bob Edwards will fire him?'

'Lester go and get those pints in and I'll tell you a little story.'

Lester walked over to the bar and Freddie sat back in his seat with a grin on his face.

'What's up Freddie?' asked Danny.

'Hold your motor Danny. Wait until Lester gets the beer in. All this talking is thirsty work mate. Okay, are we all sitting comfortably?'

'Stop pissing about Freddie. What's your mate Gary done now?'

About the same time as Freddie was chatting I was sitting outside in my car and thinking about last night. I hadn't got over the fact that it was my dad. I hadn't quite got over what I had seen going on in the cottage either. Still, it made for some valuable video. Should be worth a few quid. I started when there was a tap at my window.

'Good evening, I'm looking for the London Road?'

'Do you mean London Street?'

'You're right son. That's it. I mean Forest Street. Yes, that was the name wasn't it dear?' and the bloke turned to a shapely bird in a plunging blouse and tight skirt.

'Do we get in with you then darling?'

I eventually pulled my eyes back from their stalks and answered. 'Yes please. You sit in the back madam and you sir sit up front. You know I have to blindfold you?'

'Yes, exciting isn't it? This is our first time doing this. We're really expecting a stimulating evening if you know what we mean. We've been with other couples before at house parties of course but this is really a turn on. Oh, not too tight love. Let me breathe. You've got lovely hands. Let me hold them a moment. Feel my heart beating,' and Jesus was her heart beating, right under a smooth firm breast too.

'And you too sir,' I managed to say as I turned to my front seat passenger. 'Okay, the excitement starts folks and we'll guide you to a wonderful evening. You won't be disappointed I assure you. The drive should heighten the anticipated excitement.'

The tent pole in the bloke's pants told me that he didn't need to be driven anywhere to get excited. His bird's hands felt their way over my shoulders as I slowly tried to steer a straight line out of the village. Christ what a job I thought. Beats planting trees.

Back in the pub Freddie was explaining how his mother and Tilley Edwards used to be a wild couple and go chasing after blokes in bands. By the fourth or fifth pint Freddie was into how his mum got married first and then Tilley had to get married. By the sixth pint George cut them off 'cos the other three were pushing and shoving at Freddie to tell them what that had to do with Gary and did his mum have to get married too because she was expecting Freddie. By this time Freddie had got annoyed and fighting drunk and George wouldn't stand for it so he threw all four of them out.

Out in the forest I couldn't believe some of the things I was seeing on my cameras. This couple must have been reading some books or watching videos. There was talk about some Indian manuals, Kama or something and the three thousand or more different positions. This couple wanted to try all of them and some variations they had thought up all by themselves. At times it looked more like gymnastics, contortions, and absolute agony rather than hot and horny sex but I suppose I'm no connoisseur. I'm just a country boy and this couple looked like city folk. They had the voices that said learning, books, college and whatever else but they got their money's worth. Belle particularly could contort with the best of them and Sheena looked good in exotic clothing and veils and such. Different from last night I thought. Takes all sorts and my Gloria can handle all of it. Bloody marvellous darling; bloody great idea you coming home and coining in the cash. Christ Gary lad you might just want to give up your day job.

On the following Monday morning Freddie fucked up my day job and threatened my night job too. At the mid-morning break he took me aside and away from the rest of the crew for a quick word he said. I assumed he was going to bang on again about a foursome.

'You'd better sit down Gary. This will blow your mind man. Well it will blow something that's for sure. Probably blow your cock off,' he said and he chuckled. 'Perhaps it should have done that earlier, much earlier.'

'What are you on about Freddie? I heard George had to throw you out of the pub last night. Heard you were fighting with your mates. Christ man, you'll just have me soon if you piss off Lester and his useless band of losers.'

'Shit I wouldn't have you Gary mate. You're really fucked-up and you probably don't even know it.'

'What you talking about?'

'Don't like your dad do you Gary? Ruining your name you keep saying. Telling me that the Templetons had a long history with this forest. Proud you've always been about that haven't you?'

'Yes Freddie, yes I am. Grandfather and his dad too were good people.'

'But your dad fucked all that up didn't he?'

'Yes, my dad fucked up a lot of things. Fucked up a lot of people too, literally if you know what I mean.'

'Oh I know what you mean Gary. I really know what you mean. I even know who he fucked up. You think Walter Manson was Gloria's dad don't you? Why do you think Tilley Manson didn't want you to go out with Gloria? Why did she try and split you up? Why did we do that stupid foursome thing with Sandra all those years ago? Well Walter wasn't Gloria's dad Gary.'

'What do you mean? Of course he was. Gloria still has this deep-seated guilt trip about her dad. That's why she ran away you stupid prat. Her dad was fucking her. She told me and she couldn't stand it and so she ran away. Of course Walter was her dad. Wendell's dad too you silly bugger. Who's been telling you fairy stories Freddie Dunster?'

'Wrong Gary, so wrong mate. I don't know about Gloria and Walter but that wasn't her dad mate. Whether he was fucking her or not that's not the issue, it's who you've been fucking that's the issue.'

'What do I have to do with it? Gloria and I love each other. Get used to it Freddie, she's my girl. We play the silly game with Dora to get Tilley off my back and Gloria prefers it that way.'

'Well I can understand you loving her Gary 'cos she's family.' Freddie curled up into a ball with laughter. 'You're all one big happy family along with that wanker of a father of yours. Templeton males. You should advertise mate – we fuck anything that moves,' and Freddie rolled off the bank choking with laughter.

I was getting pretty pissed off by now. I walked over to Freddie and kicked him none too gently with my boot. 'What you on about? What are you saying?'

'I'll give it to straight you stupid bugger. Your precious father, Brian cocksman Templeton is Gloria's dad. All those years ago he balled Tilley Edwards one wild night to score another notch on his cock and never looked back. He was already married to your mum but that didn't stop him did it? Has never stopped him has it? He doesn't even know. No-one ever told him and you don't know either, but Tilley knew and Tilley didn't want you fucking your own sister now did she?'

'Get real Freddie,' and I landed another kick a bit harder this time into Freddie's ribs. 'That's crap mate. Bloody fucking crap. You're just jealous and can't get to first base with my Gloria. Just piss off and find another line.'

'Ask Tilley Gary mate. She don't like you just because you're a Templeton, or perhaps that is part of it because so is her Gloria. Fucking your own sister mate, all those years and every night now for the last little while I hear. Where were you and Gloria last night Gary? No, don't tell me. Let me guess. Balling each other's brains out somewhere.'

I kicked hard this time and caught Freddie in the crotch. Freddie cried out and the next moment we were thrashing wildly at each other. The rest of the crew heard and within a couple of minutes they had dragged us apart. Freddie grinned at me. 'Templetons,' he said, 'all alike and they all like each other. Happy families' and he spat some blood out of his mouth.

Bob Edwards took Freddie aside while two of the gang held me back 'cos I was still fighting mad. Bob came over to me. 'Got an explanation Gary?'

'I've got to go Bob. I need the rest of the day off. Freddie told me something that needs sorting. I've got to go.'

'Might be for the best,' said Bob. 'I'll run you back to the yard though before you get any other wild ideas. Cool off for Christ's sake.'

Bob ran me from the work site to the yard where I had my car. I wouldn't answer Bob's questions although he looked at me in a funny way as if he knew something I didn't. What I did learn though was that the Lord family would be away until later in the week and that the forest and the Estate were more or less empty. From the yard I drove into the village but it was too early for the pub to be open. I stopped though and looked at my watch. Only another fifteen minutes. I'll wait and catch Gloria when she opens. Have a word before this tale of Freddie's blows the whole place apart. It wasn't true. It couldn't possibly be true.

It was a beautifully clear day in Oxford and the sun shone all around the few fluffy clouds that sailed majestically across the blue skies on the light breezes that ruffled the hair and kept one cool. Majestic, scholarly, old yet modern, bustling but with quiet quadrangles, Oxford offered the resident and visitor alike a diverse array of modes and moods. The City of Spires on this Monday was full of the pomp and pageantry of scholarship. Today was a day for the gown in this "town or gown" community. The

Howard and the Lord family gathered together to see their family and friend receive her degree. A First Class Honours no less from a prestigious University and mother Deidre was quite overwhelmed. For once she was almost speechless with happiness and motherly adoration. Delaney was delighted too but he expressed himself more in tune with his civilised and cultured southern upbringing. Daniel for once wasn't his usual quiet and studious self as he too was elated both with Katya's success and his and her togetherness. Even James couldn't get over all the hugging going on. In order to fully see and explore the site of Katya's studies the entire group decided to stay until the Tuesday. Katya acted as the official guide although James wanted to get into the act with his special friend. Samantha begged off on the Monday night and took the train up to London. She had a client/partner meeting with the Peters couple and with Janet. Family lines to sort out and explanations to give thought Samantha as the train whisked her the short distance into Paddington station.

Just before eleven I heard the bolts going on the public bar door. Gloria stood there framed in the doorway.

'You must be thirsty this early. How come you're not at work? You get that couple looked after okay after last night? They were quite a laugh Gary. We should get more of that kind of clientele and we'd have a real ball. Even wanted to try some things we'd never heard or thought of. Anyway, a pint is it, and why aren't you at work? Did you say?'

'Yes a pint and a quick word, or maybe a long word but certainly words.'

'Come in then. First of the day Gary. George won't be in for thirty minutes or so. He had to go and pick up some supplies somewhere. I had to come in early to look after the place so he could go into town. Now words you say. You want to find out about your take in this business is it? I know we've never mentioned money but then we weren't sure how this would go. I've talked with Toby and how does five percent of the profits grab you? On my side I'm looking after the girls and expenses for fittings so five percent seems reasonable. Seeing as we've just started up with some initial outlays and we've had three gigs so far then I probably owe you about fifty quid Gary. That okay?'

'Gloria, Freddie's been telling me Walter wasn't your dad. All that time you weren't screwing with your dad. All those years when you thought it was your dad, well it wasn't. You never did anything wrong. Okay, he was your mum's husband but then she wasn't having any was she? So what you did was okay. That's what Freddie says anyway.'

'Freddie says eh Gary? Maybe a little bird has been whispering in our Freddie's ear, but then anyone could whisper in Freddie's ear and most of it would just fall out of the other side of his head you know. Don't think there is a lot between Freddie's ears Gary do you?'

'Where did he hear this then Gloria? He wouldn't make up something like that. That's too much for Freddie to imagine.'

'Anyway, so what Gary? What if it was true, then so what? I told you that screwing with Walter wasn't the problem. It was what it might do to my mum and her head Gary. Thought I told you that my being with Walter wasn't an issue. Taught me a lot and I've put it to good use. Last night was a good example although of course you weren't there so you wouldn't understand.'

'But Freddie told me who your dad was, or is I suppose as he is still alive if Freddie is right. Tell me it isn't true Gloria? Christ I'll go and shoot the bugger.'

'And what did this little bird whisper in Freddie's ear Gary? What managed to stay inside his peanut head?'

I looked at Gloria. 'Do you know? Do you know who Freddie said? How long have you known? Christ Gloria one of the blokes on Saturday night was my dad. I tried to warn Belle but one of the blokes out at the cottage doing who knows what was my dad, your father Gloria. There, I've said it. Freddie says your father wasn't Walter. Walter married your mum after she was already pregnant. My father fucked your mum somewhere and that fucked up her head. All those years and all because of my dad. Did Freddie hear right Gloria? Did you know?'

Gloria stood behind the bar and looked at me. She smiled and leant forwards. "Kiss me you silly bugger,' she said. 'So what? Walter's dead and no-one else is going to know or worry about it.'

'Shit Gloria, I worry about it. Freddie's threatening to tell the world, maybe even the News of the World. Now wouldn't they just love that? I can see it now blazoned all across the top of the newspaper. The headline would be "Village girl fucks father who isn't but fucks brother who is". You want to see that all around the village? Will George think that is good publicity?'

'Why should Freddie tell anyone Gary?'

'Because he's a jealous little shit. Ever since you've been back he's been wanting to get into your pants. All the foursome stuff with Dora was just an excuse to try and get back to the four of us as teenagers. When we all swapped you know.'

'Yes Gary I know. So our little friend Freddie wants to get his rocks off does he? Wants to show Gloria a good time? Well maybe we should please Freddie Gary. Maybe we should buy our little blackmailer off with a little of the other so to speak. Think I can quieten the little cocksucker do you? How about a "special just for you Freddie like I did up in London" session for our mutual friend? Come to think of it isn't it Freddie's birthday some time this week? I could give him a special birthday treat and him all in his birthday suit. Not too pretty I know but it is his birthday. Tuesday night would be good Gary. Would give me time to organise the cottage a little, something special for Freddie. I'll

411

pull him tonight or tomorrow evening and wheel him out there sometime Tuesday night. No meeting, just a blindfold and a private session for lonely Freddie. Of course I'll need a hand to move him afterwards Gary, move him somewhere where he won't come looking trying to remember what happened. Somewhere permanent Gary if you know what I mean. I don't think you should be threatened by our friend mouthing off like that. Need to keep him quiet before he gets too vocal. I can't have my family worried about such accusations now can I Gary?'

While spinning her line Gloria had moved around the bar and when she finally stopped I found her in my arms and wriggling her body against me. I jerked awake. I had been thinking as I listened to Gloria and my mind was churning with ideas about what she was saying and what I could do to help. Just when I had got some things straight in my head I found Gloria's tongue in my mouth, her arms around my neck, her breasts wriggling against my chest and her pelvis trying to grind my cock off. Her hand came free and slid down my body to feel me. 'Gloria, this is the public bar. Someone could come in. Someone might want a drink. George will be back.' Gloria stroked smoothly and wriggled some more.

'Tuesday Gary,' she whispered taking her tongue out of my mouth and nipping at my ear to get my attention. Next moment she was back behind the bar and I was feeling more in control of events. 'Sure Gloria, Tuesday,' I said and I walked out into the mid-day sunshine. Things to do Gary my lad. Quietly up to the cottage for starters and think about Tuesday night and how I was going to play this.

I went home about normal clocking off time. Surprise surprise my dad was home after his successful re-union meeting up in London over the weekend. I stayed at home that evening as I didn't want to run into Freddie or any of his mates. Dad stayed in too and chatted with mum and me. Just like a normal happy family I thought telling each other what we've been doing all day and lying in our teeth doing it. I wondered what my mother knew about any of this but my mother wasn't one for showing any emotions and kept a placid tongue in her head. When I left to go upstairs to bed dad managed to wink at me and whisper, 'You should try it son,' before I was out of the room. I lay in bed that night wrestling with thoughts of Gloria's father, my father, Freddie's mouth and then I wondered who had told Freddie. I wondered whether that scheming little shit Wendell had heard something somewhere but then it was Freddie who had decked him so Wendell wouldn't be doing Freddie any favours. Of course this could all be a vicious invention of Wendell's. No this was too clever for Wendell. Gloria hadn't been fazed. She must have known. How long had she known I wondered as I drifted off to sleep?

KISSING COUSINS

'FREDDIE IT'S YOUR BIRTHDAY TOMORROW isn't it? Thought I'd give you a special present you know. You up for it?'

'Of course Gloria. You know me, always up for a treat.'

'You've always really and truly wondered what I did up in London haven't you? I heard you've been asking Gary whether I ever told him anything, anything you hadn't heard. Intrigued aren't you? You really want to know?'

'Yes Gloria, yes. You know I never believed that story about you being a cocktail waitress and what have you. You did more than that surely? You must have and then why did that bruiser come down looking for you last year and that other old bloke just a couple of weeks ago? He said he was special and you were his friend. George was telling me.'

'Well tomorrow Freddie I'll give you a big treat and a big surprise. I'll let you see my little secret.'

'But I've seen your little secret Gloria. Remember, when we were kids, only now your secret isn't so little,' and Freddie reached out with his hands to fondle Gloria.

'Freddie, be patient,' giggled Gloria, 'wait until your birthday.'

I didn't go into the pub that night as I knew Gloria was trying to hook our unsuspecting fish and I didn't want Freddie distracted by any more aggro with me. The next day at work, the Tuesday it was, I kept as far away from Freddie as I could and made sure I was talking with the other blokes in the crew. That didn't stop Freddie looking over at me and smugly suggesting he had my number. Thought he had one up on me he did and that soon it would be pay time for Gary Templeton. Earlier, when he told me the "good news" he said he would pick the right time to tell the world what a good little "sister-fucker" I was. I was almost beside myself with rage and fear over this that I never listened to all the details but I was still seething inside. I reckoned if I got too close I would have throttled the stupid little bugger with that grin on his face. Gloria had told me it was Freddie's birthday but I didn't say bugger all to him all day. Still, he was going to get his birthday treat later that night. Gloria told me what she planned to do and what I had to do.

As it was Gloria's night off in the pub she bought Freddie a couple of pints but she didn't want him too drunk for his birthday treat and so soon after nine, just as it got dark she told Freddie she would drive him somewhere special.

'I'm going to treat you big boy to a real professional experience. This will be just like it was in London Freddie. Now, to heighten the excitement I'm going to blindfold you so you can't see where you're going. When we get there all will be revealed and I will blow your little mind.'

'As long as you blow more than that Gloria.'

'Freddie love you'll never be the same again after tonight. I'll show you things and we'll do things you've never even dreamt of. This is big time Freddie, not some little village fumble and frolic. This will be the trip of a lifetime, just you wait and see. But, to start with I'll just add a little blindfold to get you in the mood birthday boy.'

With Freddie sitting in the passenger seat complete with a blindfold over his eyes and almost wetting his pants with excitement Gloria slowly and carefully drove away from the pub. She spent half an hour up and down various back roads to throw Freddie off any memory of where they had been before slowly easing her car down the forest ride to the Ferris cottage.

'Slowly now Freddie and we're almost there. Wait until I come round to your side and I'll lead you to the promised land my lovely. A night to remember.'

You had to hand it to Gloria because she had all the patter to go with the body and the smile. She could wrap you around her little finger with the seductive routine.

'All right Freddie we are there now and I'm going to take off the blindfold.'

Freddie gasped. Gloria had stood behind Freddie and pressed herself up against him as she untied the blindfold. The light in the room was low and it came from a couple of candles. All Freddie saw was Belle Katz walking towards him waving a little dust mop and little else. At this time I was hiding in the cupboard in the room with the door partly open and so I could see most of what was going on. Belle Katz was a treat to behold. She had long fine golden hair which hung down to the small of her back. Gloria told me she was eighteen but she looked younger as she was quite short and very slender, almost waif like but she certainly wasn't anorexic. She had high set pert apple-round breasts which tried hard to peep out of the side of her modified school gymslip. The material wasn't standard High School issue either as it was a light blue colour and semi-transparent. Freddie's eyes bulged, as did his pants. To emphasise her slender waist Belle had a simple belt cinched sharply tight. This caused the bottom of the gymslip to flare a little and quite obviously there was no school policy on skirt length because the hem hardly covered the fact that Belle was a natural blond.

'Freddie my love let me make you comfortable. I'm your little pupil and you are my demanding school master. Would you like to spank me with my little duster?' and Belle swirled around and bent over to reveal a cute pink derriere.

'No, I'll do that you naughty girl,' said Gloria and she came round from behind Freddie with an old school cane and tapped Belle smartly on the behind two or three times but you could see the impact marks.

'Oo, teacher kiss me better,' said Belle and wriggled backwards towards Freddie.

'I think your school master is getting too warm little one,' said Gloria. 'Why don't you make him feel more comfortable while I get changed?'

I couldn't see but I suppose Gloria left the room and I watched Belle advance on Freddie and start to undo his shirt. It was a warm evening and Freddie wasn't wearing anything under his shirt and Belle was soon rubbing her abbreviated gymslip up against Freddie's chest while undoing the belt on his trousers. By the time Gloria stepped quietly back into the room Belle had stripped Freddie and pushed him gently back onto the bed. When Gloria came into view Freddie tried to sit up. I would have too as Gloria was wearing a see-through rose-coloured peignoir, rose-coloured high heels and wafting sweet-smelling marijuana from a little urn. She was a sight to behold and any man would have reacted.

'Now teacher, let's not get too excited shall we? We'll just have a little drink to wet your throat and then it's lesson time.' Belle offered Freddie a glass with a potent mix to heighten the senses. Freddie eagerly gulped it down and reached out for Belle. She retrieved the glass and dropped it. 'Naughty girl,' whispered Gloria. 'Bend over,' and Gloria again painted caning marks across Belle's bottom.

'Kiss me better, kiss me better,' she cried and she bent over for Freddie to soothe. 'Teacher, teacher help me. You have a lot to teach me, especially about my numbers. I get really excited when someone teaches me my numbers but you have to count with your tongue.'

All the time Belle was quietly whispering this she was straddled over Freddie and wriggling on his chest. The front of her gymslip had a zipper which Belle had opened and her two little apples were dancing in front of Freddie's face.

'So teacher dear you count one two one two with your tongue while Gloria looks after your hands. If you manage to teach me right then Gloria is going to give you a treat. Now this is one yes?' and Belle slid her nipple across Freddie's mouth. 'Just lick teacher if I've got it right.'

Freddie licked and arched his body half off the bed with the excitement. Gloria gently slid a soft piece of rope around Freddie's wrist and tied it to the bed frame.

'And this is two,' said Belle wriggling her thighs and pelvis on Freddie's chest as she slid her other breast across his panting tongue. Gloria gently tied the other wrist.

'Teacher teacher you are good. I'm learning real quick. One two, one two,' and Belle slid one breast and then the other over Freddie's tongue. I watched Freddie enter into the spirit of the experience and his body twisted and turned under Belle's thighs. He tried to bring his lower body up close to Belle's buttocks but she moved further up the bed with her knees and said, 'But I want to count to three.'

Freddie lowered his knees and enjoyed the sensation on his tongue.

'You're really good teacher and my friend here will give you your birthday present. You taught me my one two threes.'

I watched Gloria slide her hands smoothly and firmly up Freddie's legs. He arched at the first touch and then writhed as Gloria moved her hands higher. Belle moved further up Freddie's body and continued counting one two three, one two three. Freddie was torn between watching Belle and her sensual counting and the mounting pressure from Gloria as she straddled him and slowly slithered her way up from his knees to his thighs and higher.

'Happy birthday kissing cousin,' murmured Gloria as she slid higher and more demandingly higher to embrace all of Freddie. As Belle eased herself downwards over Freddie's chest and tightened her thighs I had very quietly moved out of the cupboard. I stood at the end of the bed by Freddie's tied wrists but out of sight. Freddie was completely spellbound by the panting and writhing of Belle who now was counting faster and faster as she played with herself and the demands from Gloria's body about to envelope his rampart penis.

'Happy birthday' was all he heard as I smothered the face with a pillow and knelt on either side of it to keep it in place. Belle slipped away and Gloria engulfed Freddie with her crotch and lurched forwards to pull me close to her. I felt Freddie struggle beneath me but his hands were tied, Gloria was riding his pelvis and I knelt firmly over his head. I saw Gloria start to move faster and faster and then she grabbed my head and searched for my lips frantically. She kissed hard with her lips, her tongue and her teeth. She was quite beside herself in an absolute frenzy as she rode Freddie to death and kissed and bit me at the same time.

'Gary Gary hold me, squeeze my breasts, squeeze my bum. Hold me tight.'

When she climaxed Gloria fell forward against me and I just held her. Freddie lay still between my knees. I eased myself backwards off the bed and looked at Gloria crouched there over Freddie's birthday body.

'You did it Gary. You silenced the little weasel for good. No more silly stories about sister-fucking. We're okay Gary. We can carry on as before. This can be a real money-spinner love.'

I stood there. What had I done? Sure I'd silenced Freddie. Could I go on? Gloria stood up and went over to talk to Belle.

'Gary, Gary you there mate? Things to do and places to go. We'll tidy up in here and get ourselves home with nice simple stories. You said you had this piece of shit taken care of. Here Gloria pointed scornfully to Freddie's white corpse with sunburnt arms stretched out on the bed.

'You said you would deal with him and it was best we didn't know. Okay, that's fine with us but Belle and I have some work to do here before we leave the place looking neat and tidy. You okay with that? Worked out well didn't it, just as we planned? We'll move Freddie's car from the George down to the pool by the river and ditch the keys. Belle will bog off to Bristol along the back roads so no bloody cameras will see her number plates. She's got her end taken care of. You and me Gary were together all night at my mum's place. You deal with the other and I'll see you later tonight.'

Deal with the other? Yes I thought I'll deal with the other. I had it all planned out. Outside I walked a little way into the forest and got into dad's van. He'd bought it last year, some flashy sports utility vehicle or something he called it. Bright, very comfortable for those exciting adventures with the back seats which folded down flat like a bed when the mood strikes. And, more importantly for me it had four-wheel drive. Tonight that was a useful feature. I quietly eased the van down beside the cottage and walked back inside. Gloria and Belle worked like professionals, which of course they were I realised. Jesus Gary I thought, what have you got yourself into mate? This isn't London and Gloria's other life, this is a quiet placid nothing-happens country village.

'Gary, we're nearly done in here but we need you to move our birthday boy. We want the sheets and the rope. Everything else we've tidied away. Just move the body and we'll redo the bed and then we're off. You okay? You aren't moving so fast. Do you need a hand?'

I came to and shook myself. 'No Gloria, I'm fine. The less you know about things the better. I'm fine, really I am. You did a good job tonight the pair of you. You're right Gloria, we can carry on as before. This idea works a treat. You did well too Belle. That routine is a real humdinger.'

'Sure Gary. Glad to help my friend Gloria when she needed me. Always worked well together, didn't we Gloria luv?'

Gloria gave Belle a big hug and then a tender gentle kiss. 'You're a real charmer you are Belle Katz. You're a delight to watch darling. Anyway Gary, time's a wasting. Things to do before we congratulate ourselves too far. Body Gary, body!'

I wrapped Freddie's body up in the sheets and with some difficulty slung it over my shoulder in a fireman's lift. Carefully I manoeuvred my load out to the van and eased the bundle through the hatchback. I had already spread some plastic sheets across the floor of the back and it was an easy slip off the shoulders and thump as the corpse tumbled inside. The dim lights inside the cottage went out and the two girls quietly closed the back door.

'We're off Gary. See you later.'

Gloria quietly eased her car back out of the forest to the village and set about arranging Freddie's car and Belle's exit. I sat in my dad's van and thought about my next part of the plan. When we first started this idea I had it all thought out. It seemed obvious but thinking back my mind was probably still in a rage over Freddie's accusation and any thought of a leak. Was it the best answer I thought? Sure, why not. My old granddad Edward had taken me there the first time when I was just a nipper. He had told me never to go in the cave itself as it was dangerous he said and could fall down at any time. Then just to frighten me he spun some yarn about a girl being killed there over some jewellery and that the place was haunted. Said his father had told him never to go in there. Of course after that build up for a five-year old I just had to go back and look didn't I? No self-respecting kid is going to be put off with such tales. They just make the place more exciting. Mark you, I suppose I was seven or maybe eight before I did pluck up enough courage to actually go into the cave itself. Once I realised that there was nothing special and it wasn't very exciting as it didn't go anywhere I forgot it. It was only after that whole series of events back eight or nine years ago now that I even remembered the cave existed. Then everything quietened down again until Sir Anthony decided to mount that plaque as some memorial to his son. Inside the cave itself I thought I could arrange things to look like an accident and asphyxiation. Also it was a place where no one went now, not after the plaque. Slowly and quietly I drove the van through the forest and up to the northern end of the estate. With four-wheel drive I knew I could get close to the cave and come in from the eastern side where it was a shorter walk than the way most people went. Coming up the eastern side was much rougher and most vehicles couldn't navigate this way. I coasted to a stop as close as I could get and turned off the engine. All was quiet on this mild June night, Freddie's birthday. He had just turned twenty five. Well I thought, he managed to live a little longer than his cousins. They found the treasure in this old tree and now I'm going to return Freddie to the site of the misleading cave. I could see the plaque that the Lord family had fixed on the old oak tree which stood silhouetted against the night sky by the entrance to the cave. Become a memorial now I thought; kind of a shrine. No one goes in the cave now, well not if they read that sign they don't. Seems a fitting place for Freddie. Worked on this estate nearly all of his life. Had his cousins up here and found gold. Yes Freddie, I think I can safely leave you hidden away up here you useless tosser. With some difficulty I lugged Freddie's body inside the cave holding a torch in my teeth. Now, a convenient accident scene I pondered. I went back to the van and collected a few props. Freddie had come up here to dig because he thought there was still some treasure in this cave so we have some digging implements. He's got a stove to make a brew which goes out and releases gas. Freddie's light goes out, he bangs his head, knocks himself out and the gas asphyxiates him. Night night Freddie. Just need to bang his head on one of those stalactites and hey presto an accident in the making. Let's tidy up anything else I brought that shouldn't be here. If anyone finds him and asks I can start the story that Freddie was excited about something he heard to do with more treasure. That's what the big argument and fight was all about. He didn't want to share his possible find. He was secretive was Freddie so he left his car somewhere completely different so no-one would know where he was. Funny lad Inspector, always looking for things and of course he knew the estate really well. Wouldn't have bothered him about the things to do with the cave. He'd got over the story of the twins now that all the Ferris family were dead. He never was a fan of Michael Lord so that wouldn't have bothered him either. Probably got too enthusiastic and fell over banging his head like. Liked his tea though did Freddie. Always making a brew he was. Used to take that stove with him at work sometimes. The boss was always giving him a hard time about the risk of fire but Freddie thought that stove was magic. Yes I thought. Not too hard to set-up and spin a story. Swinging my torch around I did one last look in the cave. Seemed fine I thought. Just hope it is a while before anyone thinks of looking here. Freddie's car is down by the river so why look here? I walked quietly back to dad's van and started the engine. Slowly we bumped back to a smoother part of the forest and down towards the main road. Before I left the forest I gathered up all of the sheeting and anything else unusual from the back and put the seats up. At my parent's house I switched cars and put the sheeting in my boot. It was easy to glide down our driveway back into the street before starting my engine and quietly make my way to Gloria's house. She was waiting by the door and heard me arrive.

'All fixed?' she whispered.

'Done and dusted,' I replied and folded her in my arms. 'We're home free.'

I was just going out of the door the next morning when I heard the shuffling of slippers and turning round a hand gripped my arm like a vice. 'Heathen,' whispered a voice, 'sinner, fornicator. You'll be dammed in hell Gary Templeton.'

'Sure, and good morning to you Mrs. Manson,' I replied.

'Cast out the devils and let the wicked be struck down as they speak,' she cried.

'Give over Mum, it's only Gary and you'll end up spooking our Wendell. He's only a kid remember and all that holy talk will only drive him further into his computer. I thought we'd persuaded you to leave all that behind. Wendell will think you're some character in Dungeons and Dragons. Gary get going before you get sprinkled with holy water or something. Thanks for a great night.'

I walked down the front garden path and jumped into my car. The curtains in the next house moved and a pair of eyes watched me drive away. Witnesses I thought. People who would remember where I was.

'Gary you're late. The gang's already gone.'

'Sorry Mr. Daniel. Tell me where and I'll find them. I'll tell Bob Edwards to have me do some extra over lunchtime if you like?'

'No Gary it's not that serious lad but this week hasn't been a star event for you so far now has it? Bob was telling me about Monday. Park your car, grab your gear and hop in. I've got to go and see Bob about something I forgot anyway. I'll run you out there.'

'Thanks Mr. Daniel. Sorry about earlier. Freddie and I had a falling out on Monday over something he had found and old Bob got rather pissed off at us.'

'Yes Gary. Bob told me about that. I'm not interested in what it was Gary as Bob thought it was private but keep your fights out of the forest. The crew are starting to settle down after all the disturbances of last autumn and get productive again. I don't need any more aggro on this estate. We've got some bloody-minded hikers who think they can waltz about anywhere and my dad's getting rather pissed off. Still, I think I've found an answer for them and maybe I'll get some good advice from a couple of them.'

'What they on about Mr. Daniel? Bob was saying something about drovers and rights of way for cattle or something. There haven't been any cattle here ever as far as I know. Granddad never said anything ever about cattle. You've had the sheep of Miss Stephanie but they're on your Home Farm fields and not in the forest.'

'Not for you to worry about Gary. The hiking group think they have some ancient maps showing old paths. Our worry is any of them hiking where we are operating. Just as likely to get themselves hurt and then we do have a problem. Here we are. Check with Bob and let's say no more about it. Just keep away from Freddie today.'

'Sure Mr. Daniel.'

I hopped out of the Landrover and quickly talked with Bob Edwards. He looked at me and then at Mr. Daniel. There must have been a nod or something because Bob quickly gave me a weeding tool and told me to get to work.

'He come in late Mr. Daniel? Where's his fighting mate? There was no sign of Freddie Dunster either this morning.'

'Didn't see him Bob. What did happen on Monday?'

'I'm not sure of the details Mr. Daniel 'cos I didn't see it start. I was over on the far side of the plantation and checking on the fence when I heard several shouts. By the time I got back to the gang Freddie and Gary were thumping the living daylights out of each other. Looked like Freddie was taunting Gary about something although Freddie has always been a sneaky little bugger. Anyway Gary was shouting something about it isn't true and the pair of them were rolling around in the dirt. Of course the rest of the crew weren't trying to stop them and were cheering them to start with. Then it got really nasty and we managed to pull the pair of them apart and I got everyone back to work. I was going to put Gary as far away from Freddie as I could while they were weeding. I read the riot act to the rest of the gang and things quietened down.'

'What happened going home?'

'Well right after the fight Gary upped and said he had to go and sort some things out because of what Freddie had said. I wasn't keen on having the two of them with sickles in their hands even if they were eight rows apart so I agreed. I ran Gary back to his car and he took off like a scalded cat. I docked his pay Mr. Daniel. On the way home I made Freddie sit up in the front of the gang truck but he wouldn't say a word. When we unloaded I marched Freddie back to his own car and made sure he was gone. It was weird 'cos earlier they had been snarling at each other. No, Freddie was taunting and Gary was snarling until Gary started kicking Freddie. That's when the rest of the crew waded in to separate them, before Gary did any real serious damage. But he was really kicking hard by this time Colin said.'

'What happened yesterday? I was out all day at Oxford as you know. Did anything happen yesterday?'

'Funny that Mr. Daniel. Gary seemed to ignore Freddie all day. Kept as far away from him as he could. Talked with the other blokes okay but made sure he avoided Freddie. Mark you I had my eye on both of them and I had told Freddie yesterday morning I was watching him. Told him I would put him back as a gardener if he didn't smarten up.'

'So where is Freddie this morning?'

'Well he ain't out here Mr. Daniel, that's for sure.'

'You know what you've done Gloria? You'll burn in hell. My grandmother Biddle said this family would have children of the devil. Said there would be mad ones amongst us. Put a curse on the family she did and look at you. Worse than the devil. Child of the devil.'

'Mum, Brian Templeton wasn't the devil. He was a simple man with a silver tongue and a wandering cock - a salesman with a ready grin and an ability to charm the pants off any woman. When you were young he charmed the pants off of you Mum.'

'You wicked girl. He tricked me. He teased me. He caught me at my prayers.'

'Mum I've talked with Rosemary Dunster. She's told me about the bands and the groups; about the screamers and the knickers flung on the stage. She's told me what you were like as a kid. How the pair of you used to beg and borrow to get up to Bristol to see the big name groups. You know, young girls with screaming throats, outstretched hands and ready to rip your pants off for just a touch of a singer. Then I found that old scrapbook with clippings and programmes. Amazed I was but you denied it. Well Rosemary confirmed it.'

'Lies, devil's work. Rosemary Dunster was never my friend.'

'Mum you were round there the other day. You had dressed yourself up to look like a million dollars and you went to see Rosemary. Rosemary Dunster is your cousin Mum. She was your party-going friend and I love you for it. You were alive Mum. You were wild and free and that's wonderful. You enjoyed life.'

'Brian Templeton changed all that.'

'Mum you had a fling and there was a mistake. You'd probably been fucked several times before Brian cocksure Templeton. You were what, twenty or something? None of you could still be virgins by twenty in those days. Wasn't that all the age of hippies, make love not war and free love for everyone? Didn't you all turn on and tune out? Shit, even in this God-forsaken dump there were some young people making out.'

'I'll pray for you Gloria. I'll pray you find salvation before the devil takes you away.'

'Mum I don't want to go away anywhere but I do want you back. We brought you back. Toby and I brought you back. Forget Brian bloody Templeton. It's done, past, gone, forgotten. He probably doesn't even know who he's fathered around here and he certainly doesn't care. Look at Catherine, Gary's mum. She doesn't go round dressed in old clothes and praying every moment. She knows what he's like. She gets on with her life. Dresses smart, talks with people, shops in the village. Life is for living Mum. Walter's dead God rest his soul so spread your wings and look around. Be a good idea to take that Wendell in hand for starters. If there's a devil's child it's that one.'

Gloria told me later that her mum collapsed against her at this point. She just started crying Gloria said and she sobbed and sobbed her heart out. Whatever had been driving her just up and left and Gloria had to take her into the living room and sit them both down. It was as if life itself had decided to leave Gloria explained. Fortunately this happened early in the morning and I had time to hold her and console her Gloria told me 'cos the session lasted for well over an hour. Gloria had thought after the last few days that her mum had left all that behind and now there seemed to be a relapse.

'Mum, I've got to get ready to go to work. I'm supposed to be there before eleven and George always wants something extra done before we open. You going to be all right?'

'Gloria, Gloria, what are we going to do?'

'Nothing Mum, it's all over now. You can leave it all behind.'

'But what about you and Gary?'

'Mum we'll sort that out between us. I'll explain somehow to Gary and we'll sort it out. He's a good bloke and he'll understand. He may not like his dad after this but then his mum manages to cope and I'm sure Gary will learn to live with whatever things we decide. Leave that all with me Mum. Apart from that are you okay if I go and get ready? Are you going to be all right if I leave for a few hours over lunchtime?'

Gloria told me later that she thought her mum had calmed down and had got herself back together again. What Gloria hadn't expected and hadn't known about was what her brother was up to. Out of habit Wendell bullied Dennis Edwards his cousin. He bullied him on Monday, on Tuesday and that particular Wednesday. Apart from deriving some sadistic pleasure out of all this Wendell had learnt from Tom Daley that people knew things and some of those things called information could be useful. So Wendell had heard about the enormous fight that took place between Freddie and me in the forest on the Monday. Wendell also learnt that it was Freddie who was doing the taunting and it was me who was upset. Unfortunately Dennis didn't know what I was upset about, even after Wendell had put the fear of death in him. Wendell was a hefty lad for his age and he threatened to rape poor little Dennis and that terrified him.

On the Tuesday night, the night of Freddie's birthday, Wendell sat in Tom Daley's grass-reeking computer room and shared some thoughts. Tom couldn't find anything out of the ordinary going on with any emails flying about between people in the village but he had found that Samantha MacRae was chasing birth records on the internet. Seemed Mrs. MacRae was interested in the family history of a whole array of people in the village and that in itself was nothing out of the ordinary. Given the nature of Heritage Adventures you would expect Samantha to be checking on those kinds of records, along with wedding records and death records. Last year, sometime in October, Samantha had been working with that couple from Australia and they were supposed to be related to someone in the village.

'That's it, the Templetons,' exclaimed Tom.

'But that was last year Tom. Freddie was pissing Gary off this week and Gary went ballistic.'

'Well the Templetons have never been related to the Edwards or the Biddles so that lets you out, and Freddie too because he was part of the Biddle family. I could understand it if it was anyone related to the Ferris family but they're all dead Wendell. No, it must be something that happened up in the forest. Something Freddie could do and Gary couldn't or wouldn't. Didn't Freddie find some treasure in the forest? Perhaps he wasn't going to share any of it with Gary? Go and bug those mates of Freddie. They're a pretty dim lot but they'd know. Freddie loves to brag and try and be the leader of that bunch of tossers. Lester Rainer might know. If he did he'd be glad to tell you because Gary Templeton's been going out with Dora, Lester's younger sister. That probably pisses Lester off no end. Talk with Lester Wendell. He's only a scrawny piss-artist house painter and you're bigger than him. Back him up against a wall. He'll tell you.'

Several things happened on Wednesday and Wendell didn't find out exactly from Lester Rainer but he did learn something useful that evening. I'd gone to work although a little late as I explained. Bob Edwards was on edge and sharp all day although I heard some of the reasons why over lunchtime. Two of the older blokes in the crew were discussing kids and the challenges of bringing up teenagers. I heard them both agree that it was hard these days to know what kids were doing. Most of them seemed to be buried in their computers and who could understand what they were up to? There was some talk about chat rooms, whatever they are and then one of the blokes said.

'How about you Bob?'

'What's that Dan? Sorry, my mind was elsewhere.'

'Colin here was asking about bringing up kids. His Adam is only five but already he is asking funny questions. How do you handle things with your Dennis? He's fourteen now isn't he? Didn't he play football last winter on the junior team?'

'Aye Dan. Dennis loves his football but he's a bit of a problem at the moment. Kept kind of quiet the last few days. Actually, if truth be told Frances and I are rather worried about him. He's rushed in from school like the hounds of hell are after him and won't go out anywhere.'

'Now that sounds like bullying somewhere Bob. Who here's young enough to know about the kids at school today? Who'd know about bullies in the village?'

None of the blokes on the gang spoke and I kept my mouth shut too but I could guess. Gloria's brother already had a reputation and two or three of the lads my age had already clipped young Wendell's ear a few times when we caught him bullying younger kids. Given the way his mind worked I wouldn't have put it past him to try and bugger some of them too I thought. When I got home after work I found out from my mum that my dad wouldn't be home for another night. Supposedly he was up in London at some Sales Conference and had gone up on the train. At least that was the story he had told mum. It had helped me as his van was there for last night when he was away. After a quick bite I decided to go down to the George and see that Gloria was okay. Before I left I did a quick check of the films from my video camera. I had decided to take Gloria into my confidence and tell her about the video stuff. She thought the idea was cool but wanted to check with me first before trying to sell any of them. When we set up the bedroom scene in the cottage I told Gloria it might be useful and lucrative to film some of her customers. We might even make our own porno movies I had told her. She sure had some imaginative friends and in the right places we could use some of the material as advertising. Sure, I was full of ideas me. Gloria's experiences in London had made me see green, as in easy money. Checking some of the video I found that I had some useful material, including bits of last Saturday night when our dad was there. Bastard I thought, absolute bastard buggering up my life. Christ dad, you screw up two generations of solid family traditions and then you trample all over my mum's feelings without a thought in the world. And look at her, my mum. She stands by you through thick and thin. God you're a bastard dad. Still, this video might get your attention. Broadcasting that about the village might ruin your image. We'll get some payback dad, something back for mum and me.

I packed the film carefully away in my room and changed into some fresh clothes. Feeling confident I drove down to the George looking forward to seeing Gloria. As I stepped out of the car I was approached by Lester Rainer.

'What you doing with my sister Gary Templeton? How come you're leading our Dora astray? I know you. Freddie's told us what you're like with wandering hands and wandering what other. Our Dora's just a kid and she don't know enough to say no. She likes to think she's mature but she'll get hurt and I won't have it. You hear me?'

Now Lester is a skinny little bloke but he was pissed off enough to poke me in the chest with his finger.

'Back off Lester. We've been going out as a foursome with Freddie, your mate I thought. Freddie's been the partner for Dora.'

'That's not what Freddie says Gary. He says you are going off alone with Dora while he's with Gloria. Then he told us last Sunday that there is some special secret between you and Gloria. Something to do with what Gloria did up in London. Real kinky it was Freddie said and I won't have my sister mixed up in any weird ideas you might have Gary Templeton. It's bad enough in this village with your dad running

432

around with his zipper open at every house he calls on. We don't need you banging every woman in sight and certainly not our Dora. Freddie reckons Gloria's trying to lure our Dora into the white slave trade.'

'Lester you wouldn't know a white slave trader if you fell over one mate. You've been reading too many trashy books or more likely watching too much useless tele.'

'So what's this secret thing between you and Gloria then? Freddie said he was going to tell you and that you would be real pissed off that he knew you know.'

'Nothing Lester. It's nothing.'

'That ain't what I heard Gary,' said Danny Masters as he came up beside Lester.

'Right,' said big Don Winters as he joined us. 'Freddie said you went ballistic on Monday out in the forest. Bob Edwards and the rest of the gang had to drag you apart. Freddie said you'd go ape-shit man and so you did.'

'You've got it all wrong lads. That was something we were doing in the forest. Freddie broke something special of mine and it was a kind of talisman for me.'

'Freddie told us you wouldn't speak to him yesterday. Did you talk to him today and make up then?'

'Didn't see him now did I?'

'So, as I see it Gary Freddie pisses you off on Monday. Tuesday you don't say screw all but Freddie said you looked like you wanted to bash the living daylights out of him. Now you say, Wednesday he's disappeared. How fucking convenient. What have you done Gary? You're a moody bastard at the best of times and never could stand being put down. All the time at school you had to crow over the rest of us. So where's Freddie?'

'How the fuck should I know. I'm not his keeper. We work together. Occasionally we go out in a foursome together. Jesus, you're his mates in this village. You should know where he is. You drink with him most nights. You find the silly sod.'

I brushed past the three of them and into the George.

'The usual please Gloria. I'm thirsty arguing with those three wankers outside.'

'What three wankers Gary?'

'Lester, Danny and big Don. That Lester is all pissed off about his sister coming out with us.'

'Dora's old enough to know her own mind Gary. She's fine.'

'Gloria, I know that and you know that but that Lester can't think any better than the paint brush he slaps about every day.'

Freddie's three friends stood in the George parking lot and considered what to do.

'Where's he gone Danny?' asked Lester. 'He was excited but shifty on Sunday night. He kept teasing us with that secret he knew but wouldn't say what. Said he might tell us later this week after he's spoken to Gary and Gloria.'

'He was telling me that he and Gloria had a good thing going you know,' said Don. 'Told me that Gloria was a real goer since she'd come down from London. Better than she was when they were just kids he said.'

'That's right Don, Freddie did go round with Gloria when we were all kids.'

'And he was going round with Gloria on Tuesday night,' said Lester. 'It was his birthday remember and he told us that Gloria had promised him a special treat or something.'

'Maybe we should go in and ask Gloria where he is then?' suggested Lester.

434

'Lester you'll get too wound up about your sister if you go asking Gloria. You were just accusing Gary of helping Gloria seduce her or something. Why don't you go round to his mum's house and see whether he's there. Don and I will go and see Gloria,' said Danny.

'Thought you were scared of going in there Danny? Thought you were afraid some other of your relatives might appear with that Samantha MacRae?'

'Give over,' cried Danny. 'I can't have any more relatives anywhere you big oaf.'

'Hold up you two. Danny why don't you go and talk with Freddie's mum? Don can go in the pub and ask Gloria.'

'And what are you going to do Sherlock Holmes?' asked Don.

'I'm going to see Gloria's mum,' answered Lester. 'She's weird enough to tell you anything but she might know something about Freddie. She's Freddie's aunt remember, even if she has gone all holy. Although someone told me they'd seen her all dolled up the other day looking like a young woman. Jesus, why can't these birds think straight instead of flitting from face to face?'

'Why don't I go and see Gary's mum?' asked Danny. 'If it is some secret between Freddie and Gary why don't I go and see both mums?'

'Genius you are Danny, absolutely a fucking genius,' exclaimed Lester. 'Anyone else in the village you want to go and see while you're at it?'

'Give over Lester. Good idea Danny. You go and I'll see Lester bogs off to Gloria's house. Then I'll go in and check on the white slave trader herself.'

'Don you're full of it but let's do something for Christ's sake.

Danny drove off in a great cloud of blue exhaust which didn't say much for his ability as a mechanic.

'Right Lester. Gloria's house is just down the road mate and I'll make sure you're on your way before I go and see Gloria.'

435

'Christ you're a bit of a ponce on occasions Don but I'll go. If I come back sprinkled with holy water and wearing a shroud just buy me the first pint.'

'Off mate and ask whether the silly bugger is still shagged out somewhere in Gloria's bed. He was bragging loud enough earlier on about some birthday treat.'

Lester walked down the lane towards Gloria's mum's house and wondered how best to find out without too much of an explanation. He was deep in thought mentally slip slapping his paint brush up and down when a strong shove pushed him up against the wall and an arm pressed against his throat.

'Where you going Lester Rainer?'

'Give over Wendell you stupid little prat. I'm not one of the little kids you can bully.'

'No, you're not. You're one of the older little weasels I can threaten though and I'm the one with the arm across your throat and twenty pounds extra weight. So, I'll ask again. Where you going?'

'To see your mother Wendell,' said Lester. 'Leave off with coming the heavy. I can hardly talk.'

'Why?'

'None of your business… ouch, cut it out. Christ, that hurt. What's your problem?'

'Why?'

'I'm looking for Freddie Dunster. Now back off.'

'Why?'

'Because we haven't seen him all day you stupid wanker. Hey, give over with the knee. I'll be walking funny all week.'

'Where is he?'

'I've just told you. We don't know. That's why we're looking. Jesus for a so-called smart kid you can be dense at times.'

Lester folded over as Wendell just thumped him hard in the solar plexus. He collapsed onto his knees as Wendell clapped both hands onto each ear. Crouching down Wendell grabbed hold of Lester's collar and lifted his head up.

'Listen up you pile of shit. You really are a loser. Why are you going to see my mum?'

Lester mumbled something but he was still so winded he could hardly breathe let alone talk. 'Say again tosser.'

'Freddie had something and we thought your mother might know what it was.'

'What did Freddie have?'

'Some secret.'

'What secret?'

'He had some secret about Gary Templeton.'

'What's that got to do with my mother?'

'It was something to do with your sister. We thought your mother might know,' Lester managed to whisper as he gasped for air.

'My poxy sister is in the pub, not at home.'

'Yes but she went out with Freddie last night,' gasped Lester.

And came home with Gary Templeton thought Wendell.

'You leave my mother alone,' threatened Wendell. 'She don't want to see you. Now bugger off before I redesign your bollocks again.'

Wendell gave Lester one final shove and Lester managed to stagger off still gasping for air and being careful how he walked with his already redesigned testicles. Wendell watched Lester shuffle off back towards the George and thought about his recent discoveries. Freddie Dunster is missing after going out with his sister. Maybe I should go back and ask mum about Freddie's secret. Maybe I can get her into some confession frame of mind before my sister pulls her back into the real world. Don't want that now do we sister dear? Much better if mum is living in some guilt-ridden world with prayers, visions and confessions to hear. Tell Wendell mum. I'm here to help. What does Freddie know?

Don pushed open the door of the bar and walked into the George. I never saw him as I was leaning on the bar and chatting to Gloria. On a Wednesday evening there was a mixed crowd there with several locals and one or two summer-time visitors. Two of the George's local darts team were practising. Tommy Daniels was playing against Harry Biggins, our old retired postie, and the team captain George Crawford was watching.

'George,' Don said, 'you see what happened out in the forest this past Monday with our Freddie and Gary Templeton? Heard there was some kind of fight going on out there?'

Now Don knew that George Crawford worked on the Fotheringham Estate gang and so he thought he would approach this sideways.

'Real wild it was for a moment Don. That Freddie must have said something 'cos Gary was really pissed off. I always thought those two were mates from way back but Gary went ballistic. It's a good job we were only weeding with hand tools but even then Gary thought about using his sickle. Someone grabbed that out of his hand and so Gary just waded in with his fists and his boots. He was kicking the crap out of Freddie something serious before we pulled them apart.'

'So Freddie said something George?'

'Suppose so Don although none of us knew what. Bob Edwards had us haul them apart and gave them both a bollocking. He kept them apart for the rest of the day. No, that's not true 'cos Gary buggered off. Bob took him back to the yard I think.'

'What happened Tuesday then George? Did they get back fighting again yesterday?'

'Funny that Don. It was strange yesterday.'

'How so?'

'Well for one Gary was quiet. He kept to himself a lot and didn't talk much with any of the other blokes but I saw that he kept well away from Freddie. Mark you Bob Edwards must have put a flea in his ear after the Monday fracas.'

'What about Freddie? It was his birthday yesterday you know?'

'Go on. He never said 'owt. He was his usual cheeky self but he never gave Gary a hard time. He too seemed to be avoiding being close to Gary. It was almost as if the two of them were circling around each other but never getting into a clinch if you know what I mean. Keeping their distances they were but Tuesday was quiet Don. Well quiet in comparison to Monday.'

'So after this great circling around yesterday George what happened today out on the site? Did the two cats continue this standoff? I see Gary over there at the bar and he is looking okay.'

'Well today was different again Don. First of all Gary arrived late with the boss, Mr. Daniel. After he apologised to Bob he went straight to work without another word. Actually he never said very much all day, even at lunch-time. Still, there was some serious talk going on at lunch-time about bringing up teenagers. That new bloke, Colin Entwhistle who has just moved into Enrico's old cottage was asking about raising kids. Well we all had something to say about that and Bob Edwards was drawn into the discussion. He explained that he and his missus were rather worried about their Dennis at the moment and that led into a discussion on bullying. Most of us guessed that would be Wendell Manson if that was the case but nobody came out and said that. He's Bob's nephew and none of us wanted to say 'owt. Still that kid Wendell is a real pain in this village Don but then most of you younger lads know that anyway.'

'So where was Freddie in this discussion?' asked Don.

'He wasn't there was he? Mr. Daniel and Bob Edwards both asked but no-one had seen Freddie. Perhaps he was still recovering from some birthday celebration. As he'd never let on it was his birthday on the Tuesday perhaps it was some secret thing and he's still sleeping it off somewhere. You're his mate so how come you don't know where he is?'

'You're probably right George. Still, I see Tommy and Harry are improving. Think we'll beat the Crown's dart team this Saturday? They're the opposition aren't they? Seem to remember they had a good player as captain. Bert Rawlings wasn't it?'

'You're right Don. That Rawlings is good. Still, it's a team thing and we've got five good players. Ain't that right Harry?'

'Right on George.'

Don moved away from the threesome by the darts board and looked around the room.

Outside the George Danny Masters drove off and contorted his brain trying to work out whether to talk with Gary's mum before Freddie's mum or the other way round. He was still thinking about it when he realised that he had driven past Freddie's house and was pulling up in front of the Templeton household.

'Hello Danny,' said Catherine Templeton. 'Gary's out love. I expect you'll find him down at the George.'

'No Mrs. Templeton, I didn't come looking for Gary. I'm looking for Freddie Dunster.'

'Well he ain't here either love.' Mrs. Templeton laughed and then she smiled at Danny. 'But I'll bet you a quid Danny Masters that Freddie is down there too. Where else do you lads go of an evening? I know, a wild game of darts, down a few pints and plan for an exciting day tomorrow.'

'No no Mrs. Templeton, he ain't there either. You'd lose your bet you know. No-one's seen him. He and Gary were arguing over something on Monday and then that stopped. Freddie was with us and Gloria yesterday evening but now he's disappeared.'

'What was Gary arguing with Freddie about Danny? Usually they're good chums together. Well apart from arguing about Gloria that is. So what was it this time?'

'Freddie said he had some secret. Something Gary didn't know. Something that Freddie thought would piss Gary off Mrs. Templeton.'

'Well I don't know I'm sure Danny. Gary never said anything on Monday. His dad took off on the Tuesday and Gary went to work as usual. Freddie was at work on the Tuesday you say?'

'Don't know about that Mrs. Templeton 'cos I don't work on the estate you know. Suppose so 'cos Freddie seemed fine yesterday although I didn't see your Gary.'

'Well he was here early on Danny but then he was out last night. Still, he was here first thing this morning to change his clothes and grab his lunch so he seems to be around to ask. As I said, he's down the George I think Danny. Go and ask him love 'cos I don't know anything about Freddie.'

On the way back from the Templeton's, which was a kilometre or so out of the village Danny suddenly noticed Freddie's car. It was parked just inside the edge of the woods that bordered the river. On his way out of the village Danny didn't see it because two large trees blocked the view. Right thought Danny, perhaps we'll get some answers. The silly sod's probably drunk out of his mind after last night with that fast and loose Gloria and he drove off the road somehow. Danny stopped on the verge of the road and got out. He walked over to Freddie's car and yanked open the door.

'Found you you silly sod,' cried Danny. 'We've been looking all over for you mate. We've been.....' and Danny closed his gob. The car was empty. No Freddie.

'Evening Mrs. Dunster. Is Freddie at home?'

'Danny, oh Danny, I'm glad you've come dear. I didn't know what to do or who to call. I've been so worried you know.'

'How can I help Mrs. Dunster? Is Freddie sick or something upstairs?'

'No dear, that's the problem. He's not here.'

'So where is he sick Mrs. Dunster? Where is he that he's so sick? Did he have to go to hospital? Where did he get sick? Have you called a doctor or did you say he'd gone to hospital?'

Now our Danny is not the smartest young man and his non-stop questions floored Freddie's mum before she stepped forwards and held her hand up to Danny's mouth.

'Danny, Danny listen son. Freddie is not here, that's the problem. I don't know where he is. I don't know whether he is sick or not because I don't know where he is. Do you understand now Danny? I don't know where Freddie is and I'm very worried.'

Eventually the repetition registered with Danny and he realised what was troubling Freddie's mum. Danny was about to ask "then where is he?" when it dawned on him that no-one seemed to know where Freddie was. After a moment of neural connections Danny asked the obvious. 'When did you see him last Mrs. Dunster?'

The effort to explain her anxiety to Danny and the several repetitions of the same words seemed to have taken its toll on Mrs. Dunster because she swayed as if she was going to collapse.

'Here, hold up there Mrs. Dunster. There, you okay? You had me worried for a moment. Thought you were going to faint in my arms. Can I make you a cuppa?'

Danny led Mrs. Dunster back from her door into the kitchen and helped her sit down at the table. He looked around valiantly for the kettle and the taps but before he got started Mrs. Dunster sat up straight and said, 'Just a glass of water please Danny. I'll be fine. Suppose I am worried sick. Thanks.'

As she sipped the water Freddie's mum seemed to gain strength and she turned to Danny and said, 'I last saw Freddie yesterday evening Danny. He came home from work and had his tea. Then he really took his time making himself look neat and tidy. He looked quite the smart young man. I had already given him his present earlier in the morning because it was his birthday yesterday you know. Anyway, I commented how smart and mature he looked. He told me he was looking forward to a special birthday surprise and so I just assumed it was something you, Lester and Don had arranged. You four are always doing things together you know and I guessed you might be going in to town, to a dance or a party somewhere. He looked real pleased with himself. Said he felt fine. On top of the world he told me.'

Inquiring about people wasn't Danny's strongpoint. Taking motors apart he could handle but people were another story so Danny didn't think to ask any further. It was obvious he thought. Freddie wasn't here and he, Lester and Don had seen Freddie long after his mum had so there was no point in asking her anything else.

'Thanks Mrs. Dunster. I'll go and talk with Lester and Don. Mrs. Templeton hadn't seen Freddie either 'cos I went to see her first. Maybe we'll talk with Gary Templeton.' Danny didn't notice Mrs. Dunster's reaction to Gary's name as he turned and walked out of the kitchen to the front door.

'We'll tell you as soon as we find him,' called Danny back over his shoulder as he opened the front door.

'But I'm worried about him Danny. I'm worried not knowing where he is. Freddie said he had a fight with Gary on Monday and then Tuesday it was all quiet and peaceful. That Gary knows something Danny. You talk with Gary.'

'Fine,' said Danny and he closed the front door and walked over to his car. Gary Templeton seems to know something he thought. I'll check back with Lester and Don and we'll decide what to ask Gary precious Templeton.

It was only long afterwards that I learnt any of this. At the time I was making eyes at Gloria and secretly congratulating myself on a neat and conclusive previous evening. I didn't know at the time that my world was about to slowly and ever-increasingly quickly unravel. Gloria was working behind the bar on this Wednesday night but any free time she had she was talking with Lola and Sheena. I knew that another booking had been made for the next evening out at the cottage and that the two girls were part of the service. Gloria had already told me where to meet the new customers and given me a general description of how to make contact. I was all set for my assignment as driver, guide, lookout, videographer and general dogsbody but I got my cut and thought the whole deal was a winner. Good for you Gloria I thought. Your education up in London will prove to be useful after all. Then I came back to Freddie's taunt and felt bloody mad. My sister!! Fuck it my own sister, even if only a half-sister. God dam and blast you dad. Perhaps it is you I should have smothered. Perhaps someone should cut your prick off.

ASSAULTS TIT FOR TAT

DON WALKED OUT OF THE pub just as Lester staggered back into the parking lot.

'I thought you went to see the holy holy Mrs. Manson. What'd she do, crucify you? Why you walking funny Lester?'

'I ran into that stupid son of hers didn't I? Jesus Don, someone needs to straighten out that kid before too long. I thought Freddie thumped him last week? He was crowing about giving Wendell a black eye over the weekend.'

'I gather you ran into the thumped Wendell? Anyway, what did Gloria's mum have to say?'

'Never saw her did I? Never got to their house before Wendell re-arranged my balls. Christ they hurt.'

'Well don't just stand there jiggling them. Look out, here comes master mechanic Danny in his rust bucket. Well Danny?' asked Don as he leaned in through the window.

'Learn anything useful?'

'Naw. Freddie's mum is worried sick and Gary's mum don't know 'owt. Talk to Gary she says.'

445

'Look, it's ten minutes to closing and we'll waylay Gary and take him somewhere to sort this out. Take him back into his precious forest somewhere quiet.'

'Who put you in charge Don?'

'Lester do you want to find out what happened to our mate or are you going to lament over your redesigned scrotum all night? No Danny, don't even ask. Lester met up with Wendell and asked the wrong question. Seems Wendell decided to get his own back for Freddie thumping him last week. Lester led with his balls instead of his fists and paid the price.'

'Look, Gary's car is over on the edge of the parking lot. I'll pull up alongside and we can hustle him into my motor as he tries to get into his car. You two wait there in the shadows and jump him.'

'Christ Danny, you've been watching the tele again. Think you're 007 now? Don't think your motor was one of Q's inventions.'

'Move it, it's nearly closing time.'

I'd come out of the pub that night feeling good. Sheena and Lola were looking forward to another session on the Thursday evening and I was looking forward to some more video. I had arranged with my camera contact to check over some of the material on Friday night in town. I was about to open my car door when Lester and big Don suddenly appeared. Before I knew it and not being too steady on my legs by this time I was bundled into Danny's car and off we went.

'Give over Don and get your fat arse off of me.'

'You hold still a while there fancy pants. We want a quiet word and I mean quiet.'

'Even if we have to beat it out of you,' added Lester.

Quite by chance Danny took the ride that led to the Ferris cottage although he didn't drive quite that far into the forest. As soon as he

446

was two to three hundred yards in he stopped and turned round in the driver's seat.

'Speak to him Don. Get him to speak to us.'

'Fuck off Danny,' I managed to say, 'and great this great oaf off of me.'

'Hey, I know,' exclaimed Lester. 'I was reading this book where the guy wouldn't talk. Know what they did? They tied him to a tree, naked he was, and they threatened to cut off his balls if he didn't talk. Christ, I'd like to do that to that jerk Wendell right now. Cut his balls off and see how he likes it.'

'I ain't saying anything,' I said.

'I've got some rope in the boot,' said Danny helpfully. 'Lester's got a good idea.'

'Lester's never had any idea in his head his whole life,' I said. 'I'm surprised he can even read. Pictures in this book Lester were there? Big letters, little words eh?'

'Take him outside Don and let's see how he feels trussed up. Get that rope Danny. I've got a knife.'

Well the three stupid buggers hauled me out of the car and tied me up to a tree. I suppose I was feeling tired and still quite high from last night, full of beer and looking forward to another good night to come. However, by this time I was also getting very pissed off with the three of them.

'Right,' said Lester waving his little knife about, 'Talk!'

'Fuck off Lester and stop waving that useless knife about before you stick it in yourself.'

'Where's Freddie?'

'How the fuck should I know?'

Don decided that Lester didn't have a clue so he hit me in the stomach and I puked. I had turned my head and most of it spewed over Danny who was standing beside me still fiddling with a knot.

'Bastard,' he screamed and he lashed out with a fist to my chest and that hurt. 'You puking shit.'

'Freddie?' screamed Lester dancing in front of me and waving his knife about. 'I'll cut your balls off Gary Templeton. I will I will.'

Part of me wanted to laugh at this spectacle of Lester prancing about with his itty bitty knife and then Don hit me again and another part of me threw up and I was gasping for breath.

'What was Freddie's secret? What did he tell you to piss you off on Monday?'

'Between Freddie and me,' I managed to whisper still gasping for breath. Danny grabbed me by the hair and lifted my head up. Looking me right in the eye he said, 'And now it's between all of us so tell.'

I shook my head. When I stopped Danny hit me but this time he hit my mouth and I could taste blood, my blood.

'Gary mate, you don't seem to understand we want to know. We want to know the secret, why the fight, and most of all we want to know where Freddie is. But we'll start with the secret and work our way down the list of items to tick off. Just like one of my tune-ups. Item by item Gary and number one is the secret. The secret that started all this mess.'

Don lifted his fist. I shook my head and then wished I hadn't 'cos suddenly I couldn't breathe again. With my arms tied up above my head I dam near asphyxiated and was gasping gasping. Lester had stopped prancing and was trying to undo the belt of my trousers. Suddenly this had got serious. I lifted my head and saw Don looking at me and raising his big fist again. I shook my head up and down rather than from side to side and Don lowered his fist.

'Well?' said Danny. 'Secret Gary?'

'A moment,' I managed to whisper.

'Secret Gary?' demanded Lester and he waved his knife about near my crotch.

'Freddie was going to tell Gloria and Gloria's mum about Wendell,' I managed to whisper and felt a tooth that was loose plus the blood from my cut lip.

'What about Wendell?'

I tried to take a breath but with my arms stretched above my head that wasn't easy and my gut was bruised from Don's fists. I felt like shit.

'That he was a faggot, a queer, gay. You know.'

'Everyone knows that Gary. Try again.'

'And that he's a bully and he buggers his victims.'

'And we all know that so what?'

'Well Gloria's mum doesn't,' I managed to say, 'and Gloria doesn't want her mum upset at the moment because Gloria is trying to help get her mum back into this world.' The words rushed out and I choked again and coughed. 'Now untie me you stupid prats and let's go home.'

'Crap Gary, absolute crap. That's not any secret. So, I'll say one more time, what secret?' and Don seized my shirt front and looked me right in the eye up close. I closed my eyes. Christ, now what do I do?

'See the light?' said Danny. 'See there, flashing about, on and off. Shit, I'm out of here.'

'Where Danny? I don't see fuck all,' said Lester. 'Oh shit, there, yes I do,' and Lester jumped in the back seat of the car. 'Don, come on Don. Let's get out of here.' Lester was in a right panic and Don just stood there holding my shirt.

'We'll find you Gary and we'll know,' he said and he thumped me one more time before he too turned and got in the car. Danny took off fish-tailing and I almost choked in the exhaust fumes and the dust. I hung there with my trousers and pants down around my ankles, my arms tied up above my head and my guts aching. The smell of puke wafted in from over my shoulder and I felt like shit. Suddenly a torch light flickered my way and I lifted my head.

'Rory, Rory look what I've found.'

'Aye Arnold, that's definitely the lesser-spotted species,' said Rory Flanagan, 'but it looks like it could do with a hand. Could you do with a hand mate or are we interrupting some weird yokel cult session? Arnold find some water for I think our entangled specimen here needs a little TLC. Shall I release the bondage my fine friend or will I disturb the spell and we'll all be cast into outer darkness?'

'Cut the fucking rope,' I whispered. 'Please,' I added as an afterthought.

'To be sure to be sure,' said Rory and he sawed away at Danny's hunk of rough rope. 'Arnold bring that light over here you fanatic and let me see to cut the rope and not this bloke's hands off. We'll look for the precious nightjars later.'

'And that tawny owl Rory. I know I heard him. Just before you grabbed my arm.'

'Soon enough Arnold but for the minute old boy just hold the light where I can see where I'm sawing. This rope is like an old ship's hawser and I don't think it is taking kindly to my rather blunt knife. There we are boyo. Does that feel any better now? Here we were just taking a stroll through his Lordship's forest to help with his ideas on wildlife and what should we come across but a spider's trophy.'

'Thanks,' I muttered and rubbed my raw wrists and gently inched my fingers across my sore stomach. 'Thanks for the help. Things were getting a little carried away.'

'Didn't look like you were being carried anywhere,' said Arnold flashing his torch all around the area. 'Look, you okay now because we've got to get on. We've a long night ahead of us and we want to see as

450

much as we can. Come on Rory. He seems fine. Let's go back to the ride and carry on.'

Rory turned and looked at me. 'Are you all right then mate? Are you fine? We've no wheels around this side of the forest 'cos we left them at that Education Centre and that's away off. Where've you got to go?'

'No mate, thanks I'm fine. I'll see myself home. I can follow this ride out to the road and then it's not far to the village and home. I work here so I know my way around. Thanks for the interruption. You may have saved me from a bit of aggro there. I'll be off.'

'What about a light?' asked Arnold. 'How will you see?'

'Once you've turned that torch off mate and I've stood here a moment I'll get some night vision back. Then I'll be fine on this forest ride. You can go back now to whatever you were doing. What were you doing by the way? Does Sir Anthony know about this?'

'We were talking with Daniel Lord and he wanted some ideas about wildlife, him and his girl friend Katya. Rory and I thought we would check out some of the night life too.'

'Thanks again,' I said and I filed away the thought that there could be people wandering around here at night that I wasn't expecting. The two of them flitted away and they too minimised the use of their torch. Sounded genuine enough I thought and they certainly saved me from a shit-kicking. After a couple of minutes I could see well enough to slowly walk back towards the main road and home but I felt like hell.

Mum woke me up early ready to give me breakfast before I went to work. I ached all over and had sore and rubbed-raw wrists from that stupid hunk of rope. I decided there and then I wasn't going to work that day. Sod it I thought. I did go down for breakfast but I was only halfway through when mum told me she was going out and before I knew it she had shut the door and peace settled on the house.

'You look like something the cat dragged in son. Can't hack these late nights boy? Got no stamina like your old man?'

'Dad, what you doing here?'

'Gary son it might surprise you but I live here. This is my house. The lady who just served you breakfast is my wife. I have a good job and I bring money in. I drive a nice car and I live a good life. Whereas you son, well just look at you.'

I put down my knife and fork and looked at my dad. 'Do you know what you have done? Do you know you nice man, in this nice house with the nice wife, with the nice car and the nice job what you have fucking done?' I stood up and felt the pain in my guts but I had to stand. 'You and your nice wandering cock have fucked up my life. You are Gloria Manson's father you nice arsehole. You fucked Tilley Manson and fathered Gloria and I've been going out with Gloria since I don't know when, since I was a young teenager. We love each other. We want to get married. But now I hear, now I find out that she's my sister you fucking bastard. So for years now, and pretty soon the whole village will know it, I've been fucking my sister and I didn't know it. Well Mr. nice guy, what do you say to that?'

'Could be son, could be. Let's see, how old is darling cute little Gloria right now? I must say son she is a charmer. Perhaps not as good as some of her friends though like the other night. Now that Gina bird is something else and you should see the young one.'

'You'd only just got married dad, to mum. What January and you must have fucked Tilley in February.' I stood there going through the numbers on my fingers working out the months backwards. I knew that Gloria's birthday was in November and managed to work out that she was conceived back in February. 'Why didn't you tell me you were her father? That she is my sister?'

'Hell Gary I didn't know. She was just another cunt son. It was only the once I think, coming back from some trip up to Bristol. I'd been with some mates. We'd had a few drinks and made out with a couple of hookers. I was driving back from Bristol and there she was staggering around trying to prop up Rosemary Biddle. Christ, Rosemary was right out of it and Tilley was trying to walk to the station. I offered them a lift and the silly cow said yes. What I was supposed to do? What would you have done? It was a long drive and she was a wild one. She was full of herself and putting herself about. In fact the pair of them was wild son but that Rosemary was out for the night. We had to stop because Tilley wanted a piss. Well, once her knickers were off it was like an invitation. Quick hump up against the side of the car, hot and wet. You know what it's like, especially with a young one. Back home to the village and drop the two girls off. Thanks and see you later. No problem. I never heard a word afterwards so what are you griping about? She got married to Walter Manson who was a thick bugger but that wasn't my problem. Anyway, who has rattled your cage all of a sudden? So you're balling Gloria. Fine by me. I tried the other day but she brushed me off. Lots of fish in the sea Gary my son.'

'She's my sister you stupid prick,' I shouted. 'Walter wasn't her dad you were. And all this time I've been fucking my sister.'

'No wonder she's such a nice looking girl,' said dad. 'Pretty, flirty, and full of the come on. She does wonders behind that bar Gary. George was smart to hire her back again. Absolute waste in Darlene's. Still, those girlfriends of hers have got a nice thing going somewhere down here and once a month or so I might treat myself to one of your specials. You should get a freebie son, seeing as you're part of the staff. My mates thought that was a worthwhile drive. At first they couldn't see the point of driving all this way but afterwards they realised what a benefit show the troops put on down here. That website should put this place on the map Gary. It'll rival Betty's pies,' and he laughed.

Neither of us had heard the door open and mum come in. She had been in the hall and heard virtually all of the conversation. When there was a lull in the talk she walked in and looked at both of us.

'Hello Catherine love,' said my dad. 'You were quick.'

'Forgotten something hadn't I Brian? Forget most things don't I Brian? Forget where you go, when you go, who you go with and what you do, and you do a lot don't you Brian? I suppose I've always known. Right from that first night Brian, you and me. That first night when you made your first mistake, made that first assumption and we had Gary. Yes Gary son, you were a mistake, well on your dad's part you were. It wasn't a mistake for me though Gary. I wanted your dad. I wanted a baby and I got both. Made him marry me I did Gary but I had you and that's what I wanted as well. I didn't care about all the other girls. I knew what your dad was like and nothing was going to stop him but as long as he came home here I was happy, and I had you son. You were precious.'

'But you never stopped me going out mum. You never stopped me going out with girls and you must have wondered whether I would be like dad. You never stopped me going out with Gloria. Didn't you know mum? Didn't you know that dad was Gloria's father?'

'So what Gary. I had you and I loved you. It didn't matter what you did, or what your dad did for that matter. I wanted you to do well and I was proud of you wanting to be like your grandfather. I was happy that you were happy and having a good time. You finished school and went to work at Fotheringham. You wanted to be like your grandfather and I was so happy for you.'

I couldn't take it any more. This was doing my head in. First my dad wasn't worried that I was balling my sister, his daughter that he didn't seem to know or care about and now my mum was accepting all of this like it didn't matter. Everything was lovely and fine. I stormed out of the house wanting to tear something apart. I got in my car and drove down into the village. I needed to see Gloria. I was feeling furious inside about everything. Just down the main street I saw Lester Rainer leaning under the bonnet of his painting truck poking at something. I parked in front of him and got out.

'I've a bone to pick with you,' I shouted as I swung at him. Lester tried to pull his head out from under his bonnet and partly succeeded. My fist caught him on the shoulder and he spun round. He still had a spanner in his other hand and it swung across and caught me on the edge of my bruised cheek from last night.

'You bastard Lester. I'll kill you. I'll teach you to take a knife to me you little pisser.' I swung again and this time I landed right in his solar plexus. Lester folded over and collapsed on the road. I bent over and dragged him upright by his coveralls. I propped him up against his radiator which happened to be steaming as his fan belt had snapped. Lester screamed as he put his hand on the radiator to hold himself upright.

'You shit, you bastard,' he screamed. 'You've burnt my hand, my painting hand.'

I hit him again, hard this time because I was feeling really angry at Lester, at being tied up and punched, at my dad and my mum, at everything and so I hit him. Lester collapsed into an untidy heap on the road in front of his truck. I stood back with fire in my eyes and I kicked him hard. He moaned and I got ready to kick again when suddenly a pair of arms grabbed me from behind.

'That's enough Gary. That's quite enough.' Daniel Lord pinned me from behind but I still tried to kick at Lester moaning in front of me. My boot caught his head and he jerked backwards and went quiet.

'Thanks Mr. Lord, I'll take it from here.' PC Meadows suddenly appeared and clamped his large meaty hands over my shoulders.

'Right Gary, into the car lad and quick about it. Now!'

Suddenly it all drained away and I almost collapsed under PC Meadows hands. I turned to see a concerned Daniel Lord and the burly body of PC Meadows who still held me by the shoulders. He led me away to the car and making sure I didn't bang my head he put me in the back seat. He quietly closed the door.

'Thank you Mr. Lord. Came as quick as I heard. Useful things those cell-phone gadgets. Heard you got the idea from your sister.'

'Yes constable and I've phoned for an ambulance too. I think Lester here may need some attention. Gary was kicking the shit out of him for real. The last boot was to his head. I would imagine he's got some concussion and maybe a broken rib or two. Want me to wait for the ambulance while you attend to Gary there?'

'Gary Templeton isn't going anywhere Mr. Lord and so we'll wait for the ambulance and check that Lester's still alive to do some painting later. I'll just look and see that the lad's breathing comfortably but I can see the chest is rising up and down. Be some bruising and likely concussion as you say. That Gary was right riled up when I came on the scene. Good job you happened by or something serious might have happened. No Mrs. Larkin, everything is under control love. You just go back in your shop and we'll sort this out. Good job it's this early in the morning Mr. Lord, before the tourists come thronging down this street. Might upset some of Darlene Robert's customers to see blood before their tea and crumpets. Ah, here comes the ambulance now Mr. Lord.'

I sat in the back of the police car and watched them pick Lester up on a stretcher and whisk him away. Good riddance I thought, useless little shit.

'Okay for me to have a few words Doctor?' asked Detective Inspector Field.

'Just a few sir. He's concussed and we think he's got a couple of broken ribs but the x-ray will show that. There's nothing life threatening so just a few words before we look after him.'

'Lester, I'm Detective Inspector Field. You may remember me from the George. I've seen you in there a few times. Mind telling me what that fracas was all about?'

'About Freddie Inspector, Freddie Dunster. He's got a secret, about Gary. Shit I hurt. He's done me ribs in.'

'Yes lad, the Doctor tells me you've been in the wars a little. Sorry. So Freddie's secret Lester?'

'Freddie never said and now he's gone.'

'So Freddie never told you what this secret was but you think he may have told Gary?'

'Dunno, but Gary's not told us.'

'And why was Gary trying to beat the shit out of you Lester if you don't know and you think Gary does know this secret?'

'Well we asked didn't we and he wouldn't say.'

'Who are "we" Lester?'

'Danny, Don and I.'

'Not Freddie?'

'No, I keep trying to tell you Freddie's gone missing. That's what this is all about. Haven't you been listening Inspector? Freddie's got a secret and now Freddie's missing. Find Freddie and ask him about the secret.'

'That's Danny Masters and Don Winters I assume with you, doing the asking that is?'

'Sright.'

'Okay Lester, I'll be back when the Doc has patched you up. They tell me the Doctor here is good with hands. For your painting,' Inspector

Field added when he saw Lester looking confused. Detective Inspector Field made a call back to his office. Yes, there had been a call from a rather worried sounding Mrs. Dunster and yes she had reported that she hadn't seen her son for over twenty four hours. So, it appears we have a missing Freddie Dunster who knows a secret that is concerning Gary Templeton. Well Gary Templeton can sit and stew a little thought Inspector Field. Now what was it Samantha was telling me about the Templeton family? Something about parentage that was a little surprising. I'll give her a call to check before I go and see Danny and Don. Let's see who has been asking who questions about secrets. Inspector Field couldn't make contact with Samantha who was out in the forest with Lewis and Shirley Peters looking at the Education Centre and then going on to talk with Bob Edwards. He stopped in at Taffy Williams garage in the village.

'Afternoon Mr. Williams. I'm Detective Inspector Field and I'm looking for Danny Masters. He works here I believe?'

'Right on Inspector, although work might be a rather loose term if you know what I mean. Aren't you a good friend of Miss Samantha? Know the Lord family? Heard Sir Anthony has just hired a good mechanic, young lad from Yorkshire. Daniel was in here yesterday and we were talking you know. Told that young Mr. Daniel I'd try and steal that lad from him if he wasn't careful. Daniel laughed as always and said I'd have to talk to his dad first and Sir Anthony was always a good hand at building up his own team. Fat chance I've got. Now sir, you were wanting Danny and me going on like. I'll find him.'

Inspector Field had found it was much more productive to listen to the village folk than interrupt and try and be efficient and officious. Let them come to you he thought. We'll all get there and you might learn a thing or two just listening. He smiled and remembered things Samantha had told him about watching him listen.

'Danny, I'm Detective Inspector Field,' as Terence displayed his credentials. 'I've just been talking to your friend Lester Rainer in hospital.'

'Is he sick like Freddie? Mrs. Dunster said she was sick about Freddie but she said he wasn't in the hospital. Where is Freddie and why is Lester in hospital?'

'Danny, let's get this straight son. I ask you the questions. Okay? Now, Lester is in hospital because Gary Templeton kicked the shit out of him just an hour or so ago right here in the village. And, Gary Templeton was kicking the shit out of him because you, and Lester and Don Winters were asking Gary about some secret. Right?'

'So Lester's in hospital 'cos Gary got mad, about being tied up and all. Lester went a little crazy I suppose. He must have seen it on the tele 'cos he never reads books like he said he had. He said he'd read it in a book but he never reads. Still, he had Gary going for a minute there, dancing around flashing this piddley little knife of his.'

'When Danny, when did Lester dance around flashing his piddley little knife?'

'Well last night of course. We'd all gone looking for Freddie. I'd seen Gary's mum and then I'd seen Freddie's mum. That's how I knew he wasn't in hospital because Freddie's mum said so.'

'Where did Don go, looking for Freddie?'

'He went in the pub. He asked George Crawford who works out at Fotheringham. George said that Freddie was at work on Tuesday but there was no fight like on the Monday. That was wicked that was. On the Monday they were at it like cat and dog. George said they had to pull them apart before Gary kicked Freddie's head in.'

'And Lester Danny? Where did Lester look last night for Freddie?'

'He went to see Gloria's mum 'cos we all thought she might know what Gary and Gloria were up to and Gloria was supposed to see Freddie

on the Tuesday night. It was Freddie's birthday on Tuesday and Gloria
had a surprise for him, some gift or other.'

'And what did Gloria's mum say to Lester?'

'He never saw her did he?'

'She wasn't in?'

'He never got there 'cos Wendell stopped him.'

'And Lester didn't just carry on?'

'Wendell kicked the shit out of him. Lester could hardly walk or
talk when he came back to us. Wendell had smashed his guts in. That's
probably why he was so crazy later when we talked to Gary.'

'Okay Danny. Let's see whether I can put this together right and in
some order. Monday Freddie and Gary fight.'

'Yea, but before that you've got to realise that Freddie's full of this
secret thing over the weekend. He was in the pub telling Don, Lester and
me that he had this secret and he was going to really shaft Gary. Freddie
wanted to go out with Gloria and he thought Gary was queering his
pitch. Anyway, he'd found something out that he said would shut Gary
up for good. Make Gloria his he said.'

'But he never said what this secret was?'

'Naw, he wanted to tell Gary first and watch him go ape-shit. He
couldn't wait for Monday. That's what probably led to the big fight on
the Monday at work. He told him the secret.'

'But then they both went to work on the Tuesday?'

'Suppose so Inspector. Freddie did. Don't know about Gary 'cos I
ain't seen him. Didn't see him Monday or the Tuesday.'

'And you saw Freddie on Tuesday night but not afterwards?'

'Right, so that's why we were looking for him on the Wednesday.
We wanted to hear about the birthday treat and what happened about
the secret.'

'But no Freddie and you went looking, the three of you?'

'Right but we couldn't find him and no-one had seen him. That's when Don decided we should ask Gary and so we did. When he came out of the pub.'

'And that's when Lester does this dance with the knife thing?'

'Yea.'

'Where was Lester dancing Danny?'

'In the forest.'

Inspector Field suddenly had a flippant thought and vision of Lester in white paint-covered coveralls dancing around in the forest like a sylvan elf waving a knife in one hand and a paint-brush in the other but thought better about making such a suggestion to Danny.

'The three of you took Gary for a little ride in the forest?'

'Yea.'

'He didn't object? He just came out for the ride? You could have asked him when he left the pub.'

'Don sat on him while I drove.'

'I see. So the four of you go for a ride in your car out into the forest to ask Gary where was Freddie?'

'And the secret Inspector. We asked about the secret first. Don was quite insistent we find out about the secret first.'

'So I see this little foursome in the forest all having this quiet chat although Lester is doing a special dance which you said he must have seen on television?'

'Not quite Inspector.'

'How not quite Danny? Explain son. Take your time. You drive out to the forest and Don is sitting on Gary. You all get out and....?'

'Well that's when Lester remembers this thing about the tele. So he wants me to get some rope and tie Gary to a tree while he threatens to cut off his balls if he doesn't tell us.'

'Did you tie Gary to a tree Danny?'

'Sure, but Lester didn't cut him Inspector. Lester never touched him. Don thumped him and Gary puked all over me.'

'Charming.'

'No bloody awful Inspector. Stunk it did.'

'And after being tied to a tree, thumped by Don, puked all over you and been entertained by our TV-loving Lester dancing and waving his piddley knife did Gary tell you about this secret, and where Freddie was?'

'No, we all ran away.'

'Obvious question Danny is why?'

'Some one was coming weren't they? Flashing lights we saw. Don't know how many but Lester said go and so we drove off.'

'Leaving Gary tied to the tree like the proverbial maiden at the stake when the dragon came looking for breakfast. How courageous.'

'We didn't want no trouble Inspector. We just wanted ......'

'To know the secret and where Freddie was. Yes, I think I get the picture Danny. By the way Danny, don't leave the village for a while son. I'll be back.'

Inspector Field slowly walked from the garage the four or five hundred metres to the offices of Tillson and Betts and went to find Don Winters. There he put together a similar and somewhat less jumbled up version of the same story but still no sign of Freddie after Tuesday evening and now it was Thursday morning. The search looked like it was narrowing down to talking with Gloria and what happened on Tuesday night and Gary about the secret. Inspector Field tried to call Samantha again but still got no reply from her magic mobile phone. Turned off or out of range or something Inspector Field thought. Back at his car he got a rather urgent radio message to come back into town and his office. Apparently some new evidence had just been received and he should see this. It related to Gary Templeton.

Back in his office Inspector Field looked at the hardcopy of the received email. Whoever sent it was knowledgeable enough to remove all traces of the sender so it was like an old-fashioned anonymous letter or phone call. Send the message and hang up. The email was rather blunt. It merely stated "Brian Templeton is Gloria's father". Inspector Field held the paper in his hands and thought so what? What had that to do with Freddie? What had that to do with Gary Templeton really? Wonder who sent it and why? Phone Samantha Terence remembered. She was working with that Peters couple who were really Templetons long removed. Some long-lost great grandfather or other and distant relatives.

'Terence is this important, and is it police business or are you just phoning up to say hi? I haven't seen you for a while. I've been up in London, in Oxford and then London again. I'm working with Lewis and Shirley Peters.'

'Samantha, hold it there for a moment please. This is business I'm afraid, and it does concern the Peters, well the Templeton family really. The one that is living here. When we briefly spoke over the weekend you mentioned something surprising had come to light. You'd seen some people on Friday and sort of confirmed it. You said it had to do with Gloria Manson. Am I right?'

'Yes Terence. Why do you ask?'

'I'll tell you later, well as much as I can. You found that Brian Templeton was Gloria Manson's father and not Walter Manson, right?'

'Yes Terence but how do you know all that?'

'And I know that Tilley Manson is the cousin and was the best friend of Rosemary Dunster, Freddie's mother. But, you told me they're back to being good friends just recently. Tilley Manson has changed and come back to life. All Gloria's doing?'

463

'Apparently Terence, yes.'

'So it is possible that Tilley Manson and Rosemary Dunster may be talking about old times and that might include who was the father of Tilley's baby. I'm trying to look at some dates here, looking at who knew who when and who got born when. Could Rosemary know about Tilley's baby, about Gloria? Maybe you say.'

'Terence this is still very private. My clients Lewis and Shirley Peters want to help members of the Templeton family. That's how we discovered that Gloria is a Templeton. What's all this got to do with Rosemary Dunster?'

'Freddie Dunster has been missing for over twenty-four hours and no-one knows where. I can tell you that much.'

'And you think this has something to do with Gloria and her father being Brian Templeton?'

'Maybe.'

'Terence!!'

'Sorry, can't say more. Thanks,' and Terence hung up. Should have said I'll see you later he suddenly thought. Shit, at times this job messes up my social life. Right, Gloria Manson next I think and then maybe we'll talk with Mr. Gary Templeton.

'Inspector it was Freddie's birthday. I told him on the Monday night I'd have a special treat for him. He's a nice lad even if he is a little thick. He's family but quite a way removed, second cousins or something. My mum and Freddie's mum are cousins see. Anyway, I promised Freddie I'd give him a "London Special" thrill on Tuesday evening. He's been going on and on about what I did up in London so I thought I'd treat him. I worked in Clubs up in the West End and used to dance a bit. So, I got my mum out of the house for a couple of hours and that stupid brother of mine was down Tom Daley's as usual so I had a nice quiet house to entertain my Freddie. My mum's come back to life she has Inspector and she's really cleaned up the house. It's all bright and light and looks real good now. We had a couple of pints in the George to loosen him up. After he was feeling mellow I took him home Inspector. We're consenting adults and I gave Freddie an evening he won't forget in a hurry. He left before my mum got home although he was having difficulty walking and I expect he couldn't lift his chainsaw the next day at work,' Gloria laughed. 'He couldn't lift much when he left me that night either Inspector but he's a good lad. I don't think he'll forget his birthday present. Be interested to see whether he comes back next birthday.'

'So Freddie left your house when?'

'We was here around eight and I suppose he was, well I'll say satisfied Inspector by about ten or just before. Must have left about ten but he was staggering Inspector. He managed to reach his car though and drove off rather slowly.'

'Did you see him Wednesday?'

'No, don't think so. I was working in the George last night and he didn't come in. In fact none of his crowd was in. No, Don was in but he was no sooner in and then he was gone again. He never bought a drink and none of the rest of that lot was in. So where is he then?'

'That Gloria is what I'm going to find out. Thanks for your help. You working tonight?'

'No Inspector, this girl's not working in the George tonight. Got to have some fun for myself haven't I?'

'Do you have a computer Gloria?'

'Yes Inspector, actually I suppose we've got two but I'm only just learning. A friend from London has come down recently a few times and she's been showing me how to use it. Its great for sending emails but I still seem to get it muddled up. Cheaper than the phone and neat to get pictures. I've tried sending photos too but that's a bit beyond me.'

'And the second one? You said you have two.'

'That's Wendell's Inspector, the other one. He's been doing computer things for years. He was into it long before I came home last year. Drives mum crazy as he's always stuck in his room and tied to it. She thinks he'll forget how to talk to humans next.'

Inspector Field got back in his car. Freddie's car had been found up near the river, by that swimming pool young Tony was using, and Gloria was using for her lessons with Tony. What if Gloria's "London Special" hadn't been at the house but up by the pool? Maybe we should search the pool and the river. Wonder whether Freddie could swim. I wonder whether Freddie's London Special didn't end quite the way Gloria suggested. And I wonder what Wendell does tied to his computer with secrets suddenly coming to light in that house.

Inspector Field radio-ed in to his office and his sergeant started to organise a sweep and search of the river. Freddie's car might be there by design or by default, or then again as a decoy. Still, it was a fine summer's day, the sun was shining and the search team should be happy with a day out of the office and away from the normal routine: whereas I still need to talk to Freddie's mother.

'Good morning Mrs. Dunster. I called to let you know what progress we are making with looking for Freddie. People have seen him up until around ten o'clock Tuesday evening and then it seems he disappeared. Do you know why we found his car down by the river?'

'No Inspector, not really. He can't swim and so no late night skinny dipping for my Freddie. Did that in my day of course but then we could all swim in those days. Wasn't much else to do in the summer time as kids. But my Freddie couldn't swim. I think he was a little frightened of the water Inspector. It is his car I suppose?'

'Yes Mrs. Dunster and the keys were still in it and no sign of any struggle so it got there safely. I just don't know yet who might have been driving it but we've people looking at it very carefully. Tell me, how was Freddie this past week? Was he excited, anxious, different in any way?'

'Well it was his birthday on Tuesday Inspector.'

'Yes, I'm aware of that. Several people have told me that. Anything else?'

'He was full of himself Monday morning but I expect that was the anticipation of his birthday on the Tuesday.'

'Anyone say anything special to him, anything new or unexpected? Have you had any recent visitors who may have surprised Freddie, told him things, asked him things?'

'No Inspector. We both lead a quiet life I suppose. My William's been dead nigh on ten years now and so I've led a quiet life here in the village. William's pension wasn't much Inspector and Freddie works on the forest gang up at Fotheringham you know. Sir Anthony pays okay and he looks after his people so we're not poor Inspector but then again we don't go nowhere.'

'I've just come from talking with Gloria Manson Mrs. Dunster, your niece or niece once removed I believe. She was telling me that you and her mother used to be the best of friends. Gloria also mentioned that recently her mother Tilley has come back to this world. She said that Tilley had been over here to talk with you. Is that right?'

'Yes Inspector. Tilley was over here last week. I was surprised, very surprised after all that has happened and for so long. Gloria coming home has made a difference, and Toby re-appearing I suppose.'

'Toby who Mrs. Dunster? Gloria never mentioned Toby.'

'Why Toby the Fixer of course Inspector,' Rosemary Dunster laughed. 'He was Toby the Fixer to us, to Tilley and me. When we were teenagers and going to see bands Toby was the Fixer to manage venues, gigs, groups, you name it. Anyway, seems Gloria met him up in London and now he's come down here and seen Tilley. Helped change her. Was good to talk with her Inspector after all these years. She came and forgave me. She said it wasn't my fault and now she's realised that we should forget all about it and start again. She was quite full of herself. Said now her Walter's dead and my William too we should live again like we did when we was young. She was telling me that Toby had come down and he had some friends. We could all go up to London and have a good time, just like the old days she said.'

'Was Freddie here when Tilley Manson called Mrs. Dunster? Did he hear what Tilley had to say? Freddie was keen on Gloria and he would have been interested seeing what Gloria had done and how happy Gloria's mother was with you, his own mother. Would have brought the families closer together again. Did Freddie hear what Tilley was talking about with you?'

'No Inspector, he was at work and Tilley came in the afternoon.'

'And what did Tilley forgive you about Mrs. Dunster? You said she forgave you, after all these years.'

Mrs. Dunster paused and looked at her hands in her lap. Her expression changed from the enthusiasm over her cousin's visit to the pain of the memory of the night in question.

'I fell asleep Inspector. I fell asleep and Tilley got hurt. We always looked after each other but that night I fell asleep.'

'And Brian Templeton, your helper with the offer of a lift home took advantage of you being asleep and Tilley tired helping you but still a young wild thing. Result Gloria. That was the event needing forgiveness Mrs. Dunster?'

'You know?'

'Some parts of the story Mrs. Dunster, but the question I really have is did Freddie know?'

'Parts of it Inspector. I suppose I was so surprised at Tilley coming round I felt I had to tell someone and I told Freddie.'

468

'So Freddie knew that Brian Templeton was Gloria's father.'

'I told him that Walter wasn't Inspector and I guess he worked out the rest. He's a bit thick at time Inspector God bless him but he probably worked it out in the end.'

'And Freddie may have used this "secret" to tease people?'

'Don't know Inspector. He does tease people sometimes. He isn't a big lad Inspector and that Norton Ferris used to give him a hard time when he was just a teenager. Of course my William was dead by then Inspector so there was nothing much I could do about it. He took to teasing when he thought he had something over other people. It was his only way of getting back you know.'

'Help me here Mrs. Dunster. Freddie could have teased his friends with the secret. He did a little bit with Lester, Danny and Don in the pub over the weekend. They all told me about Freddie's secret but none of them knew what it was. They did tell me it would really annoy Gary Templeton. Freddie apparently wouldn't tell his mates until after he had told Gary and made him mad.'

'Well it would annoy Gary now wouldn't it Inspector? Gary has been going out with Gloria for a long time. They all used to go out together as teenagers, and now, since Gloria has come back both Gary and Freddie are going out with her again. Freddie wanted Gloria to be his girl Inspector. He thinks she is someone special but Gary keeps getting in the way.'

'So Freddie tells Gary about Gloria's father and that causes the fight at work on the Monday?'

'Yes, I suppose. Freddie never said much about anything on Monday but he was excited about Tuesday. Gloria promised him a special birthday treat and knowing her and Freddie I can probably guess what that was all about. I don't think she just waited on tables up in London Inspector, not if she's anything like Tilley, or Brian Templeton too I suppose.'

469

'I'll go and talk with your cousin Mrs. Dunster. By the way, we've arrested Gary Templeton and I'm going to talk with him later this morning. Perhaps there I might find out a little more about the secret and Gary's reaction. Thank you for your time Mrs. Dunster and we'll find Freddie, trust me. We'll find him.'

Inspector Field left Mrs. Dunster and made a side visit to the search team.

'Nothing obvious Inspector sir.'

'His mother said he can't swim Sergeant but he might have been pushed, dumped and then again he might not. That's the trouble with searches, you never know exactly whether you are looking in the right spot. Give it today and we'll rethink this evening.'

'Right oh sir.'

Freddie taunts Gary and Gary goes ape-shit. Samantha told me that Gary left work on the Monday morning and came home, or somewhere yet he is back at work on the Tuesday and Wednesday. Suddenly he is beating the shit out of Lester on the Thursday because of Lester dancing around with a knife sometime Wednesday evening. Okay, tit for tat that could be but Freddie decides to celebrate his birthday Tuesday evening and then goes walkabout. Fine, Tilley Manson, what do you know about this and that?

'Good morning Mrs. Manson. I was round earlier talking with your daughter and you were out. Could I have a word please? You might already have heard but Mrs. Dunster has reported her Freddie is missing and we are doing a search. I've just come from her house and she recommended I talk with you. Has Gloria talked with you this morning, after I left that is?'

'No Inspector, she'd already gone to work at the pub. Come in though, come in.'

'Thank you.'

Sitting in the newly decorated bright sunny room Inspector Field noted the atmosphere and the liveliness, especially after coming from the sadness and concerns at Mrs. Dunster's.

'It appears that Gloria has brightened up everyone's lives on coming home from London? Every time I see her she is working or surrounded by people looking bright and cheerful. She certainly has become quite a draw at the George.'

'Yes Inspector, but I had to go and talk with George to re-hire her. Stupid man firing her for being with Toby and he was only having a laugh. He's a great man for a laugh Inspector. Anyway, Gloria's back now where she belongs and she's helped me Inspector. She and Toby have brought me back to life so to speak.'

'Yes,' said Inspector Field, 'that's what Mrs. Dunster was telling me. Seems you forgave her after all these years.'

'It's over Inspector. Toby and Gloria washed all that away. Washed away my sins and I went to see Rosemary and told her. Cleaned house I have Inspector. All the old stuff gone and everything new bright clean and happy-looking. I talked with Rosemary and that was probably the first time in nearly twenty five years Inspector so it was important, an important first step into the new me, the new Tilley Manson. Told her all about Toby I did, our Toby. He's a fine man Inspector. He's a negotiator now you know. We used to call him Toby the Fixer and he hasn't really changed but now he manages relationships rather than groups and bands. Fine man. So where's Freddie then?'

The Inspector had been listening, trying to hear anything new, anything that might answer that same question.

'Gloria told me you were out on the Tuesday evening?'

'Yes Inspector, until about eleven I suppose. I had talked to Mary Travers earlier in the week and she invited me to a visit at Betty's new home. I hadn't seen Katey and Paul and I was keen to hear about her

Betty's pies. Gloria had told me all about them after working at Darlene's tea-shop and how popular they were. Well, it was time I got back into knowing about things in the village and so I went to see Betty.'

'And Gloria was here alone?'

'No Inspector, Gary Templeton was here. He and Gloria have got some thing going. It's been on and off ever since she came home I suppose although I'm not keen. I don't really like him Inspector but what can I do? They're both over twenty-one and I was young once. So, Gary was here.'

'When did he leave?'

'In the morning Inspector. He went to work I suppose or went home to change and then went to work. I was up when he left 'cos I cursed at him. I just wanted him to know that I didn't like him being here even if Gloria did. Awkward Inspector it is. I love Gloria being home and I really want her to stay, along with Toby and his friends, but I don't want her taking up with Gary. She said Freddie was here earlier and that's someone I can get on with. Freddie's all right. He promised he would sort my Wendell out. That lad's a handful now Inspector. If you have children have girls, they're easier on the head than boys.'

'So you didn't see Freddie here and Gary was here all night, on the Tuesday that is?'

'Yes Inspector. What do you think has happened to Freddie? I should go and see Rosemary. She must be worried silly poor lass. Are we through Inspector 'cos I'll go and see her now?'

'And Gary Templeton left around six or so? Here all night you say?'

'That's right Inspector. Nosey parker Mrs. Young next door saw him go. She was outside supposedly putting her dustbin out but really poking her nose in.'

'Why don't you like Gary Templeton being with Gloria Mrs. Manson?'

Tilley paused.

'Can't you guess? Don't you know? Didn't that Samantha Lord tell you? Asking me she was and she already knew most of it. Polite she was to be sure and her mother was always good to me. Thoughtful people Inspector and discreet but Gloria told me that you and Miss Samantha are going out together. You make a nice couple Inspector and I wish you both every happiness, I really do. Gloria tells me you are both quite different and yet you both seem happy together. I like that. I like people who can bring two different personalities together and make a happy pair. I never had that Inspector. Things happened. Things happened too fast and I made a mistake. It wasn't Rosemary's fault that night it was me. Too young, too stoned and too full of myself. Gloria can be like that too poor love. A mistake Inspector, one mistake and my life changed. Walter never had a chance did he? Tilley Manson went to sleep for twenty five years just like Rumple whoever. But now Inspector, now I've come back. Toby and Gloria's touch and I'm back ready for another try, another kick at the poor cat.'

'Wendell was here Tuesday night Mrs. Manson?'

'Aye, tucked up in his little bedroom of horrors. Repapered my bright sunny room with black paper like a dungeon he has. Locked his door and buried his head in his computer Inspector. When he's not at school he's got his head in that computer or he's inhaling grass down at Tom Daley's. The boy's gone bad Inspector and I don't know what to do. I told Freddie to talk to him. Came home on the Thursday with a black eye Gloria said and it was a right shiner come Friday. Right mad he was about it. Rude to Miss Samantha too on the Friday when she called.'

'And Wendell is quite the expert with computers then?'

'Don't know about any expert Inspector but he's always in it. According to Gloria Tom Daley is a bit of an expert on computers. She's only just started Inspector, still learning.'

'And Wendell is at school Mrs. Manson?'

'Yes Inspector.'

'Well thanks Mrs. Manson, thank you for your time and your help. As I told Mrs. Dunster we'll find Freddie. Go and talk with her. I think you are right. She could do with a friend beside her at this time. Good morning to you.'

Back in his office Inspector Field held another piece of paper containing a brief but informative message. Also anonymous and stating "Gary Templeton was seen Tuesday night in the village".

Sitting at his desk Inspector Field sat and talked with the Detective Constable who was his partner. PC Goodfellow was in his thirties, about the same age as Terence Field. The two worked quite well together and Terence sat and discussed information to date. Between them they thought of an approach with Gary Templeton. Together they went down to the interview room and talked with me. I had calmed down a little by this time just cooling my heels. I thought about protesting but decided to keep my trap shut. They asked away for over an hour and I ended up being charged with assault and put in the cells. Inspector Field came back with PC Goodfellow and they compared notes.

After lunchtime working at the George Gloria came home to find her mother sitting worried in her newly decorated living room.

'I understand Inspector Field was here this morning Gloria, asking about Freddie?'

'Yes Mum. I explained about Tuesday evening when you were out and my giving Freddie a birthday treat. He left and you came home.'

'But you weren't here Gloria when I came home. Only Wendell was in the house.'

'No Mum, I had to go out and see Gary and then we came here for the night. Remember you saw him leaving the Wednesday morning. He'd been here all night, well most of it I suppose as we came in after you did.'

'Gloria you came in around eleven thirty love.'

'Sure Mum, I wasn't out for long.'

'Wendell tells me that Gary didn't come here until a lot later.'

'He had a couple of things to do after we was together Mum.'

'Where?'

'Where what Mum?'

'Where were you?'

'Out Mum. I'm a big girl now and living a little. Look, I know you don't like my going out with Gary but I can't just drop him cold Mum. I'll let him down gently. Actually, I've got to see him this evening. Maybe I'll explain then.'

'I've just come back from Rosemary's. You know Freddie's missing?'

'Yes Mum, that's what Inspector Field was asking about when he came here earlier. I told him what I told you.'

'You know Wendell was in all Tuesday night Gloria. He said he came home early and was shut up in his room all evening until I came home around eleven. I found him in the kitchen where he told me he was trying to find something to eat, which was a lie and he knew it. He wasn't looking in the food cupboards and the door on the sideboard in the living room was still open. He was looking for something and knowing him it was probably money.'

'So Mum? I've told you he has a problem. I've caught him looking through my things too but I clipped his ear, even though he is bigger than me.'

'He said no-one came here when I was out Gloria, no-one and that you went out soon after I did.'

'Sure Mum, I went to get Freddie from the pub didn't I? We had a couple of drinks and I entertained him. Told you, a birthday treat for Freddie; something special from the London days.'

'But not here Gloria?'

'Doesn't matter where Mum. Don't worry about it. Freddie enjoyed himself. Look Mum, I've got to go out and leave a note for Gary 'cos he's at work and I need to tell him something when he gets back. I'm going over to Catherine Templeton. Be back soon.'

Gloria decided to drive to the Templeton's house as it was too far to walk. She pulled in the driveway behind Brian Templeton's flash minivan. Useful she murmured to herself as she walked up the path and knocked on the door.

'Gloria, come in. You look a picture my lovely. Come in and I'll get you a drink.'

'Thank you Brian but I've just come to leave a note for Gary.'

'He's not here Gloria,' said Catherine walking into the room before her husband could get too cosy. 'In fact he's in gaol, well down at the police station really I suppose. Daniel Lord was here earlier and explaining what happened. You'd better sit down Gloria as this may come as something of a shock dear.'

Gloria sat down and Brian suddenly decided he had something he had to do and left the room.

'Brian's a little embarrassed Gloria, about what I'm going to say my dear. Daniel Lord broke up a fight this morning in the high street. It seems that Gary was trying to kick little Lester Rainer. Well, actually, according to Daniel, Gary was kicking little Lester quite successfully until Daniel stopped him. PC Goodfellow arrested Gary and took him into the police station and Lester is in hospital.'

'Why?'

Catherine Dunn sat on her sofa and looked at Gloria. She took her time and looked quite closely at Gloria from head to toe. She smiled. 'What do you know about Gary's activities this week Gloria, starting on Monday at work?'

'Gary got into some sort of fight with Freddie on Monday at work. I don't know the details 'cos I wasn't there but Gary explained a little to me. Then he went to work on the Tuesday and it seemed to have blown over. Neither of them said much to each other. Well that's what I overheard on the Wednesday evening when George Crawford was in the pub with a couple of the darts team. I saw Gary on the Wednesday night in the pub but I was working so we didn't talk much. I assume he went to work on the Wednesday Catherine. I haven't seen him today and so I came round to give him a note about something.'

'What was the fight about on the Monday Gloria?'

'I don't know. What would Freddie know? Probably about some thing they were doing out in the forest. Freddie was always trying to pick on Gary like he used to taunt John Ferris. Now John's gone Freddie has to pick on someone else. Those two are always trying to get one up on each other. You know men Catherine?'

'Gary left work early Monday Gloria, after the fight but where did he go? He didn't come home until knock off time and he never said anything about any fight. So where did he go? Who did he talk to? He had a fight with his dad this morning, right here in our kitchen. Wonder what that was about? Do you know? Now your mother has come back to us has she told you anything about her wild youth? She and Rosemary Biddle were quite the little devils in this village I heard, and now she is back talking with Rosemary. Your mother was telling me this the other night at Betty Traver's home.'

Gloria kept quiet and tried to look unknowing and uninterested.

'Know why Brian and Gary had a fight Gloria? Know why Brian just left in a hurry? My wandering Brian has just left again but he'll be back Gloria. He always comes back no matter where he has been. I love him and he married me Gloria so he always comes back but he does like to wander doesn't he?'

'Catherine I don't know what you're talking about. I never saw Gary today and so I never knew about any fight he might have had with his father. I never knew he and Lester Rainer had any fight although that might have been about Dora, Lester's sister. We've all been going out you know, Freddie, Gary, Dora and me. Lester was probably pissed off about that and had a go at Gary. We all know Dora is old enough to know her own mind. She thinks it's a giggle that her brother is pissed off about it.'

Catherine decided to be a little more blunt. 'Gary and my Brian were fighting over you Gloria.'

'Sorry about that Catherine but your Brian was trying to come on to me in Mrs. Digby's the other day and he got a little miffed because Mrs. Digby imagined he was in for an appointment only that wasn't what he came in for. I probably told Gary and that's what the fight was about.'

'No Gloria, it was much more fundamental than that my dear. Yes it was father and son fighting over you dear but not quite like that. Funny really but I suppose it must run in the Templeton genes. Gary had just learnt, and I assume from Freddie, that my Brian is your father and that my Gary has been sleeping with his sister all these years, and it has been all these years hasn't it Gloria? When you were a teenager before you ran away and then when you came back. Gary was upset as he never knew. I'm not sure whether Brian knew but I don't think so, although I often wondered. You were a premature baby, or so the rumour went and you don't look anything like Walter. I often wondered but then I see so many young people and I look and wonder. My Brian had a reputation when

I married him Gloria and I knew it and I didn't expect him to change. However, finding out about you did rather smack him in the face and that is why he suddenly left just now. He knew what I would say. Gary on the other hand was upset poor lad. Well, more than upset I suppose but he can lose his temper on occasions. I assume that poor little Lester was in the wrong place at the wrong time. Doesn't seem to surprise you dear. You don't seem shocked or in denial Gloria. Perhaps Tilley decided to tell you after all these years. Carrying that secret around for so long was probably why she went a little reclusive my dear. You came home and you've done a wonderful job bringing her back to life. Everyone is quite amazed and delighted with the change. She is a new woman and lovely with it. I've no doubt Brian will be trying his luck a second time. He can't help himself but he always comes back to me Gloria.'

Gloria's mind was in overdrive. Who else knew? Who else knew what was going on? What had her mum said now she was a new woman? Christ mum this is all happening too quickly and somehow I need to get a grip on things. Gary's in gaol for starters and then there's tonight to worry about. Shit, we'll have to get one of the girls to be the guide. Lola's the best bet. She keeps a cool head. I'd better go and find her as soon as I can get out of here.

'Gone quiet Gloria love. Suppose as you're family I can share some secrets with you. Brian will get over it. He always gets over any woman. But Gary, well that's another story. After Daniel Lord visited I called the police station and asked about Gary. He's under arrest for assault but all that may depend on what happens with little Lester. Troubling times Gloria don't you think?'

'I've got to go Catherine. I've got some things to sort out.'

'Yes dear, I imagine you have. Seems bringing your mother back to life was more than you expected. It has exposed a whole array of interesting memories for several people, and of course explained a few new things to some others. I'll tell Brian you weren't too bothered, about him being your father that is.'

Christ you laid back bitch Gloria thought as she slammed her car door. Taking it all in her stride and never a raised voice, and so calm and assured over her Brian. Well fuck her thought Gloria and your rather unsteady son. Jesus Gary, just learn when to act and when to think you stupid bastard. Now I can't get to you and so I'd better worry about one thing at a time and that's Lola. Looking at her watch Gloria noticed that it had gone three and Lola would be down at the cottage around four with Sheena and Gina for tonight's session. And then there was Wendell she thought. That little bugger could claim all sorts of things but it was his word against mine and he was looking for revenge after Freddie thumped him so he might be tempted to say anything. Just keep it all cool Gloria and we'll let this all slide away. Belle knows how to keep her mouth shut. And Brian, ever faithful come home to Catherine Brian will keep his mouth shut when he learns about Gary's video sessions. Those pictures will keep him quiet. Maybe I'll phone Toby and get him to lean on mum. Keep her mind on my story and forget about Wendell's vivid imagination. Yes, that will help. Toby the Fixer rides to the rescue as usual Gloria muttered with her tongue between her teeth. Bail me out of this fix Toby. Gloria pulled up at the call-box in the village just outside Mrs. Larkin's store and did some explaining to Toby. She put the receiver down feeling a little better. Toby will come through. Mum will get told.

Inspector Field along with PC Goodfellow sat in Mrs. Manson's sitting room and slowly waited while Tilley made tea. Three thirty chimed the half hour on the clock and Tilley brought a tray with biscuits and tea in from the kitchen. Terence Field explained that they had talked with a fair number of people, including Gary, and they needed to check a few facts before they went to see Lester in hospital. And no, there was no sign of Freddie in the river along where they found his car. After his tea PC Goodfellow apologised and said he'd had too much to drink and could he use the facilities. Tilley explained where and Inspector Field went back over the events of the past week including Tilley's visit to see Rosemary Dunster. PC Goodfellow found the bathroom and let the tap run in the handbasin. Wendell's door was unlocked and Wendell didn't hear anything because he was wearing headphones as he trolled the internet. He jumped when PC Goodfellow tapped him on the shoulder and motioned for him to turn down the volume.

'Good with that are you son?'

'Piece of piss most of it. Simple stuff. Some of these web sites are so crude, so poor in their capabilities. Some of these jokers are useless.'

'Been doing this long then have you?'

'Four, five years now,' boasted Wendell. 'My sister's crap though. She can manage to turn it on and that's about it.'

'So who do you talk to son, on these chat rooms eh?'

'All sorts.'

'And in the village is there anyone else you work with?'

'No, a loner me. In here most of the time. Keep to myself.'

'Who hit you lad?'

'No-one. Fell over the cables one night coming in without the light. Stupid really but we all make mistakes.'

'Sure son. I heard Lester made a mistake the other night?'

'Lester who?'

'The bloke you thumped. He's in hospital lad with broken ribs and a possible torn spleen. I was talking to him this morning. Gave us quite a description of meeting you. Last night wasn't it Wendell?'

'I only threatened him. He walked away the little git.'

'In hospital now though son. Want to tell me about it?'

'Fuck off. I didn't hit him that hard.'

481

'Let's go down and talk with your mum Wendell. Think we need a chat about bullying, hitting people, emails, and other things son. Quiet chat with the Inspector and your mother.'

For the next thirty minutes the Inspector and PC Goodfellow heard a variety of stories. Seems Freddie wasn't here on the Tuesday evening. Well Tilley was out so she couldn't really say but Wendell said not, but then it was Freddie who had hit Wendell last week now wasn't it? And Gary Templeton wasn't here all last Tuesday evening. In fact Tilley remembered that Gary and Gloria came in later but he was here all night Inspector she said. The Inspector and PC Goodfellow left soon after four. Ten minutes later the phone rang. It was for Tilley. Toby was calling from London but Tilley had already explained that Gloria and Freddie hadn't been here on Tuesday night. No problem said Toby. I'll tell Gloria and she'll handle things. Toby will fix it Tilley he re-assured her.

Sitting in his car Terence thought over the variety of stories they had heard and discussed a couple of things with his constable.

'Any suggestions constable?'

'That Wendell's nursing a big chip on his shoulder and lying through his teeth. I've heard from Timmy Meadows sir, PC Meadows that is, that Wendell spends a large amount of time with Tom Daley who is the other computer geek in this village. Likely source of our anonymous emails: likely the only people here with the smarts to make them untraceable, especially as Gary is supposed to have been seen in the village on the Tuesday night when he was not at the Manson house.'

'So where constable, where does Gloria entertain Freddie and where is Gary at that time? All of the houses have people in them so where? Maybe I should call in my amateur local sleuth. He knows the people and he knows the area. Just like our mystery of the gold coins and the bones constable.'

'That Whelks's cottage is probably still empty Inspector; the one with the golden path.'

'Good idea constable and we'll check that out. We'll check that out on our way to Fotheringham. I think we'll go and talk to Daniel Lord and I need to apologise to his sister. She told me something today that was rather relevant and I need to thank her. I cut her off rather abruptly. So constable, let's go sleuthing.'

Gloria found Lola, Gina and Sheena at the cottage relaxing. Gina had just driven down from London. After Gloria explained Gary getting himself stupidly in trouble she arranged for Lola to act as the guide. They exchanged the information they had got from Belle and the website booking. It was one bloke and he had his son with him. Apparently he wanted his son to experience some of the better things in life. The old man was in his late forties and his son nearly twenty but needs an education was the story.

The Inspector sat with his constable and Daniel in the office at Fotheringham Manor. They had just started talking when Samantha walked in and thought she should be part of the discussion because she had provided the first clue to this fracas. If it wasn't for me she had explained you would never have known what the secret was all about. Terence decided that inclusion was better than attempts at exclusion and so the four of them discussed as much of the story as Terence was prepared to tell civilians.

'What have Gary and Freddie been doing of late in the forest Daniel? And what do you think caused the fight this past Monday?'

'Bob Edwards didn't know Terence but Gary took off right there and then that Monday morning.'

'And was back at work on the Tuesday and Wednesday?'

'Late on Wednesday but yes. He wasn't in this morning but you know all about that.'

'Before this Monday?'

'They had both been doing that wash and brush up job on the cottage for the Entwhistle's Daniel,' interjected Samantha. 'Remember you told me about Gary's joke about doing the other cottage and Freddie was frightened of having to do that. Because of his cousins,' she added.

'The Ferris cottage?' Terence asked. 'You been there lately Daniel?'

'I was there with my mother and Katya a couple of weeks back,' said Daniel. 'We keep it clean. I was thinking of putting a lock on the door with the extra number of people in the forest. We've had a group of hikers through for the past three weeks. A couple of that group was interested because they offered to look at possible wildlife changes and thought the cottage would make a good base if we were serious.'

'It was left sort of semi-furnished wasn't it Daniel? You took Betty up there and she took some of the kid's things but left everything else?'

'Yes. Mum thought it would have been a better place for the Entwhistles until we discussed the history and what they might learn from folks in the village. That's why we decided on Enrico's old cottage.'

'So Gary and Freddie would know all about that cottage and that village folk would avoid it?'

'Yes.'

'But someone who didn't care about such stories and thought they could use it might think otherwise,' said Samantha. 'What did Gloria do up in London Terence? Wasn't she working at some Club? Haven't there been a few of her friends from London down over the past few months? Friends who might have been from the same Club. And, Tilley was telling me all about this Toby the Fixer. The bloke who caused George to fire Gloria from the pub but he is back in the village a few times too.'

'Samantha you have an imaginative mind like your brother,' said Terence. 'He sat and told me stories like that when we were sitting outside the Whelks's cottage.'

484

'And look where that got you Terence?' said Samantha gleefully. And,' she said, still with a smile on her face 'this time you have the owner's permission to investigate rather than having to get a search warrant like last time.'

THAT INFAMOUS COTTAGE

AROUND FIVE O'CLOCK DANIEL DROVE in the Landrover leaving Inspector Field to follow in his car with PC Goodfellow. Samantha insisted on coming as well. Fortunately, Daniel thought, Katya was still talking with her parents otherwise she would want to get in on the act too. Coming into the clearing Daniel was surprised to see two cars parked close to the cottage. He quietly eased the Landrover to a stop and motioned with his fingers for Samantha to sit patiently. Slowly Daniel opened his door and cautioned Terence to be quiet too. He walked over to Terence's car.

'Not sure about the company Terence. The licence plate on the Toyota is not local although I think I recognise the Escort. Want me to be the landlord, without our dear Samantha bowling people over or do you want to join me?'

'Maybe we'll all pay a visit Daniel. I think I know this cottage pretty well by now and I too would like to see who is visiting.'

The four of them approached the backyard door and a soft murmur of music and voices could be heard inside. Daniel unlatched the door and walked into the kitchen. Needless to say Samantha was hard on his heels.

'Good evening Gloria. Visiting the Ferris family, the Travers family or just partying?'

'Mr. Lord, Daniel, my you did give me a shock then coming in quietly like that, and with your sister too. Who's she going to bowl over? Say girls, look who Daniel has brought to the party? Inspector, it's good to see you again, so soon too. Perhaps I should introduce my friends. This is Lola, Gina and the lovely lass with the red hair is Sheena, who as you might guess with that hair is Irish.'

'Gloria may I ask what you are doing here, with or without your friends?'

'Now Daniel, why don't you just say hi to the girls and relax.'

Terence could sense that Samantha was about to explode in some form and so he decided that Daniel was a little too polite and that he should take charge. He stepped forwards passed Daniel.

'Sit ladies,' he said emphatically. 'Sit.'

After half an hour which included explanations about doing no harm, a place to party, offers of a rental fee and other dialogue Lola, Gina and Sheena left leaving Gloria with the four from the Manor. During this series of conversations Samantha had taken it on herself to walk through the cottage and take note of its appearance. She beckoned to PC Goodfellow as Terence was talking with Gloria.

'Cosy constable, very cosy,' she said as she poked around the bedroom. Pulling back some of the heavy curtaining material Samantha found one of the video cameras. Thinking before she acted she left it in position but she pointed it out to her companion. On going back into the kitchen Samantha found Gloria just leaving.

'We weren't doing any harm. In fact we were looking after the place. Looks neat and tidy doesn't it? It's certainly cleaner and smarter than when you lot left it. I'll talk with your mother Daniel Lord and offer her a rent she can't refuse. Why waste such a place? Expand your horizons. Didn't your girlfriend want to diversify or something?'

'Out Gloria, that's enough. I've no doubt Daniel and his family will be speaking to you later but for now out.'

'Okay Inspector, keep your shirt on. Christ, I think I'll go back to London and just when I've learnt to enjoy the country life. Tell your nephew Tony he's a good teacher if I don't see him again. He's a good lad. Smashing he is,' and Gloria laughed as she walked out of the kitchen and got in her car. Samantha took the opportunity to take Daniel and Terence to see her observations and discoveries in the two bedrooms.

'Constable I think we'll need a couple of search warrants. I think it is time we put Gloria and her mother together, along with Wendell perhaps. We will also pay a visit to Gary's bedroom and see whether he keeps a diary or somesuch. Gloria is now trying to tell me that she and Freddie didn't enjoy her "London Special" at her mother's house but in Freddie's car by the river. Somehow I don't find that very convincing. If it was my birthday I don't think I'd find that very special. Daniel, thank you for your advice and guidance. You may have found another scene of a tryst if not a crime although Gloria and her friends have kept this place so clean that any unexpected evidence is probably long gone. Just to be thorough I'm going to get some forensic people down here to check this place over again if you don't mind. Let's see who has been down here doing what shall we?'

The Inspector made a couple of radio calls as he returned with his constable to their offices.

All this time I had been sitting quietly bored out of my mind in my cell. I hadn't a clue what was going on and I still felt like shit from Don having hit me. My mind was a mixture of anger, pain, frustration and Gloria. Yes Gloria, my sister who I loved dearly. Christ, who else knew and who would say anything. My dad had degraded our name and my mum had just been a doormat but I wanted my name back. I wanted to be as good as grandfather. The door jangled with a key in the lock and opened. I was led out to another interview room and in came Inspector Field again along with his constable. They spent another fifteen minutes asking about the cottage, the Ferris cottage. I told them Freddie and I had cleaned up Enrico's cottage but Daniel Lord hadn't wanted anything done to the other one. Had I been there lately? No, why should I? This went on before someone came in to talk to Inspector Field and I was hustled back to my cell but not before one final question.

'Do you own a camera Gary?'

'No,' I said, 'don't know anything about them,' and away I went back to my mind and my cell.

'That's right Inspector,' said Mrs. Templeton. 'Gary doesn't have a camera. He's never been interested. You want to see his room, and you say you've got this warrant thing? Well sure, although hitting Lester Rainer is no big crime Inspector. He's more useless than Freddie Dunster. Have you found him yet by the way?'

PC Goodfellow quietly poked and pried his way around my bedroom. I heard the story later from my mum because she came up the stairs to see what the two police were up to. Carefully and thoroughly they opened drawers, checked through clothing, looked in pockets, and took everything out of my cupboard. Nothing much to see my mum said later. Most things you should have thrown away years ago Gary. They did find a couple of black cases though my mum had said. Small they were and I'd never seen them before. Don't know what they were Gary she had said. They gave mum a receipt and put them in some plastic bag along with some thin wafer like things. Flash cards or something I think they called them but I didn't know what they were either mum said. They didn't seem too excited but that Inspector is quiet and very courteous. He thanked me for my cooperation Gary she had told me. Sure I thought.

I never did hear the whole story of their similar search through Mrs. Manson's house and that involved taking away the two computers, much to Wendell's disgust. Anyway, that led to an investigation of the website on Gloria's plus several of her emails to and from Belle. Of greater interest to some of the staff at the station was the content of Wendell's computer but that never surfaced in my circumstances so I'll skip that part. I did hear the police later paid a visit to Tom Daley's and there were some high-tech discussions about some emails or other. Now I never knew what stories had been spun out of the Manson household and it seems there were several rather conflicting versions of events between Gloria, Tilley and Wendell. This all came back to haunt me as the Inspector and his trusty PC Goodfellow were back in to see me that evening. It had been a long and emotionally trying day and I was feeling at a low ebb.

'So Gary,' the Inspector said to me, 'it seems that you weren't at the Manson household on the Tuesday night until about one in the morning. Where were you son?'

'What's this got to do with Lester Rainer? You arrested me for hitting Lester.'

'Gary,' said the Inspector, 'we're looking for Freddie Dunster and you are helping us with our inquiries. You are what the press call a person of interest.'

'I never saw Freddie, not after work on Tuesday that is. I didn't go out that night until real late when I went to Gloria's.'

'What are these Gary?' and the Inspector held up two camera cases and a bunch of flash cards wrapped up in a plastic bag.

'Dunno.'

'Wonder whose fingerprints we will find?'

'Dunno.'

'The videos are interesting Gary.'

'What videos?'

'Gary I'm going to caution you son and you should think of phoning for some legal representation. I think you're going to need help. So far we've just been chatting, exchanging information but now I'm going to start recording and before I do that I'll caution you and let you think a little. We've talked with Gloria, Tilley, Wendell, your mother, Freddie's mother, as well as Lester, Danny and Don. My constable and I spent some time with Lola, Gina and Sheena at the infamous cottage at Fotheringham and we found out a few things there. Overall Gary we think we know what has happened and I even think I understand why. Samantha MacRae tells me you are ashamed of your dad but proud of your grandfather. She says you would like to put the name of Templeton up high as a proud family in this village. Her clients, Lewis and Shirley Peters also said you spoke strongly and passionately about your grandfather and the name. I remember the night in the pub when they really spooked you about long lost relatives but how you came back from the shock and stood up tall. Stood up and told them about your name and the reputation the family used to have in the village. Listening to Daniel and Samantha I have learnt quite a few things about the folk in this village and how proud several of them about their names and their families so maybe I understand a little son.'

Christ I felt shattered. He understood. That Inspector understood but he'd never really understand what I had done. He might understand why but that wasn't the point. He wanted to know where and how not why. I nodded. I just nodded, but I never confessed.

Over the next day or so the story gradually unravelled. I tried to explain that the cottage was my idea. I had wanted Gloria to stay in the village and the set-up in the cottage helped. Just look at how things were going so well with her mother and such. Slowly I tried to explain that Freddie threatened to tell the village about my sister. The Inspector understood and asked what had happened. So I told the Inspector that we fought on the Monday but you know that. Tuesday at work I just ignored the silly sod. After that I don't know Inspector. I didn't see him after that Tuesday at work. My explanation of where I was on Tuesday evening was thin with no witnesses, but the email saying I was in the village that night wasn't damming. I was with Gloria all that Tuesday night. She told me she had satisfied Freddie and kept him sweet. I had almost calmed down Inspector, almost forgotten Freddie and his vindictive taunting by the Wednesday morning. That was why I was so mad about being beaten up by Don, Danny and Lester on the Wednesday night. So mad that I lost my rag on the Thursday and tried to kick the shit out of Lester. That was why I was in here under arrest. Lester was just in the wrong place at the wrong time Inspector I told him. Apparently the police collected all sorts of forensic evidence with pillow fibres and dust from the cottage, from Freddie's car, from my car, even from Tilley's very clean house. Later in court I heard all sorts of evidence that I knew nothing about and couldn't understand. I'd pleaded not guilty and there was a whole parade of evidence that embarrassed my family which was what I was trying to hide. My dad never appeared in court although mum was there every day. The Peters, Lewis and Shirley were there briefly one day with Samantha, and my lawyer told me something about the Templeton inheritance and sharing of the wealth from Australia but I didn't really care. I don't think Gloria heard any more about any money either. Their Reginald had disgraced the Templeton name but at least he'd had the decency or the fear to change his name.

In court Gloria had decided to tell the truth. She explained that she took Freddie to the cottage for his "London Special" in her car, complete with the exciting blindfold routine. After shagging his silly brains out, although she didn't put it that way in court she brought him back into the village and dumped him in his own car. What Freddie did after that she didn't know. He was certainly capable of driving Gloria said. Then she went home and must have got in around midnight. When cross-examined Gloria described how I had come to her house soon after that needing comfort and re-assurance. She said that she explained to me that Freddie's little secret wasn't all that important. Everyone knew about the wanderings of Brian Templeton and half-brothers and half-sisters all over the West Country probably never knew each other. The judge got annoyed at this assertion from Gloria and told the jury to ignore those comments. She just looked at him and smiled as if to say you can say what you like mate but we all know. From that time onwards Freddie disappears.

I suppose the cameras and the videos did the most damage. My wanting something more did me in there. If it wasn't for the cameras Gloria and I could have denied everything. There would have been no real evidence without the cameras. Still, they weren't operating that Tuesday evening. Nevertheless it was greed I thought: looking for the easy life. Just like my dad in a way although I had my hand out and he had his cock out. I was thinking about grandfather when the guard heard footsteps in the corridor. He put down his newspaper on his chair and stood up. With his key he opened the door and I was led back along the corridor and up the staircase into the court room. I stood in the dock and looked around. The room was full and the low buzz in the room dropped as the clerk of the court stood up and addressed the jury. The clerk asked the foreman to stand.

'Members of the jury, do you find the defendant Gary Templeton guilty or not guilty of ....'

CAST OF CHARACTERS

The Lord Family

George Lord   Born 1880. Died 1946
Eldest son. Married Virginia Milne in 1908 at age of 28.

Virginia Milne   Born 1883. Died 1966
Well traveled daughter of minor gentry. Marries George in 1908 at age of 25.

George and **Virginia** have four children: **Desmond**, **Harriet**, **Veronica** and **Matthew**.

Desmond Lord   Born 1910. Died 1968
Eldest son. Married to Rosamund DeWinter in 1938 at age of 28.

Rosamund DeWinter
Born 1912. Died 1987
Only daughter of French parents. Dies 1987 at age 75 slightly gaga.

George and Virginia also have:
Harriet	Born 1912. Died 1933
Veronica	Born 1913. Alive 1999
Matthew	Born 1914. Alive 1999

Desmond and Rosamund married in 1938 have three children: **Anthony**, **Charles** and **Stephanie**

Anthony Lord   Born 1940. Alive 1999

Whirlwind meeting, romance and marriage with Sylvia Trelawney in late 1964. Anthony and Sylvia start their own company in software development called Brainware. Head of the family at Fotheringham Manor

Sylvia Trelawney   Born 1942. Alive 1999

Daughter of Cornish family in the China clay business. Marries Anthony in 1964.

Charles Lord   Born 1941. Died 1966

Meets **Helene Forcier** (age 18) in Chamonix, France. Have three children, **Marcel, Henri** and **Giselle**. Charles and Helene are killed while mountaineering in 1966 at age 25.

Stephanie Lord   Born 1942. Alive 1999

Trained as a vet but works on genetic research in sheep at Home Farm at Fotheringham Manor. In 1966 when Charles and Helene killed Stephanie takes on the adoption of Marcel (6), Henri (5) and Giselle (4).

Anthony and Sylvia Lord marry 1964 and have 4 children: **Geoffrey, Michael, Samantha, and Daniel.**

Geoffrey Lord   Born 1965. Died 1990

Eldest son. Marries Christina DeLucci in 1988 and have son Peter born 1989. Geoffrey dies in climbing accident in 1990 leaving son Peter heir to the Estate. (*Details in novel Michael*).

Christina DeLucci   Born 1965. Alive 1999

Born in Italy and only daughter of Giuseppe and Sophia. Marries Geoffrey in 1988. Son Peter born 1989. Somewhat emotional and very family oriented. Lives on Home Farm at Fotheringham with son Peter. Adopts Tony, Michael and Danielle's son in 1998.

Michael Lord   Born 1969. Died 1991

Second son and resents Lord family policy of primogeniture. Michael killed 1991 but has a son with Danielle Made called Tony (born 1989). (*Details in novel Michael*).

Danielle Made   Born 1970. Dies 1998

Born in Mozambique. Came to England in 1989 at age 18 and became mistress of Michael Lord. Has son Anthony (Tony) born August 1989. Lives in London 1989-1998 when she flees down to Fotheringham. Killed 1998 at Fotheringham. (*Details in the novel Samantha*).

Samantha Lord   Born 1972. Alive 1999

Grows up a tomboy with two brothers but her mother tries to get her to be a lady. Goes to school in Switzerland and then University in England. Marries Andrew MacRae 1993 and has son James. Moves to Canada with husband in 1996. Returns from Canada in September 1998 with son after husband Andrew MacRae killed in forest fire. Develops an interest in Detective Inspector Terence Field. Joins old school friend Janet Donaldson in Heritage Adventures Company. (*Details in novel Samantha and novel Daniel*).

Daniel Lord   Born 1974. Alive 1999

Youngest son. Daniel is 16 in 1990 and with Geoffrey and Michael when Geoffrey dies in climbing accident. Receives Forestry degree in 1996 and is in charge at Fotheringham Manor Estate. With nephew James he meets the Howard family and daughter Katya. (*Details in novel Samantha and novel Daniel*).

Charles and Helene Lord have three children: **Marcel, Henri and Giselle**

Marcel Lord   Born 1960. Alive 1999

Born in France. Adopted by Aunt Stephanie in 1966 when parents killed. Marries Marie in 1980 and have sons Jean and Philippe. International competitive yachtsman. Wife Marie lives in Dartmouth.

Henri Lord   Born 1961. Alive 1999

Born in France. Adopted by Aunt Stephanie. Grows up to be a climber like his father. Lives in Bristol and works in financial planning and investments. Has a "partner" Leslie Dauphin who is a spiteful journalist who resents Anthony/Sylvia Lord family and its traditions. Henri is a rambler/hiker as well as a climber.

Giselle Lord   Born 1962. Alive 1999

Born in France. Never really remembers her parents and is brought up by Aunt Stephanie. Develop a talent for languages. Goes to University from 1982 to 1985 with a First in Modern languages. Speaks Italian, French and Spanish and works as an interpreter for a Government office in Bristol.

Other Lord offspring include

Peter Lord   Born 1989. Alive 1999

Born August. Son of Geoffrey Lord and lives with mother Christina DeLucci at Home Farm, Fotheringham Manor. Heir to the Lord family estate after death of his father in 1990.

Tony Lord (Made)   Born 1989. Alive 1999

Born in London. Mother was Danielle Made and father was Michael Lord. Lived in London with his mother most of his life. Adopted by Christina Lord after his mother killed in September 1998 and lives with Christina and Peter at Home Farm. Keen on football and swimming.

James MacRae   Born 1994. Alive 1999

Born August. Son of Andrew MacRae and Samantha Lord. Raised by Anthony and Sylvia Lord for most of his first year. Went to Canada with parents in 1996 and returned with Samantha in 1998 to Fotheringham.

Jean Lord   Born 1981. Died 1990

Born in Devon. Elder son of Marcel and Marie Lord. Keen to sail like his father but afraid. Dies from drowning while out sailing with Michael Lord in 1990.

Philippe Lord   Born 1982. Alive 1999

Born in Devon. Younger son of Marcel and Marie Lord. Goes to Bristol House School with fees paid by Stephanie Lord.

The Howard Family

Delaney Howard IIIrd.

Manager of Forest Operations for International Paper Company in Jacksonville Florida. Married to Deidre, an outspoken voluble Yankee. They have one daughter, Katya.

Katya Howard   Born 1977. Alive 1999

Only daughter of Delaney IIIrd. and Deidre Howard from Jackonsonville, Florida. In 1998/9 is studying Forestry at Oxford University and in her final year. Special friend of James MacRae and girl friend of Daniel Lord.

The Ferris Family

Norton Ferris   Born 1925. Died 1991

Hired by Anthony Lord as a Forester in 1984 working under Ronald O'Rourke and lives with two sons in cottage on the Estate. Becomes in charge when O'Rourke dies in 1987 and bullies forest work crew especially Antonio and Enrico Branciaghlia and young Freddie Dunster. Dies in January 1991 in an accident on Fotheringham Estate. (***Details in the novel Michael***).

Idwal Ferris   Born 1960. Died 1998

Elder son of Norton Ferris. Forest labourer at Fotheringham Manor. Single. Lives with his dad and his brother in cottage on Fotheringham Estate. Fired January 1991. Leaves local area but returns in 1998 after supposedly serving time for manslaughter. Commits rape, arson, murder before being killed in 1998 at Ferris cottage on Fotheringham Estate. (*Details in the novel Samantha*).

John Ferris   Born 1963. Died 1998

Younger son of Norton Ferris. Forest labourer at Fotheringham Manor. Fired in January 1991. Rehired in May 1991. Married in 1991 to Betty Travers. Lives with wife and two children in the Ferris cottage on the Estate. Kills brother and then is killed later. (*Details in the novel Daniel*).

Betty Travers   Born 1968. Alive 1999

Eldest child of Toby and Mary Travers who run the off-licence and the greengrocers shops respectively in the village. Betty is famous for her pie-making. Married John Ferris in 1991. They live in the Ferris cottage on the Estate. Have two children, Katey and Paul. Leaves cottage to live back with her parents in the village after the return of Idwal Ferris. (*Details in the novel Daniel*).

The Branciaghlia brothers

Antonio Branciaghlia   Born 1920. Died 1990

Lived with brother in cottage on the Estate. Killed in a tree-felling accident in August 1990.

Enrico Branciaghlia   Born 1922. Alive 1999

Born near Cortina Italy. Became a woodworker. Transferred from P.O.W. Camp to Fotheringham Manor Estate. With brother trained as a forest worker and stays at Fotheringham after the war. Well respected on the Estate and in the village. Makes toys for children. Stays on in Estate cottage living alone after brother killed in 1990. Retires in 1997. Moves into Home Farm in 1998. (*Details in the novel Daniel*).

The Templeton Family

Albert Templeton   Born 1880. Died 1950

Grew up on the Fotheringham Manor Estate as a gamekeeper's assistant. Good with guns, traps, pheasant coops, and general estate work. In WWI was 34 and fought in the same artillery regiment as George Lord. Fought in Italian Alps. Married to Annie and had son Edward, born 1914. Works all his life on the estate. Is 59 in 1939 for WWII. Teaches Enrico and Antonio when they come to the estate in 1944. Dies at age 70.

Reginald Templeton   Born 1900. Died 1948

Is Albert's unknown younger brother. Labourer on Estate from 1914 (Age 14 onwards). Called up at age 17 in 1917 and goes to France in early 1918. Horrified and tries to desert. Goes AWOL at end of war in November 1918. Manages to escape to Australia and heads for the bush in Victoria working in logging. Ends up at Halls Gap in the Grampian Mountains. Changes name to Peters. Meets Marie Freidel in Victoria and marries in 1930 (age 30). Three kids born 1932, 1933 and 1935 (George, Sophia and Lazlo). Lazlo is tiny, undersize but turns into a brilliant jockey and when Reginald and Marie move to Melbourne in 1940 little Lazlo is age 5. Becomes a stable lad and a young jockey by age 16 (1951). Wins big and becomes rich. Reginald dies 1948 and leaves a 50-year time capsule. Marie dies in 1975 at age 70 but Lazlo goes from strength to strength. Shares wealth with brother and sister. Brother George marries 1954 (age 22) and has two kids (Lewis and Sharon born 1956 and 1958 respectively). Does well in business in Melbourne. Lewis marries 1980 (Age 24) to Shirley Masters. In 1999 Lewis and Shirley are 43 respectively with one child (Peter) aged 16. Come on holiday to find their roots after Lewis opens time capsule from Reginald in 1998.

Edward Templeton   Born 1914. Died 1978

Brought up on Fotheringham Manor estate as son of gameskeeper. Follows in father's footsteps. Develops a love of machinery and cars. Becomes a good mechanic for the estate. Leaves school at age 15 in 1929 and is ready to take over from father when WWII breaks out. Age 25 in 1939 and joins up. Becomes a fitter for the RAF including working on the squadron where Desmond is a pilot. Married in 1938 to Sally Ruston. Has son Brian in 1944. Takes over from his father in 1945 (Albert now 65) as head gamekeeper but also forest agent. Woodlands in need of attention after devastation of war. Lots of clearing, replanting, pruning, fencing, control of rabbits. Works well with Enrico and Antonio. Stays very traditional in forest actions. Dies at age 64.

Brian Templeton   Born 1944. Alive 1999

Becomes a salesman and a ladies man. Marries Catherine Dunn in 1973 and has son Gary. Lives in the village with wife and son.

Gary Templeton   Born 1973. Alive 1999

Grandson of Edward Templeton and son of Brian Templeton. Works as a labourer on the Fotheringham Manor Estate. Longtime friend of Freddie Dunster and Gloria Manson.

The Edwards Family

Ernest Edwards   Born 1914. Died 1988
Starts work on Fotheringham Estate in 1930. Marries Gwen Biddle in 1950. Son Bob
born in 1957. Foreman on the Estate from 1978 until 1988 when he dies at age 74.

Gwen Biddle   Born 1918. Died 1986
Marries Ernest Edwards and has daughter Tilley and son Bob.

Bob Edwards   Born 1957. Alive 1999
Son of Ernest Edwards and Gwen Biddle. Marries Frances Tetley in 1984 and have
a son Dennis born in 1985 who is mad about soccer. Worked on the Fotheringham
Estate and became foreman in 1988 on the death of his father Ernest.

Tilley Edwards   Born 1953. Alive 1999
Daughter of Ernest Edwards and Gwen Biddle. Elder sister of Bob Edwards. Marries
Walter Manson a lorry driver at age 19 in 1973. Has daughter Gloria and son Wendell.
Walter Manson a bully who was born in 1951 and dies in September 1998 in fiery
lorry crash. Tilley a good friend of cousin Rosemary Dunster (nee Biddle).

Gloria Manson   Born 1973. Alive 1999
Daughter of Tilley Edwards and Walter Manson. School friend of Freddie Dunster
and Gary Templeton. Runs away to London at age 18. Returns in October 1998 to
work at the George and Dragon Public house. Friends from London include Lola
Martinez, Gina Totti, Sheena Reegan and Belle Katz.

Wendell Manson   Born 1983. Alive 1999
Son of Tilley Edwards and Walter Manson. Computer geek, bully.

The Biddle family

Christopher Biddle   Born 1982. Died 1951
Blacksmith in village. Married Mary Jones, a Welsh tinker. Has son Jack and daughter
Gwen.

Jack Biddle   Born 1916. Died 1982
Continues as blacksmith in village. Marries Lily Ancres in 1947. Has daughter
Rosemary and daughter Violet.

Rosemary Biddle   Born 1953. Alive 1999

Marries William Dunster in 1972. Has son Freddie. Husband William dies in 1990. Rosemary is good friend of cousin Tilley Edwards

Freddie Dunster   Born 1973. Alive 1999

Son of Rosemary Biddle and William Dunster. Worked at Fotheringham Manor Estate from 1990 onwards. Friend of Gary Templeton and Gloria Manson. Village friends include Danny Masters, Lester Rainer and Don Winters.

Violet Biddle   Born 1957. Alive 1999

Ran away to Liverpool when a teenager. Has twin boys Jack and Leonard.

Jack and Leonard (Lennie) Cotton   Born 1975. Died 1991

Twins born in Liverpool. Sons of Violet Murphy (nee Biddle). Twins came back to Fotheringham in 1990.

Other Characters

Terence Field   Born 1966. Alive 1999

Detective Inspector in 1998 at time of Samantha/Daniel. Regional Crime Squad investigates September incidents at Fotheringham. Becomes friend of Samantha. City born and bred. Unfamiliar with country.

George Doone is George the landlord of the George and Dragon public house in the village.

PC Timmy Meadows is the village police constable.

Toby Dobbs is friend and later mentor of Gloria Manson from London Club scene. An old friend as Toby "the Fixer" of Tilley Manson and Rosemary Dunster. Was a rock band organizer and music promoter.

Mrs. Digby is the owner of hair-dressing salon in village

Darlene Roberts is the owner of tea-shop in the village

Ramblers include:

Rupert Oldshaw, graduate student at Oxford and son of famous film director

Ted Dexter, ex University student historian

Doris Lyon, bespectacled intense legal assistant

Mavis Taylor, close female friend of Rupert

Arnold Church, fanatic about wilderness and wild areas

Philippa Robson, believer in the word of God and anti theory of evolution

Margaret Letterman, friend of Philippa and strong supporter of the word of God

Rory Flanagan, Irish poet, musician and wildlife biologist

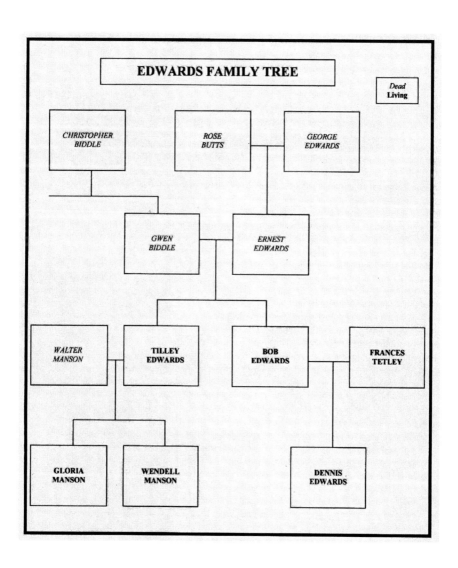

EDWARDS FAMILY TREE

Dead
Living

CHRISTOPHER BIDDLE

ROSE BUTTS

GEORGE EDWARDS

GWEN BIDDLE

ERNEST EDWARDS

WALTER MANSON

TILLEY EDWARDS

BOB EDWARDS

FRANCES TETLEY

GLORIA MANSON

WENDELL MANSON

DENNIS EDWARDS

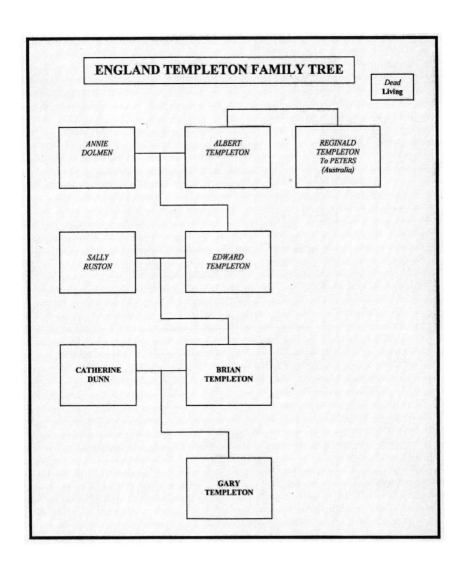

ENGLAND TEMPLETON FAMILY TREE

Dead
Living

ANNIE
DOLMEN

ALBERT
TEMPLETON

REGINALD
TEMPLETON
To PETERS
(Australia)

SALLY
RUSTON

EDWARD
TEMPLETON

CATHERINE
DUNN

BRIAN
TEMPLETON

GARY
TEMPLETON

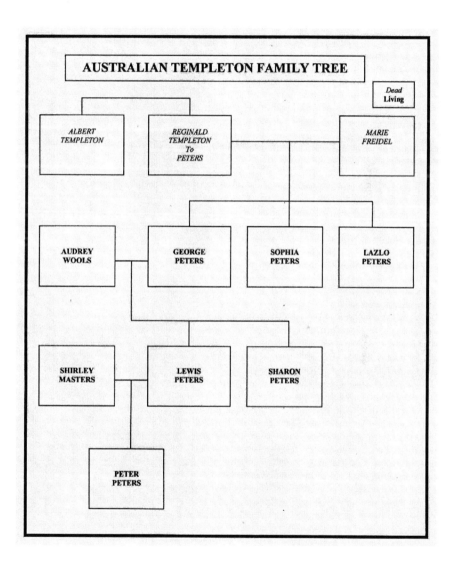

AUSTRALIAN TEMPLETON FAMILY TREE

Dead
Living

ALBERT
TEMPLETON

REGINALD
TEMPLETON
To
PETERS

MARIE
FREIDEL

AUDREY
WOOLS

GEORGE
PETERS

SOPHIA
PETERS

LAZLO
PETERS

SHIRLEY
MASTERS

LEWIS
PETERS

SHARON
PETERS

PETER
PETERS

505

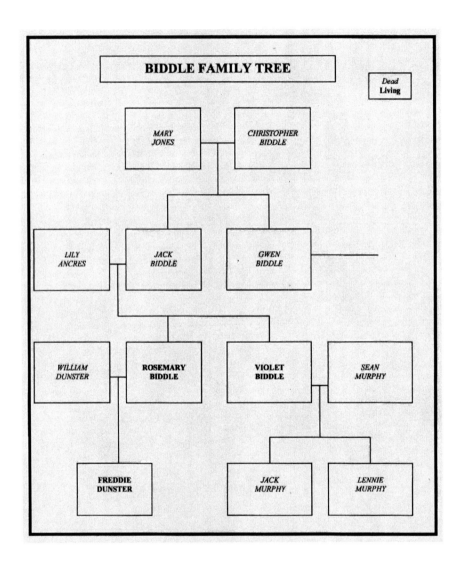

BIDDLE FAMILY TREE

Dead
Living

MARY JONES — CHRISTOPHER BIDDLE

LILY ANCRES — JACK BIDDLE — GWEN BIDDLE

WILLIAM DUNSTER — ROSEMARY BIDDLE — VIOLET BIDDLE — SEAN MURPHY

FREDDIE DUNSTER — JACK MURPHY — LENNIE MURPHY

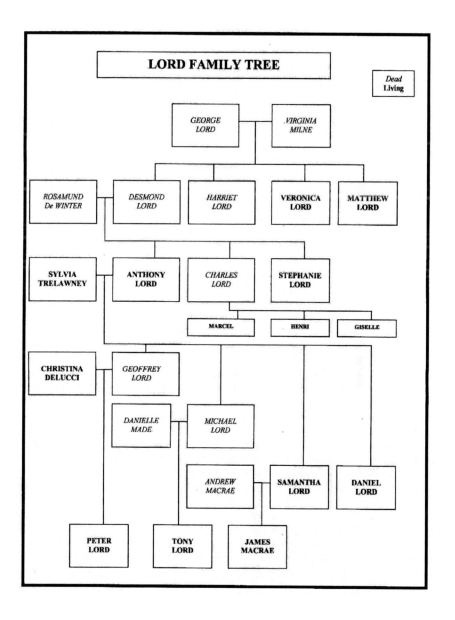

LORD FAMILY TREE

Dead
Living

GEORGE LORD — VIRGINIA MILNE

ROSAMUND De WINTER — DESMOND LORD   HARRIET LORD   VERONICA LORD   MATTHEW LORD

SYLVIA TRELAWNEY — ANTHONY LORD   CHARLES LORD   STEPHANIE LORD

MARCEL   HENRI   GISELLE

CHRISTINA DELUCCI — GEOFFREY LORD

DANIELLE MADE — MICHAEL LORD

ANDREW MACRAE   SAMANTHA LORD   DANIEL LORD

PETER LORD   TONY LORD   JAMES MACRAE

ABOUT THE AUTHOR

John Osborn was born in 1939 in Ipswich England but grew up in the East End of London where he learnt to sail. In North Wales he graduated as a professional forester and rock climbed three days a week. After working as a field forester for three years in Australia John went to Vancouver, British Columbia for postgraduate studies and the Flower Power movement of the sixties. While working for thirty years for the Ontario Ministry of Natural Resources, both as a forester and a systems analyst John sailed competitively, climbed mountains and taught survival and winter camping. He finished his professional career with three years consulting in Zimbabwe, walking with the lions. Now retired, although working part-time at the local Golf Club, John lives with his wife in Kelowna, BC where he hikes and x-c skis from his doorstep.

LaVergne, TN USA
11 August 2010
192993LV00003B/29/P